David Wishart studied Classics at Edinburgh University. He then taught Latin and Greek in school for four years and after this retrained as a teacher of EFL. He lived and worked abroad for eleven years, working in Kuwait, Greece and Saudi Arabia, and now lives with his family in Scotland.

Praise for David Wishart:

'As ever, Wishart takes true historical events and blends them into a concoction so pacey that you hardly notice all those facts and interesting details of Roman life being slipped in there ... Salve! To this latest from the top toga-wearing 'tec of Roman times!' *Highland News Group*

'It is evident that Wishart is a fine scholar and perfectly at home in the period.' *Sunday Times*

'A real gripping mystery yarn with a strong vein of laconic humour.' *Coventry Evening Telegraph*

'well-written, easy-to-read tale, full of innate humour and pace ... with intriguing twists and turns. David Wishart ... has a deep knowledge ... of Imperial Rome.' *Historical Novels Review*

Also by David Wishart

I, VIRGIL

OVID

NERO

GERMANICUS

SEJANUS

THE LYDIAN BAKER

THE HORSE COIN

OLD BONES

LAST RITES

WHITE MURDER

A VOTE FOR MURDER

David Wishart

NEW ENGLISH LIBRARY
Hodder & Stoughton

First published in Great Britain in 2003 by Hodder & Stoughton
A division of Hodder Headline
First published in paperback in 2003 by Hodder & Stoughton
A New English Library paperback

1 3 5 7 9 10 8 6 4 2

A CIP catalogue record for this title is available from the British Library

ISBN 0 340 77130 5

Typeset in Centaur by Palimpsest Book Production Limited,
Polmont, Stirlingshire
Printed and bound in Great Britain by
Clays Ltd, St Ives plc

Hodder & Stoughton
A division of Hodder Headline
338 Euston Road
London NW1 3BH

For the Edinburgh contingent:
Maggie, Rebecca and Catriona; Bea Wickens; and not forgetting Lyn Williams.

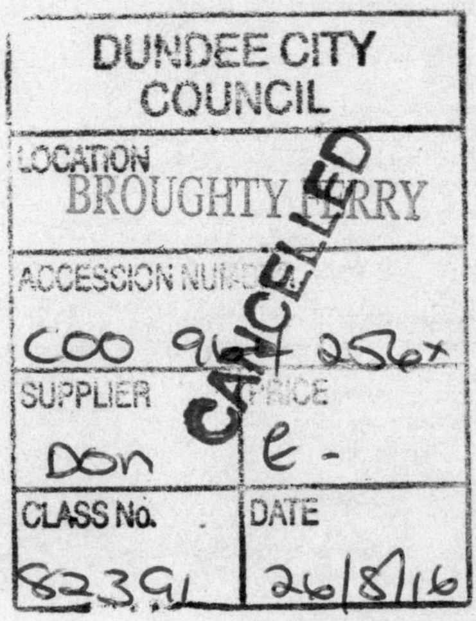

DRAMATIS PERSONAE

(Only names of main characters are given)

CORVINUS'S FAMILY AND HOUSEHOLD

Marcia Fulvina: Perilla's aunt
Marilla ('The Princess'): Corvinus and Perilla's adopted daughter
Perilla, Rufia: Corvinus's wife

Alexis: the gardener
Bathyllus: the major-domo
Meton: the chef

Dassa: the sheep
Corydon: the donkey

THE VILLAS

Bolanus, Marcus Vettius: the murdered candidate
Vettia: his sister
Draco: their major-domo

Sulpicius Severus: Bolanus's neighbour
Sulpicia: his daughter
Procne: her maid
Bion: their major-domo

Flacchus, Lucius Herdonius: Marcia's neighbour
Trupho: his major-domo

CASTRIMOENIUM

Brunna: Rutilius's wife
Concordius, Publius: a businessman; the second censorship candidate
Exuperius, Gaius: a butcher
Feronius: Bolanus's former estate manager
Gabba: a wineshop customer
Harpax: an auxiliary veteran; Rutilius's father-in-law
Libanius, Quintus: head of the Castrimoenian senate
Pontius: the wineshop owner
Rutilius, Spurius: a blacksmith
Ursus, Sextus: Concordius's right-hand man

ROMANS AND OTHERS

Decidius, Aulus: a Bovillan businessman
Licinius, Quintus: a jobbing artist
Persicus, Paullus Fabius: the current senior consul; also Marcia's nephew
Ruso, Abudius: the magistrate in charge of the Latin Festival

I

Work fascinates me. I can happily watch other people doing it for hours at a time, especially when I'm sitting in front of a wineshop with a half of the local best at my elbow. Besides, the guy with the paintbrush obviously believed in a job well done; you could just feel the concentration pouring into every letter, and if he'd been biting his tongue any harder he'd've carried it home in a bag. It's nice to see that even in these degenerate days graffiti artists have their standards.

Literacy, however, isn't necessarily a prerequisite. When he stepped back finally to inspect the result, I cleared my throat.

'Uh . . . excuse me, pal,' I said.

He turned round. 'Yeah?'

'Don't think I'm being critical, but you've spelled "tanners" wrong.'

He looked at me, then back at the wall. His thick eyebrows meshed in a scowl. 'Is that so, now?'

'Trust me.' The breeze from the hills that was doing its best to keep the town's market square cool gusted, and I caught his scent with both nostrils. Literacy problems was right: if there was one word he should've been able to spell it was 'tanner'. 'I like the lettering, though. Very striking.'

The scowl lifted and he beamed. 'I been practising that,' he said. 'What about "guild"?'

'"Guild"'s fine.'

'"Support"?'

'No problem.' I hesitated; criticism's all very well, but authors are touchy souls and you can overdo things. 'Ah . . . would the guy's name be "Concordus" or "Concordius", though?'

'Concordius.'

'Yeah. So you're missing an "i", right?'

'Damn.' He glared at the wall again, clicked his tongue, dipped the paintbrush and carefully added the single stroke. 'Better?'

'Perfect.'

'Except for the "tanners".'

Time to apply the healing balm of tact. 'Yeah, well, the meaning's clear enough. Me, I'd leave it as it is.'

'You think so?'

'Definitely. Why spoil the purity and simplicity of the line?'

His face cleared. 'Okay. If you're sure. Thanks, friend. You're a gent.' He picked up the paint can, gave his work a last approving nod and ambled off whistling across the square, leaving the air just that bit fresher.

I poured the last of the half jug and stretched out my legs. Castrimoenian may not be anywhere near the top rank of the Latian wines but cellar-chilled and drunk where it's made on a warm summer's day it has its points. And Pontius the wineshop owner had a good supplier.

The guy himself appeared with the plate of cheese and olives I'd ordered, glared at the dripping paintwork and then across the square. Not that he'd have much luck there; my graffiti artist pal was long gone to fresh walls and pastures new.

'That wall was only whitewashed last month,' he said. 'Bastard!'

'That's elections for you, pal,' I said.

'You didn't think to stop him, I suppose?'

'Uh-uh. Expressing your political opinion's a basic democratic right. And whitewashing a wall before an election's just plain stupid.'

He grunted as he set the plate down. 'Bloody tanners. They always were a bunch of shysters.'

I reached for an olive. 'You're ... ah ... not a Concordius man yourself, then?'

His mouth twisted in a grin. Not a bad lad, Pontius; not thick, either, by any means, and he'd taken my point about the wall pretty calmly. Laying on a virgin coat of whitewash two months before an election is asking for trouble, in the municipalities, anyway. One good thing about Rome, the first thing the Wart did when he took charge was hand the elections over to the Senate. Outside the city they still did the business the old-fashioned way, which was a mixed blessing. It made for interesting wineshop reading, though.

'You kidding, Corvinus?' he said. 'I run a wineshop. I can't afford to take sides and I wouldn't want to if I could. Whoever gets the five-year censor's job it's fine by me, because in the end it won't matter a straw. Politicians are all crooks anyway.'

'No arguments there, friend.' I passed him the empty half jug. 'Want to refill this for me?'

'Sure.' He disappeared inside.

I went back to the strenuous business of watching what was happening in Castrimoenium's market square. Two days up in the Alban Hills with Perilla's Aunt Marcia and our adopted kid were beginning to work their magic. Oh, yeah, I spend a fair slice of my time in the city lounging about – being one of Rome's leisured classes has to have some compensation to set against having to mix with a bunch of chinless wonders who risk blowing their brains out every time they sneeze – but even lounging in Rome's a hectic business. Castrimoenium might not be exactly a one-donkey village, but you could've fitted all of it inside one of the city regions, easy, and although the market square was far from empty it wasn't heaving. Also, if you were used to the way natives in the Big City conducted their daily business, up-and-coming election or not, the pace of life came as a pleasant surprise. Not to mention the noise level. Sit outside some of the wineshops on Iugarius or in the neighbourhood of the Julian Market for too long and you risk permanent ear damage; here even the extrovert squash-seller over on the other side of the square by the altar to Goddess Rome was keeping herself a couple of notches this side of full bellow, and closer in the noisiest contributor was a sheep so low-key its bleat sounded like an apologetic cough.

I'd closed my eyes for a moment when somebody plumped themselves down at the next table. Yeah, that'd be Gabba: this particular holiday might be only two days old, but I'd been up here often enough, and in Pontius's often enough, to know most of his regulars. Gabba was regular as a water-clock. He got through about as much liquid, too.

'Afternoon, Corvinus. I see the tanners've been round.'

I steeled myself and opened my eyes. Sure, it wasn't the poor bugger's fault, and he was pleasant enough otherwise, but nobody has the right to be that ugly. Scarecrow, nothing: Gabba's face would've frightened a pack of malnourished vultures away from a newly killed goat. 'Yeah,' I said. 'They sent in their crack speller.'

'So I see.' There was a long, bucolic pause. Pontius came with the wine: my half plus a jug and cup for Gabba. Unordered, note, but like I say the guy was a regular's regular, and like all good wineshop owners Pontius worked on his own internal timekeeping system. Gabba filled the cup, downed it in a oner and poured a slow refill. 'Barring "guild", of course,' he said. 'But people always get that one wrong.'

'Uh ... yeah.' I topped up my own cup. In the square the sheep coughed.

'The tanners're welcome to Concordius, mind.' Gabba finished the refill and poured again. 'He's a bastard.'

'Is that so, now?' I kept my voice non-committal. Me, I'm careful never to argue politics or religion, especially in wineshops, and for the same reason: if the other guy does happen to hold serious views – which he invariably does, because otherwise he wouldn't bother to bring either of the topics up – then you can spend the closing stages of the discussion looking for your teeth. Not that Gabba's opinion came as any surprise, because I'd seen exactly the same sentiment expressed about the tanners' blue-eyed boy in some of the other graffiti scattered around town.

Gabba took another swallow and reached for the jug. 'Mind you,' he said reflectively, 'Vettius Bolanus is a bastard too, so they're even there.'

'Yeah?' I tried to put the ghost of an interest into the word. Bolanus, I knew, was the other candidate in a two-horse race. Which was about all I *did* know about the subject, or want to; there can't be many topics in the world less interesting than local politics when you're not a local, while at the same time making you reach for the nearest sharp object if you are. As far as the guy's metaphorical legitimacy or lack of it was concerned, he could point to graffiti of his own, not to mention a choice specimen or two that claimed he had unnatural relations with goats and that his sister screwed slaves. Uninteresting to the outsider or not, there ain't anything either mim-mouthed or delicate about the cut and thrust of local politics. In the fruit basket of life, it's the prickly pear.

'Ah, be fair now, Gabba, boy.' Pontius had come out with a cup of wine of his own and pulled up a stool. That's something else you don't see much of in Rome: Roman landlords're friendly enough as a rule, sure, but they tend to keep the bar between themselves and the customer. Sometimes a very wise move, especially in the Subura. 'Bolanus is a different kind of bastard altogether.'

'So he is. So he is.' Gabba's eyes had strayed from his wine cup to the sheep with the cough. There was an old woman beside it and a placard that said: GOOD MILKER. 'I see old Carrinatia's trying to get rid of her Dassa again.'

Pontius grunted. 'Not surprising, is it, after the business in Veturius's cellar.'

'Right. Right.'

'And if she expects anyone to believe that sign after what happened to Publius Secundus when he gave the beast a trial last autumn she's whistling through her ear.'

Pause.

'Secundus is still having problems, then?' Gabba said.

'Off and on. Depends on the weather.'

Second pause. Somewhere a donkey brayed. I didn't think I could stand the pace. Maybe I should chip in before we all fell asleep here.

The conversational choice, it seemed, was swinging between politics and livestock. I flipped a mental coin and it came down heads. 'Uh . . . how do you mean, "different", pal?' I said.

'What?' Pontius wrenched his eyes away from Dassa.

'You said Concordius and Bolanus were different kinds of bastard.'

Pontius sipped his wine. 'Concordius . . . well, he's the pushy, self-made type,' he said slowly. 'Bolanus is the old family, damn-your-eyes variety.' He turned to Gabba. 'Fair summary, would you say, boy?'

'Very fair.' Gabba reached for the jug again. 'Couldn't've put it better myself.'

'And of course they hate each other's guts.'

'There is that, too.'

'Uh-huh.' Not much of a surprise there; certainly not considering the general tone of the pre-election graffiti I'd seen. Also, out here in the sticks where you had to make your own entertainment hating someone else's guts came pretty high on the list of popular hobbies. 'They're both local lads, then?'

Pontius cleaned an ear out with his finger. 'Bolanus is, sure. Old family, like I say; the Vettii've been big around here since men ate beech-nuts. Estate's come down a tad, especially in recent years, but they've always put in for the five-year censor's job at least once in a generation. It's a . . . what's the phrase I want, Gabba? Tip of my tongue.'

'Hallowed tradition?' Gabba sank another cupful. I wasn't keeping score, but I'd reckon the level in the jug must be getting pretty low by now. 'Family perk?'

'Yeah. That's the one.'

Sour as hell. I grinned into my wine. So much for wineshop owner's neutrality.

'How about Concordius?' I said.

'That one's just bloody well off.' Gabba refilled the cup and held up the jug. Pontius took it without a word and stood up. 'He's an incomer from the city. Got himself co-opted on to the town senate a couple of years back and makes his money from loans mostly. Property dealing. He owns quite a slice of the town, one way or another. Not that you'd notice, he's close as hell.'

'He gave us a bloody good gladiatorial show three days ago, anyhow.' Pontius was heading for the door with the jug. 'You went to it yourself, boy. Didn't hear you complaining at the time.'

'Sprat to catch a mackerel. Gladiators get you votes, specially if there's a few deaths.'

Pontius grunted. 'Some size of sprat. And he didn't skimp on the deaths, either. That'll've laid him back a good few thousands, which is more than Bolanus could afford if what—' He stopped. 'You all right, Corvinus?'

The simple answer to that was 'no': I was looking at the sheep. Or rather, I was looking at the person who was looking at the sheep. Oh, bugger; double bugger. 'Uh ... excuse me, gentlemen, this is an emergency,' I said.

I was off the bench like a bolt from a catapult, but I was too late. Money had already changed hands.

My animal-crazy adopted daughter Marilla turned and gave me one of her special smiles.

'Oh, hello, Corvinus,' she said. 'I didn't see you there.' Like hell she hadn't! I'd *seen* her not seeing me, which was why I'd moved so fast. 'Isn't she lovely?'

Only Marilla could have applied that adjective to that brute. 'Princess,' I said, 'that is a sheep, okay? Up on the farm you've got acres of fu—' I stopped myself in time. 'You've got acres of sheep. What the hell do you want another one for?'

'No one else would buy her. Carrinatia was going to sell her for chops.'

'She's a good milker, sir.' The old biddy grinned at me. 'It says so on the placard.'

Uh-huh; we'd got a weird inversion of cause and effect here. On the other hand, I wasn't going to get sidetracked. This called for desperate measures. 'Tell you what, grandma,' I said. 'Forget the whole deal, take the thing back and you can keep the money, okay?'

The Princess gave me a look that would've fried an anchovy. '*Corvinus!* That's *not* playing fair!'

'Who said it was supposed to be fair?'

'Oh, I couldn't do that, sir.' Carrinatia looked shocked; smug, too, which was worrying. 'The sale's been made.'

Bch-bch-bch, went the sheep.

'It doesn't even sound like a fu—' – I clamped my lips together – 'like a sheep.'

'She's got a cold,' the Princess said.

Oh, great. What were the bets come tonight we'd be taking turns rubbing the brute's chest with oil of camphor. At least in the form of chops she would've made a definite contribution to society. Still, that was academic now. I sighed and turned to Carrinatia. 'Okay, grandma,' I said. 'You win, you've made yourself a sale. Just tell me about the business in Veturius's cellar and we'll call it quits.'

Something shifted behind her eyes. 'Veturius's cellar?'

'Yeah.'

'I don't know nothing about Veturius's cellar, sir.'

'Is that so, now?' Either she was lying or her grammar was good enough to see the advantage of a double negative. Still, I recognised stonewalling when I heard it. And I'd bet, from the old biddy's tone and the determined look in her eye, that argue as I might she wouldn't budge an inch.

Oh, hell.

I found out about the business in Veturius's cellar from Pontius, after Marilla had gone off home in triumph leading her purchase. I wasn't surprised Carrinatia hadn't admitted to knowing anything about it. I wouldn't have, either.

Bch-bch-bch.

2

'The brute broke into Veturius's cellar and pulled the stoppers out from four jars of his best wine,' I said. '*Best* wine, note; we're talking selection here. By the time the guy found out she was on her back, legs in the air and canned as a newt.'

Perilla sniffed. 'These accidents happen. The cellar door was probably left open.'

I leaned against my dinner-couch cushion. 'Lady, I checked. The door was bolted. And the woolly bastard forced her way through a hedge and sneaked past half a dozen household slaves to get to it. That is *not* an accident.'

'I agree with Perilla, Marcus.' Marcia Fulvina dabbed her lips with her napkin. 'No sheep could possibly have the intelligence to do what you've described. The household slaves were probably covering up for themselves. Besides, it was an isolated incident.'

'You want to keep your fingers crossed over that?'

Marilla was beaming at Marcia. 'So I can keep her?' she said.

Marcia hesitated: frail, white-haired and pushing eighty she may be, but the lady is needle-sharp. Also, she knew the Princess. And Corydon. 'I don't see why not, dear,' she said at last. 'Outside. In the paddock. Tethered. With a chain and padlock. Now finish your dinner, please, and let Bathyllus clear the table.'

'But she's got a cold!'

'It's the middle of summer, and Dassa is a sheep. She won't come to any harm.' Marcia turned to me. 'You don't really mind if she keeps her, do you, Marcus?'

Gods. I had a bad feeling about this, but it was her house, I was a guest and if she wanted to take the risk there was no more to be said. 'Oh, it's fine by me,' I said. 'But when the brute cleans you out of Caecuban just remember I warned you, okay?'

The old lady smiled. 'I shall certainly remember, if and when necessary. Now. How was your afternoon? I don't get into town all that much these days, but I do like to keep abreast of what's happening. I suppose this election business is warming up nicely.'

The choice of subject wasn't as unexpected as it could've been. Marcia Fulvina might live out in the sticks, but she was no hayseed. When I'd first met her years ago in Rome she'd been married to Fabius Maximus, who in his time had been one of Augustus's right-hand men, and you can't move in these circles without picking up a taste for politics. 'Aunt' was just a courtesy title – she'd been related to Perilla's mother, but they weren't sisters – and old Maximus had been Perilla's de iure and de facto head of family. She and Perilla had always been close, and when we sprang the Princess loose from her bastard of a father it'd been Marcia who took her in. Now the kid was just as much Marcia's as ours; more so, maybe.

'Yeah,' I said. 'You could say that. It seems to be quite a needle match.'

'Oh, yes.' Marcia laid down her napkin. 'The five-year censorship always is when there's more than one candidate.' She paused, then added drily, 'And, of course, on this occasion there is the contract allocation for a new town hall in the offing. That, I'm afraid, may be of some relevance too.'

I grinned into my wine cup; like I say, where the practical aspects of politics are concerned old Marcia is no one's fool. A provincial censor isn't quite the same as his Roman equivalent, more a combination of censor, finance officer and buildings officer, which means as well as being responsible for updating the citizens' list he also controls the municipal finances and the allocation of public building contracts. Not that he has a totally free hand, of course, because all his decisions are subject to the approval of the local senate and ultimately to the central authorities in Rome; but even so he can be fairly sure that when the time comes the companies he gives the contracts to will be properly – and unobtrusively – grateful. And new town halls don't come cheap.

I was reaching for the wine jug to give myself a top-up when Bathyllus oozed in with his tray. Under normal circumstances Marcia had a major-domo of her own, but the old guy was touching seventy, he was getting pretty shaky on his pins, and when we came up for a few days he and the equally decrepit chef were shuttled down to Baiae to stay with one of Marcia's freedwomen. That could've caused bad feelings – major-domos tend to get touchy where their households are concerned – but old Laertes was an easy-going soul. Besides, we couldn't've left Bathyllus behind. He had a soft spot for the Princess too.

'Shall I clear away, madam?' he said to Marcia. Deferential as hell. That was another thing about holidays in the Alban Hills: Bathyllus is the world's number-one snob, and butlering to a real aristocrat like Marcia was the little bald-head's idea of heaven. Tough on the rest of us, mind. I could take it, just, for the duration, but towards the end it got to be a real teeth-clencher.

'Yes, thank you, Bathyllus.' Marcia looked at the Princess. 'If you've finished, Marilla.'

'Can I take an apple out to Dassa? And ask Meton for some warm oil?' Meton was our chef, currently replacing Marcia's own hash-slinger.

'Yes, I suppose so. If you really must.'

The kid grabbed the biggest Matian from the fruit bowl and disappeared in the direction of the kitchen. Perilla and Marcia watched her go, smiling.

'Pontius didn't think much of either of the candidates,' I said, while Bathyllus with lowered eyes and a murmured apology removed my dessert plate.

'They both have their drawbacks, certainly.' Marcia was cautious. 'Concordius is very much the modern-style businessman; very efficient and knowledgeable about things like market trends and valuation, no doubt, and just what Castrimoenium needs in a censor these days. On the other hand I find it difficult to take to that kind of man myself. Which sounds dreadful, I know, but really in his case I think the generalisation is justified.' She hesitated. 'Where money is concerned, I wouldn't entirely *trust* Publius Concordius.'

'Uh-huh.' I sipped my wine; no gulping, because although Marcia didn't drink much herself she kept a good cellar. This one was a twenty-year-old Alban, and practically Falernian standard. 'He's in the loans business, right?'

'Yes. Loans and property. Doing very well, too, or so I hear. He owns quite a number of large mortgages in the town, and with villas near the lake especially becoming so fashionable now at Rome the property market is booming. Vettius Bolanus, for example, could get a very large price indeed for his estate if he decided to sell it, but of course he won't. Certainly not to Concordius.'

'Bolanus is the other candidate, isn't he?' Perilla said.

'Oh, yes, very much so. I'm afraid that's the whole problem.' Then, when Perilla looked puzzled: 'Forgive me, dear; I expressed myself badly. Vettius Bolanus is the "other candidate" both in the sense that he is the second of two and also the weaker of the pair, and neither circumstance has tended to reconcile him with his opponent. The Vettii have been the leading Castrimoenian family time out of mind. When one of them puts his name forward for the censorship election it has been, up to now, a foregone conclusion and unopposed. Especially by someone who stands a good chance of winning.'

Yeah; Gabba had used the phrase 'family perk'. Some things

don't change wherever you are; magistracies and priesthoods at Rome are the same. 'Which Concordius does?' I said.

'Oh, yes. Not, though, I suspect, through any particular merit of his own.' Marcia sipped her fruit juice; Perilla had a cup of the stuff as well, from the farm's own peaches. I shuddered. 'However, Vettius Bolanus has always rather taken his position for granted, and that's not a popular attitude locally, not nowadays. His behaviour over the estate, of course, makes matters worse.'

I was getting interested despite myself; I'd always seen Castrimoenium as a quiet little place. Obviously beneath the surface it was a real hotbed of skulduggery and scandal. 'And what behaviour would that be now?'

'Oh, it's not completely unaccountable. Bolanus's grandfather supported Caesar and the young Augustus before he *was* Augustus and was still friendly with Antony, so he came through the troubles with his estate intact. It's the biggest for miles around, in area at least, although *terribly* mismanaged, or it was until recently when Bolanus got rid of that dreadful man Feronius and appointed a proper agent, since when—' She stopped. 'I'm sorry, Marcus, I'm rambling. A feature of age. Where was I?'

Rambling, nothing; personally, I'd back Marcia Fulvina's thought processes against those of nine-tenths of the buggers in the Roman Senate. At least they *were* thought processes.

'Uh . . . Bolanus's behaviour over his estate.'

'Oh, yes. I meant the business of his denying neighbours access for hunting. We take a very *laissez-faire* attitude towards trespass and poaching up here, at least where the wilder parts of a property go; there's so much ground and so much game that no one really bothers with property lines, not where the smaller animals and birds are concerned. Vettius Bolanus is different; he's very jealous over his property rights, and the fact that he isn't a huntsman himself makes matters worse. It's caused a lot of bad feeling locally, especially since the estate itself is so large.'

'And the bad feeling affects the number of votes he can expect, right?'

'Indeed.' Marcia smiled. 'What I'm saying, dear, is that Bolanus may be old Castrimoenian but he's not a terribly popular man. And because he doesn't have the hard cash he needs to buy additional popularity the election is not the foregone conclusion he considers is due him.'

Yeah; no wonder, like Gabba had said, he hated Concordius's guts. 'What about his other income?' I said. 'Or is the estate all he's got?'

'That I can't tell you, Marcus. I barely know the man personally, and also it's not a matter that I suspect he's inclined to discuss. However, he does have a certain reputation for extravagance.' She smiled again. 'Which is, I'm afraid, another point in his disfavour. Castrimoenians are simple folk in general; they don't mind a certain amount of high living, but they don't like extravagance, especially if it's the showy kind. And Bolanus is certainly showy.'

'Doesn't anyone else want the post?' Perilla topped up her fruit juice. 'I mean, if neither of the candidates is particularly popular, then—'

'This isn't Rome, dear.' Marcia took a sip from her own cup. 'Most of the local senators have business of their own to look after, and despite its advantages the censorship is no sinecure. Also, perks or not, it can be very expensive if one wants to keep up appearances, and not just at the canvassing stage.' She frowned. 'Although I don't generally have much time for Tiberius, undemocratic though it may seem on the surface, removing the election of magistrates from the public sphere has always struck me as one of his better ideas. Campaigning really is a most *distasteful* process, especially when the candidates descend to personalities, and the man who wins so often does so for quite the wrong reasons.'

Yeah; I'd agree with that. Over the past couple of days I'd seen quite a few of the graffiti on offer; one stretch had even been painted over, presumably by the opposing team, unless the guy whose wall it was on had taken exception to the sentiments expressed on political grounds. Hotbed of skulduggery and scandal was right. I reached for the wine jug. 'So who do you think will win this one, Marcia?'

She didn't answer at once. Then she said carefully, 'I don't know. Nor would I try to venture a guess. To tell you the truth, at the end of the day I don't think it will really matter.' She glanced over at the window: the dining-room had been built facing west, and the sun was disappearing behind the hills in a blaze of red. 'Speaking of which, it's a lovely evening and there's a full moon tonight. I'm off to bed myself, but why don't you and Perilla take your drinks down to the loggia and enjoy it?'

'Yeah; yeah, good idea,' I said. In Rome, sitting out in the peace of the evening isn't something you get to do all that often, not within earshot of a main road, anyway, because as soon as the sun goes down the heavy vehicles start to move in. A cup or two of wine in the garden with nothing but silence and night-birds to listen to'd make a pleasant change.

We said goodnight to Marcia. We didn't know it then, of course, but in about an hour's time the question of who would be Castrimoenium's next five-year censor would be academic.

3

'You're sure it was murder?' I set down my breakfast roll.

Quintus Libanius, the head of the Castrimoenian senate, pursed his lips behind his unsenatorial beard. Happy was something the guy didn't look. 'Oh, yes,' he said. 'Quite sure. There's no doubt about that, none at all, I'm afraid. It's all most distressing.'

Yeah, well; I'd imagine it would be. Especially for the corpse. 'Fine,' I said. 'But why come to me?'

'Marcia Fulvina is an old friend of mine, Valerius Corvinus. She has mentioned your, ah' – he hesitated – 'familiarity with cases like this on several occasions in the past, and naturally I was aware that you and your wife were spending some time here.' He looked at Perilla who was carefully honeying a roll of her own, eyes lowered. 'I will of course be contacting the foreign judge's office in Rome, but in the immediate instance I feel that your help and advice would be of immeasurable assistance. Should you care to extend them.'

Stiff as hell, sure, but that's the Roman way of doing things as far as guys like Libanius are concerned. You pull the personal strings first, and you do it formal. Translated into simple Latin, it meant that the representative of local authority wasn't going to take no for an answer.

I glanced at Perilla: no Marcia this morning, she was having a long lie, and the Princess was out tending to her sick sheep.

She didn't look too happy either, although 'pissed off' might describe it better.

'Uh . . . what do you think, lady?' I said cautiously.

Perilla set down the roll. 'Marcus, you know very well that you're going to go whatever I think,' she said, 'so don't faff around.'

I grinned; not the standard reaction, and Fuzzface Libanius looked politely scandalised, but I couldn't help that. She was right, of course; I couldn't pass this up, and as far as the holiday went two or three days of bucolic peace were about all I could take before I started itching anyway. I turned back to Fuzzface. 'You care to give me the full details?' I said.

He hesitated again. 'Perhaps . . . not while your wife is having breakfast,' he said. Ouch: that bad, eh? 'Suffice it to say that it happened late last night. Draco, Vettius Bolanus's head slave, did inform me of the death immediately, but I thought it best to leave any investigation until this morning. If you're agreeable, we might ride over there at once.'

So much for breakfast, but then I never had been a breakfast person. 'All right,' I said. 'Give me time to get a horse saddled and I'll be right with you.'

Vettius Bolanus's place was by the lakeside about a mile from town. I could see what Marcia had meant when she said that if he'd wanted to sell it he could have written his own ticket: it was prime site, and just the combination of well-set-up country house, working estate and not-quite-virgin wilderness that turns rich City businessmen gooey inside. Not just those with personal dreams of an idyllic country retreat, either: it was serviced with a good wide gravel-surfaced track, which connected with the locally maintained departmental road, and that in turn joined the Appian Way four or five miles to the south. Good communications, in other words: like Marcia had said again, wealthy City punters were waking up to the fact that even if they used a carriage they could leave Rome in summer mid-afternoon and still be sitting on their Alban veranda overlooking the lake by the time the lamps were lit, and property prices were consequently going through the roof. There was enough land here for two luxury villas easy, maybe even three, and a property developer-cum-builder who knew his business and bought the place as a parcel could clean up.

Another thing I noticed, as we rode up the track to the villa itself, was the number of new vines and fruit trees in the working parts of the farm: not all together in rows on newly broken ground, but filling gaps among the older stock. That registered too: it argued repair, not expansion. Somebody recently – and I remembered Marcia's digression about Bolanus's ex-bailiff – had been allowing the commercial side of things to slip, and whoever had taken over was in the process of putting them right. I filed that one away for future consideration.

The villa, surprisingly, wasn't walled off: the track led directly into a formal garden that stretched down to the lake itself. We walked the horses up to the main entrance where a guy in a slave's tunic and cap was waiting for us. Even at a distance I could see he was nervous as hell, which was understandable: a murder on the premises, especially where the victim's the master, tends to have that effect on the bought help.

'This is Draco, Valerius Corvinus,' Libanius said. 'Nothing's been touched, Draco?'

'No, sir.' The guy held the horses' bridles while we dismounted. He was a big man, six feet easy, but he was currently trying to lose a foot of his height like that might get him ignored. I could smell his fear even from three feet away.

'Fine. Valerius Corvinus and I will go down to the loggia. You'll make yourself available when you've seen to the horses. Is the Lady Vettia dressed yet?'

'Yes, sir.' He swallowed. 'She hasn't been to bed. She's in her room, sir, very upset. Her maid's with her.'

'We'll want to talk to her too, naturally. Later, when we've finished. Follow me, Corvinus.'

Yeah, well, I couldn't complain about Libanius's efficiency: he seemed to have everything stitched up nicely. It was a pity about the beard, though.

The loggia was tucked away in the garden's furthest corner, overlooking the lake. It was bigger than I'd expected – more of a summer-house than a loggia proper – but the design was the usual one: a stone skeleton with a solid tile roof and the actual walls made up of wooden shutters that could be folded back on themselves depending how much air and light you wanted in. Currently, as far as I could see, only the front two were open, giving the building a definite southern orientation; not that there would've been much point in opening any of the others, mind, because the surrounding bushes, sides and back, had been allowed to grow until in places they pressed against the walls. Another black mark against Bolanus's estate manager.

'He's in there.' Libanius had stopped short, before we actually got close enough to see inside. Now we'd got away from the domestic help, the guy wasn't looking so good, not to say – as far as I could see beneath the fuzz – distinctly green. 'I'd – ah – rather stay out here myself, if you don't mind.'

Uh-oh; so it was nasty right enough. Or maybe Libanius just had a weak stomach. I gave him a nod and went in.

I saw the body at once. The guy was lying just inside the door with his back to it, head twisted sideways and arms spread like he'd fallen forwards and hugged the floor. He'd been a smallish man, broad-built, and his throat had been severed ear to ear. The floorboards round the corpse's head were one brown sticky mess, and they were thick with flies.

'Oh, shit,' I murmured. I didn't blame Fuzzface for refusing to give me the details over the breakfast table, or for opting to stay out in the fresh air; I was trying hard not to breathe myself, and what little breakfast I'd managed was suddenly beginning to seem like a bad idea. A few of the disturbed flies rose lazily, and one settled on my wrist. I brushed it off, and it left a brown smear.

I stood by the entrance a while just breathing and fought the returning breakfast. Outside, Libanius was gazing out over the lake. All right for some. Yeah, fine; well, this wasn't getting the job done. I swallowed and turned round, back to the corpse.

The guy's hands were empty. He was wearing a lounging tunic, the sort you change into in the evening when there're no guests for dinner, but what there was of it clear of blood looked new and pricey: Bolanus had been a smart dresser, even on his own time. I remembered what Marcia had said about him being showy. Nothing else there, as far as I could see. No sign, certainly, of the weapon.

What else? I took a look around. The place didn't exactly show signs of daily use, and it was pretty grubby. The floor was littered with the usual accumulation of minor debris that builds up when it doesn't see a broom from one month's end to the next. Someone had been eating roasted pumpkin seeds and the spiders had been having a field day in the corners, but our pal with the knife hadn't conveniently dropped anything in the process like a cloak pin or a ring with his signet in the bezel. Well, there wasn't too much else I could do for the moment, barring the unpleasant obvious. After that first examination I'd been careful not to look at the huddle on the floor, especially the face, but the flies were seriously disturbed now and the air was full of them. Without giving myself time to think, and trying to keep my tunic clear of the blood, I bent over the corpse and lugged it over on to its back. There was nothing underneath but bloodstained boards.

So. Honour was satisfied. I left Bolanus where he lay, staring up at the ceiling, and made it outside while I still had control of my stomach.

Libanius was still giving the lake his full attention. He turned round when I came up.

'You've finished?' he said.

'Yeah.' I took a big breath of clean lakeside air.

'And?'

'It seems pretty clear what happened. As far as the actual killing's concerned, anyway. My guess is the murderer was hiding somewhere outside, probably in these bushes by the door. He waited until Bolanus was past him, grabbed the guy from behind and slit his throat, then pushed him forwards into the loggia.'

Libanius grunted, and suddenly looked green again.

'Now.' I took another deep breath of clean air. 'You want to tell me the circumstances?'

'Perhaps Draco should do that, Corvinus. Here he is now.'

I looked round. The major-domo was coming along the path. Formally laid out or not, the garden – this part of it, anyway – was pretty overgrown, and the house wasn't visible. A loud shout or a scream would've reached it, sure, but that would be what it took, nothing less. Not that, judging by what I'd just seen, the poor bugger had had much of a chance at either.

'The Lady Vettia was wondering if we might contact the undertakers in town, sir,' he said. He gave the loggia a nervous glance. 'She says it isn't right that the master should be . . . should . . .' He stopped. 'Can I do that, sir? Yes or no?'

Libanius looked at me. I shrugged. 'Sure, as far as I'm concerned. No point in leaving the poor guy lying. Vettia's his sister, right?'

'Yes, sir. Thank you.' Draco turned to go.

'Hang on, pal,' I said. 'I need some answers to a few questions first. Like for starters what your master was doing out here after sunset in a place that doesn't look like it's been used for years.'

Draco glanced at Libanius.

'I haven't had the opportunity to acquaint Valerius Corvinus with the details.' Fuzzface had on his master-to-bought-help expression again. 'You'll tell him what he wants to know yourself, please.' Then, when Draco hesitated: 'Come on, man! Don't mess about!'

'He was meeting his fiancée, sir,' Draco said. 'The Lady Sulpicia.'

'Is that so, now?' I kept my voice neutral, but I noticed that after he'd given his instructions Libanius had looked away. Judging by the answer to the question, I could understand why. Not at the information itself, he'd know that already; the guy's reaction was simple embarrassment at the necessity of someone else hearing it. Fiancée or not, isolated loggias were no places for unchaperoned single women to meet their menfriends, especially after dark. And Libanius didn't exactly strike me as the permissive type. 'They, uh, make a habit of meeting out here at night?'

'Yes, sir,' Draco said. 'She was the one who found the body, sir.'

'Sulpicia is Sulpicius Severus's daughter, Corvinus.' You could've laid a Minturnian prawn on top of Fuzzface's tone and it'd keep fresh for a month. 'He owns the villa next door.'

'Uh-huh. And where's Sulpicia now?'

'At home, sir. I assume. She was quite distraught. As you can imagine.'

Yeah, that I could understand. In his present state Bolanus wasn't a very pretty sight. Coming on what was left of him unexpectedly, alone and after dark, would make anyone distraught. However, I'd reserve judgment on Sulpicia until I met the lady: anyone unconventional enough to fly in the face of social taboos, especially out here in the sticks, clearly wasn't your normal dewy-eyed virgin. Plus, of course, there was the other less savoury possibility to be considered. 'Uh . . . he seem all right when he went outside?' I said. 'Your master, I mean? Quite cheerful and normal?'

I'd simply asked the question as a matter of course, but the major-domo hesitated again. 'No, sir,' he said at last. 'To tell you the truth, he was a little . . . preoccupied. He had been, sir, for the past day or so.'

'What with?'

His face shut. 'I'm sorry, sir. That I can't say.'

'Is that a can't or a won't, friend?'

He didn't answer, which was an answer in itself. Uh-huh; well, we'd have to leave it at that for the moment. All the same, I shelved the little nugget for future consideration. 'So what happened exactly? From the beginning?'

'The master received a note, sir, delivered by one of Sulpicius Severus's slaves about an hour after sunset. He—'

'Hold on, Draco! An hour *after* sunset?'

'Yes, sir.'

'Wasn't that unusual?'

'It happens, sir, on occasion. Happened, I should say. But then the Lady Sulpicia is an unusual lady.' That came with a sniff which, although it wasn't anywhere near Bathyllus-power, was the same sort of thing. 'Also the master was out all that evening himself, which the lady may have known.'

'Out where, pal?'

'That again I can't tell you, sir. The master simply had an early dinner and went out.'

Jupiter in spangles, I couldn't believe this! One of the key features of all major-domos is that, whether he wants them to know it or not, they can tell almost to the square foot where the boss is at any given moment; and also, for that matter, if he looks 'preoccupied' have chapter and verse on what's biting him. How they do it the gods only know; maybe when they get the job they're allowed to tap into a network of extrasensory links, or maybe that comes first and the job follows. Whatever reason, it's built in with the masonry. Either Draco was the worst of the breed I'd ever met or the guy was lying through his teeth; and if so (and I favoured the second explanation) then two questions naturally followed: a) on instructions or off his own bat? and b) was this the only porky I was being fed?

Not that I'd any right at this point to push the issue, and in any case maybe he was just a duff (but truthful) major-domo. Still, it was another factor to shelve for future consideration. 'Okay,' I said. 'So Bolanus got back at . . . what time would you say?'

'Just before the message arrived, sir. About an hour after sunset.'

'And when was the meeting arranged for?'

'Practically immediately, sir. Or at least, he went out almost at once. The Lady Sulpicia would be able to tell you exactly, or the note itself, of course.'

'You've still got the note?'

'Oh, yes. The master left it on the atrium table. I assume it's still there.'

Joy in the morning! Well, that was an unexpected bit of luck, anyway. 'So. What happened then?'

'It can only have been a few minutes later. The Lady Sulpicia came hammering on the door, very distraught as I said, with the news that she'd found the master ... as you saw him, sir. I confirmed the lady's story myself, then sent one of the boys into town to Quintus Libanius here as being the most senior magistrate, and – well, that's it, sir.'

And Quintus Libanius had rousted me out practically at the crack of dawn the next morning. He'd been lucky I'd been awake and mobile enough to be rousted, sure, but in the country the cockerels go off at first light and they tend to take you with them.

Time for a little muscle. 'Okay,' I said. 'So who do *you* think did it?'

His eyes widened. 'I beg your pardon, sir?'

'It's a simple enough question, pal. You've been a slave with the household how long?'

'I was born on the estate, sir. I've been Vettius Bolanus's major-domo for seven years.'

'Fine. So you must know if he's got any enemies. Apart from Concordius, that is.' There was no point in pussyfooting around here, and the sooner we had that particular name out in the open the better. I glanced sideways at Libanius to see how he'd taken it, but Fuzzface seemed to have gone selectively deaf.

Draco's expression stiffened. 'It wouldn't be my place to

say, sir, even if I knew. I suggest you ask the master's sister.'

'All right.' I turned away. 'Let's just do that, friend. And in the process I'd be grateful if you'd let me look at that note from Sulpicia.'

That was another lady I had to meet. Concordius might be the obvious suspect, sure – even Libanius must realise that – but, me, I'd like to know why the sudden desire for a late-night rendezvous that ended up as a murder.

We went to see Vettia.

4

Vettia turned out to be a plump, homely woman in her mid-forties, dressed in a mourning mantle which contrasted sharply with a wig years too young for her. When Draco ushered us into the atrium she was sitting in a chair dabbing her eyes with a handkerchief, but Fuzzface got the benefit of a hundred-candelabra glare.

'I would like very much, Quintus Libanius,' she said stiffly, 'to have my brother's body removed to the undertaker's, or at least brought indoors. It's neither pious nor decent to allow him to . . .' She bit her lip. 'To allow . . .'

Fuzzface held up a hand. 'I've told Draco he can make the arrangements forthwith. I'm sorry, Vettia, but the delay was necessary. This is the gentleman I mentioned to you, Marcia Fulvina's relative Valerius Corvinus.'

That netted me a long stare. I'd bet from the paleness of the lady's eyes that they weren't all that strong. I also noticed that she'd been unwise enough to have her maid apply make-up to the lids and lashes, and the business with the handkerchief was having its predictable effect.

'It's kind of you, Valerius Corvinus,' she said finally, 'to give us your help. If there is anything I can do in my turn then please feel free to ask.'

Well, you couldn't say fairer than that. 'Uh . . . you could answer a few immediate questions, madam,' I said. 'If you feel up to it.'

'Yes, of course.' She tucked the handkerchief into the sleeve of her tunic, sat up straight and set her lips together. I had the weird impression, suddenly, that I wasn't talking to a dowdy middle-aged spinster at all but a rather serious – and nervous – schoolgirl facing a teacher; a rather serious schoolgirl who'd grow up into a dowdy middle-aged spinster, if you know what I mean.

'Your major-domo tells me your brother went outside to meet his fiancée,' I said. 'That she'd sent him a note shortly before.'

'That's correct.'

'Also that this wasn't – uh – unusual behaviour.'

Vettia's lips tightened a notch. 'My brother was an honourable man, Valerius Corvinus,' she said. 'I'm sure that there was no impropriety involved. And Sulpicia was his fiancée, after all. They were due to be married shortly. That makes all the difference.' She gave Libanius a straight look, and the guy coloured. 'To my mind, at least. As far as your question is concerned, no, it was not unusual.'

So that was Fuzzface told. I waited, but clearly that was all I was getting. 'Okay,' I said. 'Draco also tells me that Bolanus was ... the word he used was "preoccupied". You wouldn't know his reasons, would you?'

'Was he? I didn't notice it myself, particularly, or no more than usual, but if so I would imagine it had to do with the election. As I say, Marcus was an honourable man, and although he didn't talk about it very much, to me at least, I know for a fact that the manner in which his opponent was conducting the campaign hurt him deeply. Those horrible graffiti.' She shuddered. 'It shouldn't be allowed, Valerius Corvinus. A political election is no place for filth.'

Yeah, well; she was the guy's sister, after all. Still, there was definitely something of the desperate innocent about Vettia. Middle-aged schoolgirl was right: anyone who can reach the years of discretion and still say with a straight face that filth has no place in politics is either a politician themselves, simple in the head or blinkered. Besides, from what I'd seen scrawled on the walls of Castrimoenium there wasn't much to choose between Bolanus's supporters and Concordius's, and if Bolanus had given the okay to his share then I reckoned that Vettia, blinkers or no blinkers, was protesting too much by half. I looked sideways at Libanius. He'd got his colour back, but he had his poker face on again.

'Ah, did your brother have any enemies that you know of?' I said; then, when her mouth opened to answer: 'Apart from Concordius, that is.'

Libanius cleared his throat. 'Corvinus, I feel you may be taking things a little too much for granted here,' he said. 'Publius Concordius was Bolanus's political opponent, yes, of course he was; but that does not mean the two were actual enemies. Certainly not to the extent of murder. Please remember this.'

Well, it was a fair point, and as senior magistrate – and so technically in charge of the investigation – Libanius was within his rights to make it. Still, if his thoughts weren't moving along these lines just as much as mine were, and probably Vettia's too unless she was even stupider than she seemed, then I was a Nubian belly-dancer. As far as I was concerned, the other guy in the censorship race was firmly in the suspects bag already. What I was after were other possible avenues. I nodded to him and turned back to Vettia.

Her schoolgirl eyes were wide open. 'But of course he didn't have enemies!' she said. 'Why on earth should anyone hate Marcus?'

I kept my face straight: there was no point in indicating the logical fallacy in *that* little offering by suggesting that if he'd been universally loved he wouldn't be out there in the loggia with his throat slit. The question was yet further proof if I needed it that where basic, everyday nous was concerned Vettia wasn't quite up to speed with the rest of humanity. 'Okay,' I said. 'How about people who might've borne him a grudge for some reason?'

'Oh.' The lady looked happier at that one; probably because

it suggested the blame could be firmly placed on the other guys' shoulders. 'There's Feronius, of course. And old Harpax and his son-in-law. No one else I can think of specifically.'

The second name was a new one to me, but I'd heard the first from Marcia. 'Feronius was your brother's factor, right?' I said.

'Until a month or so ago, yes. Marcus dismissed him for gross inefficiency. He went' – she hesitated – 'rather unwillingly. One of our own freedmen has the post now.'

'Uh-huh.' I remembered the plugged gaps in the vines and orchards on the road in. Estate factors are a landowner's bugbear. Unless they're watched closely, a lazy or an inefficient factor – or worse, one on the make – can wreck what's often only a marginally profitable estate faster and more thoroughly than a plant disease or a crop failure, especially since the slaves who do the actual work couldn't, by definition, care less about the state of the master's balance sheet. And *rather unwillingly* was a euphemism if I'd ever heard one. 'What's he doing at present, do you know?'

'I really have no idea.'

'I think you'll find, Corvinus' – Libanius's tone was carefully neutral – 'that he's employed by Publius Concordius.'

My eyebrows lifted. 'Is he, now?' Well, I couldn't say Castrimoenium's chief magistrate didn't play fair at handing out gratuitous information, anyway.

'In a very minor capacity, yes. As, so far as I understand it, a collector of interest instalments on loans.'

I nodded; add another one to the bag. Feronius was definitely one for a chat. The suspect list was filling up nicely. 'Who's this Harpax?'

Again, it was Fuzzface who answered. 'A retired soldier. He took his settlement parcel of land in the neighbourhood twenty-odd years ago, and his daughter married the local smith.'

'So why the grudge?'

'He and his son-in-law are both incorrigible poachers.' Vettia frowned. 'Marcus was very patient with them, very patient indeed, but a time does come when you have to draw the line. Also the old man isn't quite ... right. His daughter does her best, I'm sure, but people like that shouldn't really be allowed to mix in society.'

'Not quite right?'

'Oh, he's not mad, Corvinus,' Libanius said quickly. 'Don't form that impression. In fact, he's somewhat of a local hero. He served, as I understand it, in Germany with a cohort of auxiliaries and came away with an impressive array of distinctions. However, his experiences have left him ... scarred, one might say. I don't mean physically.'

Oh, hell; I didn't like the sound of this, reassurances or not. 'Fine. Then how do you mean?'

This time it was Libanius who hesitated. 'He was invalided out. I don't know the details, even in outline, and as I say this is ancient history, but I understand there were special circumstances and that he was honourably retired with full benefits before his official discharge date.'

'"Special circumstances"?' Jupiter, they must've been, at that: the army don't shell out compassionate discharges with full benefits all that often, especially to auxiliaries. Which would explain the local hero bit. Whatever this Harpax had done to get his piece of land and, presumably, his citizenship papers must've been pretty exceptional.

'That's all I can give you, I'm afraid.' Libanius cleared his throat again. 'He lives in town with his daughter and her husband – that's Spurius Rutilius the smith, as I told you – and they keep a close eye on him.'

'Not a close enough eye to stop the man poaching,' Vettia snapped. 'And Rutilius is just as bad, if not worse. Marcus has had endless trouble with the pair of them. He is ... *was* ... as I say a very patient man, but—'

'Well, that's as may be,' Libanius said. I had the distinct impression that, indulgent towards the bereaved woman as the guy was prepared to be, his own patience was beginning to wear thin. Also, I remembered what Marcia had said about how Bolanus's attitude towards poachers differed from the local norms, and Vettia seemed to be cast from the same mould. 'Certainly you must talk to Harpax, Valerius Corvinus, if you think fit. Now, if you agree, I think we've imposed on Vettia's grief for long enough and she will have things to arrange. Unless there's anything else—'

'The note,' I said. 'From Sulpicia. Maybe I could just see it?'

'Oh, yes. Draco did mention that. I have it here.' Vettia took a scrap of paper from her mantle pouch and handed it across.

I unfolded it and read. There wasn't much, just a request to meet her in the loggia an hour after sunset to 'talk things over', signed with an S. I looked up. 'Uh ... what "things" would those be, now?' I said.

Vettia's lips came together. 'That I don't know, Valerius Corvinus. Obviously whatever they were they were private, and if you really need to know then you must ask Sulpicia herself.'

'Yeah. Yeah, I'll do that.' I folded the note up again. 'Do you mind if I keep this?'

'So long as you return it to Sulpicia when you see her, no, not at all.'

We thanked her and left.

So; I reckoned I'd made a good start. The first, and most obvious, move was to have a word with the murdered man's fiancée: check the timings, generally look the lady over and satisfy myself that the arranged meeting and the murder were just coincidences. Not that that meant they were unconnected, of course; quite the reverse. If someone had been staking out Bolanus's villa, waiting for an opportunity to get him alone, then the rendezvous in the loggia would've given him all the opening he needed.

'I'm afraid I'll have to let you introduce yourself this time, Corvinus,' Libanius said as we remounted our horses and started back towards the road. 'I have business in Bovillae. Arrangements for the Latin Festival.'

Yeah, I knew that was coming up, in eleven days' time. The Latin Festival's held every year, although not on any specific date, in the sanctuary of Latin Jupiter on the top of Mount Alba; and although the surrounding municipalities aren't directly involved – the celebrants are all Roman, notably both of the consuls – they're expected to provide the necessary bits and bobs. Things like animals for sacrifice, slaves and attendants, accommodation and meals, for which last read slap-up civil banquets and general junketing. That I wasn't looking forward to; the current senior consul was Marcia's real nephew Paullus Persicus; he'd be dossing down at her villa, and on the few occasions we'd met we'd seriously got up each other's noses. I wasn't too eager to renew acquaintance with his foot-fetishist colleague Vitellius, either, but no doubt he'd've made his own accommodation arrangements.

'Fine,' I said. 'Just point me in the right direction and give me a push, pal.'

'Ah . . . yes.' That got me a quizzical, half-worried sideways look, and I had the definite impression that for all of two seconds Libanius was wondering if he should take me literally. That's the trouble with natural-born bureaucrats: no grasp of figurative language. 'You should have no difficulties, Corvinus. It's about a quarter-mile further on, on your left.'

We parted company at the villa gates and I carried on up the track that led between the wooded hill slopes and the reed-clad, bird-loud shores of the Alban Lake. Me, I'm a townie through and through, but I had to admit that for countryside Latium wasn't bad. Certainly peaceful. No wonder a fair slice of Rome's jaded rich were falling over themselves to buy in up here.

I found the track no bother and turned my horse's head into it. Severus's place was definitely the country-house variety rather than the working farm, which was more or less what I'd been expecting: all rural villas have their commercial side, sure, because scratch any Roman (barring, maybe, the occasional nut like my stepfather Priscus) and you'll find a practical businessman with an eye to cutting down overheads, but some are less production-oriented than others. This Severus obviously wasn't short of a gold piece or two.

The villa itself was smaller than Bolanus's, but it looked newer and more up-market and the marble-pillared portico along one side enclosing the formal garden must've cost a bomb. I walked the horse up to the door, dismounted and knocked. A door-slave in a natty orange tunic opened up.

'Yes, sir,' he said.

'Uh . . . the name's Marcus Valerius Corvinus. I was wondering if the mistress was at home. The Lady Sulpicia.'

'Not quite. But if you give me ten minutes I will be.'

I turned. A woman was striding towards me across the gravel from the direction of the woods at the garden's edge: late twenties, not all that much of a looker – her chin was too big, and too square – but you could feel the self-confidence just radiating off her in the way she walked. And from the snap of these two short sentences.

'Ah . . . you're Sulpicia?' I said. Yeah, stupid question under the circumstances, I know, but well-born Roman ladies don't often go for walks in the garden wearing a farmworker's tunic and leggings. They don't go much for the single tightly bound pigtail look, either. If she'd been holding a hunting spear and dragging a dead boar by the heels I wouldn't've been all that surprised.

'That's right.' She gave me a quick, summing look then pushed past me. 'Bion, take Valerius Corvinus round to the fishpond.'

That last order had been delivered over the lady's shoulder as she disappeared inside. The door-slave hadn't batted an eyelid. 'If you'll follow me, sir,' he said.

Well, I could see why a nocturnal meeting between Bolanus and his fiancée hadn't caused too much surprise. Unconventional was right; judging by first appearances, I'd guess that where unconventional behaviour was concerned Sulpicia could've written the manual. And there might've been a trace of redness in her eyes, sure, but 'distraught' wasn't a word that readily suggested itself.

We went through the lobby and the atrium. I'd expected, from the outside view, that the inside would be pretty impressive, but both the decor and the furniture were strictly functional: no wall paintings as such, just coloured plaster, and the couches were plain wood and fabric. Good quality, though, the best. Orange-Tunic led me through the gap at the side which gave out on to the peristyle, then across the enclosed formal garden with its bushes and flower-beds towards a small fountained fishpond with a couple of wicker chairs at its edge.

'Wait here, sir, if you please,' he said. 'The mistress won't be long.'

I sat. This I was looking forward to. If what I'd just seen of her was anything to go by, Vettius Bolanus's fiancée promised to be interesting.

5

She was a lot longer than the promised ten minutes, but when she finally arrived I could see what had caused the delay. The Huntress Camilla look was gone completely: she was wearing a stunning white mourning mantle and the pigtail had been transformed into a tight bun. The assurance was still there, though, in spades.

'Now,' she said, taking the other chair and settling the mantle around her. 'What exactly can I do for you, Valerius Corvinus? As you can see, we've had a bereavement, so I must ask you to be brief.'

Fair enough; although the shock didn't seem to have cramped her morning exercise any and I wondered whether she might be using the white mantle as an excuse. All the same, I wasn't about to squeeze this lady into the usual categories, because I could tell already that she wouldn't fit. 'That's why I've come,' I said. 'The First Speaker of the local senate asked me to look into the circumstances of your fiancé's death.'

Her lips set. 'Ex-fiancé.'

Gods! And I thought I was tactless! 'Uh, yeah, naturally, but—'

'No, you misunderstand. I didn't mean because Marcus is dead.' She adjusted a fold of the mantle with a sharp tug of her fingers. 'I meant it literally. We were no longer engaged. As of yesterday afternoon, to be exact.'

I blinked. 'Really?' I said. 'I'm sorry. I didn't know that.'

'You wouldn't. No one did, except for Marcus and myself. Oh, and my father, of course.' There was a definite edge to her voice, and you could've used the line her lips made for a ruler. 'Whether or not Marcus told anyone in his own household I really don't know, although I assume from your surprise that he didn't, or that they chose not to pass the information on. However, if your purpose in coming here is to ask me questions about what happened last night then we may as well begin with a clear field.'

Jupiter! 'Uh . . . you care to tell me why the engagement was broken off?' I said.

'No.' She shook her head. 'Certainly not. That's private. However, I can promise you it had nothing whatsoever to do with his death.'

'You're sure?'

That got me a look that would've skewered a rhino. 'Yes.'

I had the distinct impression that chasing the subject any further wouldn't be a good idea: a lady of few words, this, and no explanations. I took the note out from my mantle-pouch, unfolded it and passed it across. 'Okay. So if Vettius Bolanus wasn't your fiancé any longer then why arrange a meeting with him?'

Sulpicia glanced at the note, folded it carefully and set it aside. Her lips tightened another notch. 'Because I had things to explain,' she said.

'What sort of things?'

I thought at first she wasn't going to answer, but she did. 'We'd been engaged for six months and the wedding was imminent. Specifically, in another month, after the elections. When my . . . when the engagement was cancelled Marcus was very upset. Understandably so. How would you feel yourself, Corvinus, if you were simply given back a ring and told that it was no longer required?'

'It . . . ah . . . wasn't your doing then?' I said. Silence, and her face wasn't giving anything away, either. 'Fine. So. You arranged to meet Bolanus in the loggia an hour after sunset, yes?'

'Yes.'

'You often meet him there?'

'No, not in the loggia as such, but we did prefer the garden to the house. Or rather I did. I'm very much an outdoor person, Corvinus, which may surprise you since I spent most of my life in Rome.' She almost smiled. 'To tell you the truth, it surprised me as well when we moved here; but then Latium is a different world.'

'So why the loggia?'

'For the simple reason that we never met there usually. You've seen it, the place is a pit. I thought that perhaps it would be . . . less romantic, more formal, so more suited to the circumstances.' Her chin lifted. 'Also, I wasn't sure whether Marcus had told anyone of the broken engagement. A meeting in the villa itself with others present, or potentially so, would have embarrassed both of us.'

Well, that made sense of a kind, I supposed. And this lady was a deep one, that stuck out a mile. 'How about the timing?' I said.

She looked blank. 'Timing?'

'Were you on time? Early? Late?'

'I'm normally very punctual. However, on this occasion I wasn't particularly looking forward to our talk, so I was slightly late. Not by much, though; no more than five minutes.'

'You didn't see anyone? Hear anything?'

'No. Certainly not "see". I heard some rustling in the bushes at the edge of the path, but there are often small sounds at night that far from the house and I ignored them. Of course if I'd known what—' She stopped; I had the distinct impression that, despite the front, the lady wasn't quite as composed as she looked. 'If I'd known what had happened to Marcus,' she went on steadily, 'then I might have investigated, but at that point I didn't.'

Yeah; I'd believe that. Sulpicia was no soft-centre. Bloody stupid though it would've been, I could imagine the lady taking to the undergrowth after a prowler. 'So he was dead when you found him?' I said.

'Oh, yes.' She closed her eyes for a moment. 'Yes, he was. Obviously so. I ran to the house and told Draco. I don't remember much about that part, I'm afraid. Nor, to tell you the truth, am I particularly proud of myself for the way I acted.'

'Uh-huh.' I looked down. The hand on the mantle was shaking, despite the composure in the lady's voice. 'That all you can tell me?'

She nodded. 'Yes. Yes, it's all I know.'

'Except for why the engagement was broken off.'

Suddenly, the steel was back with a vengeance. 'Corvinus, I will not be interrogated! I've already told you that that is private. It had nothing at all to do with Marcus's death.' She stood up. 'Now if you'll excuse me—'

'Is your father at home?'

She paused. 'Yes. I think he's in his study. Why do you want to know?'

I hadn't moved. 'You mind if I have a word with him?'

'Personally I couldn't care less. But whether you may or not is for him to decide.' Her jaw set and took the rest of her face with it. I'd been wrong about her not being a looker; you just had to shift your perspective a bit. 'I'll send Bion to ask if he's free. Now if you're quite finished—'

'Yeah. Yes, I am.' I stood up. 'Thanks for your help.'

'Don't mention it.' Icy as hell.

'Oh, one more thing.'

'Yes?'

'Nothing to do with the murder. I was just wondering. You have any connection with the consul?'

'*What?*' For a moment, she looked fazed.

'Ex-consul, rather. Last year's model, Sulpicius Galba. You have the same family name.'

'Oh.' The fazed look disappeared, and she smiled. 'No. No, not really, no relation at all. He and my father are very distant cousins, but that's as far as it goes.'

'Right. Right.'

'I'll send Bion out with my father's decision. Good-day, Valerius Corvinus.' She turned.

I watched her disappear in the direction of the portico; nice body, too; you could tell even with the mourning mantle. I'd bet that, on her own terms, Sulpicia would be quite a catch. It'd have to be on her own terms, though, that went without saying.

Decision. Funny choice of word . . .

I sat down again and stretched out my legs. It'd been a busy morning, the sun was creeping round towards noon and I could've murdered a cup of wine. Maybe after I'd talked to Sulpicius – *if* I talked to Sulpicius – I could treat myself to an hour or two at Pontius's. I didn't have all that much to go on yet, but a half jug of Castrimoenian in the shade would be just the thing to kick-start the brain cells.

It was a good five minutes before Orange-Tunic came back out. 'Decision' was right, after all: I'd guess that whatever had been going on behind the scenes it had involved some considerable thought on someone's part.

'The master will see you, sir,' Bion said. 'This way, please.'

We went back through the atrium then upstairs to the study. Orange-Tunic knocked, then opened the door and stepped aside.

'Come in, Valerius Corvinus.'

You can tell a lot about a person from the state of their study. Me, I like a comfortable couch you can catnap on, a wine jug and cups and a window opening on to the street. Perilla's is wall-to-wall shelves crammed with books, a couch reserved strictly for reading, an upright chair and a no-nonsense writing desk.

Sulpicius Severus's study you could've used for a Market Square banker's office.

The guy suited the last part of his name, too: poker-backed, impeccably mantled, late fifties, iron-grey hair and a face that looked like if he tried a smile it'd crack along the lines and fall apart in shards. He was sitting at a desk with nothing on it but a neat pile of wax tablets and a pen.

'Sit down,' he said. I pulled up a solid wooden chair. No couches here. No upholstery, either. 'You wanted to see me.'

Jupiter! He'd've gone down a bomb as a schoolteacher. I caught myself glancing at the side of the desk to make sure there was no birch in evidence. 'Yes, sir. I'm—'

'I know who you are.' He didn't sound like he approved much, either. 'Quintus Libanius has asked you to look into the death of Marcus Vettius Bolanus.'

'Uh . . . yeah. I understand that your daughter was engaged to be m—'

'Sulpicia will have told you that the engagement was terminated shortly before he died. I simply wished to confirm that with you. She will also have said that this had nothing to do with his murder. That is also true.'

He was beginning to get up my nose: no mean feat after less than a minute's exposure. Also, I was damned if I was going to let him interrupt me a third time without blood being spilled. 'Hang on, pal,' I said.

That stopped him dead. It also got me a look that would've curdled milk.

'*Pal?*'

'Make it friend, then.' I sat back and crossed my legs. '"Shortly before" would seem to be – correct me if I'm wrong – a matter of hours. Now if you're sure that had nothing to do with Bolanus's death then fine, but I'd like to make my own mind up. And that sort of suggests that I really do need to know the reasons. From what your daughter said – or rather didn't say – I take it you were the one who pulled the plug.'

I could almost hear him counting up to ten. The red flush gradually faded and the hands on the desktop unclenched.

'Valerius Corvinus,' he said carefully, 'I have no intention, now or ever, of telling you why the marriage contract between Vettius Bolanus and my daughter was annulled. That was a private matter affecting only the three of us, the man is now dead, and in any case, Libanius or not, you have absolutely no authority to conduct any kind of interrogation. Now if you have no other business with me I would be grateful if you left.'

I got to my feet. Well, he was within his rights, and as far as his point about authority was concerned he was spot on: as head of the local senate Libanius exercised a judicial function, sure, but it stopped short of letting him appoint an official investigator; that had to come from the foreign judge's office in Rome. As things were, I could ask, but I couldn't insist. 'Thank you, sir,' I said, 'for your time.'

Maybe he hadn't thought I'd give way so easy, or maybe his conscience was pricking him; but in any case he frowned. 'Don't think I don't sympathise with your efforts, Corvinus,' he said. 'We can't have murderers running around loose. However, I honestly believe that anything I could tell you would be of no constructive help. As for my own opinion of Vettius Bolanus . . .' He stopped. I waited, but there wasn't any more. He picked up the pen and turned back to his tablets. 'Good-day, sir. Bion will show you out.'

Orange-Tunic was waiting in the corridor outside. He led me downstairs without a word.

I collected my horse and rode off slowly back up the track in the direction of town. Unsatisfactory though it'd been, the visit hadn't turned out a total waste of time, far from it. Although he'd set my teeth on edge, Sulpicius had struck me as pretty straight; the kind of man my father would've pigeonholed as 'a good, sound sort'. Obviously, he hadn't liked Bolanus – that was clear from his final words, if nothing else – and equally obviously the dislike had been recent: men like Sulpicius are careful who they pledge their daughters to, and they don't break bargains lightly. So what could the reason have been?

Clearly, something about the guy he'd just found out; something bad enough to put the wedding preparations totally on the skids. With men like Sulpicius, nine times out of ten the sticking point is the guy's morals, or lack of them, in either the sexual or the criminal sense: find out, via a reliable third party, that your darling daughter's future husband screws ballet dancers or goats, or that he's siphoning off the not-so-petty cash from the coffers of Aqueducts and Sewers, and you can't tear up the marriage contract fast enough. Unfortunately, Sulpicius's type also suffered from pride: having once let the bugger inside the ranks of the family – even in a prospective capacity – he'd feel himself debarred from blowing the whistle. He wouldn't have any more to do with the man personally, sure, but his own code stopped him from taking the next, public step, and wild horses wouldn't drag him into it.

That last was the clincher. If I wanted to know the answer to the Cancelled Wedding Mystery then I'd have to get it some other way, because neither Sulpicius nor his daughter would spill.

Sulpicia, now; that was another problem. Her father had had a down on Bolanus, sure, but I'd got the distinct impression that although she'd toed the party line like a dutiful daughter she hadn't signed all the articles. There was the mourning mantle for a start: obligatory for a family member, or of course at the actual funeral, but an ex-fiancée didn't rate mourning at home, especially where the break hadn't been amicable. And dutiful daughters whose fathers have just told them they're cancelling the cake don't arrange after-sunset meetings with their erstwhile betrothed to 'explain things'. I hadn't asked Sulpicius whether he'd known about that, but I'd bet a fistful of gold pieces to a kick in the teeth that he hadn't. I'd be interested to know what the outcome might have been *vis-à-vis* the wedding if Bolanus hadn't got himself murdered.

Also, under that cool, self-possessed exterior the lady had been *angry* . . .

The thought had come from nowhere, and it made me jerk the reins so the horse almost shied. Carefully, I laid it out and looked at it, playing over what she'd said and, more important, how she'd said it, trying other words instead of angry. Given the implications of the mourning mantle and the arranged meeting, *grief-stricken* ought to have fitted, but it didn't; but then I suspected that Sulpicia didn't do grief-stricken, not when she had herself firmly under control, anyway, which was probably most of the time. No, whether it made sense or not, *angry* was the perfect word. And the anger wasn't directed against Bolanus; it was directed against her father . . .

I shook my head. Hell, what I needed was that half jug.

I passed through Lake Gate and headed for the market square. At this time of day – early afternoon – Rome would've been heaving, but like I said Castrimoenium's a laid-back place where the logistics of getting from A to B don't involve constant vigilance against oncoming single-minded old biddies with shopping bags, misanthropic donkeys or broad-striper litters whose outwalkers reckon they have an automatic right of way even at corners.

Which meant that, especially perched up on top of a horse, I could look around and let my mind wander. I hadn't been this route all that often – the road to Marcia's led through the north-east quadrant of the town – and although, unlike Rome, Castrimoenium is more or less the same all over there are differences. The houses here, for example, were in better condition; there was even one that wouldn't have looked out of place up on the Pincian, with a high wall pierced by an iron gate through which I could see a stretch of lawn and a line of marble statues. To the immediate left of the gate was a slave with a bucket and brush, scrubbing at a large patch of what had been lettered artwork. I grinned. Yeah, well; if my graffiti artist of the day before had been anything to go by, any decent stretch of wall was just asking to be used as a political document. Now Bolanus was dead it was all academic, of course, but that little nugget of news would take time to filter down.

The slave had got most of the surface paint off, but it had soaked into the plasterwork beneath and the graffito was still clear enough. It showed a crudely drawn head surmounted by a cap. The lettering underneath said: CONCORDIUS.

I rode on, my brain buzzing.

Interesting, right?

6

'Afternoon, Corvinus.' Pontius was sweeping the wineshop floor when I came in. 'What can I get you?'

'Half a jug and some bread and cheese would go down nicely, pal.' I leaned my elbows on the bar.

Pontius set the broom against a table, came round the other side and reached for the wine flask. 'I hear you're involved with the murder,' he said.

I wasn't surprised: news travels fast in a small town like Castrimoenium, and the news that one of the municipality's great and good had had his throat slit would've been all over the place by the time the first cock stopped crowing. 'Yeah,' I said. 'So it seems.'

He poured the wine into the half jug and fetched a cup from the shelf. 'The poor bugger was butchered, so I'm told. Bits everywhere, blood spattered all over the walls.'

I sighed. 'Uh-uh,' I said. 'Just a simple throat-cutting.'

'Ah.' He looked disappointed; gods, I hate this fascination with gory details. Give the story a few hours' currency and you've got something that even old Aeschylus wouldn't touch with a buskin. 'You sure?'

'Trust me. I saw the body.' While he was slicing bread I sank the first welcome cup. Delicious!

'Concordius'll be doing handstands, anyway.' He shot me a quick sideways glance and then said casually, 'You – ah – talked to him about it yet?'

'No.' Yeah, well, that line of thought was pretty obvious, even from a nodding acquaintance with the case. I'd bet that Pontius wasn't the only guy in Castrimoenium who'd put Bolanus's political opponent's hand on the knife already. They could be right, too, for all I knew. Just because something's obvious doesn't mean to say it's wrong.

Pontius arranged the bread and cheese on a plate and passed it over. 'I hear it was the fiancée found him.' He clicked his tongue. 'Nasty.'

I was being pumped here, and I knew it. Still, that was par for the course, and it could go both ways. Also, if Pontius was in talkative-barman mode, which he clearly was, maybe I could get some answers myself. 'Yeah,' I said. 'Uh . . . she isn't a local, is she?'

'Nah.' Pontius pulled up a stool of his own. 'Sulpicius moved from Rome about five months back. Villa used to belong to an old guy called Ammianus. When he died his widow put it up for sale and went to Bovillae to live with her sister. Sulpicius's made a lot of improvements, mind. The place was a real mess inside and out, had been for years.'

I was staring at him. 'They only came here five months back? You're sure?'

'Sure I'm sure. February, it'd be. Ammianus caught a chill last November and he was dead by the Winter Festival. Property stood empty a couple of months before Sulpicius bought it and moved in.'

There was something out of kilter here. I concentrated on topping up my wine cup. 'Uh . . . I thought Bolanus and the daughter had been engaged since January.'

'Yeah. That's right. Wedding was to be after the elections. Tough on the prospective bride, right? Woman that age, she can't expect to get many more offers, especially if she's stuck out here.'

'So they were an item before she came to the district?'

'Naturally. It's not uncommon, Corvinus, her father and Bolanus being business partners, like.'

I almost spilled my wine. 'Sulpicius and Bolanus were business partners?'

'Sure. They co-owned a quarry. You didn't know?'

Shit! 'No, I didn't know,' I said. 'What quarry's this?'

'It's a big concern up Caba way. Sells building stone to companies all over the region. Rome, too.' He grinned. 'I told you, Corvinus, I don't take sides where elections go, but a lot of people say that's why Bolanus was so keen to get the censor's job. With the new town hall in the offing that could be a very handy little contract. Badly needed, too, from what I hear. Politics is a dirty business, right?'

I took a mouthful of wine. Yeah, well; I'd known about the town hall side of things already from Marcia, so that didn't come as much of a surprise. Sure, any decision Bolanus made as censor would have to be cleared with the senate, but so long as the winning bid was reasonable that part of things wouldn't be a problem as far as the guy's colleagues were concerned. Pontius had said it himself, politics was a dirty business: a lump sum judiciously lodged or a favour promised would've squared most of any opposition, and in any case 'one hand washes the other' could be the politician's motto. The other aspect, though, was something else again.

'Uh . . . how do you mean, "badly needed"?' I said.

Pontius's shoulders lifted. 'Story is, the company's in difficulties. They're not getting the orders any more.'

'Yeah? And why would that be, now?'

'I'm no businessman, Corvinus. I just hear rumours. But the quarry's been slimming down for the past six months, selling off slaves, cutting the free labour. That's all I can tell you.'

Six months, eh? That'd make it January. Could be coincidence, sure, but the back of my neck was itching. 'So if I wanted to find out more,' I said, 'who would I go to?'

Pontius shot me another look; the guy was no fool, and

even to me the question had sounded too casual. 'Barring Sulpicius?'

'Yeah. Barring Sulpicius.'

'The chief overseer used to be a man by the name of Coxa. Whether he's still there or not I don't know, but he's your best bet. You'd find him at the quarry itself. Head towards Caba and you can't miss it.'

'Right. Right, thanks.' I made a start on the bread and cheese, and chased it down with a swallow of wine. 'Incidentally, is there any rumour about Concordius being a freedman?'

Pontius blinked and frowned. 'What?'

'Only I was passing a house on the way here from the Lake Gate. Someone had drawn a picture on the wall of him wearing a freedman's cap.'

The frown was replaced by a grin. 'Big place with a huge garden? Fancy iron gates?'

'Yeah, that's it.'

The grin became a laugh. 'The cheeky bastard! That's Concordius's own house, Corvinus. A freedman's cap, you say?'

'Yeah.'

'Cheeky's right, then. Freedmen aren't eligible to run for censor. They aren't even allowed into the bloody senate, except as honorary non-voters.'

'Yeah, I know. I thought maybe that was the point. Hence the question.'

'Hang on.' Pontius was suddenly serious again. 'Let's get this clear. You're actually saying Concordius might be a freedman, right?'

'Not me. Whoever was responsible for that piece of graffiti.'

'Pal, that is *stupid*.'

'Look, I'm not saying anything. I'm *asking* if there's a rumour going round that he is. From the artwork that seems a reasonable assumption.'

'Uh-uh, no way, never. Not that I've heard, anyway. Sweet

Hercules, it wouldn't make any sense! The guy's a senator already, and they check these things. Someone's throwing muck in the hope that it sticks, that's all. It happens in every election; truth isn't an issue.'

I poured out some more of the wine. Yeah, he was probably right. Before Concordius'd be eligible for election to censor he'd have to be voted – or co-opted, at least – on to the senatorial body, which would entail submitting a birth certificate, proof of citizenship and a note from his banker guaranteeing that he met the relevant financial requirements. The last would be no problem, because if I could rely on my various informants he wasn't short of a few gold pieces, and that, when you came right down to it, was the biggie: municipal senators, unlike our home-grown broad-stripers, are expected to pay for the privilege of their rank by subsidising the local building programmes, social services and entertainment from their own pocket, and that sort of thing doesn't come cheap, especially when the pockets concerned aren't particularly numerous or well lined. As they wouldn't be, in city terms anyway, out here in the sticks. I didn't for a moment think that someone like Quintus Libanius would turn a blind eye to an illegality just to get a well-padded wallet on the strength, but under the circumstances I couldn't see him being over-zealous in checking the formal paperwork, either. And enough money'll buy you anything, even a handful of forged documents . . .

The hairs stirred on the back of my neck. Hold on, Corvinus, hold on! There was another aspect to this, and if you threw that into the pot then you were really talking high stakes. The censor's job didn't just involve controlling municipal finances. He was also responsible for revising the citizen roll; which meant, in effect, weeding out present voters whose names, for one reason or another, shouldn't be on it. Say a prospective censor had found out, for example, that one citizen had been laying claim to a status that he hadn't got; add to that that the citizen concerned wasn't just an ordinary punter, but a member of the senate who'd put himself up for the censorship in opposition to the first guy and looked like winning; say that the citizen in question knew that the first guy knew and intended to use the information in advance to get him out of the running . . .

I sat back, bread and cheese forgotten. Oh, shit. It was possible, sure it was, all of it. And it meant that I really did have to talk to Concordius.

'By the way, Corvinus. You interested in a wine-tasting competition?'

I brought my attention back. Pontius was running a cloth over the counter. 'Hmm?' I said.

'It's what you might call an annual event. To coincide with your Roman pals' celebration of the festival.' He rinsed the cloth out. 'Sort of cocking the snook, a little opposition ceremony of our own.'

'I might be. Tell me more.'

'It's simple. Like I say, it's a competition. Everybody puts in five silver pieces; two come back to me, three go into the pot. I set out six cups of wine apiece, all Latian. Everyone gets a card with the names of ten Latian wines on it. The guy who matches up the most out of the six wins the pot. Interested?'

'Sure!' Hell; I hadn't wanted to go to the festival anyway, and this sounded a lot more fun. 'Pontius, that is brilliant!'

'Yeah, well, you Romans aren't the only ones with good ideas. I warn you, though, the opposition's pretty stiff. Gabba's won it three years in a row, and there're a couple more of the lads who've come pretty close.'

'What're the ten wines?'

Pontius shook his head. 'Uh-uh. That's secret. They're all Latian, sure, but I change them every year. Have to, otherwise the buggers'd be in training from the Winter Festival on. And like I say you only get six out of the named ten.'

'You've got a deal, friend,' I said. 'And this is in eleven days' time, right?'

'Eighteenth of the month, as ever is.'

I turned my attention to the bread and cheese. If I was to beard Concordius in his den then I wanted to do it on a full stomach.

'It's a lie!' The man's huge hairy hands were flat on the study desk, stubby fingers splayed, and his face was beetroot red. 'Tell me who said it and I'll peg the bastard out for the crows. Repeat it yourself and I'll have you for slander.'

Yeah, well, I hadn't thought he'd just shrug it off with a disarming smile; Concordius wasn't the disarming-smile type. Far from it.

'Nobody said it, pal.' I leaned back in my chair. 'I just got it from a picture on a wall. And I'm not claiming it's true, either.'

He was calming down, but not by much. 'There's a lot of garbage scrawled on walls in an election campaign, anyone knows that. And only a fool believes more than half of it.'

Yeah, that was true enough; however, the trick was knowing what part you *could* believe. I'd hit the guy right away with the freedman accusation just to see how he'd react and all I'd got was simple knee-jerk rage, but that didn't mean there wasn't something in it. That I could check on later. 'Fine,' I said. 'So let's move on to Vettius Bolanus. You care to give me a thumbnail sketch? From your side of the fence?'

Concordius grunted. If the guy had had less hair I'd've described him as pig-like, but as it was he was more like a wild boar minus the tusks: big, muscular, in-your-face aggressive, and a depilatory manufacturer's nightmare. You could've spread him out and used him for a doormat.

'Bolanus,' he said, 'was a slimy, stuck-up, patronising, two-faced, five-star bastard. That do you?'

Sure it would. For an off-the-cuff thumbnail sketch it was pretty articulate, in fact. 'Uh . . . so you didn't like him, then?' I said. 'Personally, I mean.'

One side of Concordius's mouth twitched into what could've been a smile, although there wasn't much humour in it. 'Your sort make noises about not speaking ill of the dead,' he said. 'Frankly, if you handed me Vettius Bolanus's urn right now I'd spit in his ashes.'

'My sort?'

One hairy finger jerked towards the purple stripe on my tunic. 'Purple-stripers. The old-boy network. I've worked my way up the ladder, Corvinus. *Worked*, you understand? Bastards like Bolanus, they were born at the top, they think the upper rungs belong to them however incompetent they are. I'll make ten times better a censor than he ever would.'

'Is that right, now?'

'Sure it's right. You know why?'

'Tell me.'

'Because I'm not part of the network. Never have been and never will be, which is absolutely fine by me. I'm a businessman. To that crowd it may be a dirty word, but this isn't the Republic, the world's changed. They may not like it but the bastards're caught, and they know it. Businessmen are what they need to survive and what's important today is the bottom line on a balance sheet, not poncing around playing at things. You understand me?'

'Yeah. Yeah, I understand.' I did, too: the guy had a point, even if it did go with a chip on the shoulder the size of a tree-trunk. 'So what you're saying is that Bolanus was no businessman, right?'

'He couldn't turn one silver piece into two to save his life. And as far as ready cash went he didn't have a pot to piss in.'

'Uh-huh. Still, I was told he was co-partner in a quarry over at Caba.'

'That's right. So?'

'So at least he had business interests.'

Concordius chuckled. 'Having business interests don't make someone a businessman. Maybe you were also told that the company's on its way down the tubes. That proves my point. Plus it was his main reason for running for censor.'

'The town hall contract?'

That got me, for the first time, a look that was almost respectful. 'You've done your homework, haven't you? I told you. Bolanus was a slimy hypocrite who played the old-boy network for all it was worth. Sure the town hall contract. He'd dug a fucking hole for himself, business-wise, and like all these bastards do he was hoping his pals in the senate would give him a gentlemanly hand out. Only to do that he had to be censor, didn't he? And he was finding that just his name and his poncy accent weren't enough any more to get him there. That annoyed him like hell, especially since he couldn't afford to match me buying votes.'

Yeah, all that made sense. Bristles and foul mouth or not he was no fool, Concordius, far from it. 'You, uh, happen to know why his company was on the skids?' I said. 'Just for information?'

'"Just for information", eh?' He leaned back and sucked on a tooth, considering me. The small eyes under their mat of black hair had narrowed, and they were very, very sharp. 'You aren't as gormless as you look, Corvinus, are you?' I said nothing. He shrugged. 'Okay. One thing about being a businessman, you know when to make deals. I'll make you one now. The bastard's dead and good riddance but he's got friends, and if I'm to be censor, which I am now, I'll have to work with them whether we like each other or not. That's another thing about business. I want you off my back, purple-striper, and I'm willing to pay. With your "just for information" for starters. Deal?'

Pause; *long* pause. I looked into the clever, piggy eyes and shook my head slowly. 'Uh-uh. No deal, pal. Not on those terms.'

He flushed. 'Then, Corvinus,' he said slowly, 'you can just

go and play with yourself. Now leave me alone. I've got work to do.'

I found my own way out. The slave had finished scrubbing the graffito off the wall, but you could still see the outline, if you looked hard enough.

7

I'd had enough for one day, and in any case Perilla would be getting restive. Not to mention our chef, Meton: I hadn't applied for written permission excusing me dinner, and the fact that we weren't at home wouldn't make one iota of difference to the touchy bugger. Apropos of which, I hoped that when I got back there'd be an absence of laryngitic sheep together with a presence of mutton chops on the dinner menu, but that was about as likely as a tap-dancing oyster. Dassa, I suspected, was going to be a feature of life on the Alban farm until she popped her ovine clogs from natural causes.

I handed the nag over to one of Marcia's slaves to put away and went inside. Bathyllus was waiting with the usual jug and cup.

'You had a successful day, sir, I trust?' he said.

I trust. Shit, I really hated this super-butler business. Marcia wasn't even around to hear him. I stripped off my now pretty grey-looking mantle, handed it over for disposal and took charge of the drinks. 'Yeah, not bad, little guy, as far as it went. The mistress around?'

'The Lady Perilla is in the garden, sir. The Lady Marcia is resting upstairs. The Lady—'

'Right. Right,' I said hastily. 'Where do I stand *vis-à-vis* dinner?'

'Dinner will be served in about half an hour, sir, giving you ample time to change.' That was *definitely* a sniff: bastard! 'The chef is offering hare with calf's-brain stuffing in a lovage sauce plus a roast fowl with forcemeat dumplings and a *compote* of fruits for dessert.'

'Good. Good.' I poured a cupful of wine: I might be rationing myself at Marcia's, but the welcome-home belt was sacrosanct. 'Uh . . . you having problems with your adenoids, pal?'

'No, sir.' Sniff.

'Great. Well, so long as you're fit and happy that's the main thing. The garden, you said. For Perilla.'

'Yes, sir.' He butlered off. I headed for the peristyle.

I thought that, as usual, Perilla would be deep in a book but she was crouched over a clump of flowers with Alexis, the last member of the household team we'd brought with us from Rome. Alexis was doing something to the flowers in the clump with a small stick while she looked on in fascination.

I coughed. Perilla turned round, smiled and straightened. 'Ah, Marcus. You're back.'

I gave her the usual coming-home kiss. 'Yeah. What's happening here, then?'

'Alexis is showing me how to fertilise flowers.'

'He is *what*?'

My smart-as-paint gardener was on his feet as well now and red as a peony. If that's what these red flowers are. 'Uh . . . you do it with a hare's-tail brush, sir.' He held up what I'd taken for a stick. 'It reproduces the action of the bees. You see, the flower is the female part of the plant and when the bee goes into it to collect pollen it also—'

I held up a hand. Quickly. 'Yeah. Yeah, I get the idea. In outline, anyway. I won't ask you what the little bugger does when it gets there or how a brush can do the same job, but—'

'It's absolutely fascinating, dear.' Perilla was beaming. 'Alexis has this theory that under controlled conditions you could modify any plant you liked by treating the flower with pollen taken from another plant which shows the desired features. The pollen is similar in nature to male sperm, seemingly – or so Alexis tells me – and introduced into the female flower it—'

'Perilla—'

'... results in a seed, and hence a later plant, which shows features of both the originals. Yes, dear?'

I hesitated. 'Uh ... Perilla, how can I put this? You don't think that maybe a situation where a mistress and a slave are alone in a garden on their hands and knees furkling about in a flower's private parts together could be sort of misconstrued, do you?'

'Don't be silly, Marcus. Besides, I was just watching. Alexis was doing all the work.'

I bit my tongue.

'It's all based on sound philosophical principles, sir.' Alexis had his earnest look on. 'Each part of each plant contains all the elements of itself in miniature, in the appropriate proportions. If you wanted a blue poppy, say, you could treat a succession of plants with cornflower pollen because cornflower pollen contains a high proportion of the element of blueness. Or you could produce cucumbers the size of marrows by treating the flower with marrow pollen which contains large amounts of the elements of bigness. At least, that's the theory. It may require modification.'

'Alexis—'

'I'm experimenting at the moment with peas, sir.'

Holy bloody Priapus! 'Alexis, I really do not want to know any of this. Just shut up, okay?'

The guy went as purple as a mutated cauliflower. 'Yes, sir.'

'And put that ... that *brush* thing away.'

'Yes, sir.' He tucked it behind his ear. I winced.

'Now just push off, will you? And leave the plants alone, at least while the mistress is around to see. You get me?'

'Yes, sir. But—'

'No buts, pal. We'll forget this ever happened, which is maybe for the best. Agreed?' He turned to go. 'Oh, Alexis?'

'Yes, sir?'

'I'll have a job for you tomorrow. I want you to go and check up on something for me at the Citizen Births office in Rome.'

'Yes, sir.' He hesitated. 'Ah . . . I would like to say that all experiments are done in a strict spirit of scientific enquiry, sir. Honestly.'

'Yeah, sure. Go on, sunshine. Just make certain you conduct them in private next time, okay?'

'Yes, sir.' He went.

Perilla was glaring at me. 'Marcus Corvinus, that was really childish!'

'Not from where I'm standing, lady.'

'They are *plants*, for heaven's sake!'

'I thought you were the one who was good at metaphors. In fact, it wasn't even a metaphor, was it?'

'*Marcus!*'

I laughed; keeping my face straight for any length of time while I'm winding Perilla up is never easy. 'Okay. Joke's over. You have to admit it was pretty weird, though. Although for interest I'll admit it beats dead-heading roses.'

Perilla was grinning as she stretched up to kiss me. 'Corvinus, you are a pure, one hundred per cent pig! Alexis *believed* you! And you know how sensitive he is. It could set his research back months.'

'Yeah, well, perhaps the world isn't quite ready for giant cucumbers.' I took a swallow from my wine cup and carried it and the jug over to the table beneath the trellised vine. Perilla followed, and we sat down. I stretched until my joints cracked. 'Jupiter! That's better! Bathyllus said Marcia was resting. She all right?'

'Oh, yes. Nothing serious, just a touch of sun. And Marilla's out with Corydon. So, Marcus.' She rearranged her mantle. 'How far have you got?'

Bringing the lady up to date took a good fifteen minutes and two cups of wine. By the time I'd finished she was looking pensive.

'So you think Concordius did it after all?' she said.

'It's a reasonable assumption.' I took the top off my third cup. 'Not him personally, of course. He'd be capable of actual murder, sure, but he's the sort of man who'd buy a throat-slitting like any other service. Certainly, though, if we're going by pure *cui bono* then he's the obvious bet as the prime mover. The killing itself is pretty straightforward: all the killer would have to do would be to shadow Bolanus and wait his chance.'

'You don't think that argues against Concordius being responsible?'

'How do you mean, lady?'

'Well, let's say for argument that Concordius really is an ex-slave, and he knew that Bolanus had found out. Surely any murder plan which involved waiting wouldn't be an option. He'd want the man dead as soon as possible, to prevent him passing on the information to someone else.'

'Yeah, but he'd still need an opportunity, Perilla. Bolanus was a public figure, and you know how public figures behave at election times. They like to be seen in company, because company means support. I can't say for sure, but I'd bet that when Bolanus went out to meet Sulpicia it'd be the first time he'd been on his own all day. The same goes for any other day since the election campaign started.'

'Then why hadn't he made the information public already?'

'The impression I get is that he wasn't a talker. Maybe he was saving up his bombshell for the right moment.'

'Mmm.' She leaned her chin on her palm. 'If that's so then why the graffito?'

'That could've just been preparing the ground, or even a bit of devilment. It would've been easy to slip one of the local odd-job merchants a couple of silver pieces to go round under cover of darkness with a brush and a bucket of paint, make Concordius sweat before the axe fell. After all, what could the guy do? Apart from commit murder, of course, but even political opponents don't often view that as an option.'

Perilla frowned. 'This meeting with Sulpicia. I know that coincidences do happen, but you don't find this one a little too pat, do you?'

'Sure it's pat, lady; on the surface, at least. And if there is a direct, *a priori* connection then that means one of two things. Either Sulpicia was in on the murder herself or someone else knew about the note and used the meeting for their own purposes. The first's possible, sure, but it isn't likely. Why should Sulpicia want her fiancé – or ex-fiancé, rather – dead? And she was against breaking off the engagement, that I'd swear to.'

'All right. So who could have known about the note?'

'The slave who took it. And, when it was delivered, anyone in the Bolanus household, including his sister Vettia and the major-domo. They'd certainly know that the guy had gone outside, and if he left it behind him – which he did – they'd know the rest as well.' I took a swallow of wine. 'The only problem there – barring the obvious one of motive – is the time factor. The note was delivered to Bolanus personally, and Draco said he went out almost immediately. That doesn't give us much of an opportunity window. If the murderer was someone in the house then they'd only have had, say, ten or fifteen minutes max to decide on the killing, work out an excuse if necessary to be on their own, find a suitable murder weapon, get out to the loggia, slit the guy's throat and get back before they were missed. Without picking up any tell-tale bloodstains in the process. Also, of course, they'd have to *know* that they had that ten or fifteen minutes, which they naturally wouldn't. And all that, believe me, adds up to one hell of a problem. I think we can scratch the Bolanus family.'

'Agreed.' Perilla hesitated. 'What about the slave? The one

who carried the note? Oh, I don't mean him or her personally, but could they have told someone else? Been under instructions to do so, perhaps?'

I sat back. That was one aspect of things I hadn't considered, but the lady was right. We assume when we give a slave a message to carry that the guy will simply do as he's told; slaves, most slaves anyway, aren't too strong on original thought, and they don't have – or can't afford to have – any personal axes to grind. The trouble is, it's an assumption based on generalities: we forget that, slave or not, the guy's still a person, not the equivalent of a carrier pigeon. The snag was, of course, that a slave would have to be either pretty stupid or pretty pissed off before he allowed himself to betray the trust, because if he was found out the rest of his existence would be nasty, brutal and short, and probably involve a rack and a red-hot iron. Besides, slaves who aren't trustworthy aren't given messages to carry, certainly not personal ones. If this guy or girl – and I'd have to find out which before I was much older – had peached to anyone then the peachee had to be someone who outranked the young mistress. And for a slave in the Sulpicius household that could only be one person . . .

'Marcus?'

I refocused. 'Yeah?'

'I asked if you thought the slave who delivered the note could've told someone else about the meeting.'

'Yeah. The girl's father.'

Perilla was quiet for a long time. 'Ah,' she said at last.

'"Ah" is right, lady. I had my doubts about Sulpicius already, but this is extra. And it opens a few more possible angles. No answers, just questions.'

'Such as?'

'The big one is what prompted him to break off the engagement. And, now, whether he thought a broken engagement was enough repayment.'

'You think he's a possible murderer?'

I took my time over that one. 'Yeah,' I said slowly. 'Yeah, I'd go for that. Given certain circumstances. Not Concordius's kind, though: hatred wouldn't come into it, whatever the reason. Sulpicius wouldn't kill just because of hatred. If he killed anyone it wouldn't be murder, it'd be execution. Sulpicius would make a good executioner.'

Perilla shuddered. 'Don't!'

I topped up my wine. 'Of course, there is the other possibility, and that's a whole new field in itself.'

'"Other possibility"?'

'That we are talking coincidence, and the murder had nothing to do with the meeting per se. Or not directly, at least. The killer was just staking Bolanus out, waiting his chance, and seeing him go out to the loggia provided the opportunity.'

'I thought we'd already covered that. With Concordius.'

'Uh-uh.' I shook my head. 'Oh, sure, Concordius – or his agent – is the prime suspect for that angle, but he isn't the only runner. Bolanus wasn't liked. There was a guy called Feronius, for a start.'

'The ex-bailiff. Yes, you mentioned him.'

'Right. Actually, there's a tie-in there. Quintus Libanius told me he's working for Concordius now. If we're looking for an agent and thinking in terms of a premeditated murder plan then he's a definite bet. Then there's the local military hero Harpax and his son-in-law. I don't know much about that side of things yet, but they're worth a look. If the meeting and the murder were a pure coincidence then one of these two – or both – are pretty fair suspects because they'd have an independent reason for being in the right place at the right time.'

'How so?'

'They're poachers, Perilla. Last night was a full moon, and one gets you ten every hunter and poacher in Castrimoenium was out and busy. If they'd caught sight of Bolanus on his own and vulnerable they might just have seized their chance.'

'Would they have come that close to the house?'

'That I don't know. Me, if a bastard like Bolanus had warned me to keep clear of his land I might have made a point of it if only to cock a snook. But that's just me. I haven't met either of them so I can't judge.'

'Hello, Corvinus. How was the murder?'

I looked round. Marilla was leading Corydon the mule through the garden gate.

'Princess, you do not want to know,' I said. 'And if Aunt Marcia sees that brute anywhere near her flower-beds she'll sell him on for rissoles.'

'Oh, but I do want to know.' Marilla kissed the mule's nose and he licked her face. I winced. 'And Corydon's very well-behaved. He wouldn't touch Aunt Marcia's flowers.'

The mule snickered. Maybe it was my imagination, but the way the brute was eyeing up Alexis's experimental patch didn't augur well for the future of botanical research.

'Just keep a firm grip on his halter, dear,' Perilla said. 'Did you have a nice ride?'

'Oh, yes. I went into town to get some medicine for Dassa's throat.' She pulled a small bottle from her belt-pouch. 'I was just taking it to Meton. He's going to help me give it to her.'

I blinked. 'Meton? *Meton*'s going to help you?' That I just didn't believe. If Meton thought of animals at all it was in terms of a matching sauce. The guy's mental processes were so straightforward you could've used them to draw lines.

'He's very fond of Dassa. He says she has possibilities.'

'He says *what*? What the hell does that mean?' Unless, of course, he was thinking recipes, but Dassa was no epicure's dream, and even Meton had enough sense to distinguish between a pet and a candidate for the meat-safe.

'I don't know.' She pulled Corydon away from a newly

fertilised whatever-it-was. 'Now tell me about the murder. Was there much blood?'

'Marilla, I really *don't* think murder is a healthy subject for a young girl.' Perilla was frowning. 'Where did you get the medicine?'

'In town, like I said.' Was it my imagination, or was the Princess blushing slightly? 'From Hyperion.'

'Who's Hyperion?'

'The local doctor. Only he's not just a doctor. He and his wife have a herbs-and-simples shop. Aunt Marcia buys from them sometimes.'

'Uh ... these would be herbs and simples for humans, then,' I said.

'Oh, yes. But Hyperion treats animals as well and he says the medicine should work on sheep. And Dassa really does have a nasty cough.'

At which point someone did cough, behind me. I turned round in the chair. Not Dassa; Bathyllus.

'Dinner will be served shortly, sir,' he said, 'if you and the two mistresses are ready.' He eyed my still unchanged tunic and sniffed.

'Yeah, okay, little guy.' I stood up. Shelve the sleuthing for one day, the hare and the roast fowl were waiting.

'I have laid out an evening tunic for you in your room, sir. And a fresh mantle. Should you care to avail yourself of them.'

'Fine, fine. Message received and understood. I think I might just slum it, though, for one evening.'

The temperature dropped to sub-glacial. 'As you please, sir. "Slum it", sir. Certainly, sir.'

I sighed. Yeah, well, maybe I'd give way on this one: putting Bathyllus's nose out of joint was not something you did lightly. 'Okay, sunshine,' I said. 'You win. Got to keep the flag flying, right?'

'Yes, sir. My thoughts entirely.' Sniff.

I went up to change. Still, I'd made a good start. Tomorrow I'd send our botanical genius to Rome to check up on Concordius, and maybe ride over to the Caba quarry myself. Things were coming along nicely.

8

I was off the next morning reasonably bright and early. Caba wasn't far, no more than four or five miles as the crow flew, but hills being hills the distance was almost twice that, and the last stretch zigzagged up the dominating height of Mount Alba itself. I found the quarry no bother: from a distance, it had showed up as a scar cutting through the screen of pines, beeches and oaks that covered the mountain's sides. The access road was a respectable track made from stone chippings, wide enough for the carts that would be needed to transport the blocks down to the Appian Way, although I'd guess most of the Rome-bound traffic went in the other direction, up towards the Latin Road. Certainly the track was quiet enough, and I hadn't passed any wagons on the way.

The quarry itself was quiet, too. These places, usually, you can hardly hear yourself think for the constant hammering and the rumbling of the stone carts, but although there was work going on there wasn't a lot of it. I remembered what Pontius had said about the slimming down over the past six months. Judging by what I could see, the Caba quarry company was downright emaciated.

A group of four slaves were working a saw, squaring off a huge irregular block, while the fifth stood by with the ladle and water bucket. I dismounted, tied the horse to a handy bush and went over to them.

'Morning, lads,' I said. 'I'm looking for a guy by the name of Coxa.'

The four sawyers stopped at once, wiped the sweat from their eyes with the backs of their hands and stood panting, arms dangling, taking the chance of a rest when it was offered. That I could understand: in the quarry, rest-times would be in pretty short supply. Quarry slaves, like the poor buggers who work in the mines, are the lowest of the low, complete dead-enders; either they're too stupid for any other kind of work – which is saying something given the rich variety available – or they're troublemakers or habitual criminals who their ex-masters have finally given up on and sold for what they'll fetch. Which isn't all that much, generally, because in their new line of work they don't tend to live all that long. One of the gang at least fitted into that latter category: he only had half a beard because where the rest of it should've been – chin to temple, the whole right-hand side of his face – was a puckered mass of purple brand-scar tissue. I could just make out the letters FUG. Runaway. Whatever the poor bastard had run from, it must've been pretty bad to make him risk this.

The man with the ladle set it down and gave me a long slack-jawed stare.

'Master Coxa don't work here no more, sir,' he said finally.

'No problem, pal. In that case, maybe you can point me towards the overseer, whoever he is.'

'In the shed. Talking to the boss.'

He picked up the ladle again. Conversation over, evidently. And the rest-time. I left the poor sods to it and carried on further in.

There were a few more slaves working on the quarry proper, breaking off slabs of stone from the cliff face with wedges and mallets, but not all that many: business must be bad, right enough. The shed was at the far end, tucked away behind several piles of sawn blocks that occupied a flat stretch near the exit road ready for loading. I climbed the steps, knocked and entered . . .

Then I did a double-take.

Yeah, right; 'the boss'. If I'd been thinking, I'd've known what to expect.

'What are you doing here, Corvinus?' Sulpicius said; and the way he said it didn't exactly suggest he was thinking in terms of a hug of welcome.

When in doubt, take the fight to the enemy. And if Sulpicius wasn't that exactly, he was the next thing to it. 'Checking up on Vettius Bolanus's business interests,' I said. 'You didn't mention you were partners when we talked, did you?'

He purpled to the wattles: not with embarrassment, either. 'I didn't mention it,' he snapped, 'because it was none of your damned business. It still isn't. And now you'll oblige me by leaving, please.'

But that I wasn't having, not from no one. 'It's a long ride from Castrimoenium, pal,' I said, which got me another glare, 'and I haven't asked my questions yet. You don't want to answer them, that's fine, but we have to go through the motions here.'

The other guy in the small room – we were practically cheek by jowl – was staring at me, mouth half open. He had a freedman's cap on, sure, but my guess was, overseer or not, he didn't have much intellectual edge on the rest of the staff. 'You want me to call a couple of the lads, sir?' he said.

'No, Primus. Not yet.' I was getting the sort of look that Medusa the Gorgon would've given half her snakes for. 'If Valerius Corvinus wishes to act like a boor that's his affair.'

'Right.' I leaned a boorish shoulder against the door jamb. 'First question: the company's in difficulties and you're having problems getting orders. You care to tell me why?'

'Who gave you that information?' The purpling went up a notch.

'Friend, I can see for myself. You haven't got enough men out there to keep a single builder supplied for more than a couple of days max. Unless he specialises in one-seater latrines, that is.'

'Valerius Corvinus, you are being needlessly offensive!'

'Offensive, yes. Needlessly, no. I'm just wondering why I'm getting the run-around, that's all.'

'Vettius Bolanus's death has nothing to do with this business!'

'You like to let me decide that, maybe?'

'No! And I have no intention of answering your question. Not for any reasons of concealment but simply because it's none of your damn concern!'

'Okay,' I said, shifting my weight. 'Let's try another one. Where's Coxa?'

Sulpicius blinked: he hadn't been expecting that one. I didn't miss Primus's quick sideways look at his boss, either.

'What?'

'I was told the overseer here was a guy named Coxa. So what happened to him?'

'He left my employment. Primus here is his replacement.'

'You mean he was fired?'

I didn't think Sulpicius could get any angrier without spreading himself suddenly all over the walls of the hut, but he did. He was controlling it well, though, I'd give him that. 'I mean he left my employment,' he said. 'Corvinus, once again this is none of your business.'

'So when did he leave?'

'Just over six months ago. Now will you please—'

'Six months?' It was amazing how often that figure was cropping up. The start of the new year must've been a busy time up here in the Alban Hills. 'You mind if I ask why?'

Instead of answering, Sulpicius turned to Primus. 'Fetch Harpus and Auster.' Then, to me: 'I've tried to be polite, but you've made it impossible. You'll go now, this minute, or I'll have you escorted from the premises.'

Well, he wasn't going to tell me anything anyway, and I'd bet a flask of the best Alban to a poke in the eye with a stick that the whole thing would turn out to be a mare's nest. Jupiter, I hate these mule-stubborn, ramrod-spined buggers! I held up my hands, palm out. 'Fine. Fine. I'm going. One last question, nothing to do with business. Who carried your daughter's letter to Bolanus's house the night of the murder?'

I'd fazed him again, but he recovered quickly. 'Her maid Procne, naturally.'

'Right. Good.' I turned away. 'Thanks again for your help. I'll see you around.'

I didn't wait for a reply – he probably hadn't made one, anyway, certainly not one I'd've wanted to hear – but walked straight back to where I'd left my horse.

Well, I'd got something out of that little interview after all, and it had set me thinking. I'd been wrong: Sulpicius had known that his daughter was meeting Bolanus, or at least that she'd sent him a note. The question was, *when* had he known? After the event, or before it?

The answer to that made all the difference.

It was past noon when I rode through Castrimoenium's Caba Gate and up the street towards the market square. Arcadian landscape with shady dells where fauns lurk at noonday playing their reed pipes to languid dryads or not, I was hot and dusty and my tongue was dry as a razor strop. I parked the horse at the water-trough where she could make her own arrangements for liquid refreshment and headed across the square to Pontius's.

There was a guy sitting at the table under the trellis with a jug and lunch in front of him. Not one of the locals, that was sure, I could see that even from this distance: sharp city-bought mantle (plain, no stripe) impeccably draped, carefully barbered hair, age just the right side of thirty and that lounging, all-the-time-in-the-world look about him that didn't so much say 'out-of-town' as shout it. When I got closer, though, I saw the clean-cut city-slicker image was marred by a beaut of a shiner: his left eye was almost completely hidden by a purpling bruise that extended down past the cheekbone.

I gave him a nod and went inside. Pontius was finishing off his own lunch at the bar. He turned round.

'Hi, Corvinus,' he said. 'Hot enough for you?'

'Yeah.' I pulled out my purse. 'Make it a half jug of the usual, pal. And some of that sliced sausage. When you're ready.'

'Sure.' He got up, went round the other side of the bar and began putting things together.

I perched myself on a stool. 'Who's the guy out front?'

'Artist from Rome.' Pontius poured the wine into a jug. 'Been here a couple of days staying at old Mama Dastidia's.'

I raised my eyebrows. 'Is that so, now?' You didn't see many artists around, certainly not out here in the sticks, and certainly not *echt* Romans with Saepta mantles and Market Square haircuts. 'What kind of artist?'

'Wall paintings. He's making the rounds of the big villas touting for orders.'

Yeah, that made slightly more sense: like I say, the big money was moving into the Alban area in a big way, and there'd be a definite niche for a wall-painter hunting commissions. Still, he didn't fit the usual frame for an artist, not at all. For a start, most of them were Greeks, from Greece proper or, more commonly, from the Greek cities to the south. You didn't often get a Roman who could do anything with a paintbrush better than slap on a coat of whitewash; even ordinary Romans, and this guy was no ordinary Roman. The lad sounded interesting. 'Seems like he picked up more than a painting order recently, from the look of his face,' I said.

Pontius arranged the sliced sausage on a plate with a small loaf. 'Yeah. He had a spot of bother down in Bovillae, couple of days back. It happens from time to time. Romans aren't too popular in some quarters locally.' He added a handful of pickles and grinned. 'Saving your presence, Corvinus.'

I grunted, collected the jug, the wine cup and the plate and moved outside.

The guy looked up and smiled.

'You mind if I join you?' I said.

'Not at all. Glad of the company.' Cultured voice, too, despite the plain mantle.

I sat. 'Name's Valerius Corvinus.'

'Quintus Licinius.'

'Uh-huh.' Not an Aventine name, far from it; very far from it. Curiouser and curiouser. Still, I didn't comment, just poured the wine and took a restoring couple of swallows. 'Pontius says you're an artist.'

The smile widened. 'That's right. Specialising in murals. I do a good Battle of Gaugamela, if you're interested.'

'Not me, pal. I'm not local, just here on holiday.'

'Pity.' He didn't seem too worried, though: business must be good. 'That's my best seller. You'd be amazed how many bankers and fish sauce manufacturers want themselves painted in as Alexander.'

'Uh-uh.' I grinned back; I was beginning to like this guy. 'That wouldn't surprise me at all. You're from Rome?'

Licinius hesitated. 'Yes. Yes, I am, as a matter of fact.' *So?* his tone said.

'It's just that I'd bet a year's income to a pickled anchovy the number of middle-class Romans who could handle anything more complicated than a still life with cross-eyed pigeon you could count on the fingers of one hand. And even then you'd have fingers to spare.'

'Maybe. It's just something I'm good at and enjoy doing, that's all.' *Definitely* reticence; defensive reticence at that. Well, I could understand his attitude: in Roman pukkah society painting as a hobby ranked with flute-playing, acting and selling yourself under bridges. Doing it for a living put you right into the untouchable class.

Even so, curiosity was one thing but if he didn't want to volunteer the information then wineshop etiquette didn't allow me to press him any further. 'Market around here's certainly wide open,' I said as I made a start on my bread and sausage. 'New villas are going up like mushrooms.'

'Yes. That's what I thought.' He took a sip of his wine. 'You say you're on holiday?'

'Sure. My wife's a sort of niece of old Marcia Fulvina. We come up from Rome now and again.'

'Fabius Maximus's widow?'

I'd picked up my own wine cup. Now I set it down. 'Yeah, that's right,' I said. Now that was really interesting: he'd know of Marcia, sure – anyone in the interior decorating business out for commissions would've done his homework where prospective local customers were concerned – but Marcia had been widowed for years, well before she'd moved here, and family histories were another matter. 'How did you know that?'

He shrugged. 'You pick up these things. You here for long?'

'Just a month or so. Our adopted daughter lives with Marcia. It's practically the only time we get to see her.' We were on sensitive ground here as well; time for a subject change on my own account. I indicated his eye. 'I also heard from Pontius you had a bit of trouble in Bovillae.'

Another shrug. 'Nothing serious. A wineshop argument with one of the local hotheads. He didn't like Romans, I was obviously a Roman, we exchanged words and he hit me. End of story.'

'You didn't press charges?'

He gave me a long look. 'No,' he said finally. 'I hit him back. Just because I'm an artist doesn't mean I can't use my fists, and anyway the man was drunk. The wineshop owner locked him up for the night in a broom closet to sleep it off. There was no real damage done, and I don't like causing trouble unnecessarily.'

'You two all right out here?' That was Pontius, doing his customer check.

'Sure,' I said.

'You could bring me the other half.' Licinius held up his

empty jug. 'Maybe some more cheese and olives to go with it.'

'No problem.' Pontius took the jug and turned to me. 'I didn't ask you, Corvinus. You find Coxa okay at the quarry?'

'Uh-uh.' I shook my head. 'He doesn't work there any more. But I talked to Sulpicius.'

'Is that right now? Can't take to that man myself, too high and mighty by half. Still, he isn't a customer, so I should worry. Who's the new overseer?'

'Guy called Primus.'

Pontius snorted. 'That useless bastard! If he's in charge they're in trouble right enough.' He turned back to Licinius. 'I'll get you your wine and cheese, sir.'

'Thank you.' Licinius watched him go. He was frowning.

'You ever try him for a commission, friend?' I said, tearing off a piece of bread. 'Sulpicius Severus, I mean. Owns a big villa by the lake.'

'No. His tastes don't run to murals.' The frown hadn't shifted. 'I thought you said you were on holiday.'

'Yeah. That's right.'

'A mixture of business and pleasure, then?'

'No. Just pleasure.' Odds were, the guy would've heard of the murder – I doubted if there was anyone over the age of about eighteen months within a ten-mile radius who hadn't – but if he didn't know yet where I fitted in I wasn't going to tell him. Also, I was beginning to wonder about our pigment-dabbler here. Seriously wonder.

'So what's your interest in the Caba quarry?' he said.

Uh-huh: neither Pontius nor I had mentioned Caba. A little pen in my head moved towards a box and went 'tick'. 'Not in the quarry per se,' I said. I took a swallow of wine and tried to make the next question as offhand as possible. 'You happen to know why the company's in trouble?'

'Yes, of course.' He said it like it was the most natural thing in the world. I had to struggle not to show any surprise, or to make a half-assed, facetious remark that might've put him off. 'The story was all over Rome seven or eight months ago. You didn't hear it?'

'Uh . . . no.' It hadn't been, in the circles I moved in anyway; but then company news never did go down big with wineshop punters and Rome was a big enough place for there to be lots of different cities existing side by side. I wondered which particular one of them was Lucilius's. 'Tell me.'

'You've heard of Labici?'

'The town? Sure. It's on the other side of the Latin Road, just past Tusculum.'

'Right. Two years ago they built a new market hall there; stone walls, solid tile roof. Nine months later, come the winter, the walls began to crack. All of them. The builder was called back in and he did a repair job. Everything was fine until December last year when a wall collapsed and half the roof came down. It was market day, and bad weather, so the place was packed. Forty-three people were killed.'

Yeah, I dimly remembered hearing something about that, but in Rome tenements are falling down all the time, mostly for the same reason. You get what you pay for, and if you cut corners you know what to expect. 'Cowboy builders or a cut-price architect, right?'

He was shaking his head. 'The Labicines hadn't done any cheeseparing. That was the point. They had one of their own citizens design the building, certainly, but he was a top-notch retired legionary engineer with thirty years' experience. He chose the builders himself and he kept a close eye on them. There wasn't any problem with either the foundations or the building work.'

I was beginning to see light. 'So it was the stone at fault?'

'They bought locally, which made sense, transport costs being what they are. Alban stone's good, but it's soft, comparatively speaking. The standard practice is to leave the blocks out in the open for two or three years before they're sold. Any faulty ones will crack and shear, and they're broken up for rubble. The ones that survive go to the builders.'

Standard practice, eh? Yeah, well, sure, it might've been at that, but it was news to me, and the information had come out naturally, like he thought it was common knowledge. The guy knew his stuff, all right, which was interesting in itself. Still, he was an artist, and any self-respecting artist would be a bit of an architect as well. 'And you can't tell in advance which ones are faulty, right?'

'Not unless the cracks are visible on the surface to begin with, no. Letting them season's the only sure way.'

I sipped my wine. 'So the blocks that went for the new market hall hadn't been seasoned?'

'No. Only they'd been sold and bought as such. It was in the contract.'

'And the supplier was the Caba quarry company.' Jupiter! No wonder the bastard was losing orders! Like any other business the building trade operated on trust. When the Labici market hall collapsed and word got round that he'd supplied whacky stone Sulpicius's name would be mud.

'There was an investigation, naturally. By that time the quarry's overseer had disappeared and taken the paperwork with him.'

I sat back. Pontius came out with the jug and sundries, set them down and went inside. 'You're pretty well informed for an artist, friend,' I said.

Licinius poured himself another cup of wine. 'I told you, the story's well known. And my father's in the business.'

'How did Sulpicius react? Or should I say Sulpicius and Vettius Bolanus? The two were co-owners of the company, weren't they?'

'Were they? I didn't know that.' Like hell he didn't! I was getting more than a little suspicious of Licinius. 'By the way, I hear Bolanus was murdered a couple of days ago.'

'Yeah.' He didn't sound too upset; not that he had any reason to be, mind, but taken with everything else it made the hairs stir on the back of my neck. I'd also noticed the change of subject. 'So you don't know Sulpicius, then? Personally, I mean?'

'No. I've never met him.' He stood up, took out his purse and laid a silver piece on the table. I opened my eyes wide in surprise. 'I'm sorry, Corvinus, I have to go now. I've just remembered I've arranged to see a customer this afternoon.' He grinned. 'A prospective customer, anyway, and one who won't take things any further if I fail to turn up for the appointment. It was very nice talking to you. I hope we'll meet again some time.'

Talk about a hasty departure! Gods, what was that in aid of? I watched him walk away across the square, my brain churning. Artists are odd people, sure, but not even an artist will order a fresh half jug and a plate of cheese and then five minutes later get up and go leaving them practically untouched. Not without a better reason than he'd given me. Quintus Licinius was definitely someone I'd have to think about.

I'd have to have another word with Sulpicius, too.

9

There wasn't much point in going out to Sulpicius's straight away: I couldn't be sure that he'd be back yet for a start, the afternoon was wearing on and a trip to his villa would mean passing the turn for Marcia's and another two-mile return trip. Also I reckoned that, after the events of the morning, if I showed up before the guy's temper had had a chance to cool he'd simply send me off with a flea in my ear. Time, then, for the loose ends. Like, for example, my poaching duo Harpax the retired veteran and his son-in-law Rutilius.

I'd done more than my share of unaccustomed riding these past two days, and my backside was telling me to wear out sandal leather instead of skin. I got directions from Pontius for Rutilius's blacksmith shop, left the mare parked by the trough fraternising over a drink with a friendly stallion, and headed off into the town's back streets.

Prime address it wasn't, and even 'address' was pushing it. There had been a street here at one time, but most of the other houses had given up the struggle, and apart from the place I was looking for all it had to offer was a few half façades of mud brick separated by stretches of weed-covered waste ground. Not that what – from the sound of hammering and the glow of the forge – had to be the Rutilius property was all that much better. It had been built, if that's the word, as a unit, with the shop at one end and the living quarters to the side, between it and a patch of kitchen garden in which a big-boned woman was currently pinning up a line of nappies. I nodded to her and got a quick, hard look back.

'Shop', mind, was a pretty loose description in itself. Once you'd allowed for the space taken up by the forge and the anvil there wasn't all that much left, and most of that was filled with junk.

Filled with Rutilius, too; at least, I assumed the guy who was beating hell out of a flattened bar of white-hot metal was Rutilius. He was a big man, a full head taller than me, twice as wide, and even hairier than Concordius. As I came up he shoved the bar back into the glowing charcoal and wiped his brow with a forearm a gorilla would've been proud of, while the kid on the bellows pulled for all he was worth. The sudden wave of heat hit me like a gladiator's mailed fist, and I stopped.

He blinked at me under a mass of hair soaked with unwiped sweat. I saw his eyes take in the Roman mantle and the purple stripe and he scowled.

'Yeah?' he said.

I came a step closer, which was just about my limit. The day was warm enough as it was, without the heat of a bellows-driven charcoal fire to add to it. 'Uh ... your name Rutilius, friend?' I said.

Instead of answering, he turned back to the iron bar, now changing colour from flame-yellow to white, gripped it with the tongs and pulled it clear. Then he put it down on the anvil. The hammer clanged and sparks flew like tiny silver meteors. I waited until he'd beaten the thing into submission and returned it to the forge.

'That's me,' he said.

'Marcus Valerius Corvinus. I'm looking into the death of Vettius Bolanus.'

'Is that so, now?' He cleared his throat and spat into the flames. The gobbet of phlegm sizzled for no more than a split second. 'There's nice. And?'

Well, we'd got a friendly one here, right enough. No point in beating around the bush. 'Ah ... I'm told you two didn't exactly see eye to eye on local hunting rights.'

He stopped what he was doing long enough to give me a considering stare. Then he gripped the bar with the tongs and turned it, thrusting it further into the charcoal. 'I've got work to do,' he said. 'Piss off, Roman.'

Friendly was right. Still, two could play at that game. 'No problem, pal,' I said. 'Actually it was your father-in-law Harpax I really wanted to talk to. If he's around at present just point me in his direction and I'll leave you to it.'

Rutilius set down the hammer. Slowly. Then, without taking his eyes off me, he waved his hand at the kid operating the bellows. The pumping stopped. 'You leave the old man alone,' he said. 'He had enough grief from that fancy stuck-up bastard while he was alive, and he doesn't need any more now he's dead. And he can't tell you nothing about the murder. Nor can I.'

'Fine,' I said. 'But what kind of grief would that be, now, exactly?'

Rutilius spat into the coals again and picked up the hammer. 'I told you, Roman,' he said. 'I'm busy and I don't have the time to answer mealy-mouthed fucking questions. Now push off before I—'

'*Spurius!*'

I turned. The woman I'd seen hanging out the washing was standing there with the empty basket still in her hands. She was glaring at Rutilius, but she didn't say any more. The air crackled. Finally, the big man looked over his shoulder at the bellows kid, nodded, scowling, and reached for the iron bar with the tongs he still held in his left hand.

The woman made a movement with the basket towards the house. 'Come in, whatever your name is,' she said. 'My husband's right. He has his work to be doing and he doesn't have the time to spare. Any questions, you can ask me.'

I followed her in silence. Behind me came the angry clang of metal on metal.

At least the place was tidy and clean, which from the condition of the outside I hadn't been expecting. The walls were plastered and whitewashed, and the floorboards were scrubbed into a grey shine. That, though, plus a solid wooden table with matching benches and a dresser, was about it for the internals, except for a cradle with a sleeping baby in one corner and an old man sitting in a wicker chair and carving a piece of wood. He looked up as we came in.

'Uh . . . Valerius Corvinus,' I said.

He nodded and went back to his carving. Now my eyes were getting used to the dimness I could see that the thing was a toy cow. There were half a dozen other wooden animals on the dresser.

The woman had put the basket down. 'Now,' she said. 'Just what do you want?'

None too friendly, sure – I wasn't exactly taken with the friendliness and general good humour of the family as a whole – but I guessed that was just the lady's style, and it fitted her appearance. Big-boned was right; she wasn't all that much smaller than I was, and the hands that'd held the basket were large, red and beefy. Her hair was covered with a scarf, but there was enough of it showing for me to see that it was blonde; real blonde, not just what passes for it in Rome or comes out of a bottle. Harpax himself might be an easterner – his name was Greek, at least, and he had the up-country out-in-the-sticks northern Greek look to him – but his daughter was pure beer-and-pork-dumpling German.

'No hassle, lady,' I said. 'Quintus Libanius of the senate asked me to look into Vettius Bolanus's death. All I'm doing is talking to people who might've had a' – I paused fractionally; I'd been going to say 'grudge against him', but even I could see that wouldn't go down well – 'a difference of opinion with him recently.'

Harpax – the old guy had to be Harpax – looked up. 'Bolanus was a swine,' he growled. 'He's better off dead.'

His daughter stiffened and shot him a glance that was more than halfway to a warning. 'Dad,' she said, 'just let the man ask his questions and go, will you?'

'Best he hears that now, direct.' Harpax laid the wooden cow and the knife down on the floor beside him. 'Twenty years ago if a puffed-up bag of dung like Bolanus had talked to me like he did I'd've cut his throat myself. You hear me, boy?'

'I hear you,' I said. He wasn't kidding, either. Usually, someone says something along those lines and you know it doesn't mean anything except that they hated the other person's guts. Just occasionally, you get a tough, quiet-spoken guy like Harpax who's simply stating a fact. The hairs stirred on my neck. 'This . . . uh . . . would be in connection with the poaching, would it?'

Harpax scowled. 'Screw the poaching. Only a tight-arsed little lawyer like Bolanus would trouble over a few hares. If he'd sued me in any town on the mountain the jury would've thrown him out on his ear and laughed while they did it. That would just make him a bastard. Bolanus was a swine.'

'So what was the disagreement about, then?' I said.

'I told you, boy. He was a bag of dung. What he needed wasn't laughing at, it was killing.'

'Dad.' The woman was looking nervous.

He ignored her. Setting his huge hands on the arms of his chair, he pushed himself to his feet. 'See here, Corvinus,' he said.

Standing, old or not, he was still a powerful man; no invalid, either, because once he got going he moved easy enough. And I could see where his daughter got her size from, even without a German mother. He went over to the dresser, reached inside and brought out a wooden box.

'Dad, Valerius Corvinus isn't interested in—'

'Shut up, Brunna!' He brought the box back, set it on the floor, opened it and took out a thin, flat object wrapped in linen. He unwrapped it and handed it to me. The thing was a rectangular sheet of bronze with writing on it. 'You know what that is, boy?'

I glanced at the top line. 'Sure. A military discharge certificate.'

'And this?' He held out a small scroll.

This time I didn't have to look. 'Your certificate of citizenship, right?'

'Right. There was a land grant, too, once, but the land's sold and the money spent long since. I'm no farmer, me, or a saver. I've never had the patience. Now.' He reached back into the box and took out a smaller box. Then he lifted the lid and carefully – so carefully that whatever the thing was could've been made of cobwebs – took out the contents. This time he didn't pass it over, just held it up for me to see. 'What about this?'

It was a dry circlet of plaited twigs and what were still recognisable as oak leaves. I stared. I'd never seen one of these, but I knew what it was. Sure I did. No wonder he was holding it like it was one of the sacred Shields of Mars.

'It's a civic crown,' I said. Sweet gods! The number of these things around, outside the purely honorary ones presented to members of the imperial family, you could count on the fingers of one hand. Shit, maybe even the fingers of one finger. I glanced at his daughter. The woman's broad face had gone solid, lips locked.

'You know what they're given for?' Harpax said.

'Saving the life of a citizen in battle.'

He grinned: old or not, he still had all his teeth. 'Screw that, son. That's only part of it.' He put the crown back in its box. 'Save the life, kill the enemy, maintain the ground. These're the rules. And the citizen saved has to make a personal, formal request to the emperor before he'll sign the chitty. That's the real bugger.'

Yeah. Also, whatever the formal rules were, the citizen saved wouldn't be some low-life squaddie, either, and you could up the ante by a similar amount on the rest of the conditions as well; otherwise there'd be a lot more of these things around. Medals and breastplate ornaments were two a penny, but oak-leaf crowns were *rare*. 'You like to tell me how you got it?' I said. I was genuinely interested, and impressed. It isn't every day you meet someone who's been awarded the civic crown.

He didn't answer at first. The big box was carefully repacked and put away. Then he came back and sat down in the chair. 'You ever hear of a general by the name of Germanicus, boy? Tiberius's grandson?'

'Uh . . . yeah.' I tried to keep the expression on my face neutral. 'Yeah, I've heard of him.'

'Best bloody general there's ever been. I'm talking history now. Alexander, Africanus, old Julius, you can keep them. Germanicus was the *best*. Understand?'

'Sure I understand.' One of the biggest crypto-traitors, too, him and that wife of his, but I wasn't fool enough to bring that up; not with someone like Harpax, not if I valued my own neck. Once a man becomes a legend truth goes by the board, and for most of Harpax's generation of army men where legends were concerned you didn't get bigger than Germanicus Caesar. 'You served with him?'

'On the Rhine, and beyond. Standard-bearer, First Thracian Auxiliaries.' He nodded at Brunna. 'Her mother was a Chattian woman. I took her in a raid. That was before the general, mind, well before. Before that bastard Varus lost us his three Eagles, too.'

Gods! We were talking ancient history here. Varus had died with his men in the Teutoburg a quarter of a century ago. Six years later, Germanicus had buried their bones. The ones he'd found, at least.

'Just tell the story, Dad.' That was Brunna. 'If you must. Quickly. Get it over.'

'Hold your tongue, woman!' Harpax snapped. 'The boy asked. I'll give him his answer in my own time.' He turned back to me. 'The general had a deputy in the campaign against Arminius, the year after Augustus died. Man by the name of Aulus Caecina. You know him?'

'Yeah,' I said. 'I've heard of Caecina.'

'He was a good soldier. Experienced. When the general pulled the army back to the Ems Caecina took his part, including us, over the Long Bridges. You know what they are?'

This was turning into a history test. I could feel myself sweating. 'Uh ... the wooden causeway through the swamps, right? Ahenobarbus laid them out for the campaigns in Lower Germany.'

'Right. You ever see that part of the world, Corvinus?'

'No, never.'

'You're lucky. It's pure hell, nothing but mud and forests. Thick, dark forests full of men who hate your guts.' He was glaring at me. 'Keep to the path, you're a sitting duck for whatever they want to throw at you; try to fight back, get to grips with the buggers and as soon as you step off the path you can find yourself breathing marsh-water. Some places, there isn't even a path to step off because the boards've rotted or been washed away; then you don't know nothing until suddenly you're in past the neck with nowhere to go but down. That's the Long Bridges for you. You with me, boy?'

'Uh ... sure.' Something cold was moving in my stomach. I glanced sideways at Brunna, and what I saw wasn't reassuring. She was looking anxious as hell. 'Yeah, I'm with you.'

'So that's where we were. On the Long Bridges. We were marching slow because of the baggage train, three, four miles a day if we were lucky. Halfway to the Ems it wasn't even that because the Germans got clever and diverted the hill streams either side of the valley. After that we couldn't move forward no more because the Bridges ahead were either washed away or under a fresh three feet of mud. Caecina had to call a halt, send men to rebuild while the rest of us fought off the attacks as best we could. We built a camp on the dry ground. Or what passed for dry ground, anyway. We were stuck there for a month.' He paused. 'You any idea what it's like, Corvinus? To spend a fucking month up to your ankles in mud behind a stockade in the German forests or drive piles waist-deep in scummy water knowing that any second you'll feel an arrow or a javelin hit between your shoulder blades?' I shook my head; I couldn't've said anything, not now. 'The days were bad but the nights were worse. That was when the howling and the chanting started. The buggers kept it up, night after night. Night after night after night.'

'Dad, stop it!' Brunna suddenly got to her feet, reached over and gripped his arm so hard I could see the knuckles whiten.

He ignored her, his eyes fixed on mine. The cold in my gut had hardened to a lump of ice. 'You couldn't sleep, boy. And when you did there were the dreams. If they were dreams, because they were always the same ones. Story is, the general had them too, that he saw old Varus coming up out of the mud with his hand stretched out and his face—' He stopped dead; just stopped, so sharply I heard his teeth click together. He was staring past me now into nothing. My gut clenched and everything went very still.

Scarred, Libanius had said. Yeah, I could see what he meant. The hairs on my scalp crawled.

'Uh . . . that's okay, pal,' I said softly. 'Your daughter's right. You don't have to tell me this.'

I doubt if he heard me. His eyes were hard and empty, and the cold in my gut was almost a physical pain; this sort of stuff I just can't handle.

Finally the eyes refocused.

'Where was I?' he said quietly, like it was the most natural question in the world.

'Dad, please—'

'*Where was I?*'

I looked at Brunna. Her face was set.

'The camp,' I said.

He grunted. 'Right. The camp it was. There wasn't no need for a guard rota. Most of us spent the night awake, because of the dreams. One time thirty or forty of the boys from the Twentieth couldn't take it any more. They slipped out of the gate and made a foray off their own bat. Next morning we found their heads nailed to the trees. Nothing else, just the heads.'

'Tell him about the crown.' Brunna was still holding the old man's arm. 'He only wants to know about the crown, Dad. Not all this old nonsense.' The woman's own eyes turned to me, appealing. I cleared my throat.

'Uh . . . yeah,' I said, trying to keep my voice normal. 'Yeah, that's right.'

Harpax frowned. 'The lads from the Twentieth Eagle were only the skin on the porridge. Finally no one could take it any more and we broke camp against orders. Caecina couldn't stop us: it would've been the Rhine Mutiny all over again. We formed up – the whole army, thirty thousand men – on the best ground we could find, a stretch of shallow mud clear of the trees. We all knew it was a mistake – we could hardly keep our feet, let alone fucking fight, and we were tired as hell – but it had to be done, and at least it would bring the Germans.' His lips twisted. 'It did that, right enough, thousands of the buggers, swinging these bloody axes of theirs. We'd got the cavalry in place on the wings but the horses weren't no use in that slather and they went down at the first charge. My Thracians were out in front, part of the auxiliary screen, and the Germans cut through us like we was rotten cloth. Not the lads' fault; like I say, we couldn't get a grip underfoot, never mind manage a decent sword-thrust. I held them together as long as I could – I had the standard, and they wouldn't give that up – but we had to give ground, back towards the Eagles proper. Old Caecina was riding up and down the line in the centre, swearing like an Aventine whore, telling the legionary boys to hold their ranks. I was no more than spitting distance from him when his horse slid and he went down. There wasn't nobody else to help and you can't leave your general sitting on his arse in two feet of mud with half a hundred beer-crazed axe-swinging buggers heading straight for him, can you, now? So I covered him with my shield, grounded the standard and waded in. The lads bunched up round me and we fought them off until the First Eagle got its finger out and moved up in support.' He shrugged; the hardness had faded from his eyes. 'That was it. The rest of the battle was a bloody shambles, but we won through in the end. Some of us. And he was a gentleman, Caecina. He didn't forget.'

'He put you forward for the crown?'

'That's right. Had General Germanicus include the request in his next set of dispatches. Plus an early honourable discharge and the full legionary gratuity. Legionary, not auxiliary. The money's long gone. Like I said, I'm no saver, never have been. But I've still got the crown.'

'Uh-huh.' I'd wondered about that part of it. The crown itself's the important thing, sure, but there'd be a fair slice of cash involved as well. 'So where does Bolanus come into this?'

Harpax flushed and looked away.

'He was threatening to take Dad's name off the citizen's roll when he became censor,' Brunna said. You could've carved her tone with a chisel.

I stared at her. 'He was *what*?'

'I told you, Corvinus.' The old guy's hands were clenched round the arms of his chair and he was shaking with anger. 'The man was a dung-bag. He deserved killing if anyone did.'

'Because of the poaching?'

'No.' Brunna hesitated. 'There's . . .' She glanced at her father. 'Dad, go and talk to Spurius for ten minutes. Please!'

I thought the old guy would refuse, but he got up without a word and left the room meek as a lamb. His daughter waited until the door closed behind him. Then she turned back to me.

I waited.

'He takes . . . fits, Corvinus,' she said finally. 'Oh, he isn't mad; you've seen that for yourself.' I swallowed. Yeah, sure I had. Jupiter! 'All the same, now and again he . . .' She stopped. 'You heard the story for yourself, and how telling it affected him. Sometimes he'll . . . slip back. We watch him, Spurius and me, the boy as well, but it can happen at any time, for any reason or for none.' Her lips formed a line. 'Night's the worst. You'll understand why, because you heard. He doesn't sleep, not at night, he hasn't done as far back as I can remember. He gets up and walks around. Not just inside the house, out in the streets or further. Sometimes it's just that, sometimes he's . . . well, he isn't here, he's in Germany, in the mud and the blood and the battle. Then things can get bad, very bad. You understand?'

'Yeah,' I said. 'I understand.'

'He can't help himself. He knows he does it and it's a shame to him. Bolanus wanted him locked away, made a non-person. As censor he could've done that.'

'Hang on, lady,' I said. 'The guy's a hero. Bolanus couldn't've just drawn a pen through his name, he'd need official confirmation.'

She was shaking her head. 'That would've meant assessment by a formal tribunal. Dad wouldn't've stood that, the shame of it would've killed him whatever they decided. Bolanus had him trapped.'

I nodded; yeah, I could see that. Men like Harpax, they're tough enough and capable enough where direct action's involved, but when they're up against this sort of thing they lose the place altogether. And they have their pride. Anyone who's been an army standard-bearer, whether legionary or not, prides himself on his own solidity. Standard-bearers, by definition, are the guys who don't crack under pressure; they can't, because it's their job not to and if they go the rest of their unit's lost. I'd bet that

Harpax's little weakness embarrassed him like hell. Especially if it was involuntary. 'Uh . . . how often are we talking about here?' I said. 'Once a month? Less? More?'

'There isn't a pattern. Except maybe it happens more often in winter, when the nights are longer.'

'So when was the last time?'

Her eyes flickered. 'About a month ago,' she said.

She was lying, I'd bet a year's income on that. Something cold touched my neck. 'You sure about that, lady?' I said quietly.

'I'm sure.' She stood up. 'And now I've helped you all I can. We both have. If you've finished I've the dinner to make.'

Harpax was in the smiddy when I passed, helping the kid with the bellows. I waved, but he didn't look up, and Rutilius gave me a glare.

I didn't know for certain, of course, but from Brunna's reaction to the question I'd risk a hefty side bet on the last time the old guy had gone AWOL being two nights ago. And either she didn't know where he'd been or she did and she wasn't telling.

There was the other possibility, too. But that one I'd have to think about.

10

I was back well in time for dinner. Perilla and Marcia were sitting under the shade of the peristyle, playing Robbers. Marilla was there too, with the laryngitic Dassa. She'd tied a scarf round the brute's neck and she was feeding her sliced-up peaches.

I gave Perilla the welcome-home kiss, pulled up a free chair, set Bathyllus's usual wine jug and cup on the table beside it, and sat down gingerly . . .

Not gingerly enough, though.

'Hell! Oh, sweet holy Jupiter!'

Marcia looked up from the Robbers board. 'You should do more riding, Marcus,' she said calmly.

'That so, now?' I had real difficulty, under the circumstances, keeping the snarl in my voice to a minimum. Me, I'd've gone for less rather than more. If the gods had meant men to ride they would've given us blister-proof rumps. 'How's the patient, Princess?'

'A lot better today. And I've been rubbing her throat and chest with warm oil. She likes that.'

'Fine. Fine.' I sniffed. 'Uh . . . a bath wouldn't go amiss either. Or maybe a dip.'

Dassa went, '*Beh-uch! Uch!*' Well, it was an improvement. And so long as Marilla was keeping a close eye on the woolly bugger we might be okay. I poured the wine and sipped, letting the soothing nectar slip past my tonsils.

'How did you get on at the quarry?' Perilla asked.

'Not too good. I fell foul of close-mouthed Sulpicius and he gave me my head to play with. There's something there, though, I'd swear to that.' A thought struck me. 'Marcia, you know anything about a young guy called Quintus Licinius? He's an artist, on the scrounge locally for wall-painting commissions.'

Marcia's eyes widened. 'Not one of *the* Licinii, surely?'

Her tone said it all. I found myself grinning. 'That I don't know, but I wouldn't be surprised. He seemed well up on a lot of things, and if he was a real plain-mantle I'll eat my sandals. You haven't come across him?'

'No, not in person. But then I don't get out much, of course, and I very rarely have visitors. How old would he be, Marcus?'

'Late twenties. Early thirties, maybe.'

'A thin boy – man, I should say – with quite sharp features?'

'Yeah, that's right.'

'Hmm. If he is a proper Licinius then he might very well be Marcus Frugi's youngest. I do remember – goodness, it must be at least twenty years ago, now! – Frugi saying he was having terrible trouble with the boy. Always in and out of the porches, looking at the pictures. I would have thought he'd have grown out of it by now, though; his eldest brother had his consulship a few years back and made a very good marriage indeed. Still, every family has its . . . characters, I suppose.'

I grinned at the momentary hesitation, and the careful choice of wording: a fine old lady, Marcia, the best, conventional to her finger-ends but polite to a fault. 'Characters' among the top families – meaning guys and girls whose behaviour didn't match the expected norms of the ruling class – weren't something that Marcia approved of, even when the norms allowed for some pretty gross peccadilloes along the way. I was a case in point. Although we got on well and always had, with respect and liking on both sides, both of us knew I'd never really fitted her idea of a husband for Perilla. She'd wade through boiling oil before she said it, though, to me or anyone else.

So: my wandering mural-painter was the aristo Marcus Frugi's son, eh? Or he could be, anyway. No wonder the guy had been reticent: there wasn't any need to hide behind a fake name, sure, but he might not want that connection made too readily. Marcus Licinius Crassus Frugi was one of the richest men in Rome, and a pillar of the business community as well as the social élite. I'd bet good money that the thought of his youngest sprog peddling his paintbrush round the villas of the nouveaux riches up here in the Alban Hills was giving him apoplexy. If he knew, of course.

Still, it fitted. It explained why Licinius had known who Marcia's husband had been; and, more important, how he'd managed to be so clued up about the Labici scam. That would be just the sort of titbit of conversation you'd expect at a movers-and-shakers dinner table over the stuffed chaffinches, and when he'd said his father was in the business he'd been putting it mildly. Frugi probably had a controlling interest in half the construction companies in Italy.

What it didn't explain, though, was the guy's relationship with Sulpicius. On the one hand, he'd been very careful to disclaim any connection at all, even to the extent of running out on me when the conversation was turning that way. On the other, he seemed to know things about Sulpicius that he shouldn't have done if he hadn't met him, like the fact that his taste in decoration didn't extend to murals. Add to all this that he'd obviously been interested in *my* interest in the guy and it made a suspicious total.

'We'll just go down to the paddock and talk to Corydon before dinner.' The Princess got up from where she was sitting cross-legged on the ground by Marcia's chair. Dassa struggled to her feet beside her. 'He'll be upset otherwise.'

We watched them go. 'She really is very good with animals,' Perilla said. 'It's only been two days and that sheep follows her around like a dog already.'

'So would you, lady,' I said sourly, 'if someone rubbed your chest with warm oil and hand-fed you peaches.'

'As a comment that doesn't quite work, dear.'

'Where did you meet this Quintus Licinius, Marcus?' Marcia asked.

'In Pontius's wineshop.' I gave them a rundown of the conversation, including the bit about the punch-up over in Bovillae.

Marcia was scandalised. 'The man attacked him?'

'Yeah. The other guy had the worst of it, mind. At least, that was the story I heard.'

'But that's dreadful! He didn't report it?'

'There wasn't any need.'

The old girl tugged at her mantle. 'That is *quite* beside the point, Marcus,' she said, 'especially if he is Frugi's son. He had an obligation. There's too much of that sort of thing happening in the region these days, and it doesn't help the authorities to do their job if people simply shrug it off. When Augustus was alive – I suppose I should call him the Divine Augustus, but I've never been able to do that – it would have been another matter entirely.'

'What about the quarry, Marcus?' Perilla said quickly.

'Uh . . . yeah.' I took a mouthful of wine. 'There's been some skulduggery up there, that's for certain. How Bolanus fitted into it – if he did – I'm not quite sure, but I can maybe make some guesses from the result.'

'Such as what, for example?'

I topped up my wine cup and leaned back carefully: shifting position, even on a padded couch, was not a good idea at present. 'Okay,' I said. 'I'll give you the events and the timings as far as I know them and see what conclusions you come up with. First, two years back, the citizens of Labici buy a load of whacky stone from the Caba quarry to build their market hall. Last December, the building collapses and no one'll touch the Caba company, co-partners Sulpicius Severus and Vettius

Bolanus, with a ten-foot pole. There's an investigation, during or shortly after which the quarry overseer, Coxa, does a runner. Also in January, Severus betrothes his daughter to Bolanus. The following month he leaves Rome and takes over the empty villa next door to Bolanus's property on the Alban Lake. Clear so far?'

Perilla was frowning. 'Yes, Marcus, of course, but—'

'Let me finish. Two days ago, the day of the murder, Sulpicius suddenly calls the wedding off; *he* does, quite definitely, not either Bolanus or his daughter, both of whom are quite understandably peeved. When in the wake of the murder he's asked for his reasons he refuses to give them. He also refuses to discuss the subject of the business partnership. Now. What do you make of all that, lady?'

'That at some time between January and two days ago, probably very much closer to the second than the first, Sulpicius learned that Bolanus was implicated in the stone fraud.'

I nodded. 'Right. It's the obvious conclusion. Up to then he'd assumed Coxa was the only person involved, and Coxa wasn't around to tell him otherwise. Me, I'd add two more points, or rather one point and a question. Sulpicius couldn't've even suspected at the start of the affair that his partner was a crook, because people like him don't pledge their daughters to men they're already leery of, and they sure as hell don't buy a property next door to the bugger when they have the whole of Italy to choose from. Assuming they want to move in the first place.'

'Unless they want to lull the man concerned into a false sense of security, of course. And you must admit, dear, that if Sulpicius was planning to kill his partner having him as a next-door neighbour would make things much simpler.'

'Yeah, but it would also leave him a prime suspect because now he's got motive *and* opportunity. And if he is the killer then cancelling the wedding on the very day he planned to murder the guy would be just plain stupid.'

'I wonder, Marcus – forgive me for interrupting – if that wouldn't be in character for a man like Sulpicius Severus,' Marcia said quietly. 'I'm not accusing him of murder, naturally, but I do feel that the knowledge that his projected victim was currently a friend and prospective family member would have caused him some concern. Whereas if he ended the engagement – and, no doubt, the business partnership at the same time – it would be tantamount to a formal renunciation of the friendship.'

Uh-huh; I could see what she was getting at. We were being technical here. The words 'friend' and 'friendship' to old-style Romans like Marcia and – I had to agree – Sulpicius go a long way beyond expressing a personal relationship; they may not even involve liking. 'Friendship', in its technical sense, is the whole shooting-match, social, moral and business combined, so a formal renunciation is a big deal: the guy who does the renouncing breaks contact completely, returning the ex-friend to the status of a stranger. Or, rather, it goes one step beyond; it implies that if push comes to shove in future the ex-friend is more likely to be treated as a personal enemy and knows it from that moment on. It was a good point. If Sulpicius had found out that Bolanus was crooked renouncing friendship with him formally, in the old-fashioned way, would be just the sort of thing a guy like him would do. And it fitted the theory: I couldn't believe that Sulpicius would be devious enough or hypocritical enough to plot a murder months in advance and still go through the charade of friendship, but if he'd discovered his partner was a wrong 'un when he was actually in place, as it were, then it became much more of a possibility. And where the guy himself was concerned he would take the trouble to square his pukkah-Roman conscience first . . .

'What was your question, Marcus?' Perilla asked.

'Hmm?' I refocused.

'You said you had one point to make and a question.'

'Oh, yeah. I was just wondering about the betrothal itself. Why did it come so late?'

'How do you mean?'

'The daughter must be pushing thirty. Sulpicius and Bolanus had been partners for years, and a marriage is a common way of cementing the two halves of the business. So why didn't the engagement happen before?'

'She could have been married previously. Widowed or divorced.'

I looked at Marcia. She was shaking her head. 'I don't believe that's possible, Perilla,' she said. 'Of course, I could be wrong – the family only moved from Rome recently, and I knew nothing of them before they came to the district – but at best it's most unlikely. If there were no unpleasant circumstances involved the existence of any previous marriage would naturally have come up; while if there were it's not a fact that could be hidden for long.' She paused, then added delicately, 'Should either Sulpicia or her father have wanted to hide it, of course.'

Jupiter! I hadn't thought of that one! The old bird had a more suspicious mind than I did! 'Uh . . . yeah,' I said. 'Yeah, I agree. The other thing that puzzles me is why January? January specifically, when the company was on its uppers?'

'Hardly a suitable time for drawing up a marriage contract, certainly,' Marcia murmured. 'Yes, dear, that is rather curious.'

'Perhaps Bolanus agreed to a quid pro quo,' Perilla said. 'A promise to put more money into the business in exchange for his partner's daughter.'

'Uh-uh.' I took a mouthful of wine. 'That wouldn't work. Apart from the fact that it's the wrong way round – the guy would expect a dowry rather than offer a bride-price – money isn't the company's problem. It isn't struggling through lack of investment, it's lost public confidence. Also, I get the impression that where solid cash is concerned Sulpicius has a lot more of it than Bolanus did. In fact, six gets you ten that the guy needed whatever profit he made from the stone scam to finance his election campaign.'

'If Bolanus had sold his estate to a developer he'd have had plenty of money.'

'Sure, no argument. But Bolanus wouldn't sell up, nohow, no way, never. And if you tell me that Sulpicius was marrying his daughter to him for the sake of an estate that was appreciating in value I'll ask you again, why wait until January? There's been no sudden boom. Alban Lake property prices have been going up steadily for years.'

'Then I can't answer the question. Can you?'

I reached for the wine jug. 'No. Not yet. But the answer's important, that I'd swear to.'

'You think Sulpicius is the killer?'

'He's a good bet at present, sure, but he's not the only runner, even barring our friend Concordius.' I poured. 'I haven't told you yet about the talk I had with the local military hero.'

'Harpax?' Marcia frowned.

'Yeah. Seemingly Bolanus was all set to strip the old man of his voting rights.'

'He was *what*? But he couldn't—' She stopped, then went on more slowly. 'Yes. Yes, I suppose he could, as censor. Or at least try to. He would have grounds, certainly; technical grounds, at least. Not that they would get him very far. Harpax has a lot of friends in Castrimoenium. And in Rome.'

'Just the attempt would've been enough,' I said. 'So you, uh, know the situation there, do you?'

'Everyone does. Everyone, also, turns a blind eye. Quite rightly so, in my opinion.' Marcia's chin lifted. 'And, Marcus, let me say at once that under these circumstances even if he was the killer my sympathies lie totally with Harpax. If Vettius Bolanus was planning such a disgraceful course of action then he was a very mean and spiteful person and fully deserved all he got.'

Ouch; you don't cross a tough old boot like Aunt Marcia. 'You know Harpax better than I do. Could he have done it?'

'Physically, yes. You've seen him yourself, Marcus. He may be old but he's not feeble, far from it, and he was, of course, a soldier. If you ask me *would* he have done it I'm not so sure. Certainly if they'd met by chance, or Bolanus had come to him, and words were passed then yes again, I think in the heat of the moment it would be extremely possible. Going specially to Bolanus's villa, lying in wait for the man and killing him in cold blood – well, that's another matter. No, I don't think Harpax would be capable of something like that.'

Yeah; those were my feelings too. Still, the old boy couldn't be dismissed out of hand. 'When he's rational, sure,' I said. 'How about in one of these turns he takes?'

Marcia hesitated. 'It's . . . not beyond the bounds of possibility, given certain circumstances,' she said. 'In themselves they're quite harmless: he is suddenly, simply, back in the German forests, talking to people who are not present about things and events that have no relevance to his present surroundings. However, for the onlooker – and I've been one myself – it is extremely unnerving.' She pulled at her mantle. 'The important thing is that one must not interfere. I remember that happening only once, many years ago. Harpax broke two of the man's ribs, and had he been armed might well have killed him. Now, of course, his daughter and son-in-law keep a close eye on him, and no harm is done. If – and I'm not saying this is probable, or even likely – but *if* neither were present, and Bolanus had made a similar mistake then Harpax might indeed have attacked him.'

'But that presupposes Harpax was already in the garden,' Perilla said.

'Indeed. Which, I would say, is the major flaw in any theory of that kind. Rutilius and Brunna are very careful, and they have a great deal of experience. The combination of circumstances involved simply could never have occurred.'

'Yeah.' I scowled; me, I wouldn't be quite so dogmatic, but then I was just an incomer and didn't know the full story. Besides, Marcia obviously had a soft spot for the old devil, which didn't surprise me. They shared the same set of bloody-minded values, for a start. 'Okay. So let's look at it another way. How about Rutilius himself as the killer?'

Marcia sat back. 'Ah,' she said.

Not exactly, from the tone, a wholehearted endorsement. 'It would fit,' I said. 'The guy's got a motive: he didn't like Bolanus personally, and the man was trying to disenfranchise his father-in-law. He's the de facto head of the household, and he didn't exactly strike me as the type who'd knuckle under easily.' I glanced at her, but her face wasn't giving anything away. 'You're the local expert. What do you think?'

'I think that perhaps your impression of him is a little' – she hesitated – '*unbalanced*.'

Uh-huh. The polite, Marcia-style phraseology that in translation meant I was talking through the top of my head. 'Yeah? How so?'

'Spurius Rutilius is a more complicated person than you might imagine, certainly on the basis of a single meeting. Yes, he has a high regard for Harpax and is very much a family man. Also you would, I suspect, have found him quite ... abrasive.' I grinned; Jupiter, she could say that again! 'That I would have expected because like, unfortunately, many of the local people he dislikes Romans in general and makes no secret of the fact. On the other hand, he is no bone-headed fool. Far from it. He knows, for example, far more history than I do.'

'Uh ... is that right, now?' I said cautiously.

'Rutilius may be a common blacksmith but until he died four years ago his father ran the town school. Out of choice, I may say. Although he wasn't wealthy he was a very educated man, freeborn, from a good local family, and history – Latin history, not Roman – was his principal hobby. Rutilius inherited it, although not the taste for schoolmastering, hence his present occupation. His interest in history, however – especially of the pre-Roman period – is quite genuine and always has been.' She smiled. 'When we go round to Lucius Flacchus's for dinner tomorrow, Marcus, you must ask him about Spurius Rutilius. He's quite a protégé of Lucius's.'

I glanced at Perilla, eyebrows raised, and the lady had the decency to look embarrassed. I hadn't actually met Marcia's nearest neighbour Herdonius Flacchus officially, but I'd heard enough about him in the past from Marcia to know that this was one dinner party I wasn't going to enjoy. Like my stepfather Priscus the guy was an antiquities nut, and these buggers are best avoided.

'The invitation came after you'd left,' Perilla said. 'I was going to tell you later.'

Yeah, sure; probably an hour before the event, when it was too late to cancel. The lady can be devious sometimes. Still, what was done was done. I sighed. 'Fine, fine. I just hope you've packed your sauce-proof mantle.'

'Nonsense, dear.' Perilla sniffed. 'Besides, it'll take your mind off murder for one evening.'

That I doubted, if Flacchus was anything like Priscus. Quite the reverse. At least the food would be edible: there could only be one chef like Mother's Phormio.

'It'll be quite an outing for me,' Marcia was saying. 'Lucius has asked before, but it's always been so much trouble. I thought you and Perilla would enjoy a little company. And Marilla, of course. Not living in Rome, she does tend to miss out rather on the social aspect of things.'

I grinned despite myself: Marcia could be pretty devious too, when she put her mind to it, but the housebound old lady pose wasn't fooling anyone. And the Princess would've eaten out in the stables every day if Marcia let her. I topped up my wine cup. 'Okay,' I said. 'I'll survive. Probably.'

'Don't be silly, Marcus!' Perilla snapped. 'It's only a dinner party!'

'And if you do need any incentive,' Marcia said, 'Lucius has the best collection of Latian wines in the district.'

'Is that so, now?' I said.

Devious was right.

11

By next morning there was still no sign of Alexis back from his trip to the records office in Rome, so I took another trip myself out to Sulpicius's villa. This time, thanks to the information from Licinius, I was ready for the bastard. I found myself whistling as I rode through the villa gates and up the box-hedge-lined drive.

Orange-Tunic opened up at the third knock. He didn't seem over the moon to see me, but word had no doubt filtered down to the servants' quarters that Valerius Corvinus wasn't exactly flavour of the month.

'The master at home this morning, pal?' I said.

That got me a look about as open and friendly as a constipated oyster's. 'He's out on the estate, sir.' *So piss off*, the tone said.

I gave him my best smile. 'No problem, friend. I've a good pair of legs and they haven't been getting much exercise these past few days. Just point me in an approximate direction and I'll find him, okay?'

'I'm afraid, sir, that I don't know—'

'Who is it, Bion?' A woman's voice, from behind the lobby's inner door, that I recognised as Sulpicia's even before she came out. 'Oh. Valerius Corvinus. You wanted to see my father?'

She was out of mourning – the funeral would be over, now, and barring the immediate family there wouldn't be any call for it – and wearing a stunning blue mantle that wouldn't've disgraced a formal dinner; earrings and a necklace, too. Hardly everyday morning wear for a country villa in the Alban Hills. I remembered the rough tunic and leggings of the last occasion. Not a lady who believed in doing things by halves, obviously.

'Uh, yeah,' I said, putting my lower jaw back where it belonged. 'We have a bit of unfinished business to discuss.'

'He's on the preserve. It's his latest project and he likes to keep an eye on it.' She smiled. 'I'll take you, if you like. Give me a moment to change into something more sensible.'

'There's no need for that, lady.'

The smile widened. 'But, Corvinus, I can't possibly go like this!'

'Ah . . . I meant if you just tell me how to find the place—'

'It'd be quicker if I took you. And I don't mind, honestly.' She turned. 'Bion, Valerius Corvinus is to wait in the atrium. Fetch him a cup of wine. It's not too early for a cup of wine, Corvinus?'

'No. No, that'd be great.' Not in Bion's view, obviously: the guy was looking like he'd quite happily spit in the jug. 'Oh. One thing. You think I could have a short word with your maid?'

'Procne? What on earth for?'

'She carried the note, didn't she? The one arranging the meeting. I, ah, wondered if she might've told anyone about it beforehand.'

'Why should that matter?' And then, when I hesitated, she said more gravely, 'Oh, I see. Of course. No, I'm sure Procne wouldn't have done anything like that. She's been my maid since I was a girl, and she's very reliable. But I'll send her down as soon as she's helped me out of my mantle and you can ask her yourself.'

Bion led me in and parked me on the couch by the pool with a face that would've soured milk. The wine came, though, and it wasn't bad. I was halfway down the cup when Procne arrived.

'You wanted to see me, sir,' she said.

She might've been in her thirties but she was a real looker, and she knew it. No country bumpkin, either. Slaves – barring a certain class of slaves, sure – don't usually have access to make-up, but some ladies let their maids use the basics, and Procne was clearly one of the lucky ones. She'd made good use of the privilege, too, without going over the top. The eyes that were measuring me demurely from under the blackened lashes were a lot less innocent than the mild little voice would suggest.

'Uh, yeah,' I said. 'The mistress tell you what about?'

'She said you wanted to know whether I'd told anyone about her meeting her fiancé in the loggia, sir. No, I didn't.'

'No one? Not even her father?'

I'd been watching for a flicker, but it didn't come. Mind you, if Sulpicia had told her what the question would be she'd have had plenty of time to get her act together, and from the look of her I'd bet she wouldn't even need that.

'No, sir. But the master knew already. She told him herself as soon as she got back from her afternoon ride, just before she sent me round.'

I kept my face expressionless. 'Uh-huh. And he didn't mind? That she was making an assignation with Vettius Bolanus when he'd broken off the engagement?'

The smile was there and gone in a moment; a sly smile. 'Oh, it wouldn't make any difference to the mistress what the master thought. If she wants to do something she does it. The master realised that long ago.'

Yeah, I'd believe that. I'd bet Sulpicia was a real handful, especially to a straight-down-the-line traditionalist like her father. And he didn't have a wife to help him out, either. 'Uh, he's a widower, right?' I said.

'Yes, sir. The old mistress died of a fever eighteen years ago. He never remarried.'

Eighteen years? A long time. Sulpicia would've been, what, ten or eleven, say, and I'd bet she'd been running wild ever since.

'All right, Corvinus? You've finished?'

I turned round: the lady herself, changed back into her dryad outfit, her hair caught back in a bun held by a ribbon and looking sexy as hell. Eat your heart out, Hippolyta. Running wild was right.

'Yeah. Yeah, I've finished.' I looked at Procne. The eyes were mostly hidden again by the thick lashes, but the glance I got back was a long way from demure. 'Thanks for your help, Procne.'

'You're very welcome, sir.'

'We'll take the horses, if you don't mind,' Sulpicia said. 'I was going out anyway.'

Bugger, this was a conspiracy; didn't anyone walk in the country? I was beginning to hate the feel of leather under me, and I'd been looking forward to a stroll through the woods. Still, there was no point in grousing, and at least the company was good. 'Sure,' I said, gulping down the last of the wine. 'No problem.'

We went outside. One of the stable slaves brought round her horse – it was a black stallion, much bigger and more powerful than my mare – and we mounted up. Sulpicia watched me critically.

'You're not a rider, Corvinus,' she said.

'Uh-uh.' I reached for the reins. 'You've noticed already?'

'It would be difficult not to. You have a seat like a sack of turnips.'

'Thanks, lady.'

'Don't mention it.' Her serious look vanished, and she laughed. 'Never mind, we'll take it easy.'

She wheeled the stallion, crouched low over his mane and dug her heels in, heading fast as an arrow for the broad side track that led past the stable block and into the woods. Castor, if this was taking it easy I was a Nubian belly-dancer. I swore under my breath and followed.

She may've been showing off but she was pretty good, far better than me, and I had the impression that even if she'd been on her own she'd still have taken the first, clear stretch through the orchard beside the villa like she was riding the last lap in a Circus horse-race. Luckily, the track was more overgrown once we hit the woods and she slowed enough for me to catch up and draw level. I was breathing hard. Sulpicia hadn't broken sweat.

'That's better,' she said.

Yeah, well, it depended what you were making the comparison with. It beat a kick in the head with a hobnailed sandal, sure, but that was about as far as I'd go, personally. 'You, uh, like riding, then?' I said.

'I'm out most days. Twice, usually. And the countryside up here is marvellous.' She looked at me, amused. 'You don't think so?'

'It's okay. But give me Rome any time.'

'Oh, Rome's marvellous, too. But here you have to make your own excitement. Don't worry, the preserve isn't far. You could've done it on foot, if Bion hadn't been such a sourpuss.'

Now she told me. We rode in silence for a bit. Slowly.

Finally she said, 'Have you made any progress? In finding Marcus's killer?'

'Depends what you mean by progress, lady.' I ducked my head to avoid a homicidal branch. 'I'm still at the weeding-out-options stage.'

'Which options would these be?'

I hesitated. Sulpicia didn't come high on the suspect list at present, sure, but there again she certainly hadn't dropped off the end altogether; not with that all-too-pat night-time rendezvous on the tablets. Also, I couldn't very well admit that my prime reason for talking to her father was that I thought there was a fair chance he'd put paid to a lot more than Vettius Bolanus's wedding plans. 'Just options,' I said.

'Then I hope you're better at solving puzzles than you are at riding.'

'I couldn't be any worse.'

She laughed and urged the stallion into a trot. I let my mare carry on at her own pace.

I'd noticed in the last couple of minutes that we'd passed two or three cock pheasants strutting around at the side of the track and giving us evil looks as they picked about in the undergrowth. Big, plump birds, top grade. Not wild local ones, either: my guess would be domesticated Syrian imports. Which surprised me a little: maybe Sulpicius wasn't quite as uninterested in the commercial side of country villa ownership as I'd thought. Not that that was all that strange, because even the high-class property owners who'd consider it slightly infra dig to mess around with the traditional rural estate staples such as vines and fruit trees aren't above turning an extra copper or two towards expenses by supplying the luxury market at Rome with farmed game, not just pheasants but real exotics such as ostriches and flamingoes. Sometimes animals as well, boar or even bears. It's a risk, sure – exotics are expensive to buy, breed and keep, and the market is pretty fickle – but if it comes off you're quids in, and to be able to tell your guests that the marinated camel's hump they're eating was delivered fresh that morning from your own estate ranks pretty high where dinner-party one-upmanship's concerned.

Suddenly from the other side of the intervening greenery there came an eerie, despairing howl that made my scalp crawl. My horse half shied and stopped, ears laid back, but Sulpicia's didn't pay any attention and the lady herself didn't bat an eyelid. Oh, yeah; peacock. Luxury market was right. We must be getting close. I smoothed the mare's nose to quieten her and urged her forwards until we were level again. 'Uh . . . you have any problems with poachers at all out here, by the way?' I said.

Sulpicia shook her head. 'No. Not that I'm aware of, at least, but the preserve is Father's concern, not mine. Why do you ask?'

'No reason. Just interest.' A white lie: I'd been gauging direction, and from the position of the sun I'd reckon the path we were following ran more or less parallel to the lakeside track which served both Sulpicius's villa and Bolanus's; not too far from it, either. Also, that we'd come pretty close to the boundary between the two estates; which meant that the loggia where Bolanus had been killed wasn't all that far off, maybe as little as a couple of hundred yards away. Close enough for a poacher to slip across the dividing line on the off-chance, anyway. Or anyone else, for that matter. 'Does your father come out here a lot, then?'

'Oh, yes. He likes to feed the birds himself rather than trust the estate slaves to do it. Father takes everything he does very seriously. Especially where monetary investment is involved, which in this case of course it is.' She reined in beside a break in the bushes. 'This is as far as you can go on horseback, so I'll leave you here, if you don't mind. There isn't really a path as such, but go as straight as you can and you can't miss it.'

'Yeah, right.' I dismounted. 'Thanks a lot.'

'You're welcome. Give him my regards.' Without another word she turned, dug her heels into the stallion's flanks and galloped off the way we'd come. The pheasants scattered, cursing.

Jupiter! Better her than me: a gallop down that path with the overhanging trees was just asking for trouble. Strange woman, though: *Give him my regards.* I tied the halter to a handy bush and shoved my way through the undergrowth.

It wasn't far, maybe fifty yards or so. I had to admit that the guy had the thing well organised. The trees and vegetation had been cleared in a wide circle around a natural pool, and there were a couple of dozen open cages with feeding troughs. Also, birds everywhere, not just pheasants but swans, peacocks and hens and a few sad-looking cranes, practically beak to beak and tame as pet sparrows. All in all, a real on-the-claw delicatessen that would've had Meton reaching for his sauce book.

Sulpicius was standing with his back to me by a high, closed-in aviary chock-full of busy ortolans and fig-peckers.

'Your daughter says to give you her regards,' I said.

He whipped round. Pleased to see me was something he wasn't. 'What the hell—'

I indicated the birds. 'Impressive collection. You have anything on special offer today?'

If he'd been a bird himself, he'd've swelled to twice his size and ruffled his feathers. As it was, he just turned five shades of purple.

'Valerius Corvinus,' he said, 'this is nothing short of persecution, and I am getting very tired of it.'

There was an empty grain-bucket next to me. I upended it and sat down, then wished I hadn't. *Less* riding, Marcia; *less*. 'I'm sorry to hear that,' I said. 'Still, the fancy table-birds business makes a change from dealing in whacky building stone. You have an outlet in Labici?'

That got me the sixth shade. 'Get off my property!' he snapped. 'Now!'

I shook my head. 'Uh-uh. Not yet, not until I've finished. I started off nice, pal, by asking questions. Now I'm going to give you the answers and tell you what I think they mean. What happens after that is up to you.'

'I have no intention of discussing—'

'Two years ago the Caba quarry supplied unweathered stone to the municipality of Labici with the result that the market hall it was used to build collapsed. The quarry overseer Coxa did a runner, but my bet is that the person really responsible, or at least jointly responsible, for the sale was your partner Vettius Bolanus. I think you found this out somehow and that three days ago, the day of Bolanus's murder, you faced him with the accusation and formally terminated friendship. The only question left of the bunch, *pal,* is whether you terminated Bolanus a few hours later. Me, I'm keeping an open mind on that one, but I'd be prepared to offer reasonable odds. Now, you still want to play oysters or would you consider letting me have your side of the story?'

One of the peacocks spread its tail and screamed into the silence. We both ignored it, and the silence lengthened. Finally Sulpicius took a deep breath. If looks could've killed I'd've been rissole.

'Ten days ago,' he said carefully, 'I had a letter from Coxa, delivered anonymously to the quarry. The man admitted he sold the stone knowing the consignment was unweathered but was unwilling to shoulder all the blame. He claimed that Bolanus had put him up to it and pocketed most of the money paid by the building contractor. I was inclined to dismiss the accusation as malicious, but I felt it my duty to pursue the matter further. I went to our bankers in Rome. They told me that Bolanus had been withdrawing large amounts of cash from the company account, as he had a perfect right to do, over a period of several months. However, these withdrawals I had no knowledge of, nor, as far as I was aware, had they any purpose where company expenses were concerned. Under the circumstances, I decided to raise the question with Bolanus in person. Now does that satisfy you?'

'This was three days ago, right?' I said.

I thought for a moment he wasn't going to say anything else, but finally he nodded. 'Yes. The interview was ... most unpleasant. At first he categorically denied any involvement in the Labici business, but then I showed him Coxa's letter and told him about my talk with our bankers.'

'And?'

Sulpicius lips tightened. 'He simply shrugged it off. He then suggested that his withdrawals so far should be set against my daughter's dowry and that, if I were to agree to his continued use of the account as a source of funding for his political campaign, on his election to censor he would guarantee that the company received the stone order for the new town hall. Both of these suggestions left me no alternative, naturally, but to tell him I was formally renouncing friendship and that his engagement to Sulpicia was at an end.'

Yeah; straight down the line. 'So why the hell didn't you tell me all this before?' I said.

'Because, as I informed you, it was none of your business!' Sulpicius snapped. 'It still isn't.'

'The bastard was a crook. Why protect him?'

'He was my neighbour, and – at the time – my daughter's fiancé. That should be reason enough. I considered a renunciation of friendship sufficient. Your suggestion that I went further and killed the man I find simply incredible, not to say extremely insulting. Now please leave, Valerius Corvinus. That is all I have to say.'

Gods in heaven, I'll never understand guys like that! 'You knew your daughter made an arrangement to meet Bolanus that evening. In the light of what happened at the interview you didn't try to stop her?'

That got me a hard stare. Then his lips twisted into what would've been a smile if he'd been capable of one. 'I have long given up,' he said, 'trying to stop Sulpicia doing whatever she wants to do, when she wants to do it. You've met her yourself. Do you wonder?'

Well, maybe not. 'She knew why you were breaking off the engagement?'

'Of course she did. I was very careful to give her the full details.'

'Yet she still sent the guy the note?'

'Yes.'

'She, uh, provide any explanation?'

He was still staring at me like I was something that'd passed through the peacock's digestive tract. 'She said' – the words came carefully and without expression – 'that it didn't matter.'

'She said *what?*'

'That it didn't matter, Corvinus. You heard me quite correctly, I'm sure, on the first occasion.' He turned away. 'Now leave me alone, please. You're distracting the birds.'

I left.

12

She said that it didn't matter.

What the hell did that mean? I thought it over as I rode back towards the villa. Strait-laced or not, Sulpicius had done the right thing in breaking contact with Bolanus: he was a caught crook, self-confessed, and once Sulpicia knew it, which I'd no reason for doubting that she did, then the lady ought to have been grateful for the escape. Sure, if Sulpicius had told me she hadn't believed him then there'd be no problem: we'd have the old story of the wilful daughter taking the part of her wrongly accused lover and making an assignation against her father's wishes to pledge her support. But she had believed him; she simply thought it didn't matter.

Okay, so *why* didn't it matter? There were three possible reasons that I could think of. The first – the most obvious one – was that she was head over heels in love with the guy. You get women like that: the man may be a complete bastard, more crooked than a stepped-on snake, chase after everything in a skirt and treat her worse than the slave who cleans out the privy and she still thinks the sun shines out of his backside. For all I knew, that could be the explanation: I'd never met Bolanus so I'd no way of judging how attractive he'd be to women, and even that wouldn't've helped because where women are concerned you just can't make rules. However he came across to the rest of humanity, to Sulpicia he could've been Hercules, Apollo and

Adonis all rolled up into one perfect bundle. Certainly, she'd chosen to wear mourning for him where it wasn't necessary, let alone politic, and any time I'd heard her speak of the guy she'd been on his side rather than her father's; but somehow I couldn't imagine a woman like Sulpicia going overboard for anyone.

Reason two was more convincing: the fact that Bolanus was a crook didn't matter because, to Sulpicia, it was irrelevant, or at least unimportant. It might even be a plus. You get women like that, too, especially in Roman high society, and Sulpicia had spent most of her life in Rome. Men as well. They're the other side of the coin from the Sulpiciuses of this world, the straight-down-the-line good old damn-your-eyes rigid moralists who take the old-fashioned Way of the Ancestors on board in its entirety and won't budge from it an inch, whatever it costs them or other people. These guys – and girls – are the moderns; often, they're the successful ones in politics or business or society because they've got no moral code at all, or if they have they don't allow it to get between them and what they want. Sulpicius might've viewed Bolanus's actions as a crime, but to a modern they'd be nothing worse than a piece of smart business practice. It didn't mean that he or she was necessarily evil or wicked; just that, where morality was concerned, they used a different set of scales.

Which brought me to the third reason. Bolanus's crime didn't matter to Sulpicia because she knew he was a dead man walking . . .

If that one held then we were back to the direct link between the meeting and the murder: Sulpicia, for reasons of her own, had set Bolanus up and either killed him herself or stood by while someone else did the job. It was possible, sure, in practical terms, completely possible: send the note which brought him outside where he was vulnerable, then 'find' the body and put on an act for the family. The problem with that was I just couldn't see it happening. Sulpicia had no reason to want Bolanus dead; she hadn't, so far as I knew, been against the marriage, even if her father had arranged it, and from my experience of the lady she wasn't one to keep any opposition to herself, so I would've heard, one way or another: she was marrying Bolanus because *she* wanted it, not her father. There was always the chance, of course, that Sulpicius's revelations had tipped the balance completely the other way, but in that case I'd've expected a stronger immediate reaction than 'it doesn't matter'. Also, like I say, she still seemed genuinely fond of the guy. And from what Draco had said, her shock at finding his body had been real enough to set it beyond simply good acting . . .

Ah, hell; leave it. Other things beckoned. I'd reached the end of the forest track now and was back in sight of the villa. Not that I was going to call in: I'd had enough for the time being of the Sulpicius household, the sun was nearly overhead and all that riding had given me a thirst. Also, I had Herdonius bloody Flacchus's dinner party to think of. Perilla had brought out the three-line whip, and I was under strict instructions to be back home in time for a bath and a leisurely change before we all trooped next door for the festivities. Make it an easy afternoon, then. Which meant Pontius's wineshop.

All in all, I reckoned I deserved it. The morning hadn't been wasted, far from it. I'd got the confirmation I needed that Bolanus had been a wrong 'un, and that visit to the bird preserve had thrown up some interesting possibilities. Whether Sulpicia had known the whys and wherefores of the case or not, the place would've drawn poachers like wasps to honey, and Bolanus's loggia would've been hardly more than a step away, which was relevant where Harpax and Rutilius were concerned. Sulpicius, too; I wasn't done with Sulpicius, not by a long chalk. That outraged denial and the guy's ultra-respectability didn't mean a thing. The downside of the old Roman code is that you don't forget or forgive an injury, and if fate puts an enemy within your grasp you take what's offered with both hands. Sulpicius had hated Bolanus worse than poison, that I knew for certain; and the fact that he was an honourable man by his own lights didn't make that hatred any less. The guy's moral scruples might have stopped him exposing his partner in public, sure, but that would only have made things worse: through Bolanus he'd lost his personal and professional reputation – I'd bet good money, incidentally, that that was why he'd moved down here from Rome – a good slice of his income and a large amount of actual cash into the bargain, and there wasn't a thing he could, or would, officially do about it. Also – and I didn't, knowing Sulpicius's type, take this lightly – at the final interview Bolanus had added insult to injury by metaphorically spitting in Sulpicius's eye. For your strait-laced Roman that would put the lid on it. The only thing worse than being betrayed by someone you considered to be a friend is the discovery that the traitor is no gentleman.

Oh, yes, Sulpicius had hated Bolanus all right, however much he wrapped his feelings up in fancy language. Certainly enough to kill him if chance offered. Which, with the meeting in the loggia, it had.

I took it easy on the ride into town, so it was well past noon when I arrived. There was only one customer in the wineshop, propping up the counter, and that was a guy I hadn't seen before. He had a jug and a cup beside him and if he wasn't quite at the newt stage he was more than halfway there. Pontius gave me the eye as I came in, nodded in his direction and lifted his shoulders.

'Afternoon, Corvinus,' he said. 'The usual?'

'Yeah. And something to go with it.'

'I've got some cold beans in oil and sage. That do with a bit of bread and sausage?'

'Fine.' I leaned on the counter – sitting was a pleasure I intended to put off for a minute or two – and glanced sideways at my co-barfly. He wasn't all that prepossessing, a little runt with a permanent five o'clock shadow and a tunic that'd survived at least three identifiable dinners. He noticed me looking, grunted and went back to nursing his drink.

'No Gabba this afternoon?' I said to Pontius. It was past the old guy's time.

'Nah. His wife's taken him into Bovillae to buy herself a new pair of sandals. Castrimoenium isn't good enough, seemingly.' He set down the filled half jug and a cup.

'Is that right, now?' I poured and drank. Lovely. I was sorry for Gabba; his wife was a clothes nut and laboured under the delusion that his was a valid second opinion, which it wasn't. Gabba's dress sense was even worse than mine.

'How's the case coming?' Pontius ladled the beans out of an earthenware pot into a bowl.

'Don't ask, pal. Just don't ask.'

He grinned. 'That bad?'

'Uh-uh. I just want to give the brain a rest for a while. Vettius Bolanus can take a lunch break.'

The runt at my elbow turned an eye on me like a five-day-old poached egg. 'Vettius Bolanus,' he said carefully, 'can go and fuck himself. Whatever particular corner of Hades he's currently frying in.' He upended the jug into his cup. Only a dribble came out. 'And then he can take an encore.'

I raised my eyebrows.

'Now, Feronius,' Pontius murmured. He sliced the sausage, put it on a plate with a hunk of bread and passed it over to me. 'No ill of the dead in here, please.'

I'd turned to face the runt properly. Feronius, eh? Bolanus's ex-bailiff, sacked for mismanagement. I'd been meaning to look this guy up, but so far I hadn't had the time. 'Is that so?' I said. 'Now there's an unusual sentiment, pal.'

He scowled at me. 'What's your angle, Roman?'

'Quintus Libanius has asked Valerius Corvinus here to look into the murder,' Pontius said placidly. 'And we'll have none of that attitude, thank you very much, or you can drink elsewhere.'

I held out my hand towards him, palm down, where Feronius couldn't see it. 'No offence, friend,' I said. I indicated his empty jug. 'That one's a corpse. You like some of mine?'

The drunk hasn't been born who'd pass up an invitation like that. He emptied the dregs of his cup and pushed it over. I filled it and topped up my own. 'Whoever slit Bolanus's throat did the world a favour,' he said. 'Me, I'd shake his hand.'

'Right. Right,' I said.

'You want to know why?'

'Because Bolanus was a bastard?'

That got me another poached-egg stare. 'Yeah. Correct. You knew him?'

'Uh-uh.' I shook my head and reached for the spoon. 'Just a lucky guess. I hear you used to work for him and he fired you.'

Feronius drew himself up, as far as that was possible for a half-filleted drunk. 'I resigned,' he said. 'No one talks to me like that, no one.'

'Talks to you like what?'

'He claimed I was running the estate down on purpose. Me!' He drained the cup and held it out. I refilled it. 'Can you imagine that?'

'Terrible,' I said.

'The place had been falling apart for years. He wouldn't put the money in that it needed to keep going, him and that stuck-up vinegar-titted sister of his. Spent it on carriages and fancy toy monkeys. I told him, if you're not prepared to make the losses good then the best thing to do is sell up and go off to Rome where you can eat and drink yourself silly on the proceeds and have all the monkeys you like. But would he listen?'

'That kind never do,' I said.

'That's the truth of it.' He took another slug of wine. Shit; at this rate I might as well order the other half. 'He could've done. Sold out, I mean. Got a good price, too, considering the state of the place. He had the offer, but the bugger wasn't having any. Where he is now, it serves him right.'

I spooned in some of the beans and chewed. Time for

something more than the sympathetic ear. 'So who was doing the offering?' I said casually.

Not casually enough. He tapped his nose. 'That's none of your concern, Roman. It was a good offer, though, like I say. He should've taken it at the time.'

'Concordius?'

It wasn't quite a shot in the dark, because Marcia had told me that Concordius was into property and he'd been trying to get his hands on the Bolanus estate for years. However, I wasn't prepared for Feronius's reaction. The guy had lifted his cup. Now he set it down slowly, and the scowl was back. 'Concordius can fuck himself too,' he said.

'Yeah? I thought he gave you a job. After you were . . . after you resigned.'

'Some job. Collecting interest on loans as second-stringer for that bastard Ursus. And me an estate bailiff. The bugger'd no sense of gratitude.'

I let that last little nugget pass, but not unmarked. 'Who's this Ursus?'

'Concordius's muscle.' He took another swallow of wine. 'Muscle being the operative word. Ursus is muscle all the way up to his fucking scalp.'

'So Concordius is in the loans business?' I'd known that already, sure, but I needed to keep the poisonous little runt talking.

'Right. 'S why he'll be elected, isn't it?'

'Is it?'

'Sure. Money's short around here. Half the voters owe him already, the other half think if they need cash with Concordius as censor they'll get a good deal. Me, I could tell them different, because where wriggling out of paying his debts is concerned that bastard's an expert. Sodding ingrate.'

He gulped wine and held the empty out for more. Jupiter, the guy could drink! I filled the cup. Pontius was giving me looks, but I ignored them and he moved off to polish the other end of the counter. 'Tell me more about Ursus,' I said.

The little piggy eyes peered at me suspiciously. 'Why do you want to know?'

'Just interest. Besides, I'm pouring.'

'Just interest, right?' He grunted, then shrugged and downed another swallow. 'Fair enough, Roman; it's no skin off my nose, anyway. I told you, Ursus does Concordius's collecting for him. Used to be a chaser until he got his wooden sword. Not Rome, Capua.'

'That so, now?' I leaned back and mulled that little piece of info over. It fitted; chasers are the heavier type of gladiators, picked for weight and stamina. They aren't, normally, the arena's brightest intellects, chaser tactics largely being summed up by the maxim 'Run 'em down, hammer 'em flat'. To last long enough for honorary retirement the guy must've been pretty good at his job; not a complete bonehead, either, despite what Feronius said, albeit within certain fairly narrow limits, because boneheads don't last long on the sand any more than weaklings do. And Capua, although it isn't Rome, is one of the best provincial centres for sword-fighters in Italy.

The other relevant point was that most retired gladiators stay in the game, either as trainers for the up-and-coming youngsters or as advisers to the army. Some, a few, opt out, open a wineshop and drink themselves into an early, flabby death. That leaves a very small minority who hire themselves out as muscle to various legitimate or, usually, not-so-legitimate enterprises. These buggers are the real hard cases; the ones who've got the taste for violence and can't leave it alone. I'd bet that Ursus was one of these.

All of which made him a pretty interesting character.

Feronius's cup was looking empty again. I slopped in some more of the wine. 'He been with Concordius long?'

'Long enough for word to get around that falling behind on repayments is not a smart move.' We'd obviously moved on to the bosom-buddies stage, because Feronius reached over and helped himself to a piece of my sausage. 'Two, three years, maybe.'

'You get a lot of trouble?'

'Nah. Not enough for Ursus's liking, certainly. A twisted arm's usually enough.' He chewed and scowled. 'He's not complaining, though, the bastard. Concordius pays him well, and he has his other little bit of interest locally.'

'Yeah?' I took a mouthful of my own wine. 'And what would that be, now?'

The scowl changed to a leer. 'Say who and you'd be closer to the mark.'

'Is that so?'

'Oh, he's a proper swordsman all right, our Ursus. Popular, too, and not just with the local good-time girls, either, if you know what I mean.'

Pontius, still keeping out of things at the counter's far end, levelled a finger. 'Now you just be careful what you do with that mouth of yours, Feronius,' he said. 'We don't want no trouble here. A word out of place and you're out. Understand?'

Feronius reached for the wine jug and helped himself. 'Come off it, Pontius boy,' he said. 'I was asked and I'm answering. Ursus may be a bastard but if he can pull something a bit above his own class then I say good luck to him. Besides, the sour-titted old bitch is happy enough with the arrangement, by all accounts. And as far as I'm concerned if it means that fucking brother of hers is spinning in his urn the oftener Ursus screws her the better.'

'That's it!' I didn't think Pontius could move so fast, but he did, the whole length of the counter in a blink. 'Walk!'

'Come on, Pontius.' Feronius reached for his cup. 'There's no need for this, okay? I only—'

Pontius's hand came down and gripped his wrist. 'You were warned!' he snapped. 'Now walk or I'll throw you out myself!'

The ex-bailiff pulled away, spilling the wine. 'It's no secret,' he said sulkily. 'And it's true enough.'

'Out! You're barred!'

'Okay, okay.' Feronius got to his feet, steadying himself against the counter. 'You suit yourself, boy. You're the loser. There's plenty other places in town if you don't need my custom. Thanks for the drink, Roman.'

I nodded. He winked at me, made it to the door, and lurched outside.

Pontius watched him go. He reached for the bar cloth and wiped up the spill, frowning. 'Drunken sod,' he said. 'I can do without that sort in here. And you're just as bad for encouraging him.'

My brain was buzzing. Sweet holy gods! I was remembering the graffito I'd seen accusing Bolanus's sister of screwing slaves. Ursus wasn't a slave, sure, but as an ex-gladiator he was the next thing to it, and graffiti artists weren't on oath. I took a slow sip of my wine. 'Uh ... he was talking about Vettia, right?' I said.

The cloth paused. 'Look, Corvinus, I don't mind a bit of scandal or bad-mouthing, and in an election it's normal, but that kind of stuff's just plain filth and I'm having nothing to do with it.'

'You mean it's a lie?'

'I mean it's none of my business. Yours either. All I know is that Vettia's a lady and you don't spread that kind of filthy rumour about a lady, ever. Truth doesn't come into things.' He wrung the cloth out into the sink like he was wringing Feronius's neck. 'Now if you want to come in here you'll follow the same rules as everyone else or take a hike yourself, okay?'

Well, it was his wineshop and he had the right to draw his own lines. Even so, a possible link between Concordius's hard man and Bolanus's sister was one that I had to follow up. This guy Ursus was someone I just had to meet.

There was no point in trying to get any more out of Pontius, because he had shut up tighter than a disapproving oyster. I finished my late lunch in frigid silence and headed back to Marcia's.

13

'If Bolanus's sister has a thing going with Concordius's right-hand man then it opens up a whole new can of worms,' I said.

Perilla leaned back against the hot-room wall of Marcia's bath-suite and mopped the sweat out of her eyes with her towel. 'You don't have it as fact, dear. All you have is a graffito supported by a wineshop rumour.'

'Not even that. Pontius nearly hit the roof when Feronius brought out his little nugget. I didn't know the guy was such a crypto-puritan.'

'Could it be true?'

'Maybe. I've only met the lady once, and that was just for five minutes. Still, I wouldn't be all that surprised. She's a spinster of a certain age, she struck me as the slightly desperate type, mutton dressed as lamb, and that kind get funny ideas sometimes, especially shut away on their own in the country. She wouldn't be the first high-class lady to lose her sense of proportion over a gladiator. Also, Pontius didn't exactly fall over himself to deny it.'

'Bolanus would hardly have approved.'

'Damn right. But then I'd bet a month-old anchovy to a fifteen-pound sturgeon he didn't know a thing about it. Otherwise she'd be cooling her heels at some cousin's place five hundred miles away and Concordius'd be looking for a new debt-collector.'

'Hmm.' Perilla put her chin on her hand. 'So if it is true then how does it affect matters?'

'Like I say, it opens up a whole new angle.' I mopped my own face: up here in the Alban Hills there wasn't any shortage of wood, and when Marcia's slaves stoked the bath-house furnace they didn't do it by halves. 'If there is a connection with the murder then there's two possibilities that I can see, not necessarily mutually exclusive. One is that this Ursus is playing the game off his own bat, the other that he's following instructions from his boss And both would give him a prime motive for killing Bolanus.'

'Very well. Let's take the first.'

'Okay. In that case the aim is simple monetary gain, combined with getting rid of an awkward impediment. Like I say, the odds are that Bolanus knew nothing of the affair. Maybe he never did, right up to the time of his death, or maybe he found out and threatened to cause trouble. Whichever it was – and it wouldn't really matter – my bet is that the business as far as Ursus was concerned was coming to a crisis. Whichever of the two, Vettia or Ursus, originally made the running, I'd lay good money that Ursus would want to legitimise the relationship. And if so then Bolanus would be a prime fly in the ointment.'

'Legitimise?' Perilla was staring at me. 'You mean Ursus intended to *marry* Vettia? But Marcus, that's—' She stopped. 'No, perhaps it isn't so very silly after all. I don't know, I've never met the woman so I can't judge.'

'Right. Me neither, to all intents and purposes. And I don't know Ursus at all. Still, if we're building a scenario we can take it as a working hypothesis. Vettia may not be much of a catch in herself, especially for a guy who seems to have no problems pulling the talent, but her money's something else. And the only way he'd get his hands on that is through a proper wedding ceremony.'

'*Does* Vettia have money in her own right?'

'It's a fair assumption, lady. She's old local aristocracy. If she follows the usual pattern she'll have an income of her own plus her dowry capital. It may not be a fortune in Roman terms but I doubt she's short of a silver piece or two. She'd certainly have more than a guy like Ursus could expect in a wife.'

'And would she actually go to the length of marriage, do you think?'

'Absolutely. Vettia isn't the type to think in terms of a roll in the shrubbery; no way, never. That graffito and Feronius aside, I doubt if up to now she's even allowed Ursus as far as first base.'

'Hmm.' Perilla twisted a damp lock of hair. 'There wouldn't be a legal barrier, certainly. Not if Ursus is free. He is, isn't he?'

'Sure. As far as I know. He might've been a slave in the past but he isn't now, and he couldn't be for the thing to work. All the same, if we're talking motive then the legal aspect's crucial.'

'How so?'

'Because before the marriage could be made official they'd need the written permission of Vettia's head of household. And up to three days ago that would've been Bolanus.'

The lady was quiet for a moment. Then she said, 'Ah.'

I nodded. '"Ah" is right. That's the nub. There may not be a legal bar on a freeborn woman taking up with a freedman, but six gets you ten if Vettia asked her brother for permission to marry an ex-gladiator she'd still be waiting when hell froze over. From Ursus's standpoint, Bolanus had to go.'

Perilla's eyes widened. 'But, Marcus, she must realise he's only after money! Or suspect it, at least. Anyone would!'

I shrugged. 'Maybe she does, and she doesn't care. Not that I'd place any bets, mind. I may be wrong, but the lady didn't strike me as too bright. In that sort of way, anyway. She seemed to think her brother was a paragon of virtue, for a start, which we know he wasn't.'

'Wait a moment.' Perilla was frowning. 'Surely killing Bolanus would only postpone Ursus's problem. Before he could marry

Vettia he'd still have to get legal permission from the new head of family. Who is that, do we know?'

'Uh-uh.' Hell; that was an angle I hadn't considered, and with *cui bono* in mind I should've done, not just where Vettia's potential matrimonial plans were concerned but in terms of the estate itself. Bolanus might not have had much in the way of actual cash, but by all accounts whoever inherited the stretch of land by the lake would be sitting on a potential goldmine. Normally, of course – and subject to the terms of the will – the property would pass automatically to the dead man's eldest son, but in this case . . .

'Marcus?'

I blinked. 'Yeah?'

'Your eyes narrowed.'

'Yeah. I was just thinking. Bolanus was on the point of getting married himself, right?'

'The engagement had been called off. You told me the girl's father had cancelled it.'

'Fine, but that wasn't common knowledge. As far as his family was concerned there was to be a wedding within a couple of months.'

'So?'

'So if it did go ahead, and the result was the patter of little feet – little *male* feet – then whoever's name is currently at the top of Bolanus's will would find himself short of one very valuable stretch of prime development site.'

Perilla sat back on the wooden bench. 'Oh,' she said.

'Right. As far as murder goes the present heir would have a motive in spades. The timing may be pure coincidence, but we need to add another name to the suspect list. Not that that should prove too difficult, because the terms of the will should be public knowledge.'

'If Bolanus left a will.'

'The chances are he did. But even if he didn't we're talking about the nearest male relative. I can get that information from Libanius tomorrow. Sure, the guy's probably some meek-mannered family man who wouldn't cheat on his water-rate, but it's something to check out.'

'Very well.' Perilla used the towel again. 'Leave him for the present and go back to Ursus. If he was responsible then how do you see the actual murder?'

'That's easy enough. He waits for Bolanus to turn up for the meeting in the loggia and—' I stopped. Hell. 'Vettia had to know, didn't she?'

'Oh, yes. Otherwise how would *he* have known? If Ursus was the killer then Vettia must have been involved. Partly so, at least.'

'There's still a snag. Sulpicia's note wasn't sent until less than an hour before the murder. Vettia wouldn't've had time to get a message to Ursus. And even if she did she'd still have the problem of sending it.'

'Both true. I can't suggest a solution to either objection.'

'Nor me.' Bugger! There had to be, though, despite the logistics; if the scenario was valid, of course. 'Still, that's a detail. The main drawback is that I can't see Vettia conniving at the murder of her own brother; at any murder, for that matter. Not for any reason. Ursus may be the murdering type, but Vettia isn't.'

'Could she have told him inadvertently?' Perilla was twisting her damp lock of hair. 'Ursus could have claimed he wanted to talk to Bolanus; attempt to persuade him into accepting an engagement, say.'

'Uh-uh. It's an idea, sure, but we still come up against the timing difficulty. Vettia wouldn't have had the time or the means to get a message to the guy. And if he was planning to meet Sulpicia then he wouldn't be alone, or at least not for long. Also, Vettia may not be the sharpest intellect in the world but even she would've put two and two together after the event, and I'd swear she didn't feel any responsibility for her brother's death. Which she would've done if she'd known he was there and that she was the reason. No, the only way he could've known in advance is if someone else—' I stopped.

'Marcus?'

'Hold on.' Yeah, it would fit. Sure it would. 'How about Procne?'

'Who?'

'Sulpicia's maid. Oh, sure, she says she didn't tell anyone, and Sulpicia claims she's trustworthy, but personally I wouldn't trust that lady an inch. Sulpicia used to meet Bolanus regularly in the garden, and Procne'd be the one person who'd know about the meetings in advance every time, because she was the one who carried the messages. If Ursus did want to find out the best times to catch the guy alone, unprotected, then a standing arrangement with Procne'd be the obvious way of doing it. And that would get rid of both our objections at a stroke. All Procne would have to do would be to make sure Ursus knew about the meeting in the loggia before she delivered the real message to Bolanus.'

'But why should Sulpicia's maid pass on the information to Ursus?'

'Feronius said Ursus is a ladies' man. He may have his sights set on Vettia, but according to Feronius she wasn't the only one running after him. I've seen Procne, Perilla, and she's no shrinking violet herself. She's a natural for Ursus.'

'Marcus, dear, that is pure speculation.'

'Sure it is. No arguments. All the same, like I say it'd solve the whole problem in one, wouldn't it?'

Perilla sniffed. 'Not quite. There is still a timing difficulty. Even if this Procne did tell Ursus about the meeting she'd have to do it in good enough time.'

'True. But then we don't know what arrangements they had. If any. It's a working theory, anyway.'

'All right.' She tucked the curl of damp hair behind her ear. 'You mentioned two possibilities.'

'What?'

'That Ursus was playing his own game and that he was working for Concordius. What about the second?'

'Uh . . . yeah. Right.' I wiped my face clear again with the towel. Shit! Maybe theorising at bathtime wasn't such a good idea after all. It was definitely too hot for brainwork, and I could've murdered a cup of Setinian. 'In that case, the engagement business is a sham. Or at least an afterthought of Ursus's. Concordius, through Ursus, was using Vettia as an in in his campaign against Bolanus. Why and how exactly I don't know, I haven't thought this one through – maybe the opportunity just arose, or maybe he engineered it – but it needn't affect the format of the murder any. Ursus just kills Bolanus as Concordius's agent, not off his own bat.'

'Because Concordius wanted Bolanus's estate?'

'Yeah. Or that's the obvious reason, anyway.'

'But if that was his motive then it wouldn't work. Even if he did engineer a marriage between his agent and Bolanus's sister it would get him nowhere because as a single woman Vettia can't inherit and the property would pass to a stranger. He would be left in the same position he was in. So why should he bother?'

Hell's teeth. Theorising in the bathroom was definitely a mistake: my brains were beginning to ooze out of my ears. I shifted irritably on the bench. 'Gods, Perilla, I don't know!' I said. 'It's just a theory, right? Concordius knew Bolanus himself wouldn't sell. Maybe he thought the new owner would be more amenable. Maybe he has a deal set up with the guy already. Maybe he just did it on the fucking off-chance.'

'Don't swear. The other problem is one of degree. Even if Concordius *did* think murdering Bolanus would net him the estate then he would still have to want it very badly indeed for some reason. Or, of course, if his motive didn't involve the estate he'd have to want Bolanus put out of the way for a reason equally compelling. Personally, I would be asking myself what the nature of the reasons might be.'

Oh, Jupiter! 'Ah . . . I'm not with you, lady,' I said.

She sighed. 'Marcus, it's simple. If Concordius was prepared to go to the length of murdering Bolanus then the game has to be worth the candle. To Ursus it is. If he's acting for himself then his motive, as you said, is perfectly straightforward: he makes a very profitable marriage above his station. Assuming, naturally, that he and Vettia between them can get the new head of family's permission, which at present, because we don't know who the man is, is a moot point. Yes?'

'If you say so.'

'As far as Concordius is concerned I'm not so sure that the murder *would* be worth while. Even with Bolanus dead and that particular impediment removed Concordius would still have to buy the estate. Granted, now perhaps he *could* buy it, but he would still have to spend the money. Similarly, he can't simply have wanted Bolanus dead to ensure his own election to censor since by all accounts he was already the stronger candidate. So how does he gain? If he is ultimately responsible, and Ursus only an agent, then he must do somewhere along the line. It's just a question of—' She stopped. 'You're not listening, are you?'

True. I grinned. 'That's because my brain's stopped working, lady. Look, let's call it a day, right? Time for the scrapers and oil.'

'If you like. We've still got plenty of time. Flacchus won't be expecting us for two hours yet. And the permutations are fascinating.'

Gods! I was married to a salamander; a *thinking* salamander at that! I stood up. 'Come on, Aristotle, call it quits. Besides, like you said at the start we don't even know that Vettia is involved with Ursus. The whole thing might be the product of a drunk's imagination.'

Not that I believed it, mind; still, another ten minutes of slow cooking combined with a wife on cerebral overdrive and I'd be going to Flacchus's as a dried-out husk. Sleuthing could wait until tomorrow.

* * *

When we got back to the atrium red as a pair of cooked Baian crayfish, Marilla was in residence, deep in conversation with another kid I didn't know. They looked up.

'Hey, Princess,' I said. 'Who's your friend?'

'Oh, this is Clarus. Hyperion's son.' The Princess was even redder than I was. 'I did mention him. Hyperion, I mean.'

'Oh, yeah. The sheep doctor.' I grinned. The other kid – he was a bit older than the Princess, seventeen or eighteen maybe – shuffled his feet and gave me a nod. 'Nice to meet you, Clarus.'

Grunt.

'He's helping me with Dassa's cold.' She turned to Perilla. 'Is it all right if I don't come with you to Herdonius Flacchus's? Clarus is showing me how to mix up a cough medicine, and he won't be free tomorrow.'

Perilla was smiling too. 'Yes, of course,' she said. 'What's in the medicine?'

'Honey.' Clarus pushed a tangled mop of reddish-brown hair out of his eyes. The lad was Greek, sure, but he was big-boned, and that, together with the hair colour, suggested there was more than a little Gallic blood mixed in as well. 'Marigold. Angelica. Green walnuts and rue. In a wine-lees base. My father swears by it.'

'You need to watch it carefully while it boils down, though, and that takes two or three hours,' the Princess said. 'That's why I can't go out.'

'Yeah? And where are you going to do this, then?' I asked.

'In the kitchen, of course. Meton says we can use the stove.'

I blinked. Jupiter! That was a first, and no mistake! That bastard guarded his kitchen like it was the Shrine of Vesta's Fire. Sure, the skivvies who did the cleaning and washing up were allowed past the sacred threshold, but even I practically needed a passport to get in. '*Meton* said you could use his *stove*?'

'And one of the stew pans. He's very fond of Dassa. I told you.'

My guts went cold. The stove was bad enough; Meton lending out one of his precious pans to mix up medicine for a sheep was tantamount to the priests of Mars hiring out the sacred shields for mushroom dishes. The surly, evil-minded bugger was up to something; what it was I didn't know, but it was something . . .

'Uh . . . Marilla says you're looking into the death of Vettius Bolanus, Valerius Corvinus.' Clarus's mop of hair had fallen down again. He pushed it back.

'Yeah. Yeah, that's right.'

'I . . . ah . . . don't suppose you thought of calling in a doctor, did you?'

'What for? The guy was already dead.'

'Oh, I know that, sir.' The kid shifted from foot to foot. 'It was just an idea I had. When Marilla told me. Doctors can see things other people miss. Like, uh, signs of poisoning, that sort of thing. I kind of thought if someone's trying to find out how a person died, or maybe when, bringing a doctor in might be sort of useful at times. You know?' He swallowed.

Bugger; we'd got another potential Alexis on the team, I could see that now. Still, he had a point. Not where Bolanus was concerned, of course, because a slit throat's a slit throat, but it was an interesting idea all the same. 'Yeah. Maybe it would be useful, at that,' I said.

Perilla poked me in the ribs with her elbow. 'We'd better get changed, dear,' she said. 'Have a nice evening, Marilla. Clarus, it was so nice to meet you. And if that hair of yours is bothering you too much I'm sure Bathyllus has a pair of scissors somewhere.'

'Oh, no!' the Princess said. 'I think it's lovely.'

Lovely, right? We went upstairs. Perilla was smiling.

I wasn't quite finished with sleuthing for the evening, though, because while we were waiting for the carriage Alexis got back from Rome. Armed with the letter I'd given him, he'd sweet-talked the clerks in the registry office into showing him the original documentation. It was bad news: Concordius's citizenship had checked out right down the line, although his father hadn't bought his freedom until a couple of years before. Shit. Well, you win some, you lose some, and I couldn't say I was all that surprised, even though I could understand why he'd be chary of that little fact coming to light. The formal requirements are one thing, but it doesn't do to have a slave-brand too close in your ancestry if you're campaigning for office, however rich you are. Still, if Concordius was our man then the graffito lead was a dead-end. Like Perilla had said we'd have to dig deeper. He might be squeaky-clean where his election qualifications were concerned, but my gut feeling was that the hard-nosed bastard had beans to spill.

We piled into the carriage and headed off for our evening of fun and excitement.

14

Flacchus's villa wasn't all that far, although 'next door' was stretching things, as it always is when you're not dealing with proper street addresses. I was impressed. The place wasn't as up-market as Sulpicius's, but it'd obviously been there for a hell of a long time, and over the years it'd grown into something about twice the size of Marcia's. Interestingly decorated, too, as I noticed when the door-slave answered the knock and let us in: there were the usual geometric floor mosaics and naturalistic wall paintings that you'd find in any classy villa where the owner wasn't up to speed with modern trends, sure, but the atrium was full of the kind of stuff you'd see in chi-chi antique shops in the Saepta, with prices overrunning the tags, including a life-size bronze chariot with a warrior in a horned helmet standing beside it. Not my taste, but it must've cost a mint. I was glad my stepfather Priscus wasn't with us; we'd've needed hooks to get the old buffer as far as the dinner table.

'Impressive decor,' I said to Marcia.

She was looking pretty impressive herself. Marcia Fulvina might not go to dinner parties often, but when she did she pushed the boat out. I hadn't met Flacchus yet, but if the lady had been twenty years younger that combination of silk mantle, expensive jewellery and seriously pricey perfume would've had me wondering. 'Oh, Lucius is quite a collector, Marcus,' she said. 'Mind you, a lot of these things have been in the family for generations. They're all Latin, of course; the Herdonii have always been very proud of their roots.'

'The master's in the garden, sir,' the door-slave said. 'If you'd care to follow me?'

We went along a back corridor and out into a portico hung with flower baskets.

'Ah, you've arrived.' A tiny guy in a smart embroidered party mantle was hurrying towards us, hand outstretched. 'You're most welcome. *Most* welcome.'

'Good evening, Lucius,' Marcia said.

Maybe I hadn't been so far out in my reckoning after all, because the old lady was almost dimpling. Yeah, well; if first impressions were anything to go by, for an antiquities nut firmly in the Priscus class Flacchus didn't seem all that bad. Sure, there was nothing to him but skin and bone, he was well on the wrong side of sixty, and if he wasn't exactly doing a sprint for the urn he wasn't all that far off the finishing line; added to which I'd just bet from his brisk nerviness that he was like one of these highly strung little terriers you get that's nice as pie one moment and'll go for your ankles the next. On the plus side, though, at least he didn't look like he'd been dug from a pile of Egyptian sand and have a personality to match; and where these guys are concerned that's practically obligatory.

He let go of Marcia's hand and turned to me. 'You must be Valerius Corvinus,' he said. I held out my own hand and had it crushed between fingers like steel springs. 'And your wife Rufia Perilla. A pleasure to see you, my dear.'

'Our stepdaughter sends her apologies,' Perilla said. 'Problems with a sick sheep.'

I thought maybe Flacchus would balk at this, but he just nodded. 'Oh, yes, I'd heard she'd bought Carrinatia's Dassa. It'll be a cough, no doubt. Dassa's always been very prone to coughs.'

I glanced at Perilla and raised an eyebrow, but she ignored me.

'Now.' The little guy was beaming. 'Come straight through. Everyone's here and my major-domo tells me the meal is ready to serve, so we'll just recline immediately, if you don't mind. It's such a pleasant evening that I thought we'd eat outside.'

'That sounds lovely,' Perilla said.

'This way, then.'

It was a big garden, wilder than you usually get, with bushes and trees instead of box hedges and flower-beds. I was expecting an individual-table arrangement, but there was a proper dining-room suite set up on a wide patio surrounded by rose trees, trellised apricots and tall-standing candelabra for the lamps, plus a couple of incense pans to keep the insects off.

'This is nice, Lucius,' Marcia said. 'Very festive.'

'Oh, it's quite ordinary; *quite* ordinary.' Flacchus rubbed his hands. 'I eat out here most evenings in summer.' Yeah; I'd bet that was popular with the bought help. Even allowing for a table you could take apart, lugging these old-fashioned couches out through the portico wouldn't be easy. Still, the old guy lived alone, so the usual arrangements would've been a lot simpler. 'You know Quintus Libanius, I think. And his wife Fictoria.'

'How are you, Corvinus.' My pal the senator was stretched out in the centre of the middle couch with a camel-faced lady to his left. I nodded to him while Flacchus introduced Perilla.

'Marcia between me and Libanius, I think, in the place of honour.' Flacchus gave a tight, jerky smile. 'Corvinus and Rufia Perilla, if you'd care to sit opposite? There. I think that is *quite* snug.' We reclined. 'I've asked my chef to prepare a special Latin meal in honour of our Roman friends. I do hope you enjoy it.'

Oh, hell; I didn't like the sound of this. Slaves were already serving the appetisers, and I gave the dishes the once-over. They seemed okay, certainly compared with Mother's – the usual raw vegetables, boiled pea-hens' eggs with a fish pickle dip, small grilled sausages, roasted quails and a leaf salad – but I'd give the pulse porridge with green bits through it a miss. That gunk was pure Phormio.

'Now.' Flacchus snapped his fingers and a couple of slaves came over with trays. 'We have wine, honey wine and a cold herb preparation my chef compounds from an old local recipe. A *very* old local recipe. Corvinus, you, I know, will have wine. I recommend it highly, but Marcia tells me you're quite a connoisseur, and I'd appreciate your views.'

Perilla had the herb stuff. I took a cup of wine and sipped . . .

Pure liquid velvet that kissed the tonsils on the way down. Hey! Maybe it wasn't going to be such a bad evening after all! 'That's Velletrian!' I said.

Flacchus took a cup for himself. 'Indeed. Indeed it is, and forty years old if it's a day. I laid it down personally. You like it?'

'Yeah. It's beautiful.' I began to relax. Dinner parties – small ones like this – I enjoy, especially if the wine's good, and Flacchus's was the best. He wasn't such a bad guy himself, either, once you'd made allowances for the jerky manner.

The slaves went round filling cups and we started in on the sundries.

Libanius cleared his throat. 'How is the investigation proceeding, Corvinus? I haven't had time to call in on you, what with everything else, but I am keeping a watching brief.' He turned to Flacchus. 'I don't know if you know, Lucius, but Corvinus here has been kind enough to help over the business of poor Vettius Bolanus.'

'Ah, yes.' Flacchus was helping himself to the pulse porridge. 'Yes, I did know, of course. Dreadful, simply dreadful; you expect that sort of thing in Rome, but not in Castrimoenium. You're making progress, Valerius Corvinus?'

'Yeah,' I said. 'We're moving.'

'Do you have any suspects yet?'

'I'm sorry, Lucius.' Fictoria set down her spoon. 'Could we perhaps *not* discuss the murder? It's hardly a subject for the dinner table after all. I'm sure Marcia Fulvina and Rufia Perilla would agree.'

'Oh, quite definitely.' Perilla gave her a dazzling smile. 'Marcus wouldn't dream of it, would you, Marcus?'

I know when I'm being warned off, even without the edge to the lady's tone. Besides, she'd made it perfectly clear before we left that if I brought the subject up myself there'd be blood spilled. Not that I minded: apart from the fact that my brain needed a break from sleuthing for the evening, the people involved were all local, and it definitely wouldn't've done to spread out any of the dirty linen over the canapés. I needed to ask Libanius about the inheritance details and the identity of Bolanus's heir, sure, but that could wait.

'Uh-uh,' I said. 'Perish the thought.'

That got me a sniff and a straight look like a bradawl, but all Perilla said was; 'Thank you, dear,' in a voice you could've used to ice prawns. I grinned quietly into my wine cup.

'How are the arrangements coming along for the festival, Quintus?' That was Marcia. 'Well, I hope?'

'Festival?' Perilla helped herself to a pea-hen's egg. I wondered if Flacchus got them from Sulpicius.

'The Latin Festival, dear. It's in nine days' time.'

'Oh, yes. Of course.' She reached for the bowl of fish pickle. 'But I didn't think the local councils were involved with that.'

'Neither we are.' Libanius looked up from his half quail. 'Not on the celebrations side, at any rate; naturally that's purely Rome's concern. Still, it's the region's biggest annual event, and a perennial administrative headache.' He reached for a pinch of pepper. 'However, to answer your question, Marcia, as far as I'm aware young Ruso seems to have things nobly in hand. A very organised fellow, Ruso. You know him, Lucius?'

'The Roman magistrate of works? No, I've heard good reports but we haven't met.' Flacchus was frowning. 'Nor will we, at least where the festival's concerned.' He looked over at Perilla. 'It may be a "Latin" festival, but as you say, Rufia Perilla, neither the

Latin councils nor the townsfolk themselves participate in it, and have not done for a century. Except, of course, to provide the infrastructure and foot most of the bills. Rome has always been very accommodating in that area.'

There was an embarrassed silence. Marcia the dinner party diplomatist looked away and I noticed that Libanius suddenly became very interested in his quail. Bugger; I'd experienced this phenomenon time and time again, especially in Latium. The old guy wasn't being intentionally rude, I was certain of that, just making a remark – if he'd known he'd caused offence he would've apologised at once, and meant it, too – but he was a Latin after all, and to a Latin Rome-bashing comes practically as second nature: there's a fault in the system somewhere, therefore it must be Rome's. Ipso facto. The best approach, I'd found, was to ignore it.

There again, I'm not Perilla. Perilla is a lovely lady in many ways, but she can be cross-grained as hell, especially when she thinks she's right, which is ninety-nine point nine per cent of the time. She doesn't get embarrassed easy, either.

'Surely,' she said, 'the reason the Latin towns don't participate is that they ceased long ago to take any interest in the proceedings. As far as playing an active part was concerned, at least.'

I shoved my elbow into her ribs but it was too late because Flacchus had already set his spoon down like it was suddenly too hot to hold. Oh, hell. Bad move, *bad* move; never show a red rag to the Latin bull, especially on his home ground.

'Come, now,' he said. 'I'm afraid that's nonsense.'

I winced. He couldn't know it, of course, but he'd just upped the ante. Me, I can use words like 'nonsense' to Perilla and get away with it three times out of four; I reckon Flacchus might've managed it, too – he was our host, after all, and if Perilla's anything it's polite – but even I wouldn't've risked pairing it with a 'come, now'. Putting the two together was just asking for trouble, dinner party or not. And Flacchus was just as bad, I could tell. Terrier was right.

I did what little I could: gave the lady another dig. Not that it had any effect, mind. Perilla ignored me.

'Is it really?' she said brightly.

'Oh, yes.' Flacchus smiled another of his jerky smiles. 'And if the Latin towns are no longer much interested, my dear, then it's hardly surprising.'

'Indeed? Marcus, *will* you keep your elbows to yourself, please!'

Flacchus picked up his spoon again. 'Why should they be, Rufia Perilla? What was originally a purely Latin festival has now been taken over completely. The process of marginalisation was quite deliberate, and it's been going on for centuries. Not just in the case of the festival, either.'

'Quite right,' Libanius grunted. His wife was nodding too.

'Absolutely,' she said.

Uh-oh; suddenly it was three against one. *Definitely* bad vibes here. I reached for my wine cup. Shit, that was all we needed. Five minutes in, and it was the Latin wars all over again. At this rate we'd be lucky to make it as far as the main course without a refight of Suessa Aurunca.

Marcia coughed. 'These olives, Lucius,' she said. 'They really are delicious. Do you grow them yourself?'

A good try, and well meant, but Flacchus ignored her. So did Perilla. Well, things could be worse. If things were heading for a not-too-genteel scrap then at least she was holding herself in; on a scale of one to ten I'd make it about six, which meant the crockery was still in one piece. The mosquitos had gone quiet, though, and that was a bad sign.

'Oh, I'm not finding fault,' she said. 'Yes, I agree, it is a pity the Latins aren't more involved with their own festival. However, since it was a Roman foundation originally then to claim that Rome has taken it over is . . . well, it isn't really possible, is it?'

June or not I could feel the temperature plummet to mid-winter Riphaean levels. Libanius's beard was bristling, and

Fictoria had opened her mouth and closed it in a line you could've used to cut marble.

Time to intervene; past time.

'Uh . . . Perilla,' I said quietly. 'Maybe you should drop the subject, okay?' And take up something more innocuous, like razor-juggling. Jupiter! It was usually me that disgraced us at parties! Wait until I got the lady home!

Flacchus beamed and waved his hand. 'Oh, no, Valerius Corvinus,' he said. 'Please. Your wife is perfectly correct, at least, according to Roman tradition, and I do like a good argument.' He turned to Perilla. 'You're interested in history, Rufia Perilla?'

'Very much so.' She shelled and dipped another egg. 'You say 'according to Roman tradition'. Are you saying the tradition is wrong?'

'The Roman historians claim that the festival was a creation of your King Tarquin to mark Rome's alliance with the Latin towns. That, I'm afraid, is a fabrication. Latins were meeting on Mount Alba long before Tarquin's time.'

'Were they?'

'Indeed they were. The Alban League towns had sent representatives yearly to the shrine of Latin Jupiter for centuries, both to worship and to discuss league policy.' He was still smiling. 'Don't believe the historians, my dear. Tarquin simply took the festival over in an attempt to control the league itself. The fact that history is always written by the victors is a very old adage, after all.'

'But the Latins were allies, surely, not a conquered people.'

Flacchus shook his head. 'I'm sorry, Rufia Perilla, but I can't agree. In name, yes, of course they were. However Rome has always – and you'll forgive me for saying this, I hope, because I'm speaking to you as a fellow historian – viewed us as subjects, not allies. When it came to the crunch.'

'Now that really *is* nonsense,' Perilla snapped.

Ouch! Crockery time, and I noticed the others – Marcia

especially – were getting distinctly restless, albeit for different reasons. 'Uh . . . Perilla . . .' I said.

'No, no.' Flacchus waved me down. 'It's quite all right, Corvinus. I'm not offended, nor do I wish to give offence. Personally, I find a discussion of these matters stimulating. And after all it is ancient history now, and *quite* academic. Still, I do feel that it's my historian's duty to emend your Roman view of things when given the opportunity. You'd agree, Libanius?'

Fuzzface stroked his beard. 'It certainly doesn't do any harm occasionally.'

'No, indeed.' Fictoria sniffed. 'On the contrary.'

Gloves off, let's hear it for Latin solidarity. Bugger; we were definitely playing Get the Roman now. I sighed and reached again for my wine cup. Yeah, well, there's only so much you can do to keep the peace, and obviously we'd got a particularly malevolent god hovering over us taking an interest in things. I'd given it my best shot, but the atmosphere was turning distinctly sour. Not that Libanius and his wife's reaction surprised me all that much; however polite and Romanised Latins are on the surface, venture too far on certain topics then listen hard and you can always hear the genteel whetting of knives. Still, the wine was good, and after several years' experience of dinner parties at Priscus's I knew the drill backwards: sit tight and say nothing.

Flacchus was holding up his cup to the slave for a refill. 'Rome has always tried to exert a spurious claim to Latium, Rufia Perilla,' he said. 'Your account of the founding of Alba itself, for example, is no more than an attempt to link the town with the Julians.'

'That, I'm afraid,' Perilla said, 'is simply not true.' Jupiter! I would *kill* that lady! 'The Julians moved to Rome from Alba. It's a historically proven fact.'

'Oh, I'm not denying that. Not at all.' Flacchus's smile was still in place, but it didn't touch his eyes. 'However, what I do object to, my dear, if you'll forgive me saying so, is your historians' subsequent creation of a spurious link between them and Aeneas's son Iulus, who was supposedly Alba's founder. The Julians had nothing to do with him, but it suited Rome – when the time came – to make the connection. And, of course, to confirm it through the invention of Iulus's descendant Romulus.'

I set my cup down. Peacekeeping, ethnic goodwill and a quiet life are fine up to a point, but they have their limits. If Flacchus was a Latin then I was Roman and proud of it, and there are things you just don't say in front of a Roman and get away with it.

'Uh . . . hang on, Flacchus,' I said. 'You're claiming that Romulus is a myth?'

Flacchus turned to me. 'No. No, indeed, and I'm sorry if I gave that impression. Romulus may well have existed. All I'm saying is that he had no connection with Alba.'

'Romulus was the grandson of the Alban king, pal. Everyone knows that.'

'Marcus . . .'

'Everyone *accepts* it, certainly. Rome has made sure of that. However, that part of the story had no existence until some five hundred years ago. Which, by coincidence, was about the time when Rome was beginning to absorb Latium as a whole into the Roman state. The legend isn't even original. I could give you a dozen parallels from Greek tradition and elsewhere. It was invented propaganda, pure and simple; an attempt to establish a historical link where none existed, and hence a claim to overlordship.'

'Is that so, now?' I was glaring at him. 'Then you can take your historical parallels, friend, and—'

'*Marcus!*' Perilla snapped.

I subsided. 'Yeah, well.'

Marcia cleared her throat. 'I really do think, Lucius, we should discontinue this topic,' she said smoothly. 'Tempers are becoming a little frayed.'

There was a long, painful silence. Finally, Flacchus blinked. 'Really?' he said. 'Yes. Yes, perhaps they are. I'm sorry, Valerius Corvinus, if I caused any offence. But you must realise that we are very sensitive to the fact that Latium is no longer an independent entity, in any sense. Our only remedy is to remind our—' He stopped, and then said carefully; 'to remind our *allies* that we are a separate people with our own history and customs which we are in grave danger of losing. And, as I say, to correct the historical record when we have the chance to do so.'

'It isn't altogether Rome's fault, you know,' Perilla said quietly. 'The main problem is that Rome is too big, and too close. It always has been; but that, I'm afraid, is simply a fact of life.'

Libanius grunted. 'That's true enough,' he said. 'Rome sucks us in, has been doing for years. The Divine Augustus tried to reverse the flow but there isn't much you can do with laws, or even grants.'

Marcia dabbed at her lips with her napkin. 'It does go the other way,' she said. 'The Alban Hills are becoming extremely popular.'

'With the Roman rich, yes.' That was Fictoria.

Marcia turned to face her. 'Such as myself, perhaps?' she said. Diplomat or not, there was an edge to her voice.

'Oh, no. You're a permanent resident, and have been for years.' Fictoria straightened a fold of her mantle. 'I meant the incomers. People who buy or build villas which are only occupied in the summer months. They bring in money, certainly, but we need population. Rome is draining that off and has been for a long time. Youngsters especially.'

'Indeed.' Flacchus was nodding. 'My point exactly. Oh, you're quite correct, Rufia Perilla; it's not altogether Rome's fault. However, to diagnose the disease and prescribe the remedy are two different things. If one could, as it were, restore the idea of Latium to the ordinary Latins then it might be a start, but that is difficult. And losing members of the old families who have resisted the urge to move, like Vettius Bolanus, only makes things worse.'

After the storm we'd hit a real downer here. Still, it gave me a chance at the change of subject, and maybe smooth a few feathers including my own. 'Uh, incidentally,' I said. 'Marcia tells me you know Spurius Rutilius.'

Flacchus looked fazed for a moment. 'Indeed I do,' he said. 'A very capable young man, with a first-class brain.' Gods! This was *Rutilius*? 'His father ran the local school and was a historian of some note. I have a great deal of time for young Rutilius.'

'He was a sort of protégé of yours, I understand.'

'Yes. Excuse me a moment.' He turned round and signalled to the hovering major-domo. 'Trupho. You can serve the main course, if you would;. I think we've all finished.' He turned back. 'Now, Corvinus. Rutilius. Yes, although "protégé" is perhaps too strong a term. I did have hopes that he might study formally, and would certainly have helped him do so, but his inclinations didn't tend that way, although he has always taken a great interest in Latin culture. Then the marriage.' He paused. 'I don't say anything against Brunna, of course, she's a most devoted wife, or indeed against her father, but I always thought that was a bit of a waste.'

'You still see him?'

'Occasionally. It's a fair way out here, naturally, and I'm very seldom in town, but yes, we do talk and I lend him books. Why do you ask?'

'No reason. I was, uh, down at his blacksmith's shop yesterday. He doesn't seem to have much time for Romans.' I was going to add 'either' but I stopped myself. No doubt the malevolent god was still hovering.

'Rutilius can be a little . . . acerbic,' Flacchus said carefully; I wasn't the only one watching my mouth. 'Also he has financial worries at the moment, which may have acted as a contributing factor. Possibly you didn't see him at his best.'

'Financial worries?'

He hesitated. Yeah, well, I supposed I was pushing it slightly; under the laws of politeness I'd no right to ask for details, and Perilla was giving me definite looks, but that little nugget was too good to leave lying. Also, I reckoned Flacchus was feeling a little ashamed of himself and might just allow me some extra leeway. 'Yes,' he said finally. 'Some difficulties with a loan repayment, I understand. The family have never been very good with money, on either side. His father was an independent property owner to begin with, and he was just as bad. Ah.' The slaves had been clearing away the first-course dishes. Now they brought in the main course. 'Roast wild piglet with mountain herbs and a fricassé of hare in a soft fruit sauce. I hope you like game, Valerius Corvinus.'

'Sure.' I watched with approval. Well, that was one fear laid to rest, at least. I'd had my doubts when I'd seen the green porridge, but if this was traditional Latin cooking then I was all for it.

I took another swallow of the Velletrian while the carver got busy with the piglet.

Difficulties with a loan repayment, eh? Now that was something that needed chasing up.

Marcia set her poker-straight back against the carriage upholstery.

'Lucius does get a little ... dogmatic at times,' she said. 'It's the reading. He does far too much of it for his own good, poor soul. I've always been very suspicious of reading myself. Poetry is all very well, if it's not too sensational, but history can be very heating.' She paused. 'Not that you improved matters with your little outburst, Marcus.'

'Uh ... yeah.' That was definitely unfair, considering it'd been Flacchus's and Perilla's game and I'd just barged in at the end, but I was having too much trouble keeping my eyes open to argue the point. We hadn't quite finished Flacchus's Velletrian, but we'd made a pretty big hole in it, and the roast pig and hare had been excellent. I'd have to ask Meton if he could find a recipe for that soft fruit sauce.

'He's a direct descendant, you know, of *the* Herdonius,' Marcia added.

'Who?' I said.

'Turnus Herdonius, dear,' Perilla said. 'The leader of the Arician Latins. King Tarquin had him executed.'

'Oh, yeah. Him. Right.' I settled down among the cushions. Not a bad evening, all things considered, after that initial spat, especially with the food and wine. There'd been another sticky patch halfway through when Libanius revealed that he was working on an epic on goats and could quote it at length if we liked, but otherwise nothing too painful. Certainly we'd had worse experiences, mostly at Mother's and Priscus's. I stared out of the window. The moon was just past the full, and the sky was cloudless and packed with stars. Another good night for poaching . . .

'He said a strange thing to me, you know,' Marcia said suddenly. 'While we were waiting for the carriage.'

'Who did?' Perilla asked.

'Lucius. He was quite . . . nervous about it.'

'Yeah?' I pulled my eyes off the scenery. 'What was that, now?'

'He said he'd had a dream. And that I should tell Paullus to postpone the Latin Festival.'

I sat up so fast I banged my head on the carriage ceiling. *'What?'*

'It doesn't make sense, does it?'

I was frowning, and very awake indeed. Paullus was Marcia's nephew, the senior consul. It was up to the consuls, naturally, to choose the festival's date, but with only a few more days to go and all the arrangements made you might as well try to stop the sun coming up. Marcia was right; it didn't make sense. No sense at all.

'What kind of dream?' Perilla asked.

'He didn't say, dear. Just that. That Paullus should postpone it. He's an odd man, Lucius, very *intense*. As you saw.' She sighed. 'It's probably nothing; he does get these fancies occasionally. And to write to Paullus on the strength of a dream would just be silly.'

'Yeah,' I said. 'Yeah, it would.'

I sat back against the cushions, my brain churning.

15

Maybe traditional Latin cooking wasn't quite as suited to Roman stomachs as I'd thought, because I was up and down to the privy all night. Finally, just after dawn, I gave up trying to sleep and crawled downstairs, wasted to a shadow and guts rumbling.

Bathyllus was laying the table outside under the trellis for breakfast. 'Good morning, sir,' he said brightly. 'You slept well, I trust?'

Some questions are just too stupid to answer. I gave the unobservant bastard my best poached-egg stare and belched.

'Ah.' The brightness faltered. 'Perhaps not, then.'

'Just make it dry bread and a cup of boiled water this morning, little guy.' I lowered my shattered, totally emptied body into a wickerwork chair. 'And tell Meton that if he even thinks of making a compilation of local recipes for future use I will personally scrub out his omelette pan with wire. Especially if it includes one for' – I belched again – 'hare in a fucking soft fruit sauce. You get me?'

'Yes, sir.' He fiddled with a plate. 'Ah . . . how is the mistress this morning?'

Sore point. Whatever I'd eaten, it hadn't affected Perilla – that lady has the constitution of a horse – and my frequent trips downstairs hadn't got me much sympathy after the first half-dozen or so, barring a muttered: 'Oh, *Marcus*! Not *again*!' from beneath the blankets. A comfort in times of trial Perilla isn't. 'She's okay. But she may be late down.' My stomach rumbled again, sending unmistakable messages to my brain. I got up quickly. 'Uh ... give me another ten minutes, will you, Bathyllus?'

You don't want to know about the next part, you really don't. Not that very much happened. I came back white and shaking.

There was a cup of gunk on the table, beside the plate with its dry bread and the jug of warm water. Bathyllus was hovering.

I pointed. 'Uh ... just what exactly is that, pal?'

'A stomach cure, sir. Meton recommends it. He says he had the recipe from his mother.'

I picked it up, sniffed and gagged. Sweet holy gods alive! 'Bathyllus—'

'It comes with Meton's personal guarantee, sir. He says to drink it hot.'

'He tell you what was in it?'

'Ah ... no.' The little bald-head hesitated. 'I could ask, of course, but—'

'Right. Right.' Stupid question, even if Bathyllus had known the answer; judging by the smell I'd be better off ignorant. I shuddered and eyed the concoction with misgivings. Well, Meton might be a thrawn sod, but he was honest enough by his own lights, and an unsolicited personal guarantee was his professional bond. Besides, after what I'd been through in the last eight hours I'd try anything, and if it killed me then that was all to the good. I held my nose and drank the stuff down ...

The next ten seconds weren't pleasant. Not pleasant at all.

Bathyllus held out a napkin for me to wipe my streaming eyes. 'According to Meton his mother wasn't much for the fripperies, sir,' he said. 'It explains a lot, really.'

Right; I'd go for that. The held nose hadn't been enough, not by half. From the aftertaste Meton had got the main ingredient for his potion from Marcia's henhouse floor and the chickens hadn't been all that well themselves recently. Eyes still streaming,

I grabbed for the water jug, filled an empty cup and rinsed my mouth out.

'Better, sir?'

Not the word I would've used. Not even close.

'That was a *cure*?'

'So Meton claims. It takes, he says, about fifteen minutes to work its way through the system.'

Yeah, maybe; only what he hadn't said was that it took most of your guts with it. Kicking and screaming, at that. 'I might just skip breakfast altogether, sunshine,' I said.

'Very well, sir.' Bathyllus hesitated. 'You're going out?'

I'd thought more in terms of lying on the living-room couch and groaning, in between pointless dashes to the privy, but – and I hate to say this – the bloated feeling in my belly was already showing signs of easing. Magic; it had to be magic. Sadist or not, Meton's mother was also obviously a genius. 'I might do,' I said.

'I'll have the stable slaves bring your horse round.'

I shook my head. 'Uh-uh, pal. No horses, not today.' Easing gut or not, I couldn't've taken another day in the saddle, and after ten or twelve nocturnal trips to the latrine that part of my anatomy had had enough grief to be going on with. 'The walk'll do me good. Also if I do have to make a rush for the undergrowth I'll be that much quicker.'

'Indeed, sir.' Bathyllus came as close as he ever did to smiling. 'You're sure about breakfast?'

'Yeah. And, uh, thank Meton for me. I owe him one.'

I'd been planning on going into town anyway. Top of the list of things to do was to find Concordius's ex-gladiator pal Ursus, but after Marcia's little revelation the night before I also needed more info on Herdonius Flacchus. Eccentric the guy might be, but I didn't believe in dream messages, especially when they coincided so neatly with dinner invitations. I'd be paying our Latin historian a visit in the near future to discuss his reasons for asking Marcia to have her nephew postpone the festival, sure, but a little preliminary background from a third party wouldn't go amiss. All of which meant a tête-à-tête with Pontius.

It was good to be walking again, even if there was dirt track beneath my sandals rather than pavement flags, and I had to admit that Meton's cupful of gunk was working wonders. My gut had stopped churning, and although it wasn't exactly a happy little chappie it hadn't shown any desire to send me into the bushes grabbing fistfuls of leaves. Also, the weather was perfect: warm but not hot, with a sky over Mount Alba clear as spring-water and blue as a Coan silk mantle.

This business with the festival was odd. Sure, it might be nothing – or at least nothing to do with Bolanus's murder, which was all I was interested in – but it was as out of place as an owl at a wedding. And it had rattled Marcia, which was an aspect of things I didn't take lightly, not by a long chalk. Roman-born or not, the lady was as much a local as any of them, she'd known Flacchus for years, and where assessing people was concerned she was a very smart cookie indeed. Trouble was, even if Flacchus's story of a dream was pure moonshine – which I'd bet it had been – the Latin Festival was no big deal. Oh, yeah, sure, it was a major date in the religious calendar and had been for more than five centuries, but that was as far as things went, nowadays, and it wasn't saying much. All that happened was the consuls came down from Rome, sacrificed to Latin Jupiter at his shrine on Mount Alba, then went home to bore the pants off the Senate for the remainder of their term. It was a junket, pure and simple, and an outmoded junket at that.

Finding and talking to Ursus was more urgent. I didn't like the sound of that guy at all, not one bit; and if he was involved with Bolanus's sister – which I'd bet a new mantle to a bootlace he was – then as a suspect he had motive and opportunity in spades.

My stomach was still behaving itself when I reached Castrimoenium; enough, maybe, to risk a wineshop crust and some watered wine to dip it in. I was through the town's edge and crossing the market square heading towards Pontius's when I noticed the small crowd in the far corner near the altar to Goddess Rome. I thought at first it was something to do with the elections: candidates themselves are barred from making campaign speeches, naturally, but there's always some extrovert partisan ready to cry up his man or slag off the opposition in public, and street loafers in a provincial town like Castrimoenium take what entertainment they can get. However, if it was a political meeting then it was the quietest and best-behaved I'd ever met with, and, besides, Concordius was the only one still in the race so there wouldn't be much point.

Curiosity won. I strolled across.

Two or three of the guys at the back turned round when they heard me coming, did a double-take and pretended they were only there by accident, or slid away from the group like they'd been greased, putting me in mind of schoolkids legging it when the teacher shows up. Shit; what was going on here? The first thing I thought of was a corpse: the crowd had that same ghoulish feel to it you get when some poor bugger's been fitted for an urn before his time and the bystanders are waiting for the Watch to show up with the stretcher. I pushed through to the altar itself, not that there was much opposition, and found what was exciting all the interest.

I'd been nearly right with the murder theory, only the victim hadn't been human. Not in any sense. The Goddess Rome didn't have a face any more, because someone had beaten it off with a hammer.

The hairs rose on my neck; I may not be religious, but some things you don't mess with, and cult statues and altars come pretty high on the list. I turned to the guy next to me. 'What happened?' I said quietly.

He shrugged, but I noticed the fingers of his right hand were locked into the sign against the evil eye.

'Dunno,' he said.

The crowd was melting away now fast as a dawn mist, which was understandable: I might not be much, but I still had a purple stripe on my tunic and if you were counting Romans then I was all there was currently on offer. Plus, I was angry. Like Romulus, the Goddess Rome is something special to anyone born inside the Boundary Line; the feeling isn't a matter of choice, it's bred in the bone, and rational thought doesn't come into it. The crowd had known that, sure they had, which was why they'd disappeared into the woodwork.

The bastard who'd smashed her face in had known it too. That was the whole point.

My pal mumbled something about having a shop to look after, and he would've been gone too like the rest of them but I gripped his wrist so hard he yelped.

'*What happened?*'

'She was like that this morning, sir, first light.' I let the wrist go and he started rubbing it, without relaxing his fingers from the sign. Not looking at me, either. 'I don't know nothing more about it, me.'

'No one heard anything?' He shrugged again. 'Sweet Jupiter, he must've used a fucking sledgehammer!'

'I don't know nothing ab—'

I turned and walked away, towards the wineshop, gut troubles forgotten, angry as hell and shaking. Holy gods! Things like this just didn't happen! Maybe in the eastern client-kingdoms where religious tolerance was a dirty phrase, but certainly not in Italy, less than twenty miles from Rome. Whoever had done it, the bugger was sick.

I went into Pontius's. There were three loungers at the bar, but they took one look at me and were out of the door like ferrets. Pontius was leaning on the counter. He straightened slowly. I didn't say anything. He reached into the sink, drew out a cup and began drying it. There was a long silence.

'You've been across the square, then,' he said at last.

I nodded.

'It happened in the night, Corvinus. No one saw a thing.'

'Yeah, I'll bet,' I said. 'And I'll bet that no one heard anything, either. Funny how often selective blindness and deafness seem to go together, isn't it, pal?'

Pontius set the cup aside. 'Look. I don't approve any more than you do, clear? Nor would most of the people in the town.'

'Only most? Pontius, that is an *altar*!'

'A Roman altar.'

I stared at him. Sure, I didn't expect Pontius to feel the same anger I felt, not as a Latin; still, the words – and the tone – made me feel sick. You find altars to the Goddess Rome in every market town in the empire. Yeah, okay, fair enough, like the imperial statues most of them are bought and paid for by locals who want to stand in well with the governing power, but that doesn't mean they're any the less sacred for that. And it doesn't matter a rotten anchovy where you were born. 'You really think that makes a difference?' I said.

He put the dishcloth down. 'Come on, Corvinus, I'm not judging, I'm surely not justifying, but you know what I'm saying. You get these bastards sometimes, and there's no good denying it. Still less spreading the blame where it's not deserved.'

I knew what he was saying, all right, and it still made my gorge rise. 'Politics and sacrilege are two different things, pal, if you can call something like that politics. And I'm not altogether sure I am maligning the good folk of Castrimoenium. Whoever bashed the goddess's face in must've made enough noise to wake the dead, and there were plenty of interested ghouls out there ten minutes ago. You're telling me no one heard a thing, let alone stuck their heads out the window to see what was going on and who was doing it?'

'That's what I'm telling you. And as far as I know it's the truth.'

'You like to swear to that, maybe? By someone other than Goddess Rome?'

He picked up the cup he'd been drying and replaced it on the shelf with the others. Took his time over doing it, too. Then he turned to face me squarely. 'Listen, Corvinus,' he said. 'Take my advice and don't make too much of this, right? What's done is done. You're upset, sure, but like I say you get these bastards sometimes. Make trouble and you only play into their hands. Sure I'll swear, if you want me to, because to tell you straight I haven't made it my business to find out otherwise, and I won't do, either. Like, I'd guess, most of your so-called ghouls out there. Now. This is a wineshop. You going to carry on playing the insulted Roman or do you want a drink?' He hefted a flask. 'Free. On the house. Call it an apology if you like, on behalf of the ghouls.'

Yeah, well; maybe I was making a mountain out of a molehill after all, at least where Pontius was concerned. Whoever had committed the sacrilege, it hadn't been Pontius. And the little fracas had done wonders for my stomach. I took a deep breath and let it out. 'Okay,' I said. 'Tirade over.'

He poured slowly, almost formally: one for me, one for himself. We drank in silence.

'So,' he said, 'what brings you into town this early?'

'Ursus. Your pal the foul-mouthed drunk's colleague. You happen to know where I can find him?'

Pontius gave me a sharp look over the top of the wine cup. 'Feronius is no pal of mine,' he said. 'And I think I made it pretty clear to him and you where I stood. You want to talk to Ursus, fine, but I can guess your reasons and I'm having nothing to do with them. Not in any way. I'm sorry, Corvinus, but this time I can't help you.'

Hell. Still, I couldn't force the guy, and I couldn't deny the fact that he was right, either. Also, I'd lost my temper quite enough for one morning. I'd just have to ask elsewhere. I shrugged. 'Fair enough. So tell me about Herdonius Flacchus instead.'

His eyes narrowed. 'What?'

'Herdonius Flacchus. The old guy who has the villa near Marcia Fulvina's.'

'I know who Flacchus is.' He was still watching me closely. 'Why should you be interested in him?'

'No particular reason, for the present. I'm just covering the options.' I sipped my wine. 'We had dinner over at his place yesterday evening. He – ah – doesn't have much time for Romans, does he?'

Pontius set his cup down like it was made of Syrian glass. 'Listen, Corvinus,' he said. 'I don't know what sort of game you're playing here, but I'm getting tired of it. And to hell with your "no particular reason". Flacchus is well respected in Castrimoenium. If you think he had anything to do with Vettius Bolanus's murder then say so, but in that case you're a bigger fool than I took you for. As far as him having no time for Romans is concerned, that's garbage, pure and simple.'

'Is it?'

He gave me a long stare like I'd just crawled out from under a stone and pissed in his lunch. Finally, he shook his head. 'Jupiter, man, you Romans amaze me, you know that? Someone up there must really like you as much as you claim they do.'

'Yeah? How so?'

'Because you're so bloody naïve and swollen-headed that if they didn't instead of being masters of the world you'd still be perched on your seven fucking hills minding the goats.'

I blinked, as much at the f-word as anything else: Pontius wasn't a swearing man. 'Come again?'

'You believe everyone loves you as much as you love yourselves. Then when you find that they don't you assume they hate you.'

'Oh, come on now, pal, that's ridiculous.'

Pontius sighed. 'Look, Corvinus, I don't want to quarrel with you, right? I run a wineshop, I keep my mouth closed and my opinions private. That way I don't lose customers. Even so, it's not ridiculous. And I'm not blaming you, that's just the way you're made. The bastard who smashed up the altar, sure, he hates Romans, no argument, but he's only one end of the scale and luckily for all of us he's in a minority. All the same, the scale exists, and if you're ever going to understand Latins you've got to look at things through our eyes. We don't hate you, most of us anyway. We're just not Romans, and incredible as it may seem we don't want to be. Now, do you understand that or should I start drawing pictures?'

I grinned; yeah, well, when you thought about it he had a point. Not just where Latins were concerned, either: my guess was that if push came to shove he'd have at least nine-tenths of the empire on his side of the table, pax Romana or no pax Romana. 'And this is relevant to Flacchus, right?' I said.

'Sure it is. He's a Herdonius. The Herdonii fought Rome under your kings, they fought her again when your Senate wanted to grab Latium and they see themselves as Latins first, second and last. I'm not denying that, and nor would Flacchus. All the same, there's a difference between knowing who you are yourself and having no time for someone else, let alone hating them. Flacchus would agree with that, too. Now.' He reached for the wine jug. 'You want another drink or would you like to spit in my eye instead?'

I laughed. 'Neither, pal, I'll be on my way. But thanks for the lecture.'

'You're welcome, Roman. Any time.'

I went out into the sunlight. The market square had busied up, but there was no crowd now round the goddess's altar; if anything, people were ignoring it. *Look at things through our eyes,* Pontius had said. Well, although I was enough of a Roman to feel a tinge of resentment over that little diatribe I could see where he was coming from. Rome might be the best thing that ever happened to Italy and the provinces, no argument, but that didn't mean to say, human nature being what it is, that we should expect them to vote us very high in the popularity stakes. Success don't come cheap, no way, nohow, and it has to be paid for. Still, I hadn't expected an easy-going guy like Pontius to go quite so hard for the throat as he had done. It just went to show that all Latins were touchy, clannish bastards at heart, and even when you thought you knew them they could still surprise you.

So. What did I do now? Pontius couldn't be the only source of information about Ursus in town, sure, but he'd been my best bet, and the alternative of going round to Concordius's place and rattling his bars wasn't really viable, not at this stage of the game. On the plus side, Meton's potion seemed to have done the trick completely and my stomach had quietened down. Maybe a fact-finding mission to another wineshop was in order; or . . .

I stopped. Rutilius. Flacchus had mentioned that the guy was having problems with a debt repayment, and Ursus was very firmly in the debt-collecting business. That was enough of a tie-in to justify at least a look-see. And I'd nothing else to do, anyway.

Okay. So we'd have another word with the friendly blacksmith.

16

He was at work in the forge when I arrived. I thought maybe he'd give me my head in my hands right off, but although he didn't exactly look ready to hang out the flags when he saw me coming at least he stopped hammering long enough to give me a scowl from under his mating-caterpillar eyebrows.

'Well, Corvinus?' he said. 'What is it now?'

Uh-huh; *definitely* not the red carpet treatment. We'd best take the softly-softly approach here, especially since I hadn't seen any signs of Brunna in evidence. This time it was just him and me and the hammer. 'No big deal,' I said easily. 'I'm, uh, sorry to interrupt you again when you're busy, pal.' I indicated the pile of finished bars of various lengths stacked against the wall to one side. They looked like the parts to a set of wrought-iron gates. 'Business good?'

He hefted the hammer and brought it down. 'Good enough to pay the bills.'

That was an opening, if I wanted one, but my guts told me if I brought up the subject of the loan repayments this early I'd be out faster than I could whistle, maybe even minus a tooth. 'Yeah, well,' I said. 'That's about all anyone can expect these days. Commission, is it?'

'From one of the new villas by the lake. At least these bastards buy locally sometimes.' The hammer came down again on the red-hot metal. Sparks flew. 'Mind you, it isn't altruism. Prices they charge in Rome, plus the carriage, means it's common sense.'

Altruism, eh? Now there was a word you didn't hear a blacksmith use all that often. Flacchus was right, Rutilius was no monosyllabic oaf. Also in comparison with how he'd been three days ago he was almost chatty. Maybe his wife had had a word with him. 'Is that so, now?' I said.

He paused, hammer raised. 'Look, Corvinus, I don't want to hassle you, but you said it yourself, I'm busy. The customer wants these finished by tomorrow morning and that's a big job. Ask whatever questions you've got and then piss off, okay?'

Well, that was fair enough. And although he still wouldn't win any prizes for hospitality at least he was trying. 'I was over at Herdonius Flacchus's for dinner last night,' I said. 'I understand you two know each other quite well.'

The hammer came down, but the stroke hardly dented the bar. Face expressionless, Rutilius moved the iron on to the coals, laid the hammer and tongs down and reached for the water-skin hanging from a nail in the beam beside him. He swigged, then poured water into his palm and wiped his face and bare chest before answering.

'Yeah,' he said. 'Yeah, that's right. I do. Known him all my life. He'll've told you that, too, no doubt. So?'

Odd; I'd struck a nerve somewhere, that I'd swear to, but what it was the gods alone knew. Rutilius was as edgy as a cat in a dog pound. 'He seems a nice old guy,' I said.

'Yeah, Flacchus is all right.' He stretched out his hand for the tongs.

'He was telling me you had an interest in history. Local history.'

The hand came back empty and he gave me a long considering look. 'Is that so, now?'

'Do you?'

'Sure.' His massive shoulders lifted. 'Always have done. I got it from my father. Just because I beat iron for a living doesn't mean I'm thick.'

'No. Flacchus made that pretty clear.' I paused; it could've been my imagination, but I would've sworn his eyes flickered when I used the name again. 'He, uh, also mentioned you'd been having financial worries recently.'

The eyes hardened. 'Now that, Roman, is none of your concern.' He took another swig from the water-skin and hung it back up on its nail like he'd quite happily do the same for me. Not a good subject, obviously. Not at any time.

I held up my hands, palm out. 'No argument. We all have them, pal, no problem, that's not the point. It's just I'm trying to trace someone in the loan repayment business. Concordius's agent Ursus. I thought maybe you might be able to tell me where I can find him.'

His eyebrows drew together in a scowl. 'Ursus? What do you want with Ursus?'

I shrugged. 'Just a word. You know him?'

Instead of answering, Rutilius moved round to the back of the forge, reached up for the bellows handle and gave it five or six smart pulls. The furnace roared, sending out a blast of heat that made my forehead bead with sweat. 'Why bother coming all this way to ask me?' he said. 'You want to talk to Concordius's agent, it makes sense to start with his boss. Anyone'd tell you where to find him.'

I shrugged again. 'It's a private matter. No point in bringing the boss into it unless I have to. Still, like I said at the start it's no big deal. If you can't help then—'

'I never said that. Most days Ursus has lunch at the cookshop next to the shrine of Mercury, just off Market Square on the Bovillae side. You'll probably find him there.'

Hey, co-operation! Grudging, sure, but unexpected all the same. 'Fine,' I said. 'Fine. Thanks.' Lunch, right? Plenty of time, then: the sun couldn't be more than halfway to noon, and Market Square was no more than a ten-minute walk. That's one advantage of being in a small provincial town.

Rutilius gave the bellows lever another half-dozen effortless pulls before letting it go, then came back to the anvil and picked up the hammer and tongs.

'You want anything else,' he said, 'or is that it?'

'Your son taking time off?'

That got me a fresh scowl, but he answered readily enough.

'Yeah, him and Brunna and the younker are at my sister's in Bovillae for a couple of days, helping with her new baby.'

'Your father-in-law too?'

He gripped the gate bar with the tongs, pulling it out of the fire and on to the anvil. 'Sure. Harpax likes kids. Always has.'

'So you're on your own at present?'

'I don't keep a mistress in the cupboard, Corvinus. Sure I'm on my own. I'd be with them, but there's work to do here.' He turned the bar and brought the hammer down.

I stepped back to avoid the sparks. Maybe it was accidental, but most of them seemed to be thrown up in my direction. Well, at least he was still talking. 'By the way,' I said. 'You hear about the business with the altar?'

Rutilius looked up sharply, hammer poised. 'What altar would that be, now?'

'The Goddess Rome's in Market Square. Someone smashed her face in last night.'

'Is that so?' He carried on working the metal for three or four strokes, then rested the hammer-head against it and looked up. His own face was running with sweat, but it was expressionless. 'No, Corvinus, I didn't know. They catch the guy?'

Yeah, well, he might've been telling the truth, but personally I wouldn't risk a bet. Not unless I spotted any flying pigs first. 'Uh-uh. The usual thing: no one didn't see nor hear nothing.'

'Shame.' I remembered what Pontius had said about a scale for Latins. From Rutilius's tone I'd rate him about a notch clear of the bottom end, if that. 'Still, the arselickers in the senate'll foot the bill no problem, won't they? Can't have a damaged Roman altar on show. Bad for the town's image, that.'

'Not with the Latin Festival coming up, certainly,' I said. 'Mind you, I doubt if a sculptor could do a replacement in time.' I was watching him closely. 'Then again, maybe that was the idea, right?'

Rutilius had picked up the hammer. He laid it down again. 'What's that supposed to mean?'

I kept my tone friendly. 'Just a thought. The ceremony itself is on Mount Alba, sure, but there'll be quite a few people down from Rome to celebrate it and some of them'll stay over in Castrimoenium. Not to mention the Roman locals, of course, like your villa customer. If someone wanted to send them a message, that Romans weren't especially popular, then a smashed altar to Goddess Rome slap bang in the centre of town would do the job pretty effectively, wouldn't it?'

Rutilius's eyes rested on mine for an instant. Then his shoulders lifted, he picked the gate bar up again with the tongs and shoved it deep into the coals.

'Yeah,' he said. 'Yeah, I suppose it would, at that.'

I gave him my best smile. 'Well, I've disturbed you enough for one morning, pal. Thanks for your help.' He twisted the bar, then went back round to pump the bellows lever without answering. I turned to go, then turned back and said casually, 'Oh, by the way, after last night's dinner Flacchus said something to Marcia Fulvina about getting her nephew to postpone the festival. You have any idea why that might have been?'

Rutilius stopped mid-pull. This time there was no mistake: what I saw in his eyes was shock.

'He did *what*?'

'Told her to ask the senior consul to put things on hold,' I said. 'Odd, right?'

'Why the hell should Flacchus do that?'

'That's my question.' I leaned my shoulder against the door jamb. 'Seemingly the old guy had a dream. Me, I'm a born sceptic where dreams are concerned, but you know him better than I do. You think it's likely yourself?'

Rutilius pulled hard on the lever and the flames in the forge roared. 'Flacchus puts a lot of store in dreams,' he said. 'Always has done. If it was a convincing enough one then he'd feel he had to mention it, at least.'

'Right. That would be it, then.' I nodded and straightened up. 'Well, thanks again for your help.'

'Yeah. Yeah, fine.' He let go the lever but made no attempt, this time, to pull the bar from the fire. 'You're welcome. Uh . . . is Marcia Fulvina taking things any further, would you say?'

'That I don't know, pal. It's up to the lady. And to the consul, of course. Thanks again. I'll see you around.'

I looked back just before the end of the alleyway. Rutilius was standing at the door of the forge, staring after me.

Whatever nerve I'd struck, they didn't come much bigger.

Shit; what was going on?

I was thinking hard as I walked through the maze of side streets in the direction of Market Square. So; what the hell had we got here? Something, certainly: I'd bet good money that whatever he'd said to the contrary the news about the smashed altar hadn't come as any surprise to Rutilius, which was interesting in itself. The Flacchus business, though, was even more puzzling, and worrying. That he hadn't known about in advance, no way, never, I'd take my oath on it, and it had knocked him on his beam-ends. There was some skulduggery going on to do with the festival which my blacksmith pal was in on, so much was as certain now as tomorrow's sunrise; but what it was, and whether it tied in at all with Bolanus's murder, I didn't know. One thing was sure, though: all-round good guy and pillar of the community or not, Herdonius Flacchus had beans to spill, and the sooner he spilled them the better.

I didn't know exactly where the shrine of Mercury was, but I asked a couple of kids playing Robbers round a board scratched on a pavement slab and they pointed me in the right direction. I was still way too early for the lunchtime slot and when I found it the cookshop was closed, so I took a wander through the surrounding streets until I found a square with a wineshop, carried my half jug and cup out to one of the tables below the spreading fig tree in the centre and sat down to wait.

The wine wasn't a patch on Pontius's, but I'd struck lucky with the site. Apart from the wineshop itself and a seedy-looking butcher's business in one corner, the square was residential. Most of the houses – they were two-storey, not the tenements you'd get in Rome this close to the centre – had window-boxes or pots with flowering shrubs, and just off to one side the waste water from a public fountain had been led through a conduit into a concrete pool with waterlilies covering its surface. Not a bad place to be, if you had a couple of hours to kill and nothing to do but sit and think . . .

'You're a Roman, right?'

I'd let my eyes close. Now I opened them. The guy had sat himself down at the next table with a jug and cup in front of him. He wasn't exactly big, but he made up for it in attitude. And friendly was what he didn't look.

'Uh . . . yeah.' I kept my voice level. 'Yeah, that's right, pal, born and bred. Ten out of ten for observation. Not many people notice the stripe first off.'

The guy scowled. He was shortish, balding, and no beauty; added to which someone recently had used his face for a punchbag. The bruises had reached the five-day-old raw liver stage, and he had a half-healed cut over one eye.

'You taking the piss?' he growled.

'Now why should I do that?' I said.

'Only I'm not too fond of Romans, me.'

I shrugged; if he wanted a quarrel – and it was obvious he did – then he could make all the running himself. 'That's your worry, friend. Me, I'm just here for a cup of wine and some peace and quiet. Let's keep it like that, okay?'

He shifted on the bench, gripping his wine cup, and I caught the smell of rancid meat and the sight of a blood-streaked apron. Uh-huh: not one of the local banking fraternity, then. My fellow customer here had to be the owner of the seedy butcher's business taking a break from slicing collops. 'This is Latium, not the fucking Palatine,' he said. 'You don't belong here. The sooner you realise that the better.'

I sighed. 'Now look, pal—'

Which was as far as I got before he threw the wine in my face and went for my throat.

There's not a lot you can do when you're sitting down and some gorilla jumps you without warning. I got a grip of his tunic with both hands and heaved sideways hard, toppling us both off the edge of the bench. I was lucky: on the way down the corner of the table caught him a slammer on the left temple and his grip relaxed for an instant, long enough for me to break it and land a punch beneath his bottom rib that doubled him up groaning.

Behind me I heard running footsteps and the sound of benches being pushed out of the way. I grabbed the bastard's wrist and forced him over on to his front with his balled fist halfway up his spine, then came down with my full weight on his kidneys. He kicked out a couple of times, but I shifted his wrist a notch further up and increased the pressure on his back and he collapsed again with a hiss.

'You okay, sir?'

I took my eyes off our friendly neighbourhood butcher long enough to glance up. The wineshop owner was standing over us holding one of these weighted sticks they usually keep under the counter for emergencies and looking worried as hell.

'Yeah,' I said. 'More or less.'

'What happened?'

'You tell me, pal. Bastard just went for me.'

'Shit!' The owner reached down and grabbed the guy's free

arm. I relaxed my grip on the other one and stood up slowly. 'Come on, Exuperius! That's your lot, boy!'

The man shrugged the owner's hand away and struggled to his knees. The table must've caught him an even bigger clout than I'd thought, because he was bleeding freely and groggy as hell. Also, he'd managed to get a mouthful of dirt in the struggle. He leaned forward and spat it out, then rubbed his shoulder joint and glared up at me with a hundred-candelabra scowl.

The wineshop guy turned to me. 'You want to swear out a complaint?' he said.

I hesitated. The thing was clear-cut, sure – unprovoked assault – but there'd been no bones broken. All the damage I'd suffered was a stained tunic, while my Romanophobe pal would have a few more cuts and bruises to add to his collection, a significant pain in the gut and the mother of a headache to remember me by. I reckoned I'd come out winner already, and, besides, the game wasn't worth the candle. 'Uh-uh,' I said. 'Let's just call it quits, okay?'

The owner looked relieved. 'Yeah. Right.' He turned his attention to the gorilla and jerked his thumb. 'I'd push off if I was you, you stupid bugger. Before the gentleman changes his mind.'

The guy spat again into the dust at my feet and walked off towards the butcher's shop without a backward glance. Yeah, well; so much for gratitude. Not that I'd been expecting any, mind. I watched him go while the wineshop man straightened the benches and picked up the toppled jugs and cups.

'I'll bring you more wine, sir,' he said. 'On the house. You've my apologies.'

'Not your fault, pal.' The bench I'd been sitting on had wine all over it. I pulled another one over to the table and sat down. 'That sort of thing happen often around here?'

'First time since I've had the business, and that's five years. All the same, that bastard's trouble on two legs, always has been.

He's a neighbour, sure, but the neighbourhood'd be better off without him.'

'He certainly doesn't like Romans, anyway.'

'That what it was about?' The owner took a cloth from his belt and mopped the table dry. He was grinning. 'Then he doesn't have much luck picking quarrels. You'd think maybe he'd've got the message last time.'

I'd been drying my face on the sleeve of my tunic. I stopped. 'Yeah? And when would last time be, now?'

'Four or five days ago. He went for some artist – in a wineshop down in Bovillae and got his lights punched out for his trouble. Spent the night shut up in a broom closet. Served the bastard right.'

'Uh . . . the Roman's name wouldn't've been Licinius, would it?'

'Can't tell you that, sir. He was an artist from Rome, that's all I know. He a friend of yours?'

'I've met him.' The back of my neck was prickling. 'You happen to know what the quarrel was about?'

'Nah. Could've been anything, or nothing. Probably nothing. You saw yourself.' He finished with the table. 'There you are, sir, all straight again. Give me two minutes and I'll bring you another jug.'

'Fine. Ah . . . one more thing, friend. That Bovillae wineshop. You happen to know which one it was?'

'Sure. Gaius Satrius's place, just inside the Castrimoenian Gate.' He chuckled. 'The bugger made a real mistake starting something there. Satrius is a big lad, and he runs a tight shop. He don't take no grief from anyone. If your Roman friend hadn't done the job on Exuperius already he'd've fixed his wagon himself.'

He left to get the wine, and I sat back to think. It might be nothing, sure, but it was still worth a look. That meeting with Licinius had left me puzzled. If the guy was the five-star Roman aristocrat Marcia thought he was, then there was still the question of what he was doing slumming it out here in the sticks playing the jobbing artist. Sure, everything might be above board; you got these eccentrics now and again, but it didn't happen all that often, and there was that queer business over how well he actually knew Sulpicius to solve. I owed it to myself at least to check. And Bovillae wasn't all that far.

The wineshop owner came out with the jug, plus a complimentary plate of cheese and olives. While I poured the wine I glanced over towards the butcher's shop, but my pal the Roman-hater was keeping a low profile and all there was to see was the flyblown carcass of a pig hanging from the hook at the door. This time, though, I wasn't taking any chances, and I'd keep my eyes open until the sun hit noon. Fresh bruises or not, I wouldn't trust that bastard an inch.

17

I found my way to the cookshop again and went inside. There were at least a dozen guys there already, all tunics, and from the look of them a fair cross-section of the local artisan community. Good sign: if this had been a Roman cookshop the sight of so many locals would've been a guarantee that chances were the bean stew wouldn't have you tossing your guts out an hour after you'd swallowed it and the meat patties hadn't started out in life going miaow or woof. Mind you, that said, I didn't exactly feel at home. The moment I'd opened the door the buzz of conversation had stopped, and the stares I got as I edged my way between the tables towards the counter at the far end made me feel like a Greek kebab.

The cookshop owner – it was a woman – was frying eggs.

'What can I get you?' she said.

'Uh . . .' After Meton's pharmaceutical depth-charge my guts might be behaving themselves, but fried eggs was pushing things. Also, although I hadn't cleaned the plate I'd had most of the olive and cheese nibble at the wineshop. 'Just a plain roll, thanks. And some soup, if you've got it.'

'Sure. Vegetable or bean?'

'Make it vegetable.' Beans would be pushing things, too. I leaned on the counter as she set down the skillet on the charcoal grill and reached for a bowl. 'I'm looking for someone named Ursus. He here at all?'

'Who wants him?'

I turned. Yeah, the guy at the table in the near corner would fit the description, all right. I wondered if he'd chosen his name himself – gladiators sometimes did – or if his parents had just been shit-hot prognosticators. Whichever it was, 'Bear' was right. He was even bigger and shaggier than Rutilius, but I could see why the women might go for him. He looked like he'd know it, too. 'That you, friend?' I said.

'The one and only.' He was doing terrible things with a set of perfect teeth to a hunk of meat on the bone which he held in his left hand. 'So?'

'Mind if I join you?'

'Plenty of other tables free. Maybe you should tell me your business first.'

The room had gone quiet. Or quieter, rather. For working tunics on their lunch break a strange Roman with a stripe down his tunic – not to mention the wine stains – might kill conversation, but eating was a serious business and I'd still had the champing of jaws. Now there wasn't even that. 'No hassle,' I said easily. 'I just want a word, that's all.'

He tore off another chunk of mutton, chewed and swallowed. His eyes never left my face. 'A word about what?'

'You want something to drink with that?'

I turned. The woman had set a steaming bowl of soup with a spoon in it on the counter beside a big slice of barley bread.

'Yeah. A cup of wine'd go down nicely.'

She fetched up a jug from under the counter, took a beaker from the row on the shelf behind her and filled it. Well, the place gave good measure, anyway. I fumbled in my purse and brought out a half silver piece. She swapped it for a handful of coppers. Good value, too.

I turned back to Ursus, ignoring the attentive silence round about me. 'The name's Marcus Corvinus,' I said. 'I'm looking into Vettius Bolanus's death. I thought maybe talking to you might be a help.'

You could've carved your name on the silence now. The cookshop's customers were looking at me and at Ursus, back and forward, like they were watching a game of catch-the-ball. Ursus ignored them. He stared back at me, open-mouthed but jaws moving. 'Why the hell should I know anything about that?' he said at last.

'Maybe you don't, pal. That's what I want to find out.'

He set the stripped bone down on his plate and wiped a trickle of grease from his chin with the back of his hand. The stare hadn't wavered. Finally, he said, 'Eat your soup and leave me alone, Roman.'

'Fine.' I picked up the beaker and took a sip of the wine. Jupiter! No wonder the tab was cheap! 'I'll just have to talk to Concordius himself, then.'

It was a wild bet, sure, but it came off. He frowned and caught the cookshop woman's eye. 'Hey, Publilia!'

'Yeah?'

'You mind if we use the back yard for five minutes? You can't get no privacy in this fucking place.'

'Suit yourself.' She was decanting the fried eggs on to a plate. 'And watch the language. There're ladies present.'

'Yeah. Yeah, sure.' He got up – he must've been six three, easy – and dropped a few coppers on to the table. 'I'd finished anyway, Corvinus. You want to talk, fine, but I'm on my free time here. I'll give you five minutes, like I say. That's all it'll take.'

There was a door to the right of the cooking facilities, open because of the heat, and I could see a courtyard beyond. Ursus went through it. I followed with the soup and bread. Not the wine, though. That stuff could stay on the counter.

What he'd called the back yard wasn't big, less than fifteen feet square, with walls round it, a climbing vine in one corner with a table and a couple of benches next to it and a stack of empty wine jars filling the rest of the space; maybe the proprietress had thought of going up-market at some time with an executive al fresco dining area, but if so it hadn't worked out and the place just looked sad and unused.

Ursus closed the door behind us. 'Those bastards in there're nosier than a pack of Capuan grandmothers,' he said. Yeah; I'd forgotten he'd done his time on the sand in Capua. 'No point in giving them free entertainment.' He threw himself down on one of the benches. It creaked. 'Now. What makes you think I know anything about this Bolanus business?'

I took the other bench and set my bowl and bread on the table. I'd thought about how I was going to play this and decided on the direct approach.

'You're involved with his sister,' I said.

That got me a long hard stare; not a friendly one, either. 'Who told you that?' he said at last.

I wasn't going to finger Feronius; the guy might be a prime rat but he and Ursus worked together and I owed him something for the information, if it was only making sure he didn't get his teeth shoved down his throat for telling me. 'It's fairly common knowledge,' I said.

'Is it hell!'

'Common enough for a graffito, anyway.'

He grunted. I'd rattled him, sure enough, which was the purpose of the exercise. Without taking his eyes off mine, he fumbled in the pouch at his belt, brought a small handful of something out, slipped the things into his mouth and chewed. Meanwhile, I took a spoonful of soup. It was better than the wine; a lot better. Publilia might be a poor judge of drink, but the woman could cook. 'Don't believe all you read on walls, Roman,' he said. He turned sideways briefly and blew a stream of husks on to the flagstones, then reached into the pouch for a fresh supply. 'Or what you hear in wineshops. I know the Lady Vettia to speak to, sure, but that's as far as it goes.'

'Is that so, now?' I broke off a piece of the bread, dipped it in the soup and ate it. 'Me, I heard different. You may not actually be screwing her but you've got your foot in the bedroom door. Now call me a liar.'

His jaws worked. If looks could've killed I'd've been a grease spot, but he didn't say anything.

I took another spoonful. 'My guess is you made a play for her behind her brother's back. Women like that, you never know which way they'll jump until you try, especially staid upper-class spinsters who've been sitting on the shelf twiddling their thumbs for thirty years. Some of them – most, even – will yell blue murder or spit in your face and that's the end of it, game over. Others do the same but leave their window open at night. A third kind . . . well, me, I'd bet that Vettia's the third kind. Those you don't get often. They take a look at your biceps and they're flattered. One manly hug, a few whispered promises and there's nothing left between the ears but fluff and the thought of wedding cake.' I paused. 'Second and last chance, friend. Am I talking through a hole in my head or what?'

He was quiet for a long time. Then he said, 'The lady's made no complaints. Like you say, she's full-grown, she can decide for herself who she takes up with.'

'Sure.' I tore off another piece of bread. 'Especially now with her brother dead so you don't have to ask his permission to tie the knot. All in all, she's quite a catch for an ex-gladiator. Strikes me, pal, you've been pretty lucky, all things considered.'

He half rose, his fists balled, and I tensed, but the attack didn't come. I dunked the bread while he sat down again. 'You accusing me of killing Bolanus?' he growled.

'Maybe.'

That fazed him. He leaned back and shook his head. 'You're crazy.'

'You've got motive in spades, pal, and the means part is easy. All I'm missing is the opportunity. So tell me. Where were you the time Bolanus was killed?'

'How the hell should I know? I don't know when the bastard died.'

'Four days ago. The sixth of the month, just after sunset. And if you don't then you're the only person this side of the Alban Mount who doesn't. Come on, pal, or has some netman knocked what few brains you've got out of your ears?' I was needling him, sure, but he was sweating and I had to keep up the pressure. 'You want to make a stab at it, no pun intended, or should I just jump to conclusions?'

'At home. In a wineshop.' I could see the literal sweat now beading his forehead. 'One or neither, I can't fucking remember offhand, right?' He turned away and blew the chaff from his mouth, then reached nervously into his pouch again. It seemed almost an unconscious action. 'I'll tell you one thing, though, I wasn't anywhere near the Bolanus place.'

I ignored him. 'Maybe you were just clearing the ground for the marriage,' I said. 'Or maybe Bolanus finally found out what everyone else knew and was ready to pull the plug on you. That what happened, pal? He tell Vettia he knows about your secret engagement, she goes blubbing to you and you cancel the guy first chance you get? Or was the whole thing your boss Concordius's idea from the first so he could get his hands on Bolanus's estate and sell it on to some developer?'

There was a sudden silence. Ursus stared at me like I'd suddenly developed leprosy. Then he shook his head slowly and got up. 'I don't have to listen to this crap, Corvinus,' he said. 'You've had your five minutes and I've work to do. Take my advice. Will you do that? You just go and fuck yourself, okay?'

He left without another word, slamming the door to the cookshop behind him. I went back to my soup. Yeah, well, whether Ursus was the killer or not I'd rattled the bastard's cage good and proper. And that last shot about Concordius had touched a real nerve; definitely something to follow up.

As I broke off another piece of the bread my eyes fell on the scattering of chaff mixed with spit on the flags beside the table, and my brain kicked into gear. Finally. I'd seen that stuff before, sure I had; it was scattered all over the place on the floor of Bolanus's loggia: roasted pumpkin seeds, or what was left of them, anyway. And the guy, from what I'd seen of him, was a roasted pumpkin seed addict. I got up quickly, crossed to the door and opened it; but Ursus had already gone.

Not that it mattered all that much, because he'd just shot up into the number one place. I could find him again if I wanted to; or Libanius could. What I needed now was some confirmatory details.

Maybe it was time to lean a little on Vettia.

18

Hoofing it as I currently was, there wasn't enough of the afternoon left to go all the way down to Bolanus's villa and back, especially when my run-in with the friendly butcher had left me fairly low in the sartorial elegance stakes. Besides, I reckoned I'd done pretty well that day already. Home, then, and a cup of real wine before dinner.

When I walked into the atrium with Bathyllus's obligatory jug and cup there was a stranger in a broad-striped mantle sitting in the guest chair. He got up politely.

'Ah, Marcus, you're back.' Marcia was in her usual chair by the pool. 'This is Abudius Ruso, the Officer of Buildings in charge of arrangements for the festival. He's come to ask if we need any help in connection with my nephew Paullus's stay. Ruso, this is my niece's husband Valerius Corvinus whom I mentioned to you earlier.'

'Corvinus.' The man held out his hand. 'Glad to meet you.'

We shook. Not a tall guy, older than was usual for an aedile, and that snub nose wasn't the straight-bridged Roman aristocratic hatchet. The vowels were flat, too, more Aventine than Esquiline. And Abudius wasn't a name you met up with all that often in the magistrates' lists, if at all. One of the New Men, then. Not that he was any the worse for that, quite the reverse. At least he was human: I'd rather split a jug with a guy like Ruso than Marcia's braying nephew the senior consul any day.

'Marcus, what on *earth* have you been doing to yourself?' Perilla, in the other chair, was staring at my tunic.

'Uh . . . I had a bit of a run-in with a guy in a wineshop,' I said. 'He threw a cup of wine over me.'

Marcia's eyes opened wide. 'At *Pontius's?*'

'No. Another wineshop in one of the squares behind the market-place. The guy has a down on Romans, seemingly.'

Marcia's expression had stiffened. 'You notified the authorities, of course,' she said.

'Uh . . . no. No, I didn't think it was necessary.'

'Oh, but Marcus!' Perilla said. 'You should have! Things like that just can't be allowed to happen. Did you get the man's name?'

'Yeah. Exuperius. He runs the local butcher's shop. But really I'm—'

'I agree with Perilla,' Marcia said. 'You really ought to report it, at least, even if you don't prosecute. I'll send a boy round to Quintus Libanius's first thing in the morning. He'll see to it. And I'm surprised at you. How do you expect anyone to have any respect for Rome if you let that sort of thing pass?'

'Perhaps, Aunt Marcia,' Perilla said quietly, 'the first priority is for Marcus to change his tunic.'

'Uh . . . I've got kind of used to it now,' I said. 'I'll do it before dinner. If the aedile here doesn't object.'

Ruso was grinning. 'No, Valerius Corvinus, not me. As far as I'm concerned you can wear what you please.'

Yeah; definitely a breath of fresh air. Paullus Persicus would've sniffed and made a sarky comment about bad form. I held up the jug. 'They given you anything to drink, pal?'

'*Marcus!*' Perilla snapped.

'Yes. I'm fine.' Ruso indicated the wine cup on the small table beside him. 'Besides, I have to go back to Bovillae very soon. A working dinner with members of the town senate.'

I poured myself a cup, set it on the table beside the couch, lay down and stretched. Jupiter! That was good! I was out of the way of walking now, and my legs were stiffening rapidly. 'To do with the Latin Festival?' I said.

Ruso sat. 'Yes, that's right. The head of the Bovillan senate is co-ordinating things this end, with the result that I'm back and forth between Bovillae and Rome like a weaver's bloody shuttle.' He glanced at Marcia. 'Oh, I'm sorry, Marcia Fulvina.'

'Don't apologise,' Marcia said. 'I'm quite used to it with Corvinus here.'

I stifled a grin. 'Not a popular job, then?'

'Someone has to do it. One of the aediles, anyway. I simply drew the short straw.' Ruso sipped his wine. 'But you're right, it isn't a popular job. Not so much at the Roman end as the Latin one. Your run-in today doesn't particularly surprise me.'

'Is that so, now?'

'There are some very unpleasant people around, Valerius Corvinus. They don't like Rome and they don't like the festival, not one bit.'

'No argument there, friend.' I took a mouthful of wine and refilled the cup. 'You only have to look at what happened in town last night to see that, right?'

He frowned. 'I'm sorry, I'm not with you.'

'The desecration of the altar to Goddess Rome in Market Square,' I said. 'Someone beat the goddess's face in with a hammer.'

Ruso set down his cup and stared at me, his eyes wide with shock.

'You didn't know?'

'No, I did not know,' he said softly. I noticed that Marcia's and Perilla's jaws were hanging as well. 'Holy gods! You know the circumstances?'

'Uh-uh. Nor, from what I can gather, does anyone else. It seems to've been done in the small hours, but that's as much as I can tell you.' I wasn't going to finger Rutilius; even if the guy had been obviously sympathetic suspicion wasn't proof, and with nuts like my butcher pal around there wasn't any real reason to single him out as a principal suspect anyway. 'No witnesses, no details, no nothing.'

'The authorities are investigating?'

'Presumably. Not that from the impression I got talking to the locals I think it'd get them very far.'

'No, you're probably right. Unfortunately.' Ruso was still frowning. 'Latium isn't Rome, and that reaction isn't uncommon; I've met with it myself more than once in the recent past. Still, an act of overt sacrilege is rare, and worrying. Very worrying indeed. I'll report it, certainly, when I return to Rome. The foreign judge's office will want to know, at least, if they don't hear about it from elsewhere. They're a thrawn lot, the Latins, and the festival, as I say, isn't popular with some of the more hot-headed elements.'

'I was told at dinner yesterday that that is because they feel they've been squeezed out,' Perilla said.

Ruso turned to her. 'If they have, Rufia Perilla, then it's their own fault. And it isn't even true, either, realistically speaking. My family's from Tusculum originally so I've Latin roots myself. Less than half the families in Rome can trace their city ancestry back any more than three or four generations, and a good slice of them will've drifted in from Latium under their own steam. Which means a fair percentage of the ordinary celebrants will have Latin blood in their veins somewhere. If you ask me, the beggars have damn all to complain about.' He took a mouthful of wine. 'Who was feeding you this nonsense? Not a Roman, I'll bet you that.'

'No. Aunt Marcia's neighbour. Herdonius Flacchus.'

Ruso's eyebrows rose. 'Herdonius? Now there's a good Latin name! He's a direct descendant?'

Perilla glanced at me and smiled. 'Abudius Ruso, it is *so* nice for once to find someone under the age of fifty who knows something about history! Yes, I believe he is. You haven't met him?'

'No. But as I say I don't have any dealings with Castrimoenium.

Everything's done through Bovillae. Until the actual festival, of course, when we're up on Mount Alba itself. I take it this Flacchus is' – he paused and chose the word carefully – 'an enthusiast? For things Latin, I mean?' I noticed the change of tone. The question had been casual enough, sure, but there was a professional sharpness behind it. This Ruso was no fool.

'Oh, quite definitely.'

Marcia cleared her throat. 'He also,' she said, 'asked me to put in a request to my nephew to postpone the rites.'

You could've heard a pin drop. 'He asked you to do what?' Ruso said finally.

'Seems the old guy had a dream.' I kept my voice non-committal.

'When was this, Marcia Fulvina?'

'Last night, as my niece said. After dinner.'

'He gave you no other reason?' Ruso's voice was hard now; he'd be good at his job, I could see that. He reminded me a lot of Decimus Lippillus. 'None at all?'

'No. He was most insistent, however.'

'This Herdonius Flacchus. You say he's a neighbour?'

'He owns the estate next to this one. The villa is about half a mile from here, further up in the hills.'

Ruso's face was grave. 'You've known him long?'

'Oh, yes. For many years. Since I bought the farm, in fact. Although we don't see each other very often nowadays.' Marcia cleared her throat again, and I wondered about that dimpling the previous evening. 'Lucius is rather . . . eccentric, he gets these bees in his bonnet sometimes. It's probably nothing, of course.'

The aedile shook his head. 'I'm sorry, Marcia Fulvina, I can't agree, not at all. Certainly not when the warning is taken in combination with what Valerius Corvinus here tells me. This I will definitely report, and to the consul directly. Also, naturally, I'll have a word with the man myself at the earliest opportunity.' He stood. 'Which will not, unfortunately, be today. As I said, I have to be back in Bovillae by dinner-time.

However, I'm most grateful for the information, and believe me I take it seriously, very seriously indeed. As, I hope, will Fabius Persicus.'

'You, uh, like me to call round?' I said. 'I was thinking of doing it anyway.'

Ruso gave me a sharp look. 'Your wife's aunt tells me you're looking into the murder of Vettius Bolanus,' he said. 'Yes, Corvinus. Thank you, that's an excellent idea. I'm run off my feet already and squeezing anything else in would be tricky. Besides' – he grinned suddenly – 'you've probably had more experience in that direction than I have. You'll let me know the results, of course? I'm staying in Bovillae with Agilleius Mundus the First Speaker, and I should be around for the next two days.'

'No problem, pal.'

He nodded. 'Good. Then I wish you luck.' He turned to Marcia. 'My thanks for your hospitality, Marcia Fulvina. Rufia Perilla, a pleasure to meet you.'

I got up too. 'I'll see you out,' I said.

We walked as far as the outer door. While the slave was getting the guy's horse I said quietly, 'You really take this seriously?'

He didn't answer at first. Then he said, 'Corvinus, the festival is my responsibility. I don't put much reliance on dreams, but I do recognise an oblique warning when I hear one and it's better to be safe than sorry. Yes, I take it seriously and will advise the senior consul to do the same. Certainly I appreciate your offer to talk to this Flacchus. Could I ask you do it as soon as possible, please?'

'Sure. I'll go and see him tomorrow.'

'That would be marvellous.' The guy was worried, I could see that, although he covered it well. 'A definite load off my mind. I'm most grateful. And tonight after this bloody dinner I'll have a quiet word with Mundus. He may have some ideas on the subject, or be able to provide a lead or two.' He paused. 'The main problem, however, will be convincing the senior consul himself. You know him, of course?'

'Uh-huh.' I kept my voice expressionless.

Ruso's mouth twisted in a grin. 'Ah. Then you see what I mean, I'm sure. He isn't exactly open to advice.' Yeah; that was putting it mildly: Paullus Fabius Persicus was so stiff-necked you could've used him as a clothes-prop. 'If there is anything amiss involving the festival, the gods forbid, he'll need conclusive proof before he changes the arrangements with only eight days to go. Should you find out anything concrete from this Flacchus – *anything,* Valerius Corvinus – then it's vital you forward it as soon as possible. I know I asked you to keep me informed personally, and I'd still appreciate your doing that, but a direct approach might have more effect. Persicus may believe a relative where he wouldn't a junior colleague.'

Especially when the colleague concerned isn't out of the top drawer, flattens his vowels and has a no-clout name, his careful tone said. Not that there was any rancour there, he was just stating a political fact that'd held since Rome's plebeian population had got pushy four hundred years back. Yeah, right; like I say, no fool, this Ruso. Mind you, I doubted if Persicus would listen to me either, or anyone else short of Capitoline Jove himself, and even the god would have his work cut out. Shifting that bugger away from anything he'd made his tiny mind up about would've taken the persuasive equivalent of Hannibal's troop of elephants. 'Fine,' I said. 'I'll do what I can. You've got it, friend.'

'Then again all I can do is wish you luck.' The door-slave appeared leading his horse. He mounted. 'A real pleasure to meet you, Corvinus. Don't forget to call in on me if you're in Bovillae. Mundus's place is near the market square. Anyone'll point it out to you.'

He rode off down the track and I went back inside.

'Now, Marcus,' Marcia said. 'Perhaps you should tell us more about this contretemps in the wineshop.'

I told them. 'The other guy had the worst of it, more by

luck than design. Also, it was his second pasting recently. Remember that artist Licinius I mentioned who got into a scrap in Bovillae?'

'That was the same man?' Perilla said. 'Oh, Marcus! Then you should certainly report it! He's obviously a complete thug.'

'Yeah. Yeah well, maybe.' I settled down on the couch and took a swig of wine. They had a point, sure; Quintus Libanius should be told, even if I didn't press formal charges. 'I just thought this wasn't exactly the time to stir things. From what Ruso was saying local tempers're frayed enough at present.'

'That's nonsense.' Marcia pulled her mantle tighter round her legs. 'Oh, there's always a certain amount of background dissatisfaction where Rome and Romans are concerned, but physical assault is another matter entirely. If you don't inform Libanius then I will.'

I sighed. 'Okay. I'll go and see him myself tomorrow, after I've talked to Flacchus.'

Marcia looked at me. 'You will be' – she searched for the word – '*patient* with Lucius when you see him, won't you, Marcus? I don't know what the old duffer was thinking of, but I'm quite fond of him and I'm sure there's no malice there. I felt obliged to pass the information on to Ruso, but I'd hate it for Lucius to get into trouble. These officials can be very narrow-minded sometimes.'

I sipped my wine. Yeah, well; me, I'd say Ruso's reaction had been pretty sensible myself. And Flacchus needed sweating, that was clear. 'If he'll level with me, then fine,' I said. 'Still, I'm not making any promises.'

'So how was your day otherwise?' Perilla said. 'Did you see Ursus?'

'Yeah. He's definitely on the list.' I told her about the meeting back of the cookshop. And about the pumpkin seeds.

'You're certain about the ones in the loggia?'

'Oh, yeah. Sure, someone else could've been responsible for them but it's too much of a coincidence to shrug off. And like I say he's got a prime motive. The next step is to face Bolanus's sister Vettia with the evidence, see what story she comes up with.'

'Hmm.' Perilla was twisting a lock of hair. 'And you're certain, too, that she and Ursus are having an affair of some kind?'

'I really do find that most improbable, Marcus,' Marcia said. 'The fellow's an ex-gladiator, and Vettia has always been very respectable.'

'It fits.' I reached for the wine jug. 'Also, I'll bet you a year's income against a used boil plaster that Concordius is involved somewhere down the line and that he's got his eye on Bolanus's estate.'

'But that's dreadful!' Marcia looked genuinely horrified. Like all good upper-class Romans she had firm ideas where property was concerned, and while an affair with a gladiator was bad enough it paled into insignificance beside a property scam.

'Maybe so, but again it makes sense. Ursus clammed up tighter than a virgin oyster when I suggested it.' I paused. 'You, uh, have any ideas about that, by the way, Marcia?'

'How do you mean?'

'Concordius is in the land-brokering business. He have any regular developer customers that you know of? We might be able to find an in from that end.'

'I really couldn't say.' She hesitated. 'Unless perhaps you count Decidius.'

The back of my neck prickled. 'Yeah? Who's he?'

'A local entrepreneur, very wealthy, although not specifically a developer. He has his fingers in several pies, or so I've heard.' There was the barest sniff. 'Their names are often linked.'

'Uh-huh. Local? You mean Castrimoenian?'

'No. He's based in Bovillae, although I think he does most of his business in Rome so he probably has a house there as well. And not local in the sense of being locally born, either. He's from the north, I understand. A Paduan.'

'He, uh' – how could I put this? – '*sound* at all?'

That got me a definite sniff. 'Don't be silly, Marcus, of course he isn't! That kind never are. However, I haven't actually heard anything to the contrary so perhaps he's as sound as you could expect under the circumstances.'

I had to stop myself grinning: for Decidius to have passed muster with a trouper like Aunt Marcia he'd've had to be more strait-laced than the Elder Cato. More honest, too, although from what I'd heard of the old bugger's dealings, private and public, that wouldn't be difficult. At least he wasn't an out-and-out villain. 'Yeah. Right. You, ah, don't know him personally, then?'

'Certainly not!'

Well, it'd been an outside chance. If I was going to pay the guy a visit – which I was – then a personal introduction would've eased things. Still, I supposed it'd been too much to hope for. My reasons for going to Bovillae were piling up: a talk with the owner of the wineshop where Licinius and Exuperius had had their run-in, a report to Ruso – even if I was dealing directly with Persicus, I'd have to keep him informed – and now this local tycoon. I couldn't complain that we were short of leads in this case, anyway.

'And now, Marcus' – Marcia was giving me one of her gimlet stares – 'if you have quite finished cross-examining me then perhaps you wouldn't mind going upstairs to change as you said you would. Abudius Ruso is one thing, but we should be dining shortly and your tunic is a disgrace. I don't allow Marilla to slouch around at mealtimes in dirty clothes, and I see no reason why you should set a bad example.'

Ouch. I caught Perilla's eye and she swallowed a smile. 'Right, Aunt Marcia,' I said. 'Uh . . . where is the Princess, by the way?'

'Cooking up something – literally – in the kitchen with that boy of Hyperion's. For Corydon this time. The beast has a touch of hoof-rot or some such thing. He's really quite a good influence on the child.'

'*Corydon*?'

'Don't be silly, Marcus. Clarus. Personally, I'm delighted. It's about time she was seeing youngsters of her own age, and we are very isolated out here. Besides, it's a relief to me to know she's turning out' – she hesitated – '*normal,* as it were, the poor girl.'

Yeah; I knew what she meant. It'd been worrying me, too, after what we'd pulled the kid out of.

'Perhaps we should ask Clarus to stay for dinner,' Perilla said.

'Fine by me.' I grinned. 'Although the Princess has probably arranged that already, whether he knows it or not. And she seems to be hand-in-glove with Meton in any case.'

'Oh, yes,' Perilla said thoughtfully. 'Quite definitely. She's down in the kitchen quite a lot these days.'

'The bastard's got something cooking himself, that I'm sure of, and I don't mean pork stew or donkey-hoof liniment, either. You any idea what it could be?'

Perilla shook her head. 'None at all. Something involving Dassa, certainly. Marilla knows, so it can't be anything too dreadful, but she refuses to tell; I think she may be working some sort of trade-off for the use of the kitchen stove. And Meton himself, of course, isn't even approachable.'

'How about Bathyllus?'

'He's a non-starter; the two of them are at daggers drawn again after words over an accidental charcoal delivery. Don't ask, dear. I did and regretted it. Oh, and I asked Alexis, but he's as much in the dark as we are.'

'Yeah. Right.' Well, that seemed to exhaust the possibilities. I'd got a bad feeling about this whole Dassa/Meton business – like I say, the bugger was no natural pet lover, and he'd got a twisted, devious streak in him a mile wide – but no doubt the thing'd work itself out in time. Unfortunately. We'd just have to wait and see what joys the future held.

I went up to change for dinner.

19

I set off for Flacchus's after breakfast the next morning; on horseback, because from there I'd have to go on to Vettia's place and probably Bovillae after that.

I'd been thinking hard about this festival business. If Ruso had pooh-poohed the idea of Flacchus's warning being important I might've been tempted to discount it myself, or at least put it on ice for the present; but he'd taken it more seriously than I had, and judging from what I'd seen of the guy I'd a lot of time for his opinion. So what could the business be? Nothing too drastic, that was sure: I couldn't see Herdonius Flacchus, Latin heritage nut though he was, being mixed up with major-league crime, not after the endorsement Marcia and Pontius had given him, and in any case I doubted if the festival ceremonies offered much scope for it. My bet would be some kind of engineered hitch that would bring the whole ceremony to a sudden halt mid-stream. A very spectacular, high-profile hitch, involving embarrassment for the Roman celebrants, since if I was right embarrassing Rome – and so getting a kick in for the Latins – was the object of the exercise. What it'd involve exactly I didn't know, because I didn't know the ceremonial details, but six got you ten Flacchus had been in on it somewhere. His warning to Marcia was half just that – a warning – and half a personal insurance policy so that whenever what was going to happen happened he could say he'd done his best. In any event

I didn't think it had anything to do with Bolanus's death: a silly plot hatched by a few crack-brain Latins and aimed at embarrassing Rome was streets away from murder, and, like I say, I just couldn't fit a guy like Flacchus into that sort of frame. Still, we'd have to wait for the answers until we asked the questions.

I'd expected the door to be opened by Flacchus's door-slave, but it was the major-domo himself who did it, about a second after I knocked. He stood blinking at me like I'd suddenly sprung into existence out of thin air.

'I'm sorry, sir,' he said. 'I was expecting Quintus Libanius.'

There was something screwy here. The guy's face was grey as old parchment, a muscle beneath his left eye was twitching and it looked like he'd been wearing his lemon tunic to paint the living-room.

'Uh . . . that's okay, pal,' I said. 'The master available at present?'

'No, sir.' He gave a smile that rang false as a wooden coin. 'I'm afraid he's dead.'

'He is *what*?'

'Dead, sir. In his study.' His voice was eerily calm and he spoke the words carefully, like he was drunk and trying to hide it. 'That's why I thought you were Quintus Libanius, sir. I sent for him about an hour ago and he should be arriving any moment.' He smiled his wooden-coin smile again and the hairs on my scalp crawled. 'Perhaps you'd care to come in? I'm sure the master wouldn't mind.'

'Uh . . . yeah. Yeah, right. Thanks.' Sweet gods alive! 'Ah . . . What was it? An apoplexy?' That wouldn't've surprised me too much: even though the old guy had looked healthy enough at the dinner party he must've been getting on for seventy, and these nervous, highly strung types can go out as suddenly as a snuffed lamp. But in that case why send for Libanius?

The major-domo – I'd forgotten his name – was leading me

through the atrium. 'No, sir,' he said over his shoulder. 'Nothing like that. The master was murdered.'

My guts went cold, as much at the Olympian calmness of the guy's tone as the words themselves. 'Uh ... is that right, now?' I said.

'Oh, yes.' This was weird; for all the expression in his voice he might as well've been quoting the price of eggs. 'But then you'll see that for yourself, sir.'

We'd reached the short corridor I'd gone along before that ended in the portico and garden, but this time the slave stopped in front of a door halfway along its length. He tapped on it gently – the hairs on my scalp rose another half-inch – opened it and stepped back to let me past.

'Here we are, Valerius Corvinus,' he said. 'Just go in, please.'

The room was a study with a sliding door-cum-window opening out on to the garden. The walls were lined with bookshelves – full ones, at that – and there was a big, no-nonsense desk the window side of centre where it would catch the light. Flacchus was slumped over the desk, his arm stretched out towards me. I could see the blood from here, and there was a lot of it. Yeah, well: that explained the state of the major-domo's tunic, anyway.

'Oh, shit,' I murmured. 'When did this happen?'

The slave had followed me in. 'Just over an hour ago, sir.' The same eerily calm voice. 'As I told you.'

I went across. Flacchus's face was turned to one side, revealing his slashed throat. There was a bone-handled knife lying on the floor near the leg of the desk on the corpse's right-hand side like it had been dropped or had fallen there. I pointed to it, but I didn't pick it up; best wait for Libanius. 'You see that, pal?' I said. A silly question, sure, but the guy being in the state he was I was taking things slow and simple and one at a time. 'Uh ... what's your name, by the way?'

'Trupho, sir.' Yeah; I remembered now. 'Yes, of course I see it.'

'Fine. That's great. Ah . . . it belong to your master?'

'I don't know, sir. Is that important?'

'I just thought maybe if it was your master's he might've used it on himself,' I said gently.

'Oh, no, sir.' Trupho shook his head. 'The master didn't commit suicide. He was murdered. I told you that.'

'You're certain?'

'Of course.'

'And would you, uh, care to tell me why?'

He looked at me like I was the slow one of the pair. 'Because I saw it done, sir. How else would I know?'

Everything went very still. 'You actually *saw* the murder.' I tried to match his matter-of-fact tone.

'Oh, yes. Or rather, I saw the man placing the knife beneath the master's hand before he went through the window. Then he ran off into the garden.'

Holy Jupiter! 'Did you recognise him?' I was still trying to keep my voice level.

'No, sir. But I'd know him again. A shortish, balding man with a bruised face.' He touched his right eyebrow. 'He had a cut, sir, half healed. Just here.'

I stared at him. Oh, shit; this had to be the shortest murder enquiry on record. Exuperius; it had to be Exuperius. But why the hell should my Roman-hating butcher pal want to kill Herdonius Flacchus? 'Fine,' I said calmly. 'That is just fine. Now supposing you tell me the whole story from the beginning.'

'Do you mind if I sit down, sir? I know I shouldn't, not in the master's study, but I'm not feeling quite myself at present.'

He wasn't looking too hot, either, even compared with Flacchus. Without a word, I pulled up a chair and got him sat down into it. He glanced over at the corpse and swallowed. The tic had started up again. 'Now,' I said. 'Go ahead, Trupho. In your own time.'

He swallowed again. 'The master retired to his study after breakfast. He always does that, gets up at dawn, has breakfast and works in his study until noon. He'd only been gone a few minutes when I remembered I hadn't asked him about his plans for the evening. Sometimes he goes out, and of course the chef has to know.' I nodded; yeah, I knew all about chefs. 'I knocked, then I heard a sort of . . . scuffle, sir. I opened the door and . . . saw . . . what I've described, sir.'

'The murderer fitting the dead man's hand round the knife,' I said.

His eyes widened. 'Oh, but the master wasn't dead! Not at that point. He was bleeding badly, but he wasn't dead. He died later.'

My stomach went cold. Sweet gods! 'Okay,' I murmured. 'I'm sorry I interrupted. I won't do it again. You just tell it in your own way, right?'

'I yelled. At that time of day most of the other slaves are in the kitchen, or carrying out their cleaning duties upstairs. The man wasn't to know that, of course, and I think he panicked. He moved towards me then changed his mind and ran away through the garden towards the perimeter wall. I went over to see if I could help the master but he was . . . he was choking, sir. On his own blood.' He closed his eyes. 'There wasn't anything I could do for him. Nothing at all. The master knew it, too.'

'Yeah.' I touched his shoulder. 'Yeah, okay. Still, we've got the murderer, that's one good thing.'

Trupho shook his head. 'No. There's something else.' He stood up and went over to the desk. I watched anxiously, ready to grab him if he toppled – he was looking pretty wobbly – but he made it okay, just. Carefully, not looking at the body, he picked up a wax tablet and brought it over. 'The master couldn't talk, of course. He tried, but he really couldn't. None the less it took him . . . it took him a minute or two to die, sir. He wrote this. I held the tablet as steady as I could and the master was trying very hard, but I'm afraid between us this was the best we could manage.'

He passed the tablet over. The bottom was a mess of spilled blood, but the top half was clear. Gouged out of the wax so deep that you could see the tablet's wooden backboard through it and in letters a six-year-old would've been ashamed of was the single word 'Fufetius'.

'Who's Fufetius?' I said.

'I don't know, sir. The master's never mentioned him.'

I stared at the tablet hoping something would click, but it didn't. If this was Flacchus's last message to the world, then it beat me totally. He wasn't naming his murderer, that was sure: that was Exuperius, I'd stake my whole income on it. And besides, if he'd been lucid enough to write anything he'd surely have realised that Trupho had seen the guy who'd done it and could describe him. All the same, the way Trupho told it the old buffer had been desperate to get the name down on to the wax before he died. So what the hell was he . . . ?

The door behind us opened and Quintus Libanius came in. He was looking far from happy, and I felt a twinge of sympathy; Castrimoenium's squeamish First Speaker had been having a hell of a time with corpses lately. When he saw me, he did a double-take.

'Ah, Corvinus,' he said. 'I've just sent a slave round to fetch you, but it seems you've heard already.'

'Uh-uh.' I shook my head. 'I was calling round to talk to Flacchus in any case.'

'Then that was fortunate.' He glanced quickly, nervously at the body and then looked away again. I saw his Adam's apple move. He was holding himself in well, sure, but under its covering of facial fuzz his face was ash pale as he turned his attention to the major-domo. 'So, Trupho,' he said. 'What happened?'

The sit-down seemed to have done the guy some good, because he was looking a better colour now, and when he went through the details again he was a lot calmer than he had been with me.

'You would recognise the murderer again if you saw him?' Libanius asked when he'd finished.

'Oh, yes, sir.' Trupho glanced at me.

'No problem there,' I said. 'I can identify him myself.'

Libanius looked at me sharply. 'Can you, indeed?'

'His name's Exuperius. I had a run-in with him yesterday. He has a butcher's shop in town, just behind the market square.'

Libanius was frowning. 'Oh, I know Exuperius. I've encountered him several times in my judicial capacity and he's an unpleasant piece of work right enough. Why in the gods' name he should want to kill poor Lucius, though, I can't imagine.' His eyes strayed back to the body. 'It isn't as if—' He stopped suddenly, Adam's apple jerking. 'Ah . . . forgive me, Corvinus. We'll go out into the garden now, if you don't mind. I'm not quite used to—'

'Sure,' I said quickly. 'No problem.' The guy looked like he'd throw up any minute, and pride was involved here. Senatorial First Speakers, even if the job's not a usual part of their public duties, can't be seen to lose their breakfast in front of practical strangers and slaves. I turned to Trupho. 'You care to come as well, pal?'

We went outside through the door-cum-window. Libanius took a few restorative breaths of the clean morning air while I diplomatically inspected the scenery.

'Trupho said that while Lucius was dying he wrote something down,' he said when he had his stomach settled again.

'Yeah.' I was still holding the wax tablet. I handed it to him.

He read it and looked up, puzzled. 'Who's Fufetius?' he said.

'It doesn't ring any bells?'

'Not with me.' He laid the tablet aside. 'Trupho?'

The major-domo shook his head. He'd been doing some deep

breathing on his own account, and he was looking a lot more with things. 'No, sir. I've already told Valerius Corvinus, the master never mentioned him. Of course, I've only been with the household for two months.'

'Is that so, now?' I said.

'Before that I was his sister's major-domo in Naples, sir. A single lady, five years older than the master. She died in March and the household was broken up. Lucius Herdonius's previous head slave was in his seventies and the master gave him his freedom.'

'He still local?'

'No, sir. He went to live with his married daughter in Brindisi.'

Hell. Still, we had the name itself. Fufetius couldn't be all that hard to trace, and whatever message Flacchus had been trying to send us, important though it might be, at least we knew who'd killed the old guy. Things could've been a lot worse.

'So, Corvinus,' Libanius said. 'You're the expert. Where do we go from here? I don't mean as far as Exuperius is concerned, that's simply a matter of catching the man. This Fufetius business is another thing entirely.'

I shrugged. 'The best thing I can suggest is we go through Flacchus's desk. There might be a mention of him somewhere. A letter, maybe.'

Libanius glanced nervously back at the study window. 'Perhaps after the, ah, body has been removed and the ... the mess cleared up,' he said. 'And when we have the requisite authorisation from Lucius's next of kin, naturally. Trupho? Is that possible?'

'Yes, sir. The master's nearest relative is a nephew in Aricia. I'm sure he wouldn't mind. I'll send word to him at once, if that's all right. Also to the undertakers.'

'Yes. Yes.' Libanius was looking grey again. 'In the meantime you will make sure the desk is locked, please, and the key given to your master's nephew when he arrives. Ask him to arrange a time for me and Valerius Corvinus here to go through the dead man's correspondence in his presence. You understand?'

'Yes, sir.'

'Uh . . . Trupho?'

The major-domo turned to me. 'Yes, Valerius Corvinus?'

'This may not be the time, but did you ever hear Herdonius Flacchus mention this year's Latin Festival? Some private scheme he was in on?'

Libanius shot me a sudden, sharp glance, but he said nothing.

'What sort of scheme would this be, sir?'

'I don't know. You tell me.' I paused. 'You don't know what I'm talking about, do you?'

'No, sir. The master often spoke of the festival, of course, but he mentioned no scheme, private or otherwise.'

Bugger. Well, he sounded genuine enough, and it'd been worth a try. I sighed. It was an outside chance, sure, but a man might let something slip to his head slave that he wouldn't want generally known. 'Fine,' I said. 'We'll look after ourselves now. Go back and send your messages, okay?'

He left. There was a bench against the house wall near the corner of the villa. I walked over to it and Libanius followed me. We sat down.

'What was all that about the festival, Corvinus?' Libanius said.

'That was the question I came to ask Flacchus this morning. After that dinner party we had he asked Marcia Fulvina to get her nephew the consul to postpone the rites.'

Libanius stared at me like I'd grown an extra head. 'Why should he do that?'

'He claimed he'd had a dream. It's possible, sure, but my guess is that he was involved in some scam or other, or had been, maybe, and thought better of it.'

'"Scam"?' I wouldn't've believed that nostrils could actually flare, but Libanius's did. 'What do you mean, "scam"?'

'Uh . . . some sort of plot. To disrupt the ceremonies, obviously.'

That got me a look that would've fried a salamander. 'Lucius wouldn't have done anything like that, Valerius Corvinus,' Libanius said shortly. 'I knew the man for years. He may have had his eccentricities, and I know – as you do yourself after what he said over dinner – that he had strong feelings on the subject of the Latin Festival, but he would no more have become involved in criminal activity than I would.'

Maybe it was my imagination, but I had the impression there was more in his tone than disapproval: he sounded like maybe he was trying to convince himself of what he was saying just as much as he was me. That was interesting.

'You . . . ah . . . sure about that, pal?' I said gently. 'Hundred over hundred?'

'Yes!' Libanius frowned and chewed at his beard, gazing into nothing. I waited. Finally, he said, 'And *you* are positive, I suppose, as to the identity of the murderer?'

The shift in subject surprised me. 'Yeah,' I said. 'I told you, I had a brush with Exuperius myself. From Trupho's description it couldn't've been anyone else.'

He hesitated, then said too casually by half, 'The reason for my question is that Gaius Exuperius happens to be one of the festival poleaxe-men.'

A cold finger touched my spine. I sat back. Sure, if I'd thought about it it would've been obvious, or a strong possibility, at least. The poleaxe-men are the guys who do the heavy work at a sacrifice while the officiating priest faffs around sprinkling the barley meal, shaving a strand or two from the victim's brow and finally cutting the beast's throat. It's the poleaxe-men who make sure the animal doesn't bolt during the early stages and – more important – stun it with their hammers so the guy with the purple mantle can perform the ceremony with all due decorum. Invariably and logically, poleaxe-men are drawn from the local butcher population.

'Is that so, now?' I said.

'Indeed. I compiled the list of Castrimoenian servitors myself.'

It added up, sure it did, and Libanius's reservations or not things were looking pretty good for the theory. A Roman-hater like Exuperius wouldn't have applied for the job – and he'd have to have applied – unless he had an ulterior motive. Like, for example, being on the inside at what was purely a Roman festival. Still, there were fundamental questions that needed answering. Why did he want to be there so badly? And why the hell should he kill Flacchus?

That last one made no sense at all; murder was way out of proportion. If all Flacchus was involved in was some silly Latin plot to mess up the festival then to kill him just because he looked like pulling the plug was crazy. To balance that what you'd need would be something a whole lot bigger; something like . . .

I stopped. Oh, shit. Oh, holy Jupiter alive.

Poleaxe-men, as part of their job, come ready-equipped with the heavy hammers they use to stun the victims. Also, naturally, they're part of the main sacrificial party. It would be easy, so easy: one swing at the wrong head and it'd all be over before anyone knew what was going on. And if the head belonged to the sacrificial priest who also happened to be Rome's current consul then the political shit would really hit the fan.

It squared. And if I was right then we'd moved up into a completely different ball-game.

'Corvinus?'

'Hmm?' I refocused.

'You weren't listening. I asked you a question. Why should Gaius Exuperius murder Herdonius Flacchus?'

'Because Flacchus knew that Exuperius was the hit-man in a plan to kill the consuls at the Latin Festival. Or one consul, at least.'

Libanius's eyes widened. 'That is nonsense!' he said.

'Uh-uh. It fits, right down the line. It's the only explanation that does.'

'Lucius Flacchus would never become involved in something

like that!' He was on his feet now, and glaring down at me. 'Never!'

'Yeah, I know,' I said. 'That's the point. Flacchus was about to blow the whistle. Exuperius had to shut him up.'

'But by doing that he's betrayed himself in any case! He's a known killer!'

'That was his bad luck. The idea was to make Flacchus's death look like suicide and he bungled it. Not that it was all his fault; he couldn't've bargained on Trupho walking in. Then of course he panicked and it was too late.'

Libanius shook his head. 'I'm sorry, Corvinus, but as I said this is nonsense. Not the business about Exuperius and the consuls. For all I know you may well be right there, and it certainly sounds ingenious. But Lucius Flacchus could not possibly have been involved in an assassination plot, even in the preliminary stages. Anyone who knew him would tell you that. He was an antiquarian, a staunch Latin, and he had his quirks, yes, all of those things. But he would not have countenanced violence or anything approaching it, in any form. I've known the man practically all my life, and I assure you that is the truth.'

'Okay,' I said. 'Maybe he wasn't involved directly. Maybe he came to know about the plot somehow and wanted to nip it in the bud without naming names. Would that make sense?'

Libanius didn't answer for a good half-minute. Finally, he gave a curt nod. 'It would certainly be an improvement,' he said. 'Even so, perhaps you can tell me how Exuperius knew that Flacchus was, in your words, "blowing the whistle"? Who told him? Or did he simply guess that the possibility of betrayal might exist and take precautionary measures?'

Oh, hell; I hadn't got round to that one. Sure, just because he'd delivered that warning to Marcia didn't mean she was the only person he'd talked to, but on that side we were pretty limited.

'That's a question I can't answer, pal,' I said. 'Not yet, anyway.'

'Never mind.' Libanius was sounding almost friendly again.

'We have our murderer, and that, as I'm sure you'll agree, is the main thing. Once we catch Exuperius I'm sure we can persuade him to clear up the other details. Including, hopefully, the Bolanus business. If you'd care to come into town with me we'll collect two or three of our beefier public slaves and go to where he lives. I doubt if he'll be there, of course – not after Trupho caught him in the act – but you never know your luck. Failing that, we'll simply have to scour the hills.'

'You don't think he'll just disappear to Rome? Or Ostia, maybe?' I said. That would be what I'd've done in Exuperius's place; either town, you could've disappeared like a straw down a drain.

'He might. But then Exuperius is a Latin, Corvinus, and Latins in trouble take to the hills. We'll search them first.'

20

I was thinking hard as we rode towards town. So; we'd got our murderer, or at least our murderer where Flacchus was concerned. No doubt about that, none at all. The big question was, *pace* Libanius, could we fit him into the frame for killing Vettius Bolanus?

Points for. First, and most important, two unlinked murders so close together in a small provincial town like Castrimoenium just weren't a credible scenario, no way, never. One killer running around loose was fine; two was pushing things. The second plus was the modus operandi: both guys had had their throats cut. There was a difference, sure – Flacchus's death was intended to look like suicide while Bolanus's couldn't be anything but murder – but the circumstances themselves would've explained that. And Exuperius was a butcher by trade. Slitting throats would be a way of killing that came natural to him.

The prime problem was motive. If my festival plot theory was right then Exuperius had a motive for zeroing Flacchus, sure, but Bolanus was another matter entirely. He wasn't, so far as I knew, involved with the Latin Festival at all, and no one I'd talked to had suggested he took any interest in that side of things. So why should Exuperius have killed Bolanus? If the guy had been Roman, now, things might have been different, but—

The realisation hit me so hard I pulled back on the rein. My horse almost shied.

'Oh, shit!'

Libanius, riding beside me, turned in the saddle. 'What is it, Corvinus?' he said.

'Exuperius might've killed Flacchus, but he didn't kill Vettius Bolanus.'

Libanius frowned. 'You're sure? But I assumed—'

'Uh-uh.' I felt sick. 'He couldn't've done. The night Bolanus died Exuperius was shut up in a broom closet over in Bovillae.'

'He was *what*?' Libanius slowed his horse to a walk.

'Yeah. He had a scrap that afternoon in a wineshop. The owner locked him in overnight.'

'You're certain?'

'Not absolutely, because I haven't talked to the wineshop guy myself yet. But that's the story I heard, and my guess is that it'll check out.' Bugger; it looked like we'd got two killers after all. And if we had two killers then there needn't be a link between the murders. I felt like crying.

'Ah.' Libanius chewed at his beard. 'Then that is a definite complication. Still, let's just take things as they come, shall we? The first priority is to arrest our known murderer. Perhaps if – when – we talk with him he'll be able to shed some light.'

'You think he'll talk?'

'Oh, yes.' He set his heels to his horse's flanks. 'When we find him Exuperius will talk. That, Corvinus, I can guarantee.'

We called in by the town offices to pick up the strongarm brigade, but the butcher's shop at the corner of the square was shuttered and padlocked. Yeah, well. I supposed it had been too much to hope for; the guy must've known someone would be after him.

I glanced over at the wineshop where I'd had my little contretemps. The owner was out wiping tables; or at least pretending that they needed wiping. Curiosity's the same all over, and the head of the local senate plus four seriously muscled public slaves taking a keen interest in a neighbour's place of business is a guaranteed curiosity-rouser. I went over.

'Morning, friend,' I said. He straightened. 'You seen anything of Exuperius?'

'So you're pressing charges after all, sir?'

He didn't sound too upset about it, which wasn't all that surprising, I supposed; past grudges aside, he was already down a jug of wine and a plate of nibbles, not counting the breakages and the wear and tear on the outside furniture.

'Uh-uh,' I said. 'Not me. The bastard's up for murder.' His eyes widened. 'You know where we might find him?'

'He didn't open up today. You could try his flat above the shop, though. Entrance is round the side.'

'Yeah, right. Thanks.'

I rejoined Libanius and the lads. The corner of the square was broken by an alleyway leading to the next street, and sure enough three or four yards down it a flight of steps led up to a door at first-floor level. This was town business, and none of my concern; I waited while Libanius went up and knocked, then tried the door and stepped aside so the slave with the crowbar could jemmy the lock. The five of them went inside. A moment or two later Libanius reappeared.

'Empty,' he said. 'Do you want to take a look, Corvinus?'

'Sure.' I went up.

'Flat' dignified the place; there was the room the front door gave directly on to and the door to a smaller room beyond, but that was all you got. The standard of the furniture and fittings did nothing to help, either. What furniture there was could've been rescued from the local rubbish tip, while Exuperius had been no housekeeper: the bare floorboards were filthy and littered with the tossed-aside scraps of what must've been several months' meals and the place smelled like a wrestler's armpit. I held my breath and crossed to the door of the inner room. There were no windows here, not even shuttered ones, and the smell had had a chance to build up. I gave it the once-over and tried to breathe through my ears.

Item: a truckle bed minus the feet with a blanket that looked practically capable of walking off under its own steam. Ditto: a lidless clothes chest that was more worm-holes than wood, stuffed with tunics that hadn't seen the inside of a proper washtub since they'd been bought and would've gone to pieces at the first scrub. Ditto: a three-and-three-quarters-legged table with a jug and wine cup on top, both empty.

The fourth item, lying beside the jug, was a small glass perfume bottle. It was empty. I picked it up, took out the little cork and sniffed . . .

Uh-huh. Now *that* was interesting. I palmed the bottle and tucked it into my belt-pouch.

Libanius was standing in the doorway. 'Hardly salubrious, is it?' he said. 'How anyone can live like this defeats me. You've seen enough?'

'Sure,' I said. 'What happens now?'

'As I told you, we hunt the hills. Put the word out that the man's a fugitive. I'll also send a messenger to the judge's office in Rome with a full report, just in case he does make for the city. Don't worry. We'll catch him.'

'You think so?'

'Unless he's stolen a horse or cadged a lift somewhere then he's on foot, and if he's done either then once the word is out locally we'll know of it and that will be that. My guess, though – my *informed* guess – is that he's run for the high ground. That's usual here.' He smiled. 'Oh, yes, Corvinus, we'll catch him.'

He meant to be encouraging, sure, but I suddenly felt washed out. It was like this at the end of every investigation, even if this wasn't the end of an investigation: always, it came down to catching the guy, physically laying hold on him. And that part, necessary though it was, I didn't enjoy because the next stage was the public strangler's bowstring. Only this time it wouldn't be, not for Exuperius; not unless he was really, really lucky.

Even if he did play along with the guys asking the questions, they'd want to make sure he gave full value before he went, and they wouldn't leave off until he'd spilled all the beans in the bag. Murdering bastard though Exuperius undoubtedly was, the thought of that still made me sick to my stomach.

'Fine,' I said. 'Right. Well, you don't need me for that, do you? If you'll excuse me I'll just go across the square for a drink.'

I left Libanius staring and went back out into the fresh air.

The wineshop owner was still mopping tables.

'Yes, sir,' he said. 'What can I get you?'

'Make it a half jug, pal,' I said, pulling over a bench. 'Same stuff as last time.'

He tucked the cloth into his belt, but he didn't move. 'Uh . . . a murder, right?' he said. 'The bugger finally killed someone?'

Jupiter! These ghouls really make me sick! Still, I gave him what he was angling for. 'An old man by the name of Flacchus. He had a farm off the Caba road.'

The guy's jaw dropped. '*Herdonius* Flacchus?'

Yeah; Pontius had said that Flacchus was a local celebrity. 'Uh-huh. That's the one.' I sat down. 'Did Exuperius, ah, mention him ever?'

'No, sir. Not in my hearing. But then he's never been a talker, keeps himself to himself, even when he's drinking. A bit of a loner, always has been.'

I nodded. 'Right. Right.' I left a space before the next question. 'How about girlfriends? He have a regular at all that you know of?'

The wineshop owner laughed. '*Exuperius*? No decent woman'd take up with that bastard. Nor any of the other sort, neither, not even for pay. He's had two or three of them at his place in the past, sure, but no more than once, and word gets around. I've never seen inside it myself, but it's a proper pigsty by all accounts. And he's no charmer himself, that's for certain.'

Yeah, that was the impression I'd got; which was puzzling

as hell because the bottle in my belt-pouch didn't square with it. No way did it square.

'I'll bring your wine, sir.' The owner was turning to go.

'Hang on, pal,' I said. 'One more thing. Visitors in general, regular or occasional. He get any that you know of?'

'No, sir. Like I say, he keeps himself to himself when he's not in the shop, even when he comes here for a cup of wine. And the stairs to the flat are round the side. Visitors I wouldn't notice.'

While he went off to get the wine I sat back to think.

Half an hour and half a jug later I gave it up. Libanius and his happy chappies were long gone to organise the manhunt, and my brain felt tired. Okay, leave it for now. It had to be coincidence; nothing else made sense, not when you took all the factors into account. The lady would never have looked at him.

So where did I go from here? Nailing Exuperius had put a damper on the case, and for once the wine hadn't helped. My head felt thick and packed full of wool as a litter cushion. Maybe I was coming down with something.

Vettia, or Bovillae? Vettia first: the Bolanus place was nearer, and, besides, I could take in Sulpicius's place at the same time.

Vettia was at home, playing ball in the garden with a fat black puppy who couldn't retrieve for nuts. The mourning outfit was gone, and she'd added a snazzy shocking-pink mantle to the wig. The thirty-year age gap between what she was and what she was wearing didn't do her any favours.

'Ah, Valerius Corvinus.' She had a serious face on, but that had only appeared when she'd seen me coming. 'Any news?'

'About who killed your brother?' She was sitting in a chair in the rose arbour. There wasn't another one, but I perched on the low wall opposite. 'No. Not yet. I just wondered if you'd mind answering a few more questions, that's all.'

'What sort of questions?' The puppy pawed at her leg

and she pushed it away. 'Go and play by yourself, dear. Mummy's busy.'

'Just one main one, really.' I picked the ball up and threw it into the shrubbery. The puppy bounded after it and disappeared. 'What was Ursus doing in the loggia?'

Under its half-inch of make-up Vettia's face went the colour of skimmed milk and she leaned back in her chair. It took her a moment to rally.

'Who,' she said, 'is Ursus?'

Yeah, well, good try, but I'd seen the reaction and she wasn't fooling anyone. 'Publius Concordius's collection-man. Also your . . . fiancé, would it be? Subject to your new head of family's permission, naturally.'

Vettia rose like a rocketing pheasant. 'Valerius Corvinus! You will leave now! *Now*, please!'

I held out my hands, palm out, and spoke quietly. 'I'm sorry, lady. No offence intended, really, but there's no point in pussyfooting around, is there?' Silence. 'You can call your slaves and have me thrown out, sure, but I'll still want an answer, and if you don't give it to me you can give it to the praetor's rep when he finally gets here. Now which will it be?' She sat down, slowly. The look I was getting would've frozen the balls off a Cimmerian. 'Fine. Now. You want the question again?'

Vettia shook her head. 'How did you find out about Ursus?'

'You mean generally, or in connection with the loggia?'

'Generally.'

I shrugged; no sense in making this interview any more painful than it was. 'I just got lucky. As far as the guy being in the loggia's concerned, he should keep off the pumpkin seeds.' Silence again. 'Look, Vettia, let's get this clear. All I'm interested in is finding out who killed your brother. I don't make judgments and I don't spread gossip, okay? How you run your life is your own business.'

She took a deep breath. 'Very well. The answer to your

question was that he was waiting for me to join him. That was where we usually met.'

'Presumably this was before your brother was killed.'

'But of course it was!'

'How long before? An hour? Two hours?'

She blinked. 'Corvinus, we're talking at cross-purposes here. Sextus – that is, Sextus Ursus – wasn't in the loggia at all that day. I mean our meeting was two days before Marcus died.'

'You'd swear to that?'

'Yes. Yes, of course I would.'

'These pumpkin seeds, then. Ursus definitely dropped them – spat them out, whatever – two days before the murder?'

That was the crucial question, and the lady knew it. Her hands twisted together. Finally she murmured, 'I don't know. Corvinus, I really *do not know*! I can't remember, honestly.'

I sighed. Yeah, I'd believe that: Vettia might be a fluff-brained fool in some ways but she wasn't a complete idiot. And she couldn't be totally blinkered when it came to judging Ursus's character or his motives, either. I'd bet the thought that Ursus had killed her brother had occurred to her long before it did to me, and the suspicion was still there not far below the surface. 'Fine,' I said. 'Let's leave it at that. All the same, you are actually engaged to the guy, right? Unofficially, I mean?'

Her lips set and her chin came up. 'Oh, yes. Sextus asked me formally to marry him ten days ago, and I accepted.'

Ten days ago. Five days before Bolanus's death, in other words. 'You didn't tell your brother, of course.'

'No. I was . . .' She stopped. 'I thought it best to lead up to the subject gradually, and Sextus agreed. If in the event Marcus gave his permission then well and good; if not then we would have run away together.'

'He, uh, didn't have an inkling what was going on, then? Bolanus, I mean?'

'No. Or at least, I don't believe so. Marcus was an extremely . . .

self-contained man. He didn't notice things until they were laid under his nose.'

Not very strongly put, but it was the first time the lady had admitted that Bolanus was anything less than perfect. Still, she hadn't struck me exactly as being much interested in other people herself. I wouldn't like to bet that her brother hadn't guessed that something was in the wind, and if so then the chances of him having a word with Ursus – and Ursus consequently murdering him – were better than even. 'Fair enough,' I said. 'What about the money aspect of things? You have a private income, presumably?'

'Valerius Corvinus!'

I didn't apologise, just waited.

Finally, she said, 'Very well. Although it's none of your business, the answer is yes.' We were in defensive schoolgirl mode again; the hands were clasped firmly in her lap and her spine was straight as a poker. 'If you want the details, it takes the form of house rents in Castrimoenium, plus the income from a tenement building in Rome which my father bought many years ago and made over to me before he died. I am not particularly rich, certainly not by Roman standards, but Sextus and I won't starve, even without external help.'

'Your new head of family. You asked him yet to approve the engagement?'

Even beneath the make-up I could see the faint blush of colour come into her cheeks, but her voice didn't change. 'Valerius Corvinus,' she said, 'I do realise that you are concerned with finding my brother's killer, and because of that I am willing to allow you considerable latitude. However, I do feel that your line of questioning, bearing as it does on my personal life, is rather unnecessary, not to say insulting. No, I have not asked him yet, although when I do I doubt if he will raise any objections.' My surprise must've shown in my face – Ursus was obviously a fortune-hunter, and no one would sign a document of consent under these circumstances without some pretty solid assurances – because her lips quirked into what was almost a smile. 'Cousin Quintus owns a very prosperous draper's emporium in Beneventum which completely dominates both his life and his conversation. He is unmarried, suffers from chronic halitosis, is no traveller and can best be described, I think, in the single word "harmless". Furthermore, I have no intention of giving him any information regarding Sextus other than to say that he is in the loans business; which has the double advantage of being perfectly true and in his eyes constituting a thoroughly respectable qualification.'

Well, against stupidity even the gods throw up their hands. Vettia, it seemed, wasn't as undevious as she looked, and if the lady was as determined as that to go to hell in a handcart then there was nothing I could do about it. 'And this Cousin Quintus would be the heir to the property as well, would he?' I asked delicately.

'Yes. Quintus is our only surviving male relative.' Vettia sniffed. 'To be fair, Corvinus, he would not have been my brother's natural choice, had he had any other options. That was partly his reason for contracting a marriage, in the hopes of having children himself. Marcus was, as you know, greatly attached to this estate – an attachment which I do not share, incidentally; perhaps you would not, either, if you were a woman and tied to it all your life – while Cousin Quintus, as I say, has neither a connection with this area nor any desire to form one.'

'So he'll probably put the villa and the land on the market?'

'I would assume so, yes. Through a suitable local agent, naturally.'

I had to go careful here. 'Ah . . . you've talked to Ursus about this, I suppose? Since your brother's death?'

'As a matter of fact I have.' Vettia's eyes challenged me.

'And did he, uh, suggest someone suitable?'

'He did mention the name of someone who might be interested, yes, but only in passing.'

'Yeah? And who might that be, now?'

'Someone in Bovillae. Decius or Decembrius; some such name, anyway. I can't recall offhand. I'm sure Sextus would tell you himself if you asked him. He has nothing to hide.'

'Decidius?'

'Yes. That's right.'

Concordius's unsound property developer pal. Shit. It took all the self-control I had not to react. Also, not to take the lady by the neck of her tunic and shake some sense into her silly head; but that wouldn't've done any good, and besides, like she'd said, her private life wasn't any of my business. If she wanted to let herself be suckered by Ursus that was her concern; she'd had plenty of warnings. I stood up. 'Well, thanks very much, Vettia. Once again, you've been very helpful.'

She reached forward and laid a hand on my arm. I think maybe the gesture surprised even her, because the weak eyes blinked. 'Sextus didn't do it, did he?' she said. 'Murder my brother, I mean?'

I could see how badly she wanted a categorical 'No', but that was something I couldn't give her. 'I don't know,' I said, which was true enough and the best I could do.

Draco the head slave showed me out. As he opened the front door I said casually, 'Uh ... does the Lady Vettia have any relatives at all, friend? Besides this draper guy in Beneventum?'

He frowned. 'Yes, sir. Just one other; a second cousin married to a wine merchant in Naples.'

'Maybe you should get in touch with her. Suggest she drop by for a visit and have a quiet word with the lady.'

He gave me a look. If Bolanus hadn't known what was going on then I'd bet from his expression that the bought help did. 'Yes, sir,' he said. 'Thank you. I'll do that.'

The door closed behind me. Well, I'd done my best. I couldn't do any more. And if Ursus was the murderer and I nailed him then the bastard wouldn't get the length of throwing the nuts in any case. Vettia would end up really hating my guts, sure, but that was better than what the silly bitch was into at present.

I glanced up at the sun as I rode towards the lakeside track. An hour after noon, more or less. I still had Sulpicius's, sure, but with luck I'd have time to go into Bovillae and get back before dinner; see the wineshop owner, certainly, and at least check on the whereabouts of this guy Decidius. Vettia's little bombshell had been a godsend; taken with Marcia's information that he was hugger-mugger with Concordius, it couldn't be a coincidence, no way. There was a scam somewhere, I could smell it. Ursus wouldn't've given Vettia Concordius's name when she'd asked him to recommend an agent, sure – even he wasn't that crass – but if he and our Bovillan businessman were hand in glove then one got you ten it came to the same thing somewhere down the line. All I needed to do was ferret out the details.

I wondered, too, if Concordius had known in advance about the identity of Bolanus's heir. It was possible, sure it was, given the circumstances, even without access to the will itself; Ursus could've got the information out of Vettia at any time in any of a dozen ways without her noticing and passed it on to his boss. From the lady's description of Cousin Quintus I couldn't see him being much of a likely suspect himself, even with Bolanus's marriage in the offing, but if Concordius did want the estate – and at a knock-down price, too – then with Bolanus in his urn and this 'harmless' Beneventan draper holding the deeds he was laughing. Put that together with the marriage, and Concordius and his sidekick had motive and to spare.

I was just leaving the villa grounds for the main drag when a big black horse came from my right out of nowhere and flashed past me, missing the mare's nose by a whisker and going like the hammers of hell. I swore and pulled at the reins, struggling to keep my seat, while the mare bucked and shied.

The other rider slowed, turned and cantered back. It was Sulpicia, in her Diana costume.

'Oh, Corvinus, I'm terribly sorry!' she said. 'I didn't see you! Are you all right?'

'Yeah.' It was true, just; all the same, if she'd been a man I'd've given her a proper earful. I hadn't been watching myself, sure, but the lakeside road was no place for fancy riding, and if she hadn't seen me coming for the screen of trees she'd know there was a junction there and she should've been taking it easier. 'No bones broken.' I patted the mare's quivering flank.

'I was coming back from town, and I like to give Mauros his head on the last stretch. I really do apologise.'

'No problem,' I said. 'In fact, you've just saved me a trip. I was meaning to drop by and have a word with you anyway.'

'What about?'

I reached into my belt-pouch and pulled out the little phial I'd found at Exuperius's place. 'You recognise this?'

She took it. Her brow furrowed. 'No. Should I? It's just an ordinary empty perfume bottle.'

'Take a sniff.'

She uncorked it and held it to her nose. 'But that's mine! At least, that's the perfume I use.'

'Yeah,' I said neutrally. 'I recognised it. That's why I'm asking.'

'Where did you get it?'

'In a flat above a butcher's shop in town.' I was watching her carefully. Not a flicker. 'The butcher's name was Exuperius.'

That did get me a reaction, in spades. Her hand jerked hard at the reins, the black stallion's head came up and he backed away. It took her a moment to regain control, and when she did her lips formed a tight line.

'Uh . . . you know him, then,' I said.

'Oh, yes, I know him, Corvinus.' You could've driven nails into the lady's tone. I waited, but obviously that was the only information I was getting, and something told me if I asked the logical next question I'd be looking for my teeth two seconds later.

'Fine, fine,' I said.

'What was he doing with one of my old perfume bottles?'

'I don't know. I was hoping you could tell me that, lady.'

'Well, I can't,' she snapped. 'He didn't explain?'

'He wasn't there to explain. Quintus Libanius thinks he's hiding out somewhere in the mountains.'

She stared. 'Why should he be doing that?'

'Because he killed Herdonius Flacchus this morning.'

'He *what?*' There was no mistaking the genuine shock in her voice.

'Flacchus's slave saw him do it. Or at least the next best thing. He got away. Libanius and I searched his flat.' I paused. 'Which, like I said, was where I found the bottle.'

'Oh, gods!' Sulpicia was looking sick. 'That's horrible! They're looking for him?'

'Yeah. Libanius's men are up in the hills now.'

'Then I hope they kill him! The man's a brute!'

She meant it, too. Not exactly your blushing Roman rose, this lady. I wondered what she had against Exuperius; something major, anyway, there'd been real venom there. And how they knew each other in the first place. 'So you've no idea why he should have a perfume bottle of yours next his bed?' I prompted gently.

'None.' The look she gave me would've skewered a rhino. 'I certainly didn't leave it there myself, Corvinus. Should the thought have crossed your mind at all.'

'No. I didn't think you did.' That was true, at any rate: wild as she was, I couldn't imagine a woman like Sulpicia taking a roll in the hay with Exuperius, especially since the hay in question was a truckle bed so full of fleas you could practically see it move. And the loathing in her voice made me wince. 'Uh ... how about your maid?'

She laughed. '*Procne*? Be serious, please! Procne has far more taste than to sleep with Exuperius!'

Yeah, I'd go for that, too, and the answer wasn't unexpected;

I'd only asked the question in the first place because failing Sulpicia her maid was the other natural possibility. I could see the girl with the come-on eyes going for a piece of beefcake like Ursus, sure, but Exuperius was the weedy dregs. 'Fine,' I said, picking up the reins. 'Never mind, we'll just have to put it down as one of life's unsolved mysteries.' Would we hell; this needed some serious thought. 'Thanks for the chat. I'll see you later, lady.'

'You're going into town?'

'Uh-uh. Bovillae.'

'Bovillae? What's your business in Bovillae?'

'Just checking a couple of leads. Exuperius was involved in a wineshop brawl the day your fiancé was killed. Ex-fiancé. With a young Roman.'

'Oh, yes.' The loathing was back in her voice. 'Yes, that sounds like Gaius Exuperius, all right. Who was the Roman?'

'A guy by the name of Licinius. He's a jobbing artist.'

Her eyes came up. '*Who?*'

'Quintus Licinius. You know him?'

'I knew a Quintus Licinius slightly in Rome, yes. Licinius Crassus's son. He isn't in Latium, though, or not that I'm aware of. And if your Licinius is a jobbing artist, as you say, then no doubt the name's coincidental.' Her face cleared. 'It's probably someone else entirely.' She jerked on the rein, pulling the stallion's head round. 'Well, Corvinus, I'll let you get off. I'm sorry again about almost running you down.'

'That's okay, lady. I'll see you around.'

I rode off in the direction of the Bovillae junction with the Castrimoenium road, my brain buzzing. That little encounter had been interesting.

21

Bovillae was bigger than Castrimoenium, but not by much. I found the wineshop no bother, just inside the town's Castrimoenian Gate: a tight little place that looked thriving, as it would be in that position. I moored the horse to a post by the drinking trough outside the door and went in.

There were three punters propping up the counter. They gave the purple stripe on my tunic its usual once-over and two of them moved pointedly away to sit at one of the corner tables, leaving one man nursing his drink on the end.

'What'll it be?' the guy behind the bar said. My Public Fountain Square pal had been right: he was big, and he didn't look like he'd take no nonsense from nobody.

I glanced up at the wine board. 'Half a jug of Fregellan?'

He reached for the wine jar, hefted it with one hand and poured. I took out my purse. 'You're Gaius Satrius?' I said.

That got me a sharp look from under the heavy brows as he set the jar down and pushed over a cup. 'That's me.'

I laid a silver piece on the counter and he made change. 'The name's Marcus Corvinus,' I said. 'One of your colleagues over in Castrimoenium tells me a neighbour of his got into a punch-up here a few days ago. Guy by the name of Exuperius.'

Satrius grunted. 'Yeah. So?'

I poured out some of the wine and sipped. 'My wineshop pal said he spent the night in your broom closet.'

'That's right. Bugger was pissed as a newt so I put him in there to sleep it off. I'd've thrown him out altogether, but he often comes here when he's in town and I didn't have the heart.'

The punter at the end of the counter sniggered. 'Big-hearted Satrius, we call him,' he said.

'Can it, Titus,' Satrius growled.

'He was there until the next day?' Not that it'd make much difference. Even if, as didn't seem likely from what the wineshop guy was saying here, he'd been capable of murder in that condition, he'd still have had to get from Bovillae to the Bolanus property.

'Yeah. He left mid-morning. The bastard had thrown up all over the floor so I had him clean it up first.' He was looking at me with suspicion. 'What's this all about?'

No point being close-mouthed about it, that'd only lose me goodwill. Besides, I needed more from him than just confirmation that Exuperius was out of the running, and to keep the flow going information needs to go both ways. 'There was a murder in Castrimoenium that night,' I said. 'I'm just checking that he couldn't've been involved.'

'The Bolanus murder?'

'Yeah, that's right. You heard about it?'

'No one within twenty miles of the mountain who hasn't.' The suspicious look had changed to a definite scowl. 'What's your interest, friend? You with the Roman judge's office?'

'No. I'm only helping out.'

'That so, now?' Nevertheless, the scowl eased off a notch. Praetor's reps, I'd guess, weren't too popular around here.

I took a mouthful of the wine. 'You care to tell me exactly what happened? Just for the record? The other man in the fight was a Roman, or so I've heard.'

'That's right. Young artist guy touting locally for commissions.' Satrius grinned suddenly. 'Me, I haven't much time for Romans myself, no offence meant, but he could handle his fists, that lad. Exuperius didn't have a chance after he landed the first punch.'

'What was the quarrel about? You know?'

'Uh-uh. I was fetching a jar up from the cellar, so I missed the start.' He turned to the guy at the far end of the counter. 'Hey, Titus. You were there. You any idea?'

'Sure.' The barfly lowered his cup. 'Some fancy Roman dame over in Castrimoenium. Exuperius was bragging he'd had her and she was an easy lay. Turned out the youngster knew her and he took exception.'

Sweet gods! The hairs on the back of my neck stirred. No, it couldn't be; it had to be someone else. 'Uh . . . you happen to remember the lady's name, pal?' I said.

'Yeah.' Titus picked up his wine cup again and drank. 'Sulpicia. The Roman called him a liar and Exuperius went for him. Then it was goodnight sergeant.'

My guts went cold. Oh, shit. Even so, I still couldn't believe it; there was no way someone like Sulpicia would take up with a charmless, low-class loser like Exuperius, never, even without the evidence from my conversation with her earlier. Still, there had been the perfume bottle . . .

What was going on here?

'He mention her at all before that?' I said. 'Any previous time he'd been in?'

'Not by name. And he wasn't a talker, as a rule. But he did drop some fairly heavy hints about a high-class girlfriend who wouldn't leave him alone.' Titus sniggered again. 'He should be so lucky. Me, I think it was wind.'

Satrius had been frowning. 'Sulpicia. Wasn't that the fiancée's name? Bolanus's fiancée, the one who found the body?'

Titus set his cup down. 'Is that right, now, Satrius?' he said. 'Well, well.'

I kept my mouth closed.

'Then maybe Exuperius killed Bolanus after all,' Satrius grunted. 'To get the girl.'

'Sure he did.' Titus laughed. 'Walked through the wall, flew all the way to Castrimoenium and back, then walked through the wall again. Or maybe the girl killed her fiancé to get Exuperius. As theories go, they're both as likely as each other and I wouldn't give you a plugged copper coin for either of them.' He winked at me. 'Why don't you just ask lover-boy direct, Roman?'

'He's on the run. He killed an old guy by the name of Herdonius Flacchus this morning.'

You could've heard a pin drop, and even the two Romanophobes over in the corner raised their eyes. Satrius swore.

'Why the hell should he do that?' he said finally.

I emptied my cup and poured another belt; I wasn't going to go into the ins and outs of the festival theory in a public wineshop, and, besides, I wanted some private time to think about the new Sulpicia angle. 'I don't know,' I said. 'But the murder was witnessed by one of the dead man's slaves. If Exuperius should show up here again, hold him and call the town Watch.'

'Oh, we'll do that all right, don't you worry.' Satrius poured a cup of wine for himself from a jug on the counter. 'Not that I reckon it'll happen, mind, because the bastard'll've taken to the hills by now.' He shook his head slowly and drank. 'Jupiter's bloody balls! Exuperius, eh?'

'Incidentally,' I said, 'maybe you can tell me something else while I'm here. You know where I can find a man by the name of Decidius, by any chance?'

Satrius put the cup down. 'Aulus Decidius?'

'Probably.'

'What's Aulus Decidius got to do with this?' The suspicion was back in the guy's voice.

'Not a thing, far as I know,' I said blandly. 'I was just told he deals in local property. I thought maybe seeing as I was in the town anyway I might have a word with him.'

There was a definite silence. Titus cleared his throat and took a sip of his wine, eyes carefully on the wall. Satrius glanced at him, then back at me.

'Uh . . . you thinking of buying property hereabouts?' he said. 'Through Decidius?'

'Could be. He does a good trade?'

'Oh, yeah. Decidius isn't short of a copper piece or two, and some of it comes from property sales right enough.' Satrius hesitated, glanced again at Titus and seemed to come to a decision. 'Me, I'd be just a little careful there, though, friend. That's not a warning, just advice. Good advice.'

'He's a crook?'

Satrius's forehead creased and he sucked in his breath. 'Oh, well, now, I never said that! He's certainly a big man in Bovillae, if not the biggest, and he didn't get that way by losing out on anything he put his signature to. That's as far as I'd go, myself. You seem straight enough for a Roman and I'm just telling you to be careful, okay?'

'Got it,' I said.

'Big-hearted Satrius,' Titus murmured.

The wineshop owner ignored him. 'Far as finding his place is concerned there's no problem. Go to the centre of town, take the Arician road and it's a quarter-mile or so out on the left. You can't miss it.'

'Fine.' The jug still had a fair bit to go, but if I was to get back before dinner-time I'd have to make tracks. I passed it over to Titus. 'Finish that for me, pal, would you? And thanks a lot for your help.'

'No problem. See you around, Roman.'

I unhitched my horse, mounted, and rode along the Hinge towards the town centre. Not the ogre I'd expected, Satrius; in fact, all in all and appearances aside, he'd turned out to be a pussycat. And as far as Bolanus's death was concerned, anyway, Exuperius was definitely out. Like Titus the barfly had said the bugger would've needed wings.

The conversation had been an eye-opener otherwise, though, and no mistake. The business with Sulpicia had me sorely puzzled. I couldn't've been wrong about her, surely, especially after seeing the sad pit that was Exuperius's flat: a bit of rough on the side was one thing, women like Sulpicia might go for that just for the hell of it, but taking up with a slob like him didn't fit the picture at all. Also, there'd been her reaction when I'd mentioned his name. They weren't strangers to each other, that was sure – she'd admitted as much herself – but lovers was something else again, even on a temporary basis. That I couldn't swallow. On the other hand, it gave me a connection between the two murders. Exuperius couldn't've done the first one, granted, but if he had some sort of link with Bolanus's fiancée – and that was way beyond doubt – then it wasn't something I could ignore.

Licinius was another problem. Where the hell did our plain-clothes Roman aristocrat fit into the puzzle? He was playing some sort of game of his own, that was certain, but what exactly it was I couldn't guess. He knew Sulpicia for a start, possibly beyond Sulpicia's 'slightly', and that was definite too. How far their relationship went was a question that needed answering, and whatever the answer was the fact that he was in the area couldn't be a coincidence. On the other hand, although I'd bet our jobbing artist and Sulpicia's friend in Rome were one and the same person, the news that he was in Castrimoenium had seemed to come as a genuine surprise to her. I'd have to have a talk with Licinius before either of us were much older.

The Hinge gave out on to the market square. Aricia was to the south-west of Bovillae, so the Arician Gate would be somewhere to the left. I'd stopped off to ask an old woman selling greens from a stall in front of the town offices how to get to it when someone shouted my name.

'Corvinus! Hold on a moment!'

I looked up. Abudius Ruso was coming down the steps with a couple of greybeards in formal mantles. He spoke to them then hurried towards me. I dismounted.

'I hear Flacchus was killed this morning,' he said.

'Yeah.' I frowned. 'News travels fast, seemingly. Who told you that, pal?'

'Agilleius Mundus. Libanius sent him a message; he's sent out messengers to all the towns in the region telling them to be on the lookout for the murderer.' He was looking worried as hell. 'Did you have a chance to talk to him before he died?'

'Uh-uh. I was too late.'

'Fuck!' I raised my eyebrows: you didn't usually hear language like that from serving Roman magistrates. I was beginning to like Ruso. 'Corvinus, I don't like the smell of this. Not one bit. Also, I hear the killer was the man you had a run-in with yourself yesterday.'

'Yeah, that's right. Exuperius.' I hesitated. 'Uh . . . one thing I think you should know. Libanius tells me he was to be one of the poleaxe-men at the festival.'

Ruso's eyes came up. 'He was *what*? How did that happen?'

'He's a butcher. These're the guys they usually recruit.'

'Gods, I know that!' If Ruso had been looking worried before, he looked doubly so now. 'Who the devil approved the appointment?'

'Libanius, presumably. He made the list, anyway.'

Ruso wasn't listening. He chewed his lower lip. 'Corvinus, I really don't like the sound of all this. It may be nothing, of course, and there isn't a chance in hell of this Exuperius getting within a mile of the festival now, but it's still worrying. There was something going on, certainly. Perhaps there still is.'

'Uh . . . for what it's worth, my thought was that Exuperius might've been planning to kill the consuls.'

Ruso stared at me in shock. 'What?'

'It'd make sense. The guy would be a poleaxe-man, after all; he'd have his hammer, and the consuls – or one of them, anyway, I'm not sure how you work these things – would be right there in reach. Murdering him would be easy-peasy, and with no one expecting it he might even get away in the confusion.'

'Holy living Jupiter!' The aedile's face was grey as a month-old dishrag.

'It's possible, then?'

'Better than possible. The senior consul performs the sacrifice as officiating priest. But why should Exuperius want to kill Persicus?'

'Because he hates Romans. No.' I stopped myself. 'That's not good enough. Because the guy hates *Rome*. If a Roman consul were assassinated on Latin soil, at the Latin Festival, that'd send out a pretty strong message, wouldn't it?'

Ruso shook his head. He wasn't disagreeing, I could tell that; the shock had just numbed him. 'Look,' he said. 'Just how sure are you about this?'

'Not absolutely, it's only a theory. But, like I say, it fits. And it'd explain why Exuperius needed Flacchus dead. Whether the old bugger was involved personally or if he just found out about the plot somehow, I don't know, but my guess is that he knew what was going on and threatened to pull the plug.'

'He chose a bloody funny way to do it, then. Why faff around with Marcia Fulvina and that stupid dream story? Why not go directly to the authorities?'

A smart cookie, this Ruso. What I'd just told him had knocked the guy beam over tip, but he was already back in there punching. And the question was bang on the nail. 'Yeah; that has me puzzled as well,' I said. 'For a start, I'd bet a pickled cucumber to a bag of gold pieces that that dinner invitation was no accident, that he'd got Marcia round with the full intention of buttonholing her after the meal and asking her to have a word with her nephew. The problem is, if he'd really wanted to give the game away or at least drop a heavy hint then why didn't he tell Quintus Libanius instead, especially since he'd gone to the trouble of inviting him to the party in the first place? Also, the subject of the festival came up in the conversation. Why not mention the dream then? That way he'd kill two birds with one stone and still manage to stay out of things.'

'Pass. You're the sleuth, Corvinus. You tell me.'

I sighed. 'The gods know, pal. Me, I'm just at the asking questions stage. If you twisted my arm, though, I'd say it was because Flacchus was suffering from divided loyalties. If he'd approached Libanius he might not've got off so easily. Libanius is no fool. He and Flacchus were friends, sure, but he's the local senate's First Speaker, he takes his job seriously and he'd've wanted more. Sure, Marcia has her head screwed on, but she's still an old woman and only a neighbour. Using her as the medium would've kept the whole business unofficial. The same reason'd hold for why he didn't mention the dream at the dinner itself. Libanius would've picked him up on it, and Flacchus would've had even less of a chance of backing off.'

'What do you mean about "divided loyalties"?'

'That makes sense as well. Exuperius might've been the linchpin of the plan, but one gets you ten he wasn't the guiding force. He hasn't got the brains for one thing, and for another I can't see someone like Flacchus going out on a limb to protect a homicidal butcher. Me, I'd bet there was someone else involved, someone Flacchus knew personally and didn't want hurt. He wanted to stop the plot, not rip the lid off it. Getting Persicus to postpone the festival would give him time to talk to the guy, hopefully persuade him to call the whole thing off.'

'And instead it persuaded the man to silence Flacchus. Or have him silenced by Exuperius.' Ruso was frowning. 'Oh, yes. It's plausible, Corvinus. Very plausible. So who was the man? Who's our prime villain?'

'That I don't know. Not yet. All I have to go on is a name Flacchus wrote while he was dying. You come across anyone called Fufetius at all?'

'Who?'

'Fufetius. Flacchus knew him, sure, and he was important enough for the man to use his last moments sending us the message, but his head slave's never heard of the guy. Nor has Libanius.'

'No.' Ruso shook his head. 'I'm sorry, Corvinus, he's no one I know. It's a good Latin name, certainly, but it's not common by any means. However, I'll make enquiries, you can be sure of that, and if the man exists then we'll find him. All this, however, proves my point: if Exuperius wasn't playing a lone game and it's your belief that the consuls are in danger then Persicus has to be persuaded to postpone the rites, at least until this whole mess can be cleared up. There's too much at stake here to take any risks, and the exact date isn't important anyway.'

I nodded. 'Yeah. I agree entirely.'

'The problem is, the thrawn bugger won't listen to me, will he?' Ruso's mouth twisted. 'In fact, in my very considered opinion it'd have the opposite result, which is something I do not want to happen under any circumstances. Perhaps Flacchus had the right idea after all. Could Marcia Fulvina be persuaded to go to Rome and talk to her nephew herself, do you think? I'd make all the arrangements, naturally, and Persicus might well believe her where he wouldn't anyone else.'

'Uh-uh.' I shook my head decisively. 'It's a good enough idea in theory, pal, no arguments, but that's a forty-odd-mile round trip, Marcia's pushing eighty and she hasn't been all that well lately. Me, I wouldn't even ask. Besides, if she did go we're talking litters, not even a carriage, and with regular stops that'd take a couple of days that we just don't have. How about if I went myself? Maybe with a note from Marcia to oil the wheels?'

Ruso looked relieved. 'That'd be excellent,' he said. 'I didn't like to ask you, Corvinus, because this is really not your headache, but you'd be doing me – and probably Rome – an enormous favour. You're sure?'

'Sure I'm sure.'

'How soon could you leave?'

I shrugged. 'Dawn tomorrow morning. I'm no great rider, but I can get there in four or five hours easy.'

'First rate. Then I'll send a despatch rider to Persicus

immediately arranging a meeting for late afternoon. His office on the Capitol suit you?'

'Yeah. Yeah, that'd be fine.'

The aedile blew out his cheeks; he suddenly looked ten years younger. 'I really do appreciate this,' he said. 'The logistics of this job are hell already without having to worry about possible assassination attempts, and you've certainly lifted a load from my mind. If there's ever anything I can do in return – anything – you only have to ask.'

I grinned: Roman society's all about favours, and having a magistrate in your debt can come in handy. 'No problem, pal,' I said. 'Not that I'm making any promises, mind. Paullus Persicus isn't exactly a bosom buddy of mine, either. He may just send me off with a flea in my ear.'

'Not if you tell him what you've told me, he won't. Or if he does then he's a total fool. We can only do our best.'

'Yeah.' I hesitated. 'Oh, by the way. You happen to know someone in Bovillae by the name of Aulus Decidius?'

'Yes, of course.' Ruso's eyebrows rose. 'You have business with him?'

'It's why I'm here. Partly, anyway. I was on my way to talk to the guy.'

'In connection with Bolanus's murder?'

'Maybe. I'm just following a lead, that's all. I understand he's a pretty noted entrepreneur locally.'

'Oh, yes. In Rome, too. In fact he handles several major contracts for our office, in the building line.'

'So he's . . . uh . . . straight, then? I mean, I got the impression from a guy I talked to in a wineshop that he might not be too averse to cutting a few corners.'

Ruso laughed. 'Decidius is straight, yes, as far as I'm aware. We don't deal with cowboys, Corvinus, or if it does happen it only happens once and we make sure they live to regret it. He's a hard nut, though, and I don't say he wouldn't come out of any bargain he made ahead of the field. If that's what your wineshop friend meant by cutting corners then he's quite right, although Aulus Decidius is no worse than some I could name. What exactly did you want to ask him?'

'Oh, just a couple of questions about a deal he may be thinking of making.'

'Drop my name into the conversation, then. If you need a bit of extra leverage to prise his jaws apart I think that may do it. As I say, he does a fair amount of business with the office and if he knows you have an aedile behind you he may be more communicative.'

'Yeah. Yeah, I'll do that. Thanks.'

'Don't mention it. I still owe you.' He glanced up to where the two old guys in the mantles were twiddling their thumbs and shifting from foot to foot. 'Hell! I really have to go, I'm late enough already. Have fun with the senior consul, and persuade him if you can. And again, I really do appreciate your help.'

'That's okay, friend.' I took hold of the horse's saddle and remounted. 'I'll see you in a couple of days.'

'Fine.' He half turned, then a thought struck him. 'Corvinus, just hold on a second, will you? Let me just ask Mundus if he knows.'

'What about?' I said, but he was already running up the steps. I calmed the fidgeting horse while Ruso talked to the older of the two mantles. A minute later he came back down.

'Bull's-eye,' he said, 'I've got your Fufetius. Or at least a Fufetius.'

I stared at him. 'Yeah?' Maybe the gods were smiling on me for once. 'That's great!'

'He's an augur. Lives over in Roboraria, full name Marcus Fufetius Albus.' My face fell. Oh, shit; another bit of riding to look forward to, and I couldn't even call in on the way to Rome because Roboraria was in the other direction, well to the east and north of Caba. Fufetius might be important, but the guy would have to wait his turn.

'Got it,' I said.

'Would you like me to check him out myself? As I said, this business isn't your headache.'

He didn't seem all that enthusiastic which, given his current hectic lifestyle, wasn't too surprising. 'No, that's okay,' I said. 'I can take the Latin Road instead on the way back and call in then. Thanks again, Ruso.'

'You're welcome.'

He went back up the steps, and I urged the nag into a walk. Bugger; what had I let myself in for? Paullus bloody Persicus aside, a day in Rome I was looking forward to, sure, but I'd bet after another forty-odd miles in the saddle my rear end wouldn't be too happy with the bargain. Still, it had to be done, and at least I could squeeze this Fufetius in on the return trip. If the guy had form then we might be able to stitch up that aspect of the case, anyway.

Meanwhile, I had Aulus Decidius to look forward to.

22

I'd have to get a move on here: the afternoon was practically half gone, and time and touchy chefs wait for no man. Satrius had been right about not being able to miss Decidius's place, though; it took up half a hillside. You could see the sprawl of the villa and its surrounding gardens in the distance practically from the Arician Gate itself, and the monumental entrance to the long driveway wouldn't've disgraced Triumph Road in Rome. Evidently Decidius wasn't so much a big fish in a small pool as a whale in a bucket.

I dismounted, tethered my horse to the hitching-ring beside the fancy fountain in front of the house, went up the marble steps and knocked on the panelled door. The slave who opened it could've buttled for one of the eastern client-kings.

'Yes, sir?' he said.

'The master at home?' I asked.

'Yes, sir, he is. Who shall I say?'

I gave him all four bits. He didn't blink. 'If you'd care to wait in the atrium, sir,' he said, 'I'll see whether Aulus Decidius is receiving.'

'Fine,' I said. I followed him in and stood cooling my heels while he went to solicit an audience.

Rich was right; even though Decidius was – presumably – in the business and could get most of the furniture and fittings at rock-bottom prices, putting that atrium together must've cost him an arm and a leg. No chairs, just low couches, which struck me as odd, but from the looks of them they were top of the range, well into the luxury bracket. There was marble everywhere – the pricey coloured stuff, too, not your jobbing white – and the floor mosaics were among the best I'd seen even in Rome. Not many statues, sure, but what there were were either originals or first-rate copies. I was especially taken with a bronze of a drunken old woman clutching a wine cup. Even her fingernails were perfect.

'Ah, you like the Myron.' I turned: the guy was coming down the polished wood staircase, but if I hadn't been facing it straight on I'd've missed him. 'It's a copy, naturally, but cast only a few years after the original. I had it shipped from Athens.'

'Is that so, now?' I was trying hard not to stare, because the door-slave three steps down from him still had the edge as far as height was concerned. Decidius was a dwarf: a silver-haired sixty-year-old with a three-year-old's legs.

He reached the bottom of the flight. 'Bring us some wine,' he said to the slave. The guy bowed and exited. 'Sit down, Valerius Corvinus. Or stretch out, rather. Make yourself comfortable, in any case.'

Yeah, well; that explained the couches, anyway. Either he'd've had to have a chair specially made, in which case a visitor sitting on one normal-sized would've towered over him, or he'd end up perched clear of the ground, swinging his legs. If he could climb up at all without steps, that was. I chose one of the couches – the frame was satinwood inlaid with ivory – and reclined.

Decidius waddled over and squeezed himself up on to the one opposite. 'Now,' he said, 'what exactly can I do for you?'

This was the tricky part. 'Uh ... you know a Publius Concordius, so I understand,' I said. 'Over in Castrimoenium.'

When he was lying down if you didn't look at the legs you weren't aware of his lack of height. And the eyes that fixed themselves on mine were sharp as knives. The voice, though, was mild. 'Yes, indeed,' he said. 'Publius and I are old friends.'

'Business friends?'

'Is there another kind?'

I felt slightly nettled. I hadn't expected him to be on the defensive, exactly, but he was relaxed enough to use as a drape. 'I thought there was, sure,' I said.

'Indeed?' He smiled. 'Oh, then I stand corrected. In that case, Publius is quite definitely the business sort.'

'Fine.' Weak; he had the edge here, and I knew it. Still, there wasn't a quicker way to play things. Accusing him outright of being involved in a property scam would just get me shown the door. 'Ah . . . you work together with him on occasion, right?'

'In what way?'

'You co-operate on deals. Property deals, specifically.'

The smile had vanished. Decidius sat up. 'Valerius Corvinus, what is this about? Forgive me, but I'm very busy at present and I have to be in Rome tomorrow morning to attend an auction on the Palatine, which means a *very* trying night coach journey. Could you please come to the point before we both perish from old age and boredom?'

Shit. 'Okay. I'm interested in a lakeside estate that belonged to a guy named Vettius Bolanus. He died five days ago.'

The little man shifted irritably. 'Don't play with words, please,' he said. 'Vettius Bolanus didn't "die", nor am I either stupid or ill-informed; the man was murdered. And in what way are you "interested" in his estate? If you're considering purchasing it yourself then I'm afraid I don't offer a brokerage service; I buy for myself and then sell on. However, I would guess from your earlier questions that that was *not* your meaning, so I'll ask you again: what is this about?'

The slave – not the doorman, another guy – came in with the tray. I noticed that the wine service was Syrian glass; prime quality, too. He handed me my goblet, bowed and left. He must've been six feet, easy. I sipped; the wine was Caecuban, smooth as silk and thirty years old if it was a day.

'Before I tell you,' I said, 'I should say I'm here with the knowledge of Abudius Ruso.'

'Who?'

'Abudius Ruso. The aedile.'

'Oh, *that* chap!' Decidius's face cleared suddenly and he laughed. 'Really, Corvinus, if you think that entitles you to any sort of preferential treatment from me then I'm sorry, I must disappoint you. His father was an antiques dealer, and not a very good one, either. Not dishonest – that I could cope with, I know where I am with crooks – just not particularly good at his job. Pull some other string, if you will. That one, I'm afraid, does *not* have a bell at the end.' He cradled the glass wine goblet in both hands. 'Now. We've got off here to a very bad start indeed. Let's begin again, if you will. Unless my ability to read between the lines is gravely at fault you think I'm involved in some sort of unsavoury plot with Publius Concordius involving Vettius Bolanus's estate. True or false?'

Things were running ahead of me here; still, I found myself quite liking the sarky little bugger. 'Uh . . . true,' I said.

'Good. Thank you; now we're getting somewhere.' He took a mouthful of wine and set the goblet on the table beside him. 'And what form does it take?'

'Uh . . . Bolanus's estate goes to a cousin, and according to the dead man's sister, the chances are that as soon as the legal details are settled he'll put it on the market. The—'

Decidius held up a hand. 'Wait a moment, please. You know who this man is, presumably?'

'Not his name, no. He has a draper's business in Beneventum.'

'He's a provincial businessman, then? Not one of your Roman dilettantes with his nose up his own backside?'

'Uh . . . no.'

'Fine. No, Corvinus, I was just checking on a factor you might not have considered; you have the floor. Carry on.'

He was smiling at me; not a nasty smile, more the sort of tolerant look you might give to a serious ten-year-old having his first crack at delivering a formal speech. I was beginning to get a bad feeling about this. 'The sister herself is involved with Concordius's right-hand man. You know Ursus?'

'Oh, yes, I know Sextus Ursus. A most capable fellow in many ways, but with very little between the ears. How interesting; is she really? How do you mean, "involved"?'

'They're . . . ah . . . engaged. In a manner of speaking. She tells me Ursus recommended you as an agent for selling the property. Only as you say you don't act as a broker I thought that may've simply been a sort of warm-up ploy to get him hooked.'

'Did you, now?' I'd expected that that would've ruffled the little guy's feathers a bit, but he just sounded mildly curious. 'Actually, I misled you there; I do occasionally practise brokerage, although nowadays mostly as a favour to friends and when I have no particular interest in the property myself. To be honest with you, though, this would not have been the case with the Bolanus estate. You're quite correct; it's a prime site for development.' He paused. 'And that, presumably, is your theory: that Ursus – or rather Publius, since his assistant has some difficulty with extended trains of thought – is plotting with me to acquire the property, with a view to splitting the profits on its eventual resale?'

'Uh . . . yeah,' I said. 'More or less.'

'Then it's not unreasonable. Considered only *as* a theory, of course, because if you'd taken the trouble to find out more about me you would have realised that I wouldn't touch a scheme like that with a bargepole. Even if I were criminally inclined, which I am not.'

'That so, now?' I said neutrally.

Decidius laughed. 'You may safely take my word for it, or ask your friend Ruso, if you don't believe me. I'm a very wealthy man, Valerius Corvinus, and I'm wealthy because I'm *not* such a fool as your theory would have me be. Only fools break the law; the risks are out of all proportion to the rewards, and I don't take risks. Not that kind of risk, anyway. I can't afford to.'

'Okay,' I said. 'I'll accept that. As a working hypothesis, anyway.'

'That's most generous of you.' He was still smiling. 'As far as the property itself is concerned, yes, I would certainly be very happy indeed to buy it, especially if I had it cheaply. Land bordering on the Alban Lake is going for a premium, *if* you have the capital to develop it, which I do. Even if I did have to pay top rates I could build two luxury villas on the Bolanus property – three, if we're talking middle of the market – and still quadruple my investment.'

Well, at least he was being straight. Or he sounded as if he was, anyway. I shifted on my couch. 'So, uh, if you prefer to buy direct then how does Concordius come into things normally?' I asked. 'As a business associate, I mean?'

'Oh, it's not only Publius. I have several other friends who are on the lookout for suitable properties on my behalf, on a commission basis. And not only as – shall we say – simple gatherers of information.'

'Uh . . . I'm not with you, pal,' I said.

'Corvinus, you obviously don't understand the subtleties of the property market. As a rule absentee owners, such as the Roman gentry, feel no particular attachment for the estates they own and will buy and sell them quite happily as circumstances dictate. In the country districts, especially here in Latium, the situation is quite different. Often the estates have been in the same family for generations; they are in, as it were, their owners' bones, and the owners themselves, by and large, are conservative souls. You do get realists who'll take the money and run, but some, in the Vettius Bolanus mould . . . let's just say they're old-fashioned. They may not mind selling up, but they feel they have a say in what happens to the property when it passes out of their hands. They expect the new owner simply to take up where they left off and keep the estate intact, however unprofitable it may be. A *very* old-fashioned attitude. I have, I'm afraid, a certain reputation, totally deserved, for maximising the land's potential and selling on to the highest bidder; usually, naturally, since large amounts of money are involved, to an outsider who wants the place as a holiday home. Because of this I'm often forced to make my purchases at second hand due to the fact that the original seller won't deal with me directly at any price. Now you may say that this makes no sense, since I end up with the property in any case, and I'd quite agree; but there you are, human nature is a strange thing.'

'So your, ah, friends buy the property in their own names knowing that they can sell it on to you straight away?'

'Correct. Except that the money they buy it with is mine, not theirs. And I do add a fair commission, naturally, which depends on the estate's potential value.' He smiled. 'What a grasp of the concept you have, Valerius Corvinus!'

'And this is your usual arrangement with Publius Concordius?'

'It is. In the case of the Bolanus estate, however, the situation is slightly more complicated. Publius, I know, has been after it for years; it's quite a plum, and had he acquired it for me I would have been very happy to pay him a commission well over the normal odds. However, as you're no doubt aware, Vettius Bolanus has consistently refused to sell to anyone, certainly not to Publius, whom he disliked intensely. We had reached an effective impasse. Which' – he picked up his goblet and sipped – 'makes your theory of a plot rather intriguing.'

I blinked. 'You think there was a plot?'

Decidius laughed again. 'My dear Corvinus, I have no idea! I wouldn't be at all surprised, though; Publius is a *very* sharp fellow. I wouldn't put it past him at all to have engineered things through Sextus Ursus who, as I say, is not one of nature's brightest. Vettius Bolanus is dead, the impediment is removed; you tell me his heir would not be averse to selling, and since he is *not* a local man or a Roman he may not wholly appreciate the value of the property. Publius would know that to come forward himself as a prospective purchaser – even although he would, in effect, be only my front man – might well arouse suspicion, or even outright antagonism; I've never met Bolanus's sister, myself, so I've no way of knowing whether she shares his prejudices. This way, the deal would involve only myself and the new owner; although given the circumstances and being, I hope, an honest man I would be happy to pay the commission as usual.'

'So you'd buy it?' I just didn't believe this! 'Even under these circumstances?'

'Of course I'd buy it! As long as the sale was legal and the price was right I'd be a fool not to.'

'Even though you knew Concordius may've had Bolanus killed to get it?'

Decidius's smile disappeared like a blown-out lamp flame. 'Now *that* is a very dangerous line to pursue,' he said softly. 'I have no reason to believe that Publius would do any such thing, none at all, and you certainly have no proof. Or do you?'

'No. All the same, you said—'

'I *said* that I would buy the property so long as the sale was legal and the price right. I also said that I would be dealing directly with the legitimate new owner. Property trading uses only the present tense; who *owned* the land previously, and how he died, would be no concern of mine.' He must've noticed the look on my face because he added, 'Corvinus, this is business. I deal in facts, not theories. You tell me Sextus Ursus is engaged to Vettius Bolanus's sister and that he, through her, has given my name to Bolanus's heir in connection with a sell-on of the Bolanus estate. Very well; as I told you, I'm an honest man and I pay my debts. Ursus has acted as my agent and should the sale happen then I will pay him his commission in the normal fashion. I see nothing in all this that should cause you the remotest offence, and my conscience is, or would be in the event, completely clear.'

I stared at him. Jupiter! He'd got the whole thing stitched up!

'Speaking of debts, however' – Decidius took another delicate sip of his wine – 'and, you understand, completely off the record, your theory does have certain attractions.'

'Yeah?' I said. 'How so?'

He set the goblet back down. 'Publius is by no means poor, but his money is tied up in loans and property, and this silly election campaign of his has left him with a definite cash-flow problem. Two or three months ago he borrowed a hundred thousand from me to finance a set of gladiatorial games he was putting on. At reasonable interest, naturally, because what are friends for?'

There was a cold feeling in my gut. Sweet gods! 'Yeah. Yeah, right,' I said.

'These local magistracies are *so* expensive to buy into you wouldn't believe. And then when you are elected it's like having a hole in your purse. Myself, I wouldn't bother, but then I couldn't care less about climbing the social ladder because making money is a lot more satisfying and a lot less complicated. Publius is different; he's never forgotten he's a freedman's son and it rankles. In circumstances like that, good financial sense goes out the window.'

'Uh-huh.' The cold feeling increased. I took a swallow of my own wine. 'So he still owes you?' I said. 'And he's finding it difficult to pay?'

'Oh, yes, although I think "impossible" would be a better word. He's bound to be elected now in any case, because he's the only candidate, but the hundred thousand has already gone. And, as I say, the magistracy itself may have its perks but his expenses over the next twelve months will at least equal his income. On the other hand, if he – through Ursus – were to be responsible for getting me the Bolanus estate then I would be more than happy to set the debt against the commission, with probably a little over.'

'Hang on, pal,' I said slowly. 'What you're telling me, free, gratis and for nothing, is that Publius Concordius and his friend Ursus between them have a prime motive for murder, right?'

'Am I?' Decidius's eyes widened. 'Surely not! Why on earth would I want to do that?'

I set the goblet down; somehow, five-star Caecuban though it was, and even though what the guy was giving me here was pure gold, I didn't fancy drinking any more. 'Maybe because if they did conspire to kill Bolanus to free up his estate and were nailed for it then you'd save yourself a hefty finders' fee,' I said.

We looked at each other. Finally, Decidius laughed. He wasn't embarrassed or ashamed, just amused; and that sickened me. 'You have a very nasty imagination, Valerius Corvinus,' he said. 'However, you also – and I mean this as a compliment – have the makings of an excellent businessman.'

I got up abruptly, before I was tempted to throw the rest of the wine into his face. 'Thanks for agreeing to see me,' I said.

'You're going?'

'Sure. I got what I came for. I'm very grateful.'

I left, as quickly as I could. For the first time, I felt almost sorry for Concordius. With friends like that, he didn't need enemies.

23

I'd miscalculated drastically; it was late when I got back to Marcia's, easily inside the usual dinner slot. Bugger. I thrust the mare's reins at one of the yard slaves and took the entrance steps two at a time. Well, at least up here in the hills it wouldn't be fish, that was one good thing, anyway. Keeping a fish dinner waiting past its best-served-by time was something that really pissed Meton off. As it was, I might get away with second-degree sarcasm burns and a two-day sulk.

Bathyllus was waiting in the lobby with the jug of wine. He looked at my seriously travel-stained tunic and sniffed.

'Uh ... sorry I'm late, pal,' I said. 'They started without me?'

'No, sir.' He poured the welcome-home cup. 'It's quite all right; dinner will be delayed this evening. Meton says it will be at least another half-hour.'

I breathed again; the gods were smiling. 'Trouble with the sauce?'

'Not as far as I'm aware, sir. The chef was otherwise engaged for a large part of the afternoon, which has set things back somewhat.'

'"Otherwise engaged"?' I frowned; that wasn't like Meton. Nothing took precedence over cooking dinner; nothing. When the world dissolved in fire Meton would probably still be mixing the stuffing. 'What on?'

'I don't know, sir. He wouldn't tell me, and I couldn't see for myself because he'd bolted the kitchen door.' He handed the cup over and I downed the first restoring mouthful. 'Not even the skivvies were allowed in.'

Oh, shit; this sounded bad. 'Ah . . . he isn't hitting the cooking wine again, is he?' I said. Meton didn't go on a binge often, but it'd happened in the past and when it did it was serious. The last time we'd had to live on stale bread and takeaway meatballs for two days until he was sober enough to manage a best-of-three omelette.

'I don't think so, sir. He was quite rational when he did come out, and the Lady Marilla and her . . . *sheep* were with him.' Bathyllus hesitated over the s-word like it was prefixed by another beginning with f. His disapproving tone would've fried sardines. 'They've been spending a lot of time there recently. Or the sheep has, anyway.'

Pause. *Long* pause, while we stared at each other, bridging the master-slave divide.

'Ah . . . let's get this straight, pal,' I said eventually. '*Meton* is allowing *Dassa* in *Meton's kitchen*? On a regular basis?'

'Yes, sir.'

'Right. Right.' Oh, gods! There are some thoughts you just don't entertain. The true explanation was probably weird enough. 'That's, uh, fine. Lovely.'

Bathyllus was eyeing my tunic again. 'Perhaps a quick wash and change, sir?' he said. 'Before dinner actually is served?'

'Yeah. Yeah, maybe.' I was too distracted to argue. 'Ah . . . where's the Princess now?'

'She's gone into town, sir, on Corydon. She's having dinner at young Clarus's.'

'Uh-huh.' There was definitely a burgeoning relationship there, which was okay with me because I didn't begrudge the kid her new-found social life. The really worrying partnership was this one between Meton and Dassa. That bastard was up to something, both the bastards were, human and ovine, I'd bet my boots on it, and whatever it was our butter-wouldn't-melt-in-the-mouth stepdaughter was in it up to her cute little sidecurls. 'Ah . . . if you see her before I do, pal, tell her I'd like a word, okay?'

'Yes, sir. Certainly, sir.'

I took the cup and the jug into the atrium. Marcia was there with Perilla. The old girl was looking grey. I hadn't been looking forward to breaking the news to her about Flacchus's death, but she'd heard it already, and it had hit her pretty hard. I was glad I'd vetoed Ruso's idea of letting her go to Rome: she'd've done it, sure, especially now that the murder had raised his request to warn her nephew to the level of a dying wish.

She didn't make any trouble about writing me a letter, either.

'It's the least I can do for Lucius,' she said as she pressed her seal down on to the wax tag fastening the laces. 'Be sure and tell Paullus from me that I expect him to take the matter seriously. He can just bite on his shield-strap and get on with things for once.'

I couldn't help grinning; she might still be partially in shock, but that'd been a flash of the old Marcia. The guy might be within sight of forty and Rome's chief de iure magistrate, but to her he was still the snotty-nosed kid who didn't want to miss a party just because his brother had come down with mumps. I'd've given a lot to have seen her deliver the message in person.

'Yeah,' I said. 'Yeah, I'll do that.'

'Good. Here you are, then.' Marcia handed me the letter. She was moving slowly, and looking all of her seventy-nine years. 'Now if you'll excuse me I think I'll give dinner a miss and go to bed. Have a nice trip tomorrow, dear, and give Paullus my regards. I know you don't get on well with each other, but do try not to lose your tempers.'

When she'd gone, Perilla said quietly, 'She was very upset when she heard about Lucius Flacchus's death, Marcus. Very.'

'Yeah,' I said. 'I know.'

'So. What happened exactly? I didn't like to ask before.'

I told her the whole story, including my conspiracy theory.

'You really think that Flacchus was involved in some sort of plot to kill Cousin Paullus?' She was staring at me.

'It's a possibility, lady.' I stretched out on the couch and topped up my wine cup. 'It'd certainly explain his link with Exuperius and give the guy a reason for murdering him which otherwise he hasn't got.'

'But that's dreadful! Aunt Marcia will never believe it, to begin with, and I'm not at all sure I can myself. Flacchus was very forthright in his views, of course, but he was a scholar, a talker, not a political activist. Marcus, I really cannot see him conniving at assassination.'

'No.' I sipped my wine. 'Me neither, and that's the problem. Oh, sure, I only met the guy once and not, maybe, under the best of circumstances but Marcia's known him for years, she's no slouch at reading people and like you say she wouldn't believe it for a minute. If it were just Marcia I might discount that – the old girl obviously had a soft spot for him – but she isn't alone. When I suggested it to Quintus Libanius he practically gave me my teeth in my pocket.'

'So what's your explanation?'

'The one I gave Libanius. That Flacchus wasn't part of the plot himself, but he found out about it somehow and wanted it stopped without getting personally involved. That'd make just as much sense, especially if knew someone who *was* mixed up in it and didn't want him hurt.'

'Rutilius?'

I nodded. 'He's the logical candidate. He may not be an out-and-out fanatic like Exuperius, but he doesn't like Romans, that's for sure, and I'd bet my buttons he had something to do with smashing the Goddess Rome's face in. Also, he's no bonehead and I'd imagine he's just as steeped in Latin history as Flacchus was.'

'But Rutilius wouldn't have been a party to the old man's murder! He was practically a son!'

'No, I think the murder was Exuperius's idea.' I shifted on the couch. 'He's the real hard man in all this. Mind you, I wouldn't rule it out altogether. Look at it from Rutilius's point of view. The plot's up and running, everything's in place and suddenly Flacchus looks like peaching. Oh, he hasn't gone directly to the authorities, but it's only a matter of time and his mouth has to be shut fast. Rutilius can't risk leaving things as they are, especially since – as had to be the case – he was responsible for Flacchus finding out in the first place.'

'You think that's how Flacchus knew?'

'It's the simplest explanation, sure. Maybe Rutilius sounded him out in one of their chats, or maybe Flacchus just got suspicious for some reason and pressured him a little. I don't know for certain, but I'd guess it was something along those lines. In any case, like I say, the mischief was done and Rutilius would know it was his fault.'

'What about this man Fufetius? Where does he come in?'

'Yeah.' I cradled my wine cup. 'Yeah, that's the real bugbear. Oh, sure, he's important, or at least Flacchus obviously thought he was because the poor bugger spent his last minutes giving us the name, but that's as much as we've got. Presumably he's one of the conspirators, maybe even the top man. Still, thanks to Ruso's pal Mundus we have a possible fit in this augur guy over in Roboraria and it's not a common name, so we may've struck lucky for once. I'll—' I paused. 'You okay, lady?'

She'd gone pensive on me. 'Yes. I'm sorry, Marcus, I just had . . .' She frowned. 'No. Forget it, it doesn't matter. Of course there is another possibility, one that's not quite so melodramatic.'

'Yeah? What's that, now?'

'That Flacchus wrote down Fufetius's name not because he was a conspirator but because he could provide more information about the plot, even if he wasn't necessarily aware of the fact himself. If, as you say, he's an augur then he may well have connections with the festival.'

'Uh . . . right.' That was an angle I hadn't thought of. 'Well done, lady. We'll just have to see how things pan out.'

'You don't find it odd, though, Marcus, that Flacchus's major-domo knew nothing of him? After all, if he was someone whom Flacchus knew then surely his slave would be aware of the fact.'

'Uh-uh. Trupho's only been in the job for a couple of months. If Fufetius was an acquaintance as opposed to a friend then his name might not've come up. And he needn't even have been that. Flacchus might just've got him from Rutilius.'

'Yes. Yes, that's true.' Perilla still wasn't looking too happy about something, but she shook her head. 'Go on, dear.'

'There isn't much more anyway, not where Flacchus's death's concerned. As far as Fufetius goes there's no point in theorising until I see him myself on the way back from Rome.'

Perilla sat quiet for a moment, twisting her curl. Then she said slowly; 'We seem to have lost sight of Vettius Bolanus's murder in all this. Is there a connection, do you think, or are the two cases quite separate?'

'Yeah.' I sank a swallow of wine. 'That's another problem. My gut feeling is that they're tied in together, if only because in a small place like Castrimoenium two separate scams on the go at once is one too many. What the link is, though, I can't see. Except that it has to involve Sulpicia.'

Perilla's fingers stopped twisting the curl. '*Sulpicia?*'

'Yeah. She has – or had – something going with Exuperius.' Perilla's eyes widened and her mouth opened. 'Oh, no, I don't mean an affair. No way, never. He's a total slob and, besides, she hates his guts.'

'So what do you mean?'

I told her about the perfume bottle and the conversation in Satrius's wineshop. 'It can't be a coincidence. Sure, the most likely thing is that it's all on Exuperius's side and a product of the guy's own heated imagination, but it's a link none the less. *How* it's a link, though, your guess is as good as mine.'

'Hmm.' Perilla went back to her curl-twisting. 'Of course, someone with a really nasty mind would find the explanation simple.'

'Yeah? Then you go right ahead, lady.'

She sniffed. 'Very well. Sulpicia wanted to get rid of her fiancé. She seduces – verbally, if not physically – Exuperius, who is obviously very taken with her, sets up a meeting with Bolanus in the loggia and has Exuperius kill him; after which . . .' She stopped. 'No. It doesn't work, does it? Not at all.'

'No, it doesn't. For a start Exuperius is the one guy who *can't've* killed Bolanus, because he was spewing his guts out in a closet in Bovillae. Second, from all indications, unlike her father Sulpicia had nothing whatever against her fiancé, certainly no reason strong enough to want him dead. Third, high-class Roman ladies don't get the opportunity to seduce butchers over the chops even if they might be so inclined, verbally or otherwise, because they have kitchen staff to bring in the groceries. And fourth . . . yeah, well, you haven't met either of them, so the fourth I'll let you off with. I can't see Sulpicia lowering herself to seducing Exuperius, not for any reason. In fact, one gets you ten she wouldn't touch the guy with gloves and a ten-foot pole.'

'Well, then, how do you explain things?'

Sarky as hell. I grinned; Perilla might've pulled herself out of the mud before she'd gone too far in, but she still hated to be wrong, even temporarily. 'I don't,' I said. 'For what it's worth, my guess would be it *was* all on one side; that Sulpicia didn't play any part at all. That's not to say Exuperius's fantasies aren't relevant somewhere along the line, especially since it'd pull the two halves of the case together. They probably are; I just don't know where yet.'

'What about the perfume bottle? How did he get that?'

I shrugged. 'That's no problem, not given the guy was obsessed. It was just an ordinary glass refill, the sort you buy from the shop and pour into your own container. He'd know where Sulpicia lived and he could've got it any time for a copper piece from one of the skivvies who cleaned the rooms. The other thing that does puzzle me in connection with Sulpicia is that artist guy Licinius. He's got a link with Exuperius as well, and he seems to—'

'You wanted to see me, Corvinus?'

I turned round. 'Hey, Princess! I thought you were eating round at your boyfriend's.'

Marilla reddened. 'I did,' she said. 'Clarus's family eat early. Only he's not a boyfriend, he's just a friend who's helping me with Dassa.'

'Fine,' I said. 'Whatever. Apropos of which, what exactly is going on in the kitchen these days?'

I'd caught her off guard, which was the main idea. 'Pardon?' she said.

'Come on, Princess! You know what I mean! Between Dassa and Meton.' Gods! That'd come out wrong, but there weren't many better ways to phrase it. I glanced at Perilla. The lady was grinning, but I had the distinct feeling she was keeping out of this one.

'Meton's very taken with Dassa,' Marilla said. 'I told you. He likes to have her round about while he's working.'

Good try, but she was looking shifty as hell. 'With the door bolted?' I said. 'And the day Meton likes to have the patter of tiny hooves about the floor while he's whipping up a soufflé, let alone the patter of other things as well if the beast's not house-trained, which Dassa isn't, there'll be sheep flying over Mount Alba. Besides, whatever he's up to with her it isn't cookery. That's why we're sitting here rather than next door at the fruit and nuts stage. So spill, chicken-chops.'

Long silence; *long* silence. 'It's a secret,' she said at last.

'Yeah, well, I'd actually sort of come to that conclusion myself independently, Princess. What I was hoping for was that you might let me into it.'

'I can't do that. It was part of the bargain.'

'What bargain?'

'Meton let us – Clarus and me, I mean – use the kitchen stove to cook up Dassa's medicine and in exchange I allowed him to borrow Dassa and' – she hesitated and swallowed – 'do what he's doing with her.' She must've noticed something about the expression on my and Perilla's faces because she reddened again. 'Oh, no! It's all right, it's not anything terrible, I promise you, and Dassa doesn't mind. Not at all. Meton just doesn't want anyone to know until he's ready, and he doesn't want people to interfere.'

I'd bet! 'And, uh, what sort of time scale are we looking at here?'

'Just a few days. He says he should have her—' She stopped. 'He says he should be finished by then.'

Jupiter on wheels with a squeaker! 'Uh . . . "finished"?'

The Princess's lips clamped.

I glanced at Perilla. 'What do you think, lady?' I said. Cop-outs aren't allowed in the Corvinus household.

She fixed the Princess with her eye. 'Marilla, you swear that what Meton is doing with Dassa is completely above board?'

I raised my own eyes to the ceiling. A clever woman, Perilla, with a vocabulary streets ahead of mine, but sometimes her turn of phrase left something to be desired.

'Oh, yes.'

'And that the situation will last only for a few more days?'

'Yes. Meton has to—' She caught herself again. 'Yes.'

'Has to what?'

'Nothing. But, yes, he'll've done everything he wants to in another few days.'

'Hmm.' She tapped her fingers on the side of her couch. 'Marcus, perhaps you should have a talk with Meton yourself.'

Oh, hell! I sat up. '*Me*? *I* should have a talk?'

'You're the head of household. It's your job.'

'Now look, lady, if you think I'm going to risk—'

'But it's *all right,*' Marilla almost shouted. 'Honestly it is! No one has to talk to anyone!'

'Fine,' I said. 'I'll go for that.'

Perilla looked from the Princess to me. 'Well, if you're certain, Marcus.'

Certain was the last thing I was: just the thought of what that warped, devious bastard might be up to brought me out in a cold sweat. On the other hand, venturing on a disciplinary chat with Meton was the domestic equivalent of invading Parthia. Sure, it might be necessary eventually, but until push really came to shove I'd side with Marilla. Why commit culinary suicide before you had to?

'Let's leave it,' I said.

'Hmm,' Perilla said.

At which point Bathyllus padded in. I turned to him gratefully and got a glare and a sniff in return. Shit; I hadn't had the promised wash and change, had I?

'Dinner will be served in five minutes, sir, if you'd care to come through,' he said. 'I can if you wish put a temporary cover over the upholstery.' Bastard! 'Will the Lady Marilla be eating?'

'Uh, no, little guy, she's already—'

'Of course, Bathyllus,' the Princess said. 'I'm starved.'

I grinned. Well, she had said Clarus's family ate early, and the ride from town would've given her an appetite.

We went into the dining-room. I'd just hefted the jug and followed Perilla when my brain kicked in apropos of nothing with a gobbet of information re Flacchus's murder.

When Perilla and I had been discussing it we hadn't asked ourselves – and we should've done – how Exuperius had known that Flacchus was thinking of spilling the beans; which, of course, was the reason for killing him. Now the question and the answer came together.

I'd told Rutilius about Flacchus's warning myself, not twenty-four hours before Exuperius killed him.

Rutilius might've been practically a son to the old man, and Flacchus might've invented the dream story in the first place to protect him, but that was a clincher. If Flacchus's dream was what had tipped the scales then the only way Exuperius could've known about it was if Rutilius had told him the night before; and *that* meant forget filial loyalty, the bastard was out to save his own neck.

I was committed to Rome tomorrow, sure, but when I got back Spurius Rutilius would have questions to answer.

24

It's a funny thing about holidays in the country, but after only a few days away you feel as if you've been out of circulation for a month. I reached the city late morning, when the streets were at their busiest in any case, but Mars Incline, beyond the Appian Gate, was heaving: it was obviously a local market day, the Incline itself was chock-a-block with bag ladies and corn-dole punters with time on their hands and no work to go to and every square inch of free space either side was taken up with hucksters' stalls. Moving forward was a major problem. First District shoppers don't give way easy, especially to purple-stripers on horseback without the usual slaves with sticks to press the point, and the road-blocking potential of an Incline matron bent on making the best deal she can clinch over a pound of carrots or a couple of artichoke heads should be part of every military textbook.

As a result it took me almost an hour before I won through as far as the Aventine-Caelian gap and got within striking distance of the Circus; by which time I'd been cursed six ways from nothing by three old biddies holding a confab across the road's central gutter, almost had my kneecap broken by a misanthropic water-carrier's pole and been seriously bad-mouthed by a five-year-old pimp who took it as a personal insult that I didn't want a good time with his sister. Also, this being market day, hit with the olfactory equivalent of a fifty-catapult artillery barrage involving everything from a mixture of bring-your-own-jar fish sauce stalls through penfuls of nervous, loose-bowelled livestock to the heady scents of incense and aromatic gums. No wonder Decidius wasn't short of takers for his tarted-up lakeside properties.

You can keep the countryside. It was good to be home.

I was still too early for the consul, but I parked the horse with one of the entrepreneurially minded kids who operate a holding service near the Temple of Venus and took up the slack in Renatius's wineshop with half a jug of Spoletan and a plate of cheese and sausage; so when the time of the appointment finally came and I climbed the steps to the Capitol where Rome's current best and brightest had his office I was feeling comfortably full and at peace with the world. Which happy state lasted about as long as it took for me to find out that the bugger hadn't dragged himself in yet from his own lunch with the head of a Senate trade committee. I sat in the anteroom and fumed while the Greek clerk behind the desk polished his nails and exchanged the latest gossip with his bosom pal from Records. A good hour passed while I learned a lot, inadvertently and unwillingly, about the characters and sexual peccadilloes of the Capitol staff.

'Ah, Marcus, there you are. Haven't been waiting long, I hope?'

I glanced up. Paullus Fabius Persicus was a naturally florid man with a face like an underdone beefsteak, but he was looking even redder than usual. Evidently the lunch had been well on the liquid side; not that I could criticise. 'Uh-uh,' I said. 'Once I'd mastered the knack of thumb-twiddling the time just flew by.'

'Good. Good. We'll go straight in, then.' Skin as thick as a rhino's; or more probably he hadn't even been listening. Consulships, especially senior ones, seem to be hard on the ears while doing wonders for the tongue. 'I can only give you half an hour, I'm afraid, because I have to go out again. A delegation of Egyptian pulse-shippers.'

'Ah . . . yeah. Right.' Jupiter in spangles! All the way from darkest Latium and a backside rubbed nearly raw just to come second to a pack of bean-merchants! Somehow I didn't think Persicus was going to view the situation very seriously. I tagged along behind.

We went through the heavy oak and brass doors into the inner sanctum. Like most bureaucrats' offices it was pretty bare: the real business gets done elsewhere, like in prospective clients' dining-rooms over roast peacock and Caecuban. The only personal decoration was a three-quarters bust of Persicus himself, set against a side wall where it would be visible to both the great man behind the desk and his visitor. Persicus must've seen me looking, because he beamed and laid a hand on what, if the artist had been truthful, ought to have been a receding hairline but was a neat line of crimped marble curls.

'Good likeness, isn't it?' he said.

'Uh . . . yeah.' Well, it would've been if it'd had another couple of chins, a bag under each eye, jowls like a hamster's and an expression that didn't suggest the subject had more between his ears than pillow-feathers. 'Very lifelike.'

Persicus grunted, then moved round behind the desk. 'Got a Naxian artist fella to bang it out for me a couple of months back,' he said. 'Reasonable price, too, which isn't all that usual. You've got to watch these bloody Greeks, rob their own grandmothers if they have the chance.' He settled himself into the chair. 'Now sit yourself down and unburden. Abudius Ruso says you're here to report some nonsense about a plot at the Latin Festival.'

'It isn't nonsense, Paullus,' I said.

'That so?'

As a declaration of belief I wouldn't've rated it more than one out of ten, but there again I hadn't really expected the guy to clutch his forehead and reel backwards in consternation. I took out Marcia's letter and passed it over. 'Maybe you should read this,' I said.

He broke the seal, opened the tablet and began reading. I sat down in the guest chair and waited. Seal or not, I knew what was in the letter, and the old girl hadn't pulled any punches. The consul's vacuous expression changed to a frown. Finally, he looked up.

'Pure conspiracy theory,' he said. 'The bloody woman's gone senile. What's all this rubbish about a dream?'

I sighed mentally: with Persicus you not only had to cross the 't's and dot the 'i's, you had to remind him what the other letters were as well. Thank the gods Rome's security didn't depend on her nominally highest officials any longer, or we'd be short of half an empire before you could say 'Parthia'. 'I think that might just've been a blind on Flacchus's part, Paullus,' I explained carefully. 'He didn't want to come right out with a straight warning.'

'Why the hell not?'

I told him why the hell not; at length and in detail. The whole story, fact and theory; glossing over the tricky point that most of it *was* theory, because with Persicus simplicity was best. There's this game Perilla's clever-clever philosopher pals used to play after dinner back in Athens, where they each thought of someone and the others had to guess who it was from the answers to questions like: 'If he were a fruit, what fruit would he be?' If Persicus had been a mural, he'd've been a blank wall.

To be fair, the guy heard me out before he spoke again. 'Very pretty,' he said. 'Can't see the problem myself, though.'

'You, uh, can't see the problem.' I kept the question mark out of my voice.

'No. Ruso's nailed the bugger who was going to do the dirty deed, what's-his-name the butcher, yes? Or as good as, because he hasn't got a snowball's chance in Hades of getting inside the sanctuary without having his collar felt. Flacchus is dead, for what that's worth in worn coppers. And as far as this Rutilius fella and your Robo-wherever-it-was augur are concerned we can clap the treasonous bastards in jail as a precautionary measure until the festival's over and then examine them at our leisure. So that's the whole crew, isn't it? End of dastardly plot.'

'Paullus,' I said carefully, 'we don't *know* that they were the only ones involved, okay? And in Fufetius's case we don't even know if he's the right man. We can't take the risk. We're not asking you to cancel the festival altogether, just postpone it until later in the year when we've had a chance to clear things up. After all, it doesn't matter when it's held, does it?'

Persicus leaned back. 'Dammit, Marcus, boy, don't you try to teach me my job, all right?' he snapped. 'You want me to call Alcis in and get him to show you my diary for now until New Year's Day? There isn't another date; you couldn't slip a ruddy knife blade between the appointments, and the festival's been arranged for months. If security's all you're worried about I'll clear it with the Palace to detail a century of Praetorians and we'll have the Temple of Latin Jove stitched up tighter than a gnat's bum.'

I winced. Oh, yes, lovely; that would really put the cap on things where the locals were concerned: a squad of Rome's meanest and toughest camped for three days on their most sacred site and answerable to no one but that bastard Macro who only took orders from loopy Prince Gaius. Also if in spite of everything there was an assassination the immediate repercussions didn't bear thinking about, because Macro's men wouldn't just sit on their hands afterwards and send out thank-you notes to the municipalities for their hospitality. If our plotters wanted to stir up local resentment against Rome bringing in the Praetorians would give them it in spades; it might even trigger a general revolt, suicidal though that might be in this day and age.

'Uh . . . I don't think that's a terribly good idea, Paullus,' I said mildly.

'There you are, then.' Persicus sniffed. 'We'll have our Axemen anyway and they're protection enough. Now go home, Marcus, and don't be such a bloody fool. You can tell my Aunt Marcia the same.'

Well, I'd done reason, and that hadn't worked. Maybe losing my temper would help. I didn't have far to go, either.

'The only bloody fool in this room, Paullus,' I said, 'is you.'

Persicus's eyes bulged. '*What?*'

I tried to keep my voice level and matter-of-fact. 'Look, this isn't my concern, right? I'm just the messenger-boy. Abudius Ruso, who's the man on the spot, thinks there's a definite possibility you'll have your stupid fat fucking head beaten in unless someone can shove some sense into it first. That guy is no fool, his opinion is based on hard evidence, and I agree with him one hundred per cent. Where he fell down was believing you might listen to Marcia and me where you wouldn't listen to him. Now personally I don't think you use anything above your neck a lot anyway so it wouldn't be much of a loss, but I'm trying to take the wider view.' I paused: the senior consul's mouth was opening and shutting like a guppy's. 'Postponing the rites is no big deal. Set against what might happen if you don't, or if you celebrate them ringed with enough armed guards to put every back up between here and Velitrae, it's plain common sense. Anyone but a fool would see that in a minute. Which brings me back to the point I made earlier.'

Persicus's mouth closed. Forget red; you could've matched the colour of his face with the Wart's best mantle.

'*How dare you?*' he whispered.

'That's easy, pal. I couldn't live with myself if I didn't.' I tried a defusing grin. 'Come on, Paullus! A month won't make any difference. Forget the diary, put the festival arrangements on hold and cancel a few formal dinners. It'll be good for your waistline, it might save your neck and it'll certainly save a lot of bad feeling. I'm making sense and you know it.'

So much for the grin; he was already on his feet, hamster's jowls quivering. 'Out!' he said. How he managed it with teeth clenched so tight I could see the bones of his jaw behind the flab I didn't know, but he did. 'Get out of here now, Marcus, or I'll have Alcis throw you out!'

That I'd like to see; Persicus's secretary wasn't the throwing-out sort, and I'd bet he wouldn't want to risk breaking one of his carefully polished nails in the process, either. However, there was no point pushing things. I'd given it my best shot, and against stiff-necked stupidity the gods themselves throw their hands up and call in the dice. We'd just have to hope we had the whole case bagged before the time came to put things to the test. I stood up too.

'Fine. Fine,' I said. 'Keep your wig on, friend. I'm going.'

'I shall be writing to Aunt Marcia.' You could've used his tone to freeze rocks on a summer's day in Libya. 'Tell her that. As for young Abudius Ruso, if you see him before I do you can tell him that we'll be having a talk shortly which he will not enjoy. If I needed any confirmation of his unsuitability for office then you've amply provided it. The man's a complete disgrace to his magistracy. Good afternoon, Marcus.'

'Yeah. Right.' I turned to go. 'Enjoy your meeting with the Egyptian bean-merchants.'

But Persicus didn't answer.

Well, that had gone down like a fart at a funeral. Not that, in retrospect, I could've played it any other way, and to be fair to Ruso he hadn't had great hopes of success either. Still, it left a bad taste in the mouth, and with only – what was it? – six more days before the festival we hadn't much time to play with. Of course, there was always the chance that Persicus could be right: the plot – if there was a plot – was dead as a pickled oyster, and Ruso was chasing shadows; also, that a dozen beefy Axemen was all the protection needed. However, we hadn't got even one genuine conspirator under lock and key yet, and as for the Axemen they couldn't be on duty all the time. A killing at the ceremony itself would be most effective symbolically, sure, but there was no reason to think it was the only option and they had a whole three days to play with. The game wasn't worth the candle.

Like I'd said to Persicus, though, this whole thing was none of my concern; I was only the messenger. Fair enough: the messenger was knackered, he had another twenty-mile ride ahead of him tomorrow and that frustrating little interview had left him with a throat as dry as a short-legged camel's scrotum. Time for the other half jug, followed by a trip up to the Caelian with a takeaway cookshop dinner for a long relaxing steam in the bath-suite and an early night.

I wasn't feeling too chirpy as I made my way back to Renatius's wineshop. If that was my day in Rome then I needn't've bothered.

25

The bath and early night were a good idea, or maybe I was just getting more used to this riding lark, because I wasn't as stiff the next morning as I thought I'd be. Unlike Perilla I don't usually go a bomb for breakfast, and in any case riding with a full stomach's never a very good idea, but I had the kitchen skivvies make me up a packed lunch with a travelling flask of wine and shoved it into the saddlebag just in case.

Checking out this Fufetius Albus guy might be a sine qua non, but it was also a real bugger. Roboraria was on the Latin Road, which forked off to the left on the city outskirts and ran inland to the north of the Alban Mount itself; worse, it lay past the turnoff that led down through the foothills to Castrimoenium, so I'd not only be heading in the wrong direction but I'd have to retrace part of the route before we were back on the right track again. Still, that couldn't be helped; and like Persicus had said if our Roborarian augur did turn out to have form then we were quids in as far as the Latin Festival business was concerned. I'd just have to grit my teeth and add a few more saddle-sores to the account.

I was lucky with the weather, though. I'd made an early start, just after dawn, and by the time Rome would really have begun to warm up I was well into the cooler hill country with its rolling stretches of woodland, pasture and vineyards. Traffic down the Latin Road tends to be heavier than it is on the Appian Way because when the latter gets nearer the coast it passes through the marshy flatlands of the south-western plains, and although the road itself is well enough maintained that's not a healthy place to be, especially if – as most travellers have to do – you have to make a stop between Three Inns and Tarracum. It could be just a story, sure, and I've no experience of it myself, but some places the water's so full of little worms you have to pass it through a wine-sieve before you can even boil it.

I got to Roboraria just after noon. The town isn't all that big, but being on the main drag – unlike Castrimoenium and Bovillae – there were two or three meatball and rissole stalls outside the town gates catering for the cheap end of the travelling market, and at the last of these a balding old grandma with serious skin problems and a bad case of mumbling halitosis gave me directions to the augur's place. That turned out to be down a cul-de-sac in the more upmarket part of town, next to the fenced-off shrine to one of the local water nymphs: an old two-up, two-down property behind a railinged wall, with a shady garden in front. I tied my horse to the railings, opened the gate and went in. A couple of kids – they looked maybe five and three – were playing with a puppy on the doorstep. They looked up round-eyed.

'Does Fufetius Albus live here?' I asked.

The elder blinked at me, then without a word ran inside, leaving his brother staring. The puppy waddled over and sniffed at my ankles. I reached down and tickled it under the chin, bowling it over. The bigger kid reappeared, sucking his thumb and clinging to the tunic-skirts of a young woman who could've been the living image of the nymph next door.

'Yes?' she said.

'Ah . . . I was looking for someone called Fufetius Albus,' I said.

'That's my grandfather.' She smiled. 'I don't know if he's awake – he has a nap after lunch – but we can certainly see. What was your business with him?'

Hell; this didn't sound too promising, I could tell that already. 'I just wanted a brief word,' I said. 'About the Latin Festival. Agilleius Mundus down in Bovillae gave me his name.'

She frowned and wiped her hands on her tunic; I'd guess she'd been doing the washing-up when the half-pint thumb-sucker had fetched her. 'The Latin Festival? Grandfather's had nothing to do with that for a long time. Not for the past ten or twelve years. As for talking, you can try but I don't think . . .' She hesitated. 'Well. If you'd like to follow me anyway.'

The kid went back to the puppy and she led me round the corner of the house into another part of the garden. There was a chair set out under a spreading fig tree, and if the lady could've doubled for a nymph the old guy sitting in it would've done for Tithonus. He was scrawny as a plucked chicken, he had more wrinkles than a pickled walnut and the hands folded in his lap were nothing but skin, bone and gravemarks. He was snoring gently.

The woman laid a hand on his shoulder. 'Grandpa?' she said. 'You've got a visitor.'

The snores broke off and his eyes opened. There were no pupils, just a white film covering both the eyeballs. Forget Tithonus; what we had here was Tiresias on a very bad day. As well as being ancient Fufetius Albus was stone blind. His granddaughter glanced at me.

'Uh . . . Marcus Valerius Corvinus, sir,' I said. 'I'm staying down in Castrimoenium.'

He didn't answer, just moved his head slowly from side to side like an old tortoise. A thread of spittle ran down his jaw from his open mouth. The woman took a napkin from under the chair and dabbed at it. Shit. Add 'ga-ga' to the list.

'Yes, I thought so,' she said. 'He gets a little lost when his nap's disturbed. Maybe I can help you instead.'

I had a sinking feeling in my stomach. Having seen Fufetius Albus, I doubted that very much. If this old guy was the spearhead of a plot to assassinate the Roman consul then

I'd eat my sandals. Still, there was always Perilla's idea that he might be able to shed some light on the plot itself.

'Uh . . . the name Flacchus ring a bell with you?' I said. 'Lucius Herdonius Flacchus?'

'No. Should it?'

'How about Spurius Rutilius?' No response. 'A butcher called Exuperius?'

She was looking even more mystified. 'No. Grandfather's never mentioned any of those men. Mind you, since his stroke six months ago he hasn't spoken much at all. You say this has something to do with the festival?'

I sighed; there went the ball-game. 'Yeah. Only it doesn't matter now. Thanks all the same, but I think maybe I've had a wasted journey.'

She pushed a lock of hair out of her eyes. 'But you haven't explained what you want!'

True; but at that precise moment all I wanted was to go somewhere quiet where I could beat my head against a rock. 'There isn't any point, lady,' I said. 'I made a mistake, that's all. No eggs broken.' I looked back at the old man; his eyes were closing and he was nodding again, mouth still open. 'I'm sorry to've disturbed you.'

'Well, if you're sure.' The woman's face still wore a puzzled expression, which didn't altogether surprise me: it couldn't be very often she got mad Romans trailing out to Roboraria just for the fun of a one-way five-second conversation with her senile grandfather. 'I'll see you out.'

We left the old guy at the start of his first snore and were headed back to the gate when I thought of one last angle I could try. 'There, uh, wouldn't be any other Fufetii around here, would there?' I said. 'Your father, maybe?'

'No, Father's dead. He and my mother died within a month of each other six years ago. There's my two uncles, of course. They're the only ones on my side of the family left.'

Hey! Maybe the journey hadn't been wasted after all! 'Yeah?' I said. 'They local men?'

She shook her head. 'I've never even seen either of them. Uncle Quintus is with the Sixth Legion in Spain and Uncle Aulus married a Sicilian woman. He lives in Syracuse.' Bugger; so much for hope. 'Valerius Corvinus, I thought you wanted my grandfather specifically. Why this interest in our family, please?'

We'd reached the gate; the two kids and the puppy had gone. 'No reason,' I said. 'Not now. Like I say, I made a mistake. When your grandfather wakes up, give him my apologies for disturbing his nap.'

I untied my horse, mounted up and trotted back the way I'd come, leaving her staring. Yeah, well; around here they probably thought most Romans were three-quarters the way mad anyway, and I'd just helped confirm the general opinion.

That was that, then; scratch Fufetius Albus from the conspiracy list.

So where did we go from here?

The short-term answer was home. It'd been a long, hard day and it was well after dark when I got back to the farm. Marcia had told the slaves to fire up the bathroom furnace, so I lay on a bench and sweated away the grime and stiffness for a good hour before changing into a fresh tunic and carrying what was left of Bathyllus's welcome-home jug into the dining-room. Meton being Meton, I'd expected something cold, or maybe reheated leftovers at best, but whatever he was up to with Dassa must've put the guy into an unusually philanthropic mood because there was a hot chicken stew, green vegetables with pepper and thyme and a basket of freshly made rolls. My stomach rumbled.

The Princess and Marcia had gone to bed long since, but Perilla was still up, lying on one of the couches, reading by the light of a six-lamp candelabrum. She laid the book-roll aside.

'Feeling better after your bath, Marcus?' she said.

'Yeah.' I set the wine jug and cup on the table, kissed her then stretched out and helped myself to the chicken. 'Glad to be back.'

'How did the interview with Cousin Paullus go?'

'It didn't.' I spooned vegetables on to my plate. 'He threw me out.'

'Oh.' She frowned. 'So it was a wasted trip?'

'The festival's still on.' I tore off a piece of bread, soaked it in the gravy and chewed. 'And I don't think either Marcia or me are exactly persona grata with the higher echelons of Roman government at present. Let alone Abudius Ruso. I wouldn't like to be in that poor bugger's sandals when Persicus hauls him on to the carpet.'

'Didn't Aunt Marcia's letter have any effect?'

'He thinks the old girl's senile.' I sighed. 'Well, we did our best. And Persicus may be right, this could just be a whole lot of fuss over nothing.'

'You think so?'

I swallowed a mouthful of wine. 'No. There was a plot, at least, that I'd stake a year's income on, and my bet is it's still running. Exuperius is out of it, sure, but he wasn't the only one involved.' I spooned up a piece of chicken. 'They catch him yet, by the way?'

'Not as far as I know. Libanius hasn't been in touch, certainly.' Perilla shifted on her couch. 'How about Fufetius? Did you see him?'

'Yeah.' In between mouthfuls, I told her about my visit to Roboraria. 'If Marcia's senile then that guy's in the vegetable class. We may still be looking for a Fufetius, but if Fufetius Albus is the one we want after all then I'll pack in sleuthing and take up crochet. In his condition he couldn't mastermind a trip to the bathroom.'

The lady twisted her stray curl. 'I've been thinking about that,' she said.

'Is that so, now? And?'

'It's not a common name, but it certainly is Latin. And it has . . . connotations.'

'What kind of connotations?'

'They suggested themselves when you first mentioned it. The thought did occur, but since you told me that there was a real candidate I assumed it was coincidence. Especially because, as I say, the name is still current.'

I set my spoon down. 'Lady, you're not making sense.'

She shook her head. 'I'm sorry. Fufetius – Mettius Fufetius – was a historical figure. One of the early Latin heroes.'

'Go on.'

She smiled. 'I shouldn't need to. You really don't know your history, do you, dear? Mettius Fufetius was given the Latin leadership at the time of the Alban war with Rome under King Tullus Hostilius. We won, of course, and Fufetius was betrayed and executed; after which the town of Alba was destroyed and its people transferred to Rome.'

Holy gods! I stared at her, chicken stew forgotten. 'You're telling me Fufetius isn't a real person?'

'Marcus, I don't know. It's just an idea. Certainly, as I say, Fufetius was a historical character and viewed as a national hero by the Latins for his resistance to Rome, but the name is still extant. It's a possibility, no more.'

Shit; if Perilla was right then we were into a completely different ball-game here. 'Then "Fufetius" might not be a real name at all? It could be an alias?'

'Indeed.'

It fitted; the conspiracy part, sure, because adopting the name of a Latin hero might well be just what a modern-day anti-Roman fanatic might do, and it'd explain why, for example, neither Flacchus's major-domo nor Libanius had recognised it as anyone they knew. On the other hand, it left a whole load of questions unanswered.

'Marcus?'

'Hmm?'

'You're not listening. I asked you if I was making sense.'

I frowned into my wine cup. 'You tell me, lady. Oh, yeah, sure, the alias bit, you may have something there. But it still leaves us with the problem of who the guy is.'

Perilla sniffed. 'Naturally, dear. I never said it didn't.'

'Uh-uh. I don't mean it that way. I'm thinking of Flacchus's message.'

'How so?'

'If he wrote 'Fufetius' knowing it was only an alias then what the hell was he playing at? The guy wasn't in the Delphic Oracle business. If Fufetius were someone involved with the conspiracy in some way – as he had to be – then presumably Flacchus knew who he was; who he *really* was, aliases aside. So why faff around creating a mystery when he knew damned well no one would understand him?'

'Ah. I see your point.' Perilla twisted her curl. 'Perhaps, then, he *didn't* know who he was. The name Fufetius was all he had; perhaps because – if he did derive his information from Rutilius – it was all Rutilius had given him.'

'Lady, that won't work. Even if he did get the name second-hand, why should Rutilius be coy about it when he'd been so open about everything else? Rutilius would know who the man himself was, and for him to use an alias to Flacchus under the circumstances would be just plain pointless.'

'*Would* Rutilius know? Necessarily?'

'Sure he would. Castrimoenium's a small place. If Fufetius were a local, he'd have to know him, alias or not.'

'And if he weren't? If he were a stranger?'

'The same applies. Oh, sure, any stranger could turn up and give a false name instead of his real one and no one would be any the wiser, but this isn't Rome, we're dealing with a small, tight community where everyone knows everyone else. Strangers here have a high profile, and one who used two different names at two different times would be sussed pretty quickly. Also, where the conspiracy itself was concerned a total stranger just wouldn't make the starting line for inclusion. *Someone* on the inside would have to know and vouch for him, and before that happened he'd be strictly vetted. So we're back to the original question: if Fufetius isn't a real name then why should Flacchus write it?'

'You think it is, then?'

I rubbed my temples. 'Lady, I don't know. If it is then it'd make things a lot simpler. After all, you said yourself the name still exists. All I know is that our Fufetius isn't the old augur over in Roboraria.'

Perilla was twisting her curl again. 'There is another possibility,' she said slowly.

'Yeah?'

'It could be a nickname.'

My attention sharpened. 'How do you mean?'

'Flacchus's family name was Herdonius, and Herdonius, too, was a Latin hero, executed by King Tarquin. If our Fufetius were someone Flacchus knew well, and had done for a long time, and he held the same pro-Latin opinions as Flacchus, he might have given the man the name himself as a sort of kinship link. Or at least thought privately in those terms.'

'Perilla, that doesn't make sense!'

'Actually, it does. If Flacchus thought of the man as Fufetius in his own mind then it's not beyond the bounds of possibility that when he was dying that was the name which suggested itself.'

I shifted irritably on my couch. 'What about the Delphic Oracle angle? Why the hell should he use a nickname at all?'

'We're assuming Flacchus wrote the name on the tablet as a . . . well, as a sort of message from beyond the grave to his avengers, yes? That he was identifying, if not his actual murderer, then someone involved with the plot who had to be tracked down.'

'Right. So?'

'What if that wasn't his intention at all? In fact, the complete opposite?'

'Uh . . . you mean he *didn't* want the guy found,' I said neutrally.

'Well, yes. In a way.'

'Perilla, what the *hell* are you maundering about? I've heard some bloody stupid theories in my time but—'

'I did say "in a way", dear.'

'Gods, lady, if he didn't want the guy found then why the fuck write *anything*?'

'Don't swear, Marcus.'

'Yeah, okay, I'm sorry.' I subsided. 'Still, it's a fair question. Why should he go to the trouble of using his last moments writing down the name of a guy he didn't want traced?'

'Because he was an old man, dying, and he forgot,' she said quietly.

That brought me up short. 'Forgot what?'

'We're assuming that Flacchus meant the message for the authorities. Perhaps he didn't. Perhaps he was talking to the only other person present.'

'*Trupho*?'

'No, not Trupho.' She hesitated. 'Or at least not as such. That's what I meant when I said Flacchus had forgotten. If Fufetius was a private name, his old major-domo would have recognised it where an outsider – even, probably, Libanius – would not; and that was the whole point. Writing it – *using* it – was Flacchus's final appeal to Fufetius not to continue with the plot, in a way that would not reveal his proper name to the authorities. Only, of course, Trupho didn't understand the reference either.'

Jupiter! Talk about devious! Yeah, well, complicated as it was, the theory had a sort of twisted logic to it. And it would certainly cut the Gordian knot. 'You . . . ah . . . have anyone in mind?' I said.

'Yes, of course. Rutilius.'

I nodded. Yeah; it would have to be Rutilius, and we kept coming back to him anyway.

'What do you think of it, Marcus? As a theory?'

'Ah . . . it has its points,' I said. I could be diplomatic too, and if personally I thought the lady was being too damned clever for her own good saying something like that to Perilla was never a smart move. Me, I'd keep looking for a real Fufetius. 'Certainly we need another talk with our friendly blacksmith.'

'Oh, yes. If nothing else he must have been involved in the conspiracy. And if he isn't Fufetius himself then he may know who is.'

'Right.' I glanced at the food on the table. I hadn't eaten all that much in the end, but the combination of the bath, the wine and the brainwork had knocked me for six, and suddenly I could hardly keep my eyes open. 'Uh . . . look. You want to call it a night, Perilla? We'll take it from there in the morning.'

'Yes, of course, dear.' She reached for her book-roll. 'You must be exhausted.'

Where Rutilius was concerned I didn't know it then, but I was already too late.

26

My muscles weren't as stiff as I'd thought they'd be the next day, and I was obviously developing calluses where it mattered as far as riding was concerned. I had a fairly large breakfast – the reheated chicken stew from the night before plus a couple of the rolls – and headed into Castrimoenium.

It wasn't all that early when I arrived – I'd allowed myself a long lie and breakfast had taken longer than usual – but the forge was empty and the fire hadn't been lit. Hell's teeth; first Exuperius, now Rutilius. Sure, he could simply be out and about somewhere making a delivery, but I wouldn't mind betting that the guy had done a runner.

I left my horse tethered and knocked at the door of the house. There was no answer: Brunna and the old man must still be down in Bovillae. I knocked again and then tried the door. It was open.

I went inside; which was when I noticed the flies. Rutilius was fairly obvious too, though. He was sprawled face down on the floor in front of the chair Harpax had been sitting in the first time I'd visited. I'd've lost my bet. Our conspiratorial blacksmith wouldn't be running anywhere, ever again.

I knelt, caught him by the shoulder and heaved him on to his back. He'd been stabbed twice in the chest. The stiffness had left the corpse, and the bloodstains on the floor beneath him were dark and dry.

I sat back on my heels to think. Bugger; double bugger. There was a chair behind me, facing Harpax's, that hadn't been there the last time I was here; probably brought in from another room, although there were benches against the wall. A visitor's chair. Okay. Say Rutilius had had a visitor and they'd sat down to talk; the visitor had stood up, Rutilius had followed suit and the other guy had stabbed him . . .

Yeah, well, as a simple working scenario it would do as well as any. The precise circumstances didn't really matter; whatever the exact truth, from the undisturbed look of the room the big blacksmith hadn't suspected a thing until the knife went in, by which time it was too late.

I left the corpse and went back out to the forge. The charcoal had burned completely to a fine ash and there was no trace of heat at all in the stonework. Yeah, that matched with what was inside: the murder had to've happened longer ago than just last night. During the previous day was unlikely because the chances were that Rutilius would've been out here working, so my bet for the when of things would be two nights ago. A night-time killing would make more sense in any case; it wasn't a salubrious neighbourhood, and people who don't have the cash to waste on lamp oil tend to go to bed with the sun, so there'd be less likelihood of the killer being seen. On the other hand, Rutilius had been fully clothed, so either it hadn't been too late on in the evening or the man had been expected.

'Valerius Corvinus? What're you doing here? And where's Spurius?'

I turned. Brunna and her father were standing in the doorway. Brunna was holding the baby, and the kid who'd been operating the bellows was picking his nose and chewing on a bread ring at the same time. Behind them was a panniered donkey.

Oh, hell. This I didn't need.

'Ah . . . maybe you'd like to come in here for a moment,' I said.

Brunna frowned. 'Why would we want to do that? And I'd like an answer, please. Where's Spurius?'

There wasn't any point in covering, especially since when they went to the house they'd find the truth out anyway. 'I'm sorry, Brunna,' I said. 'Your husband's dead.'

She looked blank. 'Dead? How can he be dead?'

Harpax stepped forward quickly, edging her aside. 'What's going on here, Corvinus?' he said.

'I don't know.' Gods; I could really have done without this. Perilla's the tactful one in the family, she'd've handled things a lot better. Still, at least I'd been the one to find the body. Ten minutes later and it would've been Brunna herself. 'I just arrived. Your son-in-law's inside. He's been stabbed.'

Brunna gave a moan and turned, stumbling, heading in the direction of the house.

'Stop her, Titus!' Harpax snapped over his shoulder. The bellows kid, who'd been staring at me wide-eyed, swallowed and rushed after his mother. Harpax turned back to me. 'Now maybe you'd best tell me more,' he said softly. 'And make it quick before Titus brings her back.'

He'd taken the news on board with hardly a flicker. Yeah, I'd forgotten; the guy'd been a soldier, a standard-carrier at that; some things you don't lose, because they're in the bones. Old though he was, the eyes that were skewering me were level and hard, and not an old man's at all.

'There isn't much more to tell,' I said. 'I only got here a few minutes ago. Rutilius wasn't around so I checked the house and found him lying on the floor with a couple of stab wounds in his chest. My guess is he's been dead a day, easy. That's as much as I know.'

It was pretty clear Harpax wasn't satisfied. He threw a quick look over his shoulder. I could hear Brunna sobbing, but she was still in the alleyway so Titus must've caught her in time.

'Wait there,' he growled. 'And don't move.'

You didn't argue with a tone like that. I waited. It took

a good ten minutes for Harpax to reappear. He was alone this time, and he looked grim. 'Some things aren't a woman's concern,' he said. 'Or a child's. I've left her and the boy with a neighbour in the next street.' He straightened his shoulders. 'Right then, Valerius Corvinus. Let's you and me go and see to Spurius. And after that we need to have a little talk.'

The corpse lay as I'd left it, blank eyes staring up at the ceiling. Harpax paused in the doorway, made a clicking noise with his tongue and then without a word went through into the other room where I could hear him rummaging about. He came back with a blanket, a bronze bucket, a scrap of rag and a scrubbing brush.

'Stand clear,' he said.

I watched while he moved the body to one side, straightened it, closed its eyes and covered it with the blanket, every movement gentle but brisk and efficient, like he'd done it a hundred times before. Then he used the scrubbing brush and water on the bloodstains and mopped the floor dry with the rag. Finally, he grunted and stood up.

'That'll do him for the present,' he said, 'till he can be washed and laid out decent. Now, Corvinus. I want information.'

I glanced down at the corpse. 'Uh . . . shouldn't we contact the authorities? Libanius, maybe?'

'Fuck Libanius. He can't do anything, Spurius is dead and he's nothing but an old fool. You're the man I want. Who did it?'

The hairs stirred on my neck. There wasn't anything in the words themselves to suggest it, but judging by the tone he could just as well have said, 'Who do I kill?'

'Uh . . . I don't know,' I said.

'Is that so, now?' Harpax fixed me with a contemplative eye and sucked a tooth. 'Then we'll have to find out before we're much older, won't we? That's your job, boy. You're good at asking questions. Ask me any you like if you think they'll help to nail the bastard and I'll answer them if I can.'

'Ah . . . right. Right.' Well, that was one good thing; I couldn't complain about lack of willingness in the Rutilius household now. 'My bet is your son-in-law was involved in a plot to kill the senior Roman consul at the Latin Festival. That was probably why he was murdered, to stop him fingering the guy behind it. You know anything about that?'

Harpax's jaw had dropped. 'You serious?' he said.

'Sure I'm serious.'

He shook his head firmly. 'Then you're not as smart as I thought, Corvinus. Nothing like it. Spurius wouldn't have no truck with killing, not consuls nor no one else. I'm telling you that straight. And if he did and I found out I'd've stopped him myself. The gods know you Roman bastards have your faults, but I spent twenty years in your army and that doesn't go for nothing. So your answer's no. Ask again.'

Shit. He wasn't covering, either; I knew the truth when I heard it. Still, I couldn't be wrong, not completely: the theory made too much sense.

'Okay,' I said. 'So he may not have gone the full distance. All the same, he was mixed up with some sort of anti-Roman movement somewhere. Am I right?'

Harpax chuckled. 'If you mean Flacchus's lot, then sure. For a time, anyway. Although "anti-Roman movement"'s overcalling it because the only movement those buggers're capable of is all wind.'

I had to fight to keep my face and voice expressionless. 'Uh . . . "Flacchus's lot"?' I said.

He made as if to spit, then changed his mind. 'The Alban Brotherhood, they call themselves. Load of bloody nonsense, but there isn't any harm in them. Or wasn't, anyway, when Spurius was a member.'

'Uh . . . tell me more, pal,' I said carefully.

Maybe it was something in my voice or my look, because Harpax suddenly frowned: the guy might be no great brain – he had other strengths – but he was no fool, either.

'You think they had something to do with it?' he said. 'Spurius's death, I mean?'

'Yeah,' I said. 'Yeah, I think they might have, at that.'

'Corvinus, they're just a bunch of jokers! Oh, sure, that Exuperius is a real bastard, but even he wouldn't go the length of killing a consul.'

Jupiter! Things were going too fast for me here. 'Hold on just one second, pal,' I said. 'Exuperius is one of this brotherhood of yours?'

'He was in it almost from the start.'

Sweet holy gods! 'You know Flacchus is dead, don't you? And that Exuperius killed him?'

He stared at me slack-jawed. '*What?*'

'It happened three days ago. You didn't know?'

'We were with Spurius's sister and we've hardly been out of the house. Flacchus was murdered?'

'Yeah. By Exuperius. The guy's major-domo practically witnessed it.'

'Mars's holy balls!' Ex-standard-bearer or not, I'd rocked him. Harpax was looking at me like I'd just broken out in green and yellow stripes.

'So if Exuperius was a member of the Alban Brotherhood,' I said, 'then you can see how they might be, uh, relevant, right?'

'Yeah. Yeah.' He was still looking fazed. 'Shit. I'm sorry, Corvinus. You go ahead with your questions, boy.'

'Okay. Before Flacchus died he managed to write down the name Fufetius. That—'

I stopped; I'd been going to ask if the name rang a bell with him at all, but there wasn't any point because he'd sworn under his breath.

'All right, that's enough,' he said quietly. 'You've convinced me.' His eyes had gone steel-hard. 'Oh, yes. All the same, no more questions. I start at the beginning and take you all the way through while you keep your mouth shut and listen. Agreed?'

'Suits me,' I said.

'Fine.' He jerked his head towards one of the chairs. 'Sit down, then. It's a long story and there's no point you standing, although I'll stand myself if you don't mind. I think better on my feet.'

I sat. We faced each other over Rutilius's shrouded corpse.

'It started about a year and a half ago. Spurius'd always been keen on history, Latin history, which was why old Flacchus took an interest in him. You knew that already, right?'

'Sure.'

'Okay. So eighteen months back Flacchus tells Spurius he's starting a private club for – and I'm quoting Spurius here – "the conservation and promulgation of all things Latin".' His lips twisted like he'd bitten on something sour. 'Me – well, he's dead but I'm telling you straight, Corvinus, I'd no time for Flacchus. You get these types sometimes, windy, money to burn, time on their hands, smart enough as far as book-learning goes but with as much sense of the real world as a new-born babe. And they like playing games; games that make them feel big and important in their own heads. Know what I mean?'

'Uh-huh. And the game Flacchus was playing was Conspiracy, right?'

'You could say.' Harpax scowled. 'Although that's overcalling it by a long chalk, mind, because the club meetings were all piss and wind. There wasn't anything the authorities would've lost five minutes' sleep over if they'd known, nothing at all. All the same, the old bugger liked to pretend there was because that was part of the fun.' I nodded. Yeah; I could just imagine. It fitted Flacchus's character; he was a talker, not a doer, and he'd like to feel he was being terribly daring. 'Spurius wouldn't've touched the whole silly fucking business with a ten-foot pole, only Flacchus'd been good to him so he went to the meetings every month and tried to keep a straight face.'

'He told you about them? The meetings, I mean?'

'Sure he did. Even after Flacchus started playing silly buggers with oaths of secrecy. Mostly they were just a rehash of old grudges and old history, anyway.' He glanced down at the body. 'We were close, Spurius and me, very close, like son and father. Better. He wasn't a gabber, far from it, but he trusted me and he needed someone to talk to. Brunna was no use; you don't pass on secrets to a woman however bloody stupid they are. Me, I wouldn't even be telling you now if he wasn't dead and I didn't think it'd help you find the bastard who killed him.'

'So what about the members of this club?' I said.

'There were ten or a dozen at first; Flacchus's cronies mostly whose arms he'd twisted to get their support, but a few locals who turned up out of curiosity. Including, early on, your pal Exuperius. That lasted, oh, maybe five or six months, until the novelty wore off. You know these societies yourself, Corvinus.' Yeah, I did; all-male clubs with silly names like the Sons of Neptune or the Arcadian Swains. The buggers never actually *do* anything, they just talk in circles, pass resolutions and dress up in funny clothes to get pissed once a year. There's no harm in them; like Harpax said they're just silly ego-boosters. 'Finally there were just four left: Flacchus himself, Spurius, Exuperius and that bastard Bolanus.'

Everything went very still. 'Uh . . . Bolanus was a member of the Alban Brotherhood?' I said.

'Flacchus asked him special.'

Oh, gods! 'You know why?'

'Sure. Flacchus was a prime snob, and Bolanus could trace his ancestors back to the Latin kings. Never mind that he cared less about Latin culture than I do, he had to be in because of who he was. Spurius didn't like it either, but he'd a lot of time for Flacchus and if that was what the old man wanted it was fine with him. Understand?'

'Yeah. Yeah, I understand.' I felt numb. Sweet holy Jupiter, I'd got my link!

'Anyway, six months back Bolanus brought his new fiancée along. Flacchus wasn't too keen on that, but there wasn't much he could do.'

This time I was beyond shock. I just stared at him.

'*Sulpicia?* Sulpicia was a member too?'

'Sure. Bolanus didn't give Flacchus any choice. He told him it was either both of them or neither, and Roman-born or not she was just as much a Latin at heart as Flacchus. The old man gave way, which was when Spurius began to have second thoughts himself about the whole business. The lad is – *was* – a lot like me in many ways. Women are all right in their place, but they're different creatures after all. Sometimes them and men don't mix. You with me?'

'Uh . . . yeah. Yeah, sure. I'm with you, pal.' Oh, hell; forget the can of worms. This was like watching the lid of Pandora's box lift and all the creepy-crawlies spill out. 'What about Fufetius? When did he turn up?'

'Just wait, Corvinus, all in good time. I'm not telling you this for fun. We do it once, and we do it right, okay? Because you're the bugger with the brains and I'm expecting you to put them to good use. You got any questions along the road, that's fine with me, you ask them, but we take it by the book.'

'Fine,' I said. 'So there're five members to the brotherhood: Flacchus, Rutilius, Exuperius, Bolanus and Sulpicia. We're talking about – what – January/February here? Five, six months ago?'

'Right. That was when things began to get tricky. Up to now, it's been Flacchus's show; for what that's worth, because it hasn't been all that much. When Sulpicia joins the group the balance shifts and she and Bolanus begin to take over. Exuperius is no problem because he's fallen for her in a big way and she's leading him by the nose. Spurius – well, like I say Spurius is thinking of dropping out in any case, so it's three against one. Anyway, Bolanus finds a place about two miles outside town on the Caba road – a farmhouse that's been lying empty for years – and they hold the meetings there instead of at Flacchus's villa, the night of every full moon. The first of these, Bolanus and Sulpicia turn up with a stranger in tow. They tell Flacchus and

Spurius the stranger's name is Fufetius, only it's not his real name, right? And the stranger's wearing a heavy cloak and a mask so his face is hidden.'

'A mask?'

Harpax's hand sketched the shape on his own face. 'One of these fancy parade helmets with a full visor to the chin and slits for eyes. You with me?'

I nodded. So Flacchus hadn't had anything to go by but the name, and under the cloak and the mask Fufetius could've been anyone because even the voice would be different.

'Carry on,' I said.

'So Bolanus tells Flacchus he's fed up faffing around with words and theory. The Latin Festival's coming up, maybe it's time to make a bit of a splash, make the Latins sit up and take notice. Oh, no' – I'd opened my own mouth to say something – 'not your business with the consul. I told you, Spurius wouldn't've had no truck with murder, nor would Flacchus. Bolanus wasn't suggesting nothing violent, just a bit of a lark, something that'd leave the stuck-up Romans with egg over their faces and give the locals a laugh. Then he hands over to Fufetius, because he's the man with the ideas. They're pretty simple stuff: letting the animals out of their pens, putting burrs under their tails to make them bolt, hiding the sacrificial implements, that sort of thing. Just a bit of fun that won't do any real harm but will turn the ceremony into a Winter Festival farce. Exuperius'll be the linchpin; he'll apply for a job as sacrificer's assistant, and being a local butcher he'll get it, no problem.

'And Flacchus agreed?'

'He didn't like it more than half, boy. All the same, there wasn't much he could do. Especially since he'd been slagging the Romans off for arrogant bastards himself over the past year and saying how they should be taken down a peg. Now he'd been taken at his word there was no way he could back down. And so long as the thing was played as a joke he'd no comeback. There'd be trouble, sure, but if Exuperius was careful there was no reason why the authorities'd ever be able to fix responsibility where it belonged.'

'So when did the plan change? To assassinating the consul?'

Harpax shrugged. 'That I can't tell you, Corvinus. If it did I don't know nothing about it, nor did Spurius because that was his last meeting. Oh, he'd no objection to seeing Romans made fools of, but he had Brunna and the kids to think about and he wasn't going to get involved in any half-assed scheme that might end up in trouble. He wished them luck and left them to it. And that's as much as I know.'

I sat back. The time scale worked, sure: exactly how and when Flacchus had discovered that Fufetius had his own hidden agenda I didn't know, but I'd bet Exuperius'd been the leak. He, certainly, would have to have known well in advance, he wouldn't've had any qualms about murder and he wouldn't be averse to bragging about his role, either. Which raised another interesting question: to what extent Bolanus and Sulpicia were in on things. Because if they were then . . .

Oh, shit. Oh, holy gods.

Harpax was staring at me. 'Something wrong?' he said.

'The . . . uh . . . night Bolanus was killed. It was a full moon, right?'

'Sure.'

'So there would've been a meeting of the brotherhood?'

'Yeah. Yeah, there would. At sunset. That was the usual time.'

And Bolanus had died less than two hours later, when he arrived back home from wherever he'd been and was almost immediately yanked out to the loggia for a rendezvous with Sulpicia, who he'd just left, arranged by a note that had only reached the villa after Bolanus himself . . .

Sweet gods, it couldn't be coincidence; no way could it be coincidence. One got you ten that had been the evening Bolanus – and presumably Flacchus – found out what Fufetius was really planning: accidentally or on purpose I didn't know, and it didn't matter anyway, although Exuperius couldn't've blown the gaff because he was shut up in his Bovillae broom closet. The crucial difference was that while Flacchus hadn't had the guts to respond, Bolanus had. A joke was one thing – and I'd bet that had been all Bolanus had seen the business as, right from the start – but assassination was something else. So the guy had stormed out of the meeting threatening that if Fufetius didn't call the whole thing off he'd go to the authorities. And that that was what had killed him.

Which raised the question of Sulpicia . . .

She had to have been in on the murder. She and Fufetius had set it up together: lured Bolanus into a meeting in the loggia and then killed him. It couldn't've happened any other way.

So; I'd got half my killer. But who the hell was Fufetius?

'You all right, Corvinus?' Harpax was watching me.

'Uh . . . yeah. Yeah.' I struggled to maintain the neutral tone. This I'd keep to myself for the moment: I could still be wrong somehow, and in his present mood I didn't want Harpax going off at half-cock. 'One more question, pal. Just a minor detail. What about the altar?'

Harpax blinked. 'What altar?'

Oh, right; he'd been in Bovillae, he wouldn't know. 'Someone smashed the altar of the Goddess Rome in the market square four days back. I thought Rutilius might've been responsible.'

Harpax shook his head. 'Not him. Oh, he'd no time for Romans, but he was a lot like Flacchus in that way; for all his talk he wouldn't actually have done anything. Like I say, it was why he left the brotherhood. Maybe it was Exuperius, or maybe it was some other bastard who just doesn't like Rome. There're enough around.' He glanced back down at Rutilius's corpse and sucked on a tooth. 'So that's it, Corvinus. All I can tell you, or almost all.'

'Almost?'

'You've got everything Spurius told me. Past that, you're

on your own. There's one more thing, though, and that's mine to tell.'

'Yeah?'

'I didn't say nothing about it before, because it's part and parcel of the story you've just heard, and that was Spurius's secret, not mine. Clear?' I nodded. 'So, then. We were out hunting – Spurius and me – the night Bolanus died, in the woods near the lakeside road. Spurius was elsewhere checking traps, but me, I was near the road itself. It must've been a couple of hours after sunset, maybe a bit less, when I hear a horse coming down going hell for leather in the direction of town. I look out just as it passes, and the rider's got a cavalry helmet on. Full visor, silver-gilt. Right?'

'Fufetius?'

'Couldn't be anyone else, boy,' Harpax grunted. His eyes went back to the corpse. 'So that's it. The whole thing. It make any sense to you?'

'Yeah,' I said. 'A lot of sense.'

'That so, now?' He looked up sharply. 'Then you know who the killer was?'

'Maybe. I've got a fair idea but I'm not sure yet.'

I thought he'd balk at that, but he just grunted. 'When you are you tell me, okay? I'll take it from there.'

The hairs on my neck were stirring again. I stood up. 'You know I can't do that,' I said quietly. 'This has to be done legal.'

'Fuck that, Corvinus. Spurius was a good man, and a good son-in-law. Whoever killed him I want to know. I'm not playing around here, boy.'

'Yeah.' I felt empty. 'I know that. Still, we can't have everything we want. Oh, and I really would tell Libanius about . . .' I gestured towards the corpse. 'Okay?'

'It won't bring Spurius back.'

'No, it won't. All the same it has to be done.' I paused in the doorway. 'One other thing. Talk to the neighbours, ask if anyone saw anything. If so then get word to me up at Marcia Fulvina's place.' It was an outside chance, but worth the effort. And the old guy needed something to keep him busy, I could see that.

At least my next course of action was definite: I had to have a serious talk with Sulpicia. That lady had questions to answer.

27

Bion, the door-slave at the Sulpicius place, opened up on my second knock and gave me a look like I'd just grown four more legs and a pair of feelers. Obviously the name Valerius Corvinus was still not one to conjure with in this quarter.

'Yes?' he said.

As a greeting, it wasn't exactly welcoming. 'I wanted to talk to the mistress, sunshine,' I said. 'If she's in.'

'She went out riding two hours ago. Sir.' He moved the door fractionally forwards; conversation over, evidently, from his point of view. I leaned sideways so my shoulder was resting against the panelling, stopping the forward movement. His eyes flickered.

'How about the master?'

'He's busy in his study.'

Not even a trace of politeness now. Hell; I'd had enough of this. I gave him my best smile. 'Now that is a shame,' I said. 'Tell you what. You just run upstairs and say I'd like a word with him about his daughter being involved in a plot to assassinate the senior Roman consul. You think you can remember that or should I put it in writing?'

Bion's jaw dropped and his lips formed a word that slaves weren't supposed to use in front of visitors. I hadn't meant the order literally, but he took me at my word anyway. You could almost feel the air shift, and a moment later the only trace of him was the slap-slap of sandals running across the marble atrium floor.

Sulpicius himself was down in two minutes flat, his expression as black as a thunderstorm.

'Corvinus, what the *hell* is this nonsense?' he snapped.

Well, I'd nailed my colours to the mast good and proper with Bion and there wasn't much point in tearing them down now. 'No nonsense,' I said. 'There's a plot to kill at least one of the consuls at the Latin Festival and your daughter's in it up to her neck. That isn't theory, it's fact. Now do you want to talk out here with the whole household listening or should we go somewhere more private?'

He gave me a look that left scorch marks on my tunic. Then he said, turning; 'My study! Now!'

I followed him through the lobby and the atrium, and up the staircase, in silence. He opened the door at the top and motioned me through.

'Sit!'

I sat in the visitor's chair while he closed the door after us and went behind the desk. On it were two orderly piles of wax tablets, a stylus and an abacus. Obviously I'd interrupted the monthly accounts session.

'Now.' He faced me straight, his eyes hard. 'Explain yourself. And you had better do it well, because although I'm not exactly sure of the legal position here I intend to find out at the earliest opportunity, after which you will be very sorry indeed.'

'You heard of a society called the Alban Brotherhood?'

'No.'

'It was headed – used to be headed – by Herdonius Flacchus. Your daughter's a member.'

'That's absurd!'

I sighed. 'Look, pal, we're not going to get anywhere by locking horns like a couple of bulls in a field. You want me to explain myself, that's fine with me, but like I say this is fact, not theory and at this point I'm giving you facts, not asking for comments. Okay?'

'Corvinus, my daughter is part of this household.' Sulpicius's tone just dripped with venom. 'If she were a member of this society of yours then I would be aware of it. And I've told you before, I will not have you addressing me as "pal"!'

'All right. Point taken. My apologies, sir.' I leaned back; there wasn't any reason to antagonise the guy more than I had already. 'All the same, do you really believe that? That Sulpicia would tell you something if she didn't want to?'

He frowned, but I could see the question had gone home. Sulpicius might be a stiff bastard and currently a seriously annoyed one, but he was basically fair. 'Very well,' he said. 'You're correct, of course; on certain subjects my daughter does tend to keep her own counsel. Although in this instance I would be very surprised if what you claim has any foundation, because Sulpicia is not and never has been one for societies of any kind. What exactly is this . . . Alban Brotherhood?'

'It started up about eighteen months ago. Like I say, the head – self-appointed – was Herdonius Flacchus, and one of the other members was your ex-partner Vettius Bolanus. He was the one who introduced Sulpicia.'

'Really?' He was giving me a look like I was something the cat had brought up all over his clean study floor. 'And its purpose was what?'

I ignored the look, and the tone. 'That's the crux. While Flacchus was in charge it was just one of these silly little secret clubs you get when two or three cranks decide they're going to change the world, on paper at least. As far as I understand, originally it had the aim of preserving and promoting Latin culture, although Bolanus and your daughter changed all that. I don't exactly know what their motives were, or how far they were intending to go, but thanks to them about six months back things started to get dirty. Bolanus—'

'Just a moment.' Sulpicius held up a hand. 'Before you go

on, Valerius Corvinus, I want to know where your proof for all this comes from. Especially in regard to my daughter's involvement.'

Yeah, well; that was fair enough. And at least he was listening now. 'I got it from Harpax, the retired veteran in Castrimoenium. His son-in-law Spurius Rutilius was one of the other members.'

'"Was"?'

'Yeah, in both senses of the word. He pulled out about a month later, but more to the point the guy's dead. He was knifed at home, probably two nights ago. His family were away, and he'd been lying there ever since. I found the body myself this morning.'

'*What?*' Sulpicius's shock was real.

'So you see why I'm interested in your daughter, don't you? Three of the six members of the society dead – murdered – within eight days of each other can't be any sort of coincidence. Especially since the guy who committed one of the murders was a member too.'

He was staring at me. 'You claim that Sulpicia was one of the group,' he said. 'Very well; we'll leave that for the present. Who were the other two?'

'One was a local butcher by the name of Exuperius. He was the one who killed Flacchus.'

'And the last?'

'I don't know. Oh, I know the name, sure, for what it's worth. A guy called Fufetius.' I was watching Sulpicius closely, but there wasn't a flicker. 'My theory is that he was the guiding force, the man who took things over the edge.' I hesitated; there wasn't any way I could soften the next part. 'According to Rutilius, Bolanus and your daughter were the ones who introduced him.'

There was a long silence. Sulpicius never moved. All the colour had suddenly drained from his face and the eyes were closed. Shit; that was all I needed, for the guy to peg out on me. Finally, I reached over and touched his arm. 'You okay, sir?' I said. 'You want me to fetch someone?'

His eyes opened and he shook his head. Then, without a word, he got up and walked across the room, moving like he'd just had twenty years added to his age. He opened the door.

'Bion?' he shouted; or tried to, anyway, because the word came out hardly louder than a croak. There was a pause, and the slave's voice drifted up in acknowledgment. Sulpicius steadied himself with his hand on the jamb and cleared his throat. 'When the mistress gets in,' he said, 'you will send her up here immediately.' He didn't wait for a response, just closed the door again behind him and came back over to the desk. I glanced at his face. It was grey and lifeless as a corpse's. 'There, Corvinus,' he said. 'As you can see, I'm being co-operative. Are you happy now?'

'I'm sorry, sir,' I said quietly. 'I don't like this either.'

He waved me down. A muscle moved at the corner of his eye. 'No, I don't believe you do,' he said. 'It's not your fault. And perhaps I should apologise in my turn.' He took a deep breath and lowered himself into his chair. His colour was coming back, but he still looked like death warmed over. 'Now. A plot to kill the consuls, you said.'

'Yeah. During the Latin Festival. At least, I think that was the idea originally, although whether that's changed with the circumstances I don't know. The hit-man was to be Exuperius. He'd got himself taken on as a sacrificant's assistant.'

'And my . . . and Sulpicia knows the identity of this Fufetius person?' His voice was toneless.

'I assume so, sir. Like I say, she and Bolanus introduced him to the group.'

'It's a fair assumption, then.' Sulpicius ran a hand over his face, slowly, drawing the flesh down. The muscle next to his eye was still twitching. 'You must forgive me, Valerius Corvinus. This isn't easy. And the suddenness of it makes it worse.'

I didn't speak.

'I won't say I accept your version of events; that's for my

daughter to confirm or deny and I will not prejudge either way. However, perhaps if I tell you a little of her background it would help. When you talk with her, I mean.' His lips twisted in the parody of a smile. 'Also – and I admit I'm being selfish here – it will pass the time until she returns and can speak for herself. There's no point in sitting staring at each other in silence, exchanging pleasantries is out of the question and I have no desire to be alone with my own thoughts. It may, as I say, help you. To understand, that is. Although the gods know I find that hard enough.'

I nodded. 'Go ahead, sir.'

His fingers strayed to the abacus on the desk and he pushed a bead back and forward without looking at it while he spoke. 'Sulpicia's mother died eighteen years ago of a summer fever, when Sulpicia was ten. She always had been a difficult child, we were never close and things didn't improve over the years. I've never remarried. Perhaps it would have been better for her if I had, but I don't really think it would've made much difference. She always was wild, more like a boy than a girl but without a boy's suggestibility.' He smiled briefly. 'That's not quite the word I want, but it doesn't matter. I mean that had she been a son we could have related to each other more, even if there was the occasional father–son spat. Despite her wildness Sulpicia has always been pure woman, even when she was a child. That has made the relationship very difficult, and at times impossible. You understand me, Corvinus?'

'Yeah,' I said. 'I understand.'

'I thought, when she came of age, the best thing would be for her to marry as soon as possible. We were living in Rome at the time, naturally, and several good families expressed an interest. We aren't blue bloods, of course, we Sulpicii, but I was quite well off and Sulpicia had a decent legacy from her mother. She even attracted the attention of one of Licinius Frugi's sons; not the eldest, unfortunately, but—'

'Quintus Licinius?'

Sulpicius's fingers were still pushing at the bead. They paused. 'Yes. Yes, that's right. You know him?'

'I think I might. He's the artistic one?'

Sulpicius was old-fashioned-Roman enough to look disapproving. 'Yes,' he said. 'A pleasant boy, though, for all that, and very struck on Sulpicia. Very struck indeed. There would've been no objection to the engagement on my side.'

'But there was on hers?'

'Yes, there was on hers. And that was the end of that.'

'You know Quintus Licinius is in Castrimoenium?' I said.

'No.' He gave me a sharp look. 'Since when?'

'I don't know. He's been here a while, though.'

'Doing what?'

'Touting for mural commissions.'

'*Licinius?*' Sulpicius's eyes opened wide, and the surprise in his voice showed he'd been jerked briefly out of his reminiscent mood. 'What's one of the Licinii Crassi doing working as a jobbing artist?'

'That I don't know either, sir, but my guess now would be he's shadowing your daughter. He hasn't been in touch?'

'Not with me, certainly.'

'He's, uh, never married, then?'

'Oh, yes. His father arranged an engagement not long after Sulpicia refused him. I don't know if the marriage is still current, but from what I heard before we left Rome I wouldn't be surprised if it isn't. The two weren't suited, and there was a certain amount of friction from the start.'

'Could, uh, he and Sulpicia still be seeing each other?'

'It's possible, yes, if, as you say, he's in the area, although it's unlikely. The attraction, considerable though it was, was very much one-sided. Quintus Licinius would have done anything for my daughter – I think the word "obsessed" wouldn't be out of place to describe him – but although she was happy to use the young man she had no real feelings for him.' He hesitated. 'On the other hand, I cannot in good conscience answer you with a definite no. Sulpicia's private life has been very much a closed book to me for years; her doing, not mine. That was the root of the trouble. It is – was – in fact largely my reason for moving out of Rome to the countryside.'

I shifted on my chair. 'You like to explain that a bit, sir?'

'Do I really have to?' he said gently. 'It's obvious enough. You're a Roman yourself, Corvinus. You know what it's like there, the temptations. Sulpicia always had been wild, and as I said she matured early. I kept her in check as long as I could, which admittedly' – his lips twisted – 'was not for very long. Her friendship, if you can call it that, with young Licinius gave her the entrée into the top social levels, where codes of behaviour aren't . . . well, they aren't the sort of codes that I personally would endorse.' His eyes came up. 'It wasn't Licinius's fault. Barring his artistic leanings, he was a creditable enough youngster. I'm not blaming him. The initiative was hers; as I said she used him and his connections quite callously, and as a result there were various men over the years. If you can call them men. Fortunately she showed no particular interest in marriage to any of them, although most, I suspect, were already married or were uninterested themselves.' Again his lips twisted. 'You notice I say "suspect". I didn't *know*, and I admit I didn't try too hard to find out. Nor did I try to put any curbs on her. You'll think the worse of me for that.'

'Uh-uh.' I shook my head. 'Not me.' The old guy might've taken it hard, but that was because of who he was, not because of the situation. That wasn't unusual; it happened, like he said, at the top end of the scale more often than not, and it'd been going on for years. Most kids went through the wild stage and came out the other side little the worse – I had, myself – although some didn't; they were the real problems, and the numbers were increasing. Augustus had tried to put the brakes on, sure, and the Wart had followed suit, but some trends you just can't stop by passing laws. I'd heard the same story a dozen times. 'She, uh, didn't make the break completely, then?'

'No. I couldn't control her actions, or her morals, but I did – and still do – control the purse strings.' He smiled bleakly. 'That sounds callous, I know, Valerius Corvinus, but then a financial hold is the only hold over my daughter I possess, and in spite of everything I still love Sulpicia. I mentioned she has an income from my wife's estate. Under the terms of the will she could draw on the interest but not the principal until her marriage, and only then if she married with my consent. My wife was very like me in many ways, rather old-fashioned about these things. And although she loved Sulpicia dearly she wasn't blind to the girl's character.'

I nodded; things were beginning to make sense. 'So she was on a long leash. She could do as she liked, but only so far, until she was decently married.'

'Indeed. I'd failed myself; a husband, carefully chosen, might do better. Which, of course, was why I approached Vettius Bolanus. At that time, naturally, I didn't know the man's true character.' Briefly, Sulpicius's mouth formed a hard line. 'We'd been business partners for several years, I thought I knew him, he came from a good family and my daughter seemed to like him. Also – well, she was in her late twenties, long past the marriageable age. He was agreeable; it seemed the perfect solution. The most important thing was that Sulpicia was in favour, and that was something I thought I'd never see. Besides, matters at Rome had reached a crisis.'

'You mean the Labici business? The stone scam?'

'Oh, no.' He shook his head. 'Oh, that was a contributing factor, certainly, but it wasn't the main one. I could have survived that, both socially and financially. Anyone who knew me – and I may not have many friends, Corvinus, but those I have are good ones – knew that I wasn't personally implicated, and the rest could believe what they liked. No, the crisis concerned Sulpicia herself. I'd approached Bolanus, you see, and although we hadn't reached formal agreement matters were in train. At that point someone – *not* a friend – thought fit to acquaint me with the details of her current private life. I realised then that if the marriage were to proceed I had to remove her from Rome immediately.'

Yeah; given what he'd told me already I could see how that might be. Bolanus would know he wasn't getting a dewy-eyed virgin as his part of the deal, sure, but he wouldn't want to announce his engagement to a girl – woman, rather – who was currently occupying half of someone else's bed. Or, even worse, several someone else's beds.

'She was in the middle of an affair, right?' I said.

Sulpicius's face darkened for a moment, and I thought he was going to snap my head off in his old style. If so he thought better of it because he took a deep breath and let it out.

'I'm sorry, Corvinus,' he said. 'I can't take this quite as lightly as you seem to. Perhaps it's because she is my daughter, not some casually met acquaintance, a mere factor in your theories; or perhaps as moral individuals we see these things differently. In either case the answer to your question is no. She was at the *beginning* of an affair, which was much worse, because she was in the process of seducing the man concerned. I mean actively seducing him. Making, as my informant so gracefully put it, "the running".' He spoke the word like he was biting on a lemon. 'I couldn't, in all conscience, finalise a marriage contract knowing that. I presented Sulpicia with an ultimatum: we would leave Rome and she would break off all relations with this man before things became serious – she had no real interest in him, I knew, it was simple lust, not love – or that would be the end of it; I would formally disown her in law and although she would continue to receive the income from her mother's bequest that would be all she would ever have, for my lifetime and, if I could so arrange it, for hers.' He paused; his hands, flat on the desk now, were shaking. 'It wasn't an ultimatum I relished giving, and I did not feel especially proud of myself, but there was nothing else I could do. The marriage with Bolanus was my – and her –

final chance. I couldn't afford to jeopardise it in any way. You understand me?'

'Sure,' I said quietly. 'I understand. She agreed?'

'She agreed. I think, in a way, she respected me – perhaps for the first time – for making a stand. Certainly, as I say, she wasn't against marriage to Vettius Bolanus.' Again his lips formed that dry smile. 'Probably because she already knew, which I did not, what kind of man he really was, and found him genuinely attractive for just that reason; in the same way that some people prefer the flavour of half-rotten game to that of fresh meat.' He must have seen me blink. 'Oh, I've no illusions about my daughter, Corvinus, none at all. Fortunately love is not a rational quality, and so mine for her remains unaffected.'

'And once you had her agreement you sold up in Rome and moved here?'

'Correct. We'd already formalised the engagement, and a property near Castrimoenium – next door, in fact, to Bolanus's itself – made the obvious choice. Sulpicia was out of Rome and in a place where both I and her future husband could keep an eye on her. Also, she's an only child. When I died she would inherit and the two properties could simply be combined. It was a perfect arrangement. Or so I thought, six months ago.'

'One thing,' I said. 'The guy in Rome. The one she was mixed up with. Or hoping to be. You happen to know who he was?'

'Not his name, no. My informant retained sufficient of his natural decency to keep that from me, and it has been my conscious policy for many years to preserve my ignorance where the names of Sulpicia's lovers are concerned. However, I understand that he was one of the junior magistrates designate.'

My stomach went cold. 'Uh . . . junior magistrates? You mean quaestors and aediles?'

'That would be a logical assumption, yes.'

Oh, gods. Sweet holy gods. 'Did your daughter ever—'

But I didn't have a chance to finish the question because behind me the door opened and Sulpicia came in.

28

Bion had obviously followed Sulpicius's instructions to the letter and sent her straight up after her ride without giving her the time to change, because she was wearing her Huntress Camilla outfit with her hair tied back in a club braid. She hadn't been expecting me, that was clear, any more than at that point I'd been expecting her, because she stopped dead.

Time froze.

Me, I think it was what she saw in Sulpicius's face that did it. In any case, their eyes met and locked. I glanced from one to the other. Sulpicius had half risen, hands flat on the desk; Sulpicia's tongue flicked nervously between her lips, her eyes like a cornered cat's shifted to me, then back to her father. She turned . . .

Time restarted.

She had the advantage; she was already on her feet and she had the presence of mind to slam the door behind her. When I got it open and was out on to the landing she was already down the stairs, past the gaping Bion and haring through the atrium. I cursed and followed, stumbling over a heavy marble bust that she'd pulled down with the pedestal it had been resting on so that they lay flush across the stretch of wooden flooring outside the study door.

I took the stairs as fast as I could manage. Bion's jaw was still hanging, but he tried to stop me. I shoved him aside and sprinted for the lobby, in time to hear the front door slam.

Bugger!

Outside, one of the stable slaves was standing, hands dangling at his sides, staring down the track that led to the lakeside road. I could hear the beat of hooves in the distance; she must be a hundred yards off, easy, and going like hell. I turned towards the hitching-post where I'd left the mare . . .

No horse.

I whirled round and grabbed the slave's shoulder. 'Where is she?' I yelled. '*Where's my fucking horse?*'

He gave me a scared look. 'She cut the traces, sir, and sent her down towards the rose garden.' He pointed to where the horse was cropping grass. 'Over there.'

'She on that stallion of hers?'

'Yes, sir. I was just leading him to the stable.'

Hell's teeth! Things could've been worse, yeah – she could've dragged the mare with her and left me stranded – but all the same, as it was I didn't have a hope of catching her anyway. Not the way she rode.

That didn't mean I needn't try, mind. I sprinted for the mare, grabbed the reins – she'd cut them, but thank the gods there was enough left to hold – and struggled up into the saddle. Then I dug my heels in, crouched low over the horse's neck and gave her her head. The stable slave threw himself to one side and I galloped past him, making for the road.

She was long gone when I reached the villa gates, but I didn't hesitate over which way to go. Left would just take me further along the lake where the road petered out. She must be heading in the direction of Castrimoenium, towards the crossroads for the Appian Way and Bovillae. I made the turn as fast as I could, then dug my heels in again, lay flat against the horse's mane and forced myself to ignore the pounding motion of the gallop while I thought things through.

She'd panicked, sure, but she must have some definite aim

in mind. If she was tied in with her lover Ruso – and I'd bet my last copper piece she was – then she could be on her way to warn him that the game was up. Which meant she was heading for Bovillae. I might not be able to catch her before she reached him, but brazening things out wasn't one of their options, not any longer, and at least I might be in time to nail the pair of them before they lit out for the tall timber. My guess was they'd make straight for Ostia and take the first boat out for wherever they could get; which made finding them even more urgent.

Shit; what a mess!

I reached the crossroads and took the left-hand turn. Bovillae wasn't far, maybe five or six miles, on the other side of the Appian Way. They'd have to use that, sure, if they wanted to get to Ostia fast, but there were enough minor tracks linking the town with the road and joining it further up its length to mean they wouldn't have to retrace Sulpicia's route and risk meeting me. Neither of them was that stupid, and if they were on horseback any track would do. If I was going to chase them it had to be from behind all the way.

I'd covered just over a quarter of a mile when a guy leading a panniered donkey hove into view, coming in the other direction. Best to check. I slowed the mare and reined in.

'Hey, pal,' I said. 'Did a woman on a big black horse pass you?'

He was chewing on a bit of straw. He took it out of his mouth, inspected it carefully, and put it back.

'When would this be, now?' he said.

Jupiter! The mare skittered, eager to be off, and I quietened her with my hand and knees. 'Any time you like, friend. But my guess would be ten, fifteen minutes back.'

'Heading for Bovillae?'

I gritted my teeth. 'Yeah,' I said. 'Heading for fu— for Bovillae.'

That got me a long, considering stare. Then he turned his head aside and spat into the ditch.

'No. No women on black horses, consul,' he said slowly. 'Barring one you're the only rider I've seen. And unless your friend's changed sex, is pushing seventy, looks like a goat and has swapped her fancy horse for a clothes-rack then that worn't her.'

Oh, great; I'd bet the bugger was a riot at dinner parties. Still, there was a chance he'd only joined the road recently from one of the local farm tracks when she'd already gone past.

'You've come from Bovillae yourself?' I said.

'All the way.' He indicated the panniers. 'Got some cheeses here I'm taking into Castrimoenium for my daughter's stall. Top quality, two coppers the piece. My daughter'd charge you four. You interested?'

'Uh-uh. No thanks.'

'Suit yourself. It's your loss, friend, they're good cheeses.' He clicked his tongue and jerked on the donkey's halter.

I watched him go, feeling like the last chicken on the shop counter. The mare was still skittering, anxious to be off, and I held her in on a tight rein. Fuck; what did I do now? Sulpicia could be doing a runner on her own, sure, maybe to Rome in the first instance, in which case she wouldn't be going as far as Bovillae, but not even she couldn't've got the length of the crossroads with the Way by this time; in which case my entrepreneurial pal had to've seen her. If he hadn't, then I was headed in the wrong direction. So where could she be going?

I'd taken the wrong turn, that was obvious. The only thing was, the other two options hadn't been viable. At least, I didn't see how they could be. Straight on at the lakeside crossroads was Castrimoenium and a dead-end, the right-hand road led into the hills towards Caba . . .

Caba. My brain was trying to tell me something. What the hell was it? Something about Caba . . .

Then I had it. Harpax had said that when Bolanus and Sulpicia took over the group they'd shifted their meetings from Flacchus's villa to a farmhouse two miles up the Caba road; probably so that Ruso, aka Fufetius, could come and go with less people to notice. I couldn't be absolutely certain, but one got you ten that was where the lady was headed.

After all, I could only be wrong. And if I was I'd lost her anyway.

I wheeled the mare, jabbed my heels into her ribs and galloped back hell for leather the way I'd come. The would-be cheesemonger didn't even look up as I passed.

I found the place exactly where Harpax said it would be, two miles out in the sticks on the Caba side of Castrimoenium. If I hadn't been looking out for it I'd probably have ridden past without noticing, because 'farmhouse' was an exaggeration; it lay a good fifty yards off the road, tucked into a fold of the hillside partly screened by trees and bushes, and from its size and the tired sag of its tiled roof no farmer's wife with any pretensions to local standing would've used it for anything grander than a chicken-coop. Be that as it may, there was a tumble-down wall at the side which presumably marked off some sort of courtyard, and over the top of it peered the head of Sulpicia's black stallion. As I looked, another horse's head – a brown one, this time – joined it.

Bull's-eye! Got her!

I slowed the mare to a walk. There wasn't any point in rushing into things here: I might've found Sulpicia, but if the presence of the other horse was anything to go by she wasn't alone, and the odds were the other person in there was Ruso himself. I wasn't armed, not even with a knife, and it wasn't likely that all I'd have to do was knock on the door and the pair of them would give up and come quietly. So how did I play it? I could ride back into Castrimoenium, sure, report to Libanius and get him to detail three or four of his municipal heavies to take them into custody, but by that time the odds were they'd be long gone and on their way to Rome or Ostia and I'd be left with an empty house and the whole thing to do again. Another idea might be to carry on towards Caba, stop off at one of the farms along the way and commandeer local help, but I'd no official standing, and from my experience of the locals I was just as likely to get a long stare and a blown raspberry. Still, there wasn't much else I could—

Someone screamed; a woman, and it came from the house. Shit. I dug my heels into the mare's ribs, urging her along the overgrown track that led to the gate in the wall; then, when I reached it, threw myself out of the saddle and took the last few yards at a run. The door was half open, dangling from a single hinge. I hit it hard with my shoulder and barged through, keeping up the speed . . .

Bad move. Bad, bad move.

Something was lying just inside the threshold. My feet caught on it and I went arse over tip. I shot out my hand, palm raised, to save the worst of the fall, and the shock as it met the floor sent a stab of pain up my arm. I rolled sideways, gritting my teeth as my shoulder slammed against the beaten clay surface, turned over on to my back, gasping—

And froze, because someone was holding a sword at my throat.

Oh, fuck; nice one, Corvinus. So much for heroics.

'Where did you spring from, Roman?'

It was Exuperius. My pal the homicidal butcher hadn't been all that prepossessing the last time I'd seen him, but compared with what he looked like now he'd've been in the running for the Best-Dressed Citizen of the Year Award. Behind him, Sulpicia was pressed back as far as she could go against the wall. Her eyes were wide, she was biting her knuckle, and she looked scared as hell.

If I was still capable of breathing then maybe I'd keep doing it for a while. I took a deep breath and tried to ignore the sword-point. The hammering in my chest quietened.

'Where's Ruso?' I said finally.

Exuperius grinned. The sword-blade didn't move. I noticed now that it had blood on it.

'You just tripped over him,' he said.

Ah. I glanced back at the bundle by the door and swallowed. Yeah; so I had, at that. Well, there went the case. Whether Ruso was the guilty party or not they'd have to get a new aedile to run the festival now, that was definite.

'You killed him?'

Stupid question: he hadn't done that to himself shaving. Still, I wasn't feeling too bright at that particular moment.

'He deserved it.' The sword still didn't waver. I glanced down at it: fancy workmanship, with a silver-mounted hilt. Probably Ruso's own. The guy lay on his back, and his throat was a mess of blood. It was still wet, and as I looked the corpse's outstretched leg twitched. My gorge rose; it must've just happened, which explained Sulpicia's scream.

'Is that so?' I said.

'Sure. He would've sold me down the river if I'd been caught, just to save his own neck. So would that bitch.' Exuperius jerked a thumb at Sulpicia. 'I wasn't going to leave until I'd settled things with both of them. Now, of course . . .' He sucked on a tooth, considering.

I waited.

Finally he stepped back a little. 'All right. Let's play it that way. On your feet. And make it nice and slow.'

I didn't have any other option, because my right arm hurt like hell all the way to the shoulder and the wrist was twice the size it should've been and swelling. There might not be any bones broken – at least, I didn't think so – but it wouldn't bear my weight, and I had to use my left to push myself upright. Bugger; no chance of rushing him, then. With an arm out of commission I couldn't've out-wrestled a determined twelve-year-old, let alone a guy armed with a sword. Well, at any rate I was still alive, which was surprising. Not that I was complaining, mind.

'You've been hiding out here?' I said.

'Nah. They'd've found me if I had. But I was keeping an eye on the place. I knew that piece of garbage' – he nodded at Ruso – 'would come here sooner or later. It was where he and the bitch came to screw. They thought I didn't know, but I did. I knew everything, me.' Suddenly he stepped back and to one side. I stiffened, thinking maybe he was giving himself more room for a thrust or a cut, but the hand holding the sword didn't move. 'Now do as I say. Stand up properly.'

I stood.

'Over there to your right. You see these hooks in the wall? I want you between them.'

I glanced sideways. Sure enough there were two iron hooks cemented into the room's right-hand far wall, about a foot from the ceiling and four feet apart: the kind of thing you get in peasant houses in the country, where space is at a premium, carpentered wooden furniture's expensive and so vegetables or even spare clothes are stored in net bags and hung up out of the way. Without taking my eyes off the sword, I moved over and stood between them.

'Fine. Now take off your tunic belt.' His left hand fumbled with his own. 'You! Bitch!'

Sulpicia flinched. She hadn't spoken a word since I'd made my entrance, and her eyes had kept going back to Ruso's body. My guess was she was in shock. She lowered the hand from her mouth but still didn't speak.

Exuperius threw her his own belt. 'Take that and the Roman's. There's a stool over there you can stand on. I want the bastard's wrists tied to these hooks, and if you don't do it properly or if there're any tricks you'll join your boyfriend on the floor. Now!'

Wrists, eh? Oh, shit; this wasn't going to be pleasant.

Sulpicia bent down and picked up the belt. I took mine off, left-handed, and gave it to her, my eyes still on Exuperius's sword. She moved the stool over so it stood under the right-hand hook and I raised my right arm, wincing with the pain in my shoulder joint. I could just reach the top of the hook with my fingertips, but there wasn't going to be any way, once I was tied, that I could ease the loop over and slip it free. Certainly not with a crocked arm.

'You okay, Roman?' Exuperius said.

'Sure,' I lied. 'Never better.' Whatever his reason for asking, it wasn't sympathy, and I knew I wouldn't get any. Sulpicia fastened the belt round my swollen wrist and pulled it tight. I clenched my teeth.

Exuperius grunted. 'Like to know why you're not dead? Why I'm going to all this trouble?'

'Yeah.' My whole arm felt like it was on fire, and I had to concentrate to blank out the pain. 'Yeah, I was kind of wondering that.'

'Because you're my insurance policy, boy. Once this bitch has tied you up, her and me are going to leave.' I felt Sulpicia stiffen as she wrapped the other end of the belt round the hook and knotted it. 'She's my hostage, you see. Or sort of hostage.' He smiled. 'But that part of it's my business. I've waited long enough to have her, now she can deliver. Oh, she's guilty, all right, just as much as Ruso and me; don't waste any sympathy on her. And it's in her interests as well. She knows I'm her only chance of getting away, now her boyfriend's dead, and she'd better play along. Don't you, bitch?' Sulpicia still didn't speak, but I saw her eyes harden and her jaw clench. She tugged hard on the belt, and its leather edge dug agonisingly into my wrist. I bit my lip. 'She's caught, you see. She hates my guts, I disgust her, sure, I know all that. Still, it's the carrot and the stick, at least for now. The carrot is, she needs my muscle against you and your like until we're both free and clear, the stick is she knows if she crosses me she's dead.' He smiled again. 'Simple, yes? So here's the deal, Roman. I let you live. All you have to do in return is tell the truth: that I've got sweet Sulpicia here with me. If I'm caught it means the strangler anyway, so I've nothing to lose. But if I am caught, or if I even think I might be, I'll kill her first. Now you tell everyone that and keep them off my back, okay?'

'If she's guilty then why should I bother?' I said.

Sulpicia was moving the stool so she could tie my left hand. The breath hissed through her teeth and she shot me a glare.

'Yeah.' Exuperius chuckled. 'Fair point. I think, though, maybe her father would disagree with you, even that old woman Libanius. And if she died before her time then the senior consul might have a few regrets, too.'

'Persicus?' I frowned. 'Why should Persicus care particularly?'

'You didn't know? Well, there's no reason why you should. It was one reason he had it in for chummy down here.' Exuperius kicked Ruso's body lightly. 'Fabius High-and-Mighty Persicus was a boyfriend of our sweet Sulpicia's until she chucked him in Ruso's favour. Not that it was the only reason, mind, far from it; it just put the lid on things. Still, Persicus'd be sorry to see a face and a body like that go to the urn.' His voice sharpened. 'Come on, bitch! Hurry up!'

Sulpicia flashed him a venomous look over her shoulder, tied the last knot and stepped down. Well, that hadn't been so bad after all. My right wrist was still on fire and pounding away like hell, sure, but the pain in my shoulder had settled to a dull ache. So long as I didn't move I'd only have agony to contend with.

Exuperius had lowered the sword, but he still held it. Smart man; me, I wouldn't trust the lady either, especially now, as it appeared, the shock of Ruso's death was wearing off and she was more in control and looking more her old self again. How he expected to get through the next stage of events without finding a knife between his ribs or Sulpicia doing another runner at the earliest opportunity beat me, mind, but that was his worry. Smart was relative: however much he believed he'd got the edge on her, I knew once she had herself back in hand she could run rings round him, and his obvious interest in her was a definite blind spot.

So maybe that was something I could use. I couldn't expect Sulpicia as an ally, sure, but nor could Exuperius, because she hated him like poison. That was clear enough from every look she gave him. If I could work on that, maybe give her time to think things over, weigh the possibilities in that cool calculating head of hers we could shift the balance a little . . .

'Okay, then, Roman,' Exuperius said. 'We'll be on our way. Shout all you want when we've gone; someone'll hear you eventually.' He grinned. 'I'd've liked to kill you too, but maybe one Roman's enough for the present. And you're more useful alive. You be sure to pass on the message, you hear?'

'Wait a moment, pal,' I said.

He'd been heading for the door. He turned. 'Yeah?'

'I'm supposed to finger Ruso and the lady, right? Just how exactly do I do that?'

His brow furrowed. 'What the fuck do you mean? They're the guilty ones, they were behind the whole thing.'

I glanced at Sulpicia. She'd made a movement, but she still didn't speak.

'The plot to kill Persicus?'

'Sure. Me, I was just the cat's-paw.'

'Friend, I've got no proof of that. None. All I have is theory and three murders.' I kept my voice level. 'You killed Flacchus. His major-domo saw you run off. Okay. But for all I know you killed Bolanus and Rutilius as well, and if so then—'

'What is this shit?' He was looking puzzled. 'I never touched Bolanus, nor Spurius Rutilius neither. That was Ruso.'

I shrugged, as far as I was able to. I had to take this careful because it was the only shot I had left. Out of the corner of my eye I could see that Sulpicia was staring at me. 'So you say,' I said. 'But Ruso's dead, isn't he? He can't talk now. You ask me, pal, that's pretty convenient.'

Exuperius took a step towards me, sword raised, and my stomach muscles clenched; but he only pointed it. 'Look,' he said softly. 'I killed Flacchus, sure, but only because Ruso told me to and his mouth had to be shut or we were all screwed. I'd nothing against the old man personal. And I'm not taking the rap for the others, not if it means saving Ruso's name and this bitch's here. When Bolanus died I wasn't even in Castrimoenium. You know that.'

This was the tricky part. I put every bit of damn-your-eyes patrician arrogance I could muster into my voice and said, 'Do I?'

'Sure you do! I was locked up in a broom closet in Bovillae after a fist-fight with that poncy Roman artist. Which was why that bastard' – he spat in the direction of Ruso's corpse – 'had to do his own killing that night. Him and the bitch set it up between them after the meeting, when Bolanus threatened to blow the whistle on the festival business.'

'That's a lie!'

Sulpicia was glaring at Exuperius, and the dull, shocked look had gone from her eyes. Mentally, I breathed a sigh of relief.

'Is it, now?' Exuperius turned and regarded her coolly.

Her lips were a hard line. 'I didn't know anything about Ruso's plans for Marcus. I never even knew he'd be there, right up to the moment when he came out of the bushes and—' She stopped. The anger suddenly drained out of her and she hugged herself like she was giving herself comfort. Then she looked directly at me. 'Corvinus, all I agreed to was to send Marcus a note asking him to meet me in the loggia so we could talk things over. Just the two of us. There was no need for him to die. I could have persuaded him.'

'To agree to the murder of a Roman consul,' Exuperius sneered. 'Sure. Don't waste your breath, lady. You knew, right enough.'

'It's the truth!' She turned on him again, eyes flashing, then looked back at me. 'We were playing, we were bored and the whole thing was just a stupid game. All Marcus and I ever wanted was to have a bit of fun; the Alban Brotherhood was a joke and the festival's silly and outmoded anyway. We didn't want anyone to die!'

Yeah, looking at her now I'd believe that. There wasn't any real malice in Sulpicia; she was just an overgrown spoiled brat who'd played with fire once too often, got herself seriously burned and had nowhere to run to. 'So,' I said wearily. 'You let Ruso in on the game. Did Bolanus know you were lovers?'

She shook her head. 'I don't think so. He thought we were . . . just friends. From Rome. And that wouldn't've mattered, not to me. We only wanted to disrupt the festival, embarrass the stuffed shirts. Nothing really bad!'

'But Ruso had other ideas?'

'He hated Fabius Persicus. Oh, I knew that already, but I didn't make the connection. Ruso was ambitious, he wanted to run for city judge, but Persicus was using his influence to block him. He'd never have got on to the list while Persicus was around to spread his poison, and if he didn't then his political career was finished. Even so, Corvinus, this is hindsight. I didn't *know* he wanted to kill the consul; I didn't so much as think of it!' She was almost crying now. 'He didn't even tell us he was going to be in charge of the festival arrangements. We only found that out later by accident.'

'Uh-huh.' Well, it all sounded plausible enough, especially knowing Paullus Persicus like I did. The bugger was an arch-snob, Ruso wasn't out of the top drawer and if Persicus had his knife into him – which he obviously did – then the old-boy network would make sure the aedileship was as high as he'd go. Also, organising the Latin Festival wasn't exactly a plum job. For all Ruso's claims to have drawn the short straw I'd guess he'd volunteered, and his colleagues had been happy to let him have it. 'So how did the real plot come out?' I said. 'When did you know Ruso was planning to kill Persicus?'

'Oh, that was my fault, Roman.' Exuperius grinned. 'It was supposed to be a secret between Ruso and me, only I lost my temper with that old fool Flacchus and told him his useless bloody Alban Brotherhood were going to *do* something for once. Ruso was livid, but I reckon it was the best mistake I ever made.'

'Uh . . . how so, pal?'

'It brought everything out in the open. After that I got to thinking.' He nudged the corpse with his toe. 'That bastard'd never've let me get clear once Persicus was dead, whatever he'd told me. As the aedile in charge he'd've been on the spot and he'd make fucking sure I died as well, there and then. Then there'd only be one person in the secret, right? Like I said at the start, I was to be the cat's-paw, and telling Flacchus saved my neck. I may be in trouble enough now, but if I'd gone along with Abudius bloody Ruso I'd be dead for sure.'

I looked at Exuperius with new respect: he wasn't quite the thicko I'd taken him for. 'That's very, uh, perceptive,' I said.

'Bet your boots it is.' The grin widened and he turned for the door. 'Okay, Roman, so now you've got it all and we'll leave you to your thoughts. Don't forget to pass on the message, right? I wouldn't want—'

Sulpicia lunged; neither of us was expecting it, and she moved too fast for Exuperius to avoid the blow. I'd forgotten the cut traces; she must've had the knife all the time, cached away somewhere. Even so, he managed to bring the sword round as she drove it into his neck, and the point slipped in under her right breast and between her ribs. He jerked her towards him hard with his left arm, thrusting the sword home at the same time, then let her go. She was dead before she hit the floor.

The whole thing had taken maybe five seconds, start to finish.

Shit; oh, shit. I pulled on the hooks, ignoring the pain in my wrist, but the belts held. Exuperius's left hand was pressed to the wound, in the hollow between neck and shoulder. There was a lot of blood but he didn't seem too concerned. Probably just a shallow cut; she'd meant to kill him, sure, but there couldn't've been all that much force to a downward stab, especially since they were much of a height.

He paused, grinning, like he was considering his next move. Then he hefted the sword.

'Well, now,' he said slowly, looking down at it. 'Since I've lost my hostage after all—'

I pulled myself up with my left arm so I was clear of the floor and kicked out hard. My foot caught him in the balls and he staggered backwards, tripping over Sulpicia's corpse. The sword flew out of his hands, coming to rest beside Ruso's body. I heaved on the belts again, but I was anchored fast.

Exuperius sat up, head between his knees, retching. Finally, his chin lifted. A thread of vomit dribbled from his mouth.

'You're dead, Roman,' he whispered. 'But *slowly*.'

He got to his feet and staggered over to where the sword lay. There wasn't anything I could do; he wouldn't fall for another trick like that, and it was only postponing the inevitable anyway. Well, I'd almost made it.

I gritted my teeth and waited to die.

Exuperius stooped for the sword, picked it up and straightened, his eyes fixed on something outside the still open door—

And then he was stumbling backwards, staring at the blossoming wound under his ribs.

Harpax stepped over Ruso's body – auxiliary veterans didn't trip – contemptuously flicked Exuperius's half-raised blade aside and planted a second thrust beneath his chin; in-twist-out, fast and economical as a snake striking. Blood jetted and Exuperius collapsed in a tangle of twitching limbs.

Harpax wiped his short army-issue sword clean on the fallen man's tunic and winked at me. 'You were lucky I happened to be passing, boy,' he said.

I leaned back against the wall waiting for my heartbeat to quieten and closed my mouth, which had opened at some point in the latter stages of the proceedings and stayed that way throughout.

'Passing, nothing.' I grinned weakly. I was feeling pretty light-headed all of a sudden. Shit; that had been close, if you like. Certainly as close to an urn as I wanted to get for another forty years or so. 'What the hell are you doing out here, you old bugger?' Then, as he reached the point of the sword up towards my right-hand tie: 'And don't cut that one. That's my tunic belt.'

Harpax grunted and sheathed his sword. 'I just had a little think to myself, Corvinus.' His fingers prised the knot in the leather apart. 'If the bastard who killed Spurius was one of the Alban Brotherhood then maybe it might be an idea to check out their headquarters. Especially if the killer was this nameless Fufetius of yours.'

'Very enterprising of you.'

'I had to get out and busy somewhere. What did you expect me to do with my son-in-law lying murdered, sit at home and twiddle my fucking thumbs while you ponced about playing the great investigator?'

The loop round my swollen wrist slackened and the agony eased. I pulled my hand out. Gods, that was good! 'Don't get me wrong, pal,' I said. 'I'm not complaining, far from it. And you can insult me as much as you like. You've earned it.'

He chuckled, drew his sword and slit the second tie; Exuperius's belt. This time I didn't object: that bastard wouldn't be needing it any longer.

'So,' he said. 'Was that him?'

I undid the remains of the belt from my left wrist and rubbed my aching right arm. 'The guy you killed? No, that was Exuperius. He killed Flacchus. Your murderer's lying over there by the door. The aedile, Abudius Ruso.'

'Is that so, now?' Harpax's face was expressionless. He sheathed his sword again, walked over to Ruso's corpse, pulled the guy's mouth open and carefully spat into it. I winced. 'Hasn't been dead for long, has he? Pity I didn't get here earlier. You kill him yourself?'

'No. Exuperius did. He stabbed the woman too.'

He glanced towards Sulpicia and frowned. 'That's Sulpicius Severus's daughter, right? She involved in the murders?'

'Yeah, but—'

'Then she got what she deserved. Vettius Bolanus may've been scum and needed killing, but they were engaged. That's not nice.' He looked back at me. 'So. What happens now?'

'I hand the whole boiling over to Quintus Libanius. Let him sort it out.'

'Fine by me.' Harpax gave another grunt. 'May as well give this place the once-over first, though.' He nodded towards a closed door in the far wall. I can't say I'd noticed it earlier, but then I'd had other things on my mind than the interior arrangements. 'That'll be the bedroom. You want to check it out?'

I raised the latch with my good left hand and looked in. Sure enough, it was a smaller version of the living area, filling what was left of the ground floor, with a double bed, a clothes chest and a bedside table with a four-lamp candelabrum. The bed had been slept in, but the blankets looked clean. I remembered what Exuperius had said about Ruso and Sulpicia having used the place as a rendezvous.

I walked over and lifted the lid of the chest. Inside was a heavy cloak – the kind with a fitted hood that covered the whole head – and a silver-gilt full-face cavalry helmet. I picked them both up and showed them to Harpax without a word. He nodded.

'Yeah, that's right,' he said. 'Those're what the rider was wearing when I saw him on the lakeside road the night of Bolanus's murder. And they were what Fufetius wore when he met with the group.'

Well, that was that, then. The house had a second storey reached by an external stair, plus a separate kitchen off to one side, but there was no sign that either had been used for years; not that I'd been expecting anything else. I went back to the bedroom, wrapped the helmet in the cloak and took the bundle outside to where Harpax was waiting. Then we shut the door on the corpses, mounted up with the other two horses in tow and rode back to Castrimoenium.

All that was left to do was clean up the mess. But then I'd had enough for the day, and I reckoned I'd done my part. Harpax, too.

Libanius had had it easy so far; let him do some of the dirty work for a change.

29

'So Ruso wanted to put me in an urn, did he, Marcus?' Persicus chewed his tenth honeyed date and washed it down with a swallow of Marcia's best Caecuban. Yeah, well, he'd managed that deduction, at least. It'd taken me two whole courses to get even the basic facts of the case through his skull, and I supposed I was lucky to've managed it at all before he swanned off to the festival with his Axemen minders next morning. 'Me personally, not me the senior consul, if you get my drift. Seems a bit extreme, doesn't it? I mean, I'd no time for the man but that's no reason to kill a chap, is it?'

'He wanted a political career, Paullus,' Marcia said.

'So?'

'You'd made it abundantly clear both to him and your senatorial colleagues that you'd use all your influence to block him.'

'Damn right I would.' Persicus reached for another date. 'What's the use of having influence if you don't use it, eh? The fellah was a nobody; his father was a bloody art dealer. Sold me a dodgy painting once and then when I complained he had the nerve to claim he'd thought it was an original.'

'Did he take it back?' Perilla said.

Persicus frowned. 'Course he took it back. That's not the point, he shouldn't've made the mistake in the first place. Still, I made damn sure the son was blacklisted from then on. No one tries to do me and gets away with it. I might not've been quick enough to stop the young bugger getting his aedileship, but he wouldn't've got any further up the tree. Not if I could help it.'

'Yeah. Right.' I took a sip of my own wine. Ruso had been a bad 'un, sure, no arguments, but petty-minded vindictive bastards like Persicus made me sick to my stomach. 'So that's all you had against him? Originally?'

'Isn't it enough? Bad blood in the family. You can't have that sort running for office, Marcus. Gives the magistracy a bad name.'

I swallowed down the obvious retort: if the Senate put a bar on candidates for the magistracy on these grounds then we wouldn't have enough broad-stripers to run a chicken-farm, let alone an empire. And there were more crooks and swindlers inside the Senate House than out of it.

'There was the business over Sulpicia as well, of course,' I said.

The senior consuls's jaws paused in mid-chew.

'Oh?' Marcia had been peeling an apple. She looked up. 'You never mentioned that before, dear. What business was that, Paullus?'

'Ah . . .'

'Paullus had an affair with her before she left Rome,' I said. 'She ditched him for Ruso.'

'Really.' Marcia set the apple down and fixed Persicus with a look you could've used to ice prawns. 'And was Cloelia aware of this?' Cloelia was Persicus's wife.

'Ah . . . not as such,' Persicus said. I was getting a glare that smoked at the edges. 'We'll leave Sulpicia out of it, if you don't mind.'

'Will we, indeed?' Marcia murmured.

'Suits me.' I was grinning; point made. 'Your private life has nothing to do with me, pal. And I'm not defending Ruso, either. I'm just pointing out the fact that if he wanted a crack at the praetorship in a few years' time then you were his main obstacle.

Without you around he might have had a chance; with you actively lobbying your senatorial cronies on the appointments board he didn't have a hope.'

'That's true enough.' Persicus smirked, and my guts twisted. 'I wouldn't've lost any sleep over it either, I'll tell you that now. Man didn't deserve to be a city judge, he was a bloody upstart and you can't have riff-raff at that level. Still, it was a bit of a round-the-houses way of doing things, wasn't it? Why the hell should he kill these other fellahs along the road? Over-egging the pudding, if you ask me.'

Gods; here we went again. Getting more than two ideas into the senior consul's head at once needed major surgery and a crowbar. 'Paullus, I've already told you. None of that was part of the original plan. It was all a cover-up, or an attempt at one, right from Bolanus's murder onwards. The guy was running scared all the way.'

I could see that filtering in. 'So when you came to Rome to see me there wasn't a plot at all?' he said finally.

'Right!' Jupiter's holy balls! 'It was only really unworkable when Exuperius was caught killing Flacchus, sure, but I doubt that even if he hadn't been Ruso would've had the guts to go ahead with the original plan in any case. Like I say, all he was interested in by that stage was covering his tracks and getting out with a whole skin; which was why, naturally, he had to kill Spurius Rutilius.'

'That so, now? Ah ... remind me; he was the blacksmith fellah, correct?'

Gods! 'Correct.'

'Rutilius was the only one of the brotherhood left, Paullus,' Perilla said gently. 'Barring Exuperius and Sulpicia. He could have explained Flacchus's reference to Fufetius. He didn't know, of course, that Harpax was in on the secret too.'

'Ah.'

Too many names, too close together, even if he had heard them half a dozen times before; Persicus's eyes had glazed over.

We'd lost him, that was obvious. Maybe it was the wine – he'd had more than his fair share – but I doubted it; to Rome's current brightest and best, putting two and two together was an exercise in higher mathematics.

'What I can't understand,' Marcia said, 'is the girl Sulpicia's behaviour. On the few occasions when I met her she seemed such a nice young woman, and genuinely fond of her fiancé.'

'Yeah.' I turned away from Persicus and finished topping up my cup. 'I think she was. She hadn't an ounce of morality in her, sure, but she wasn't an out-and-out villain.'

'And you think she was telling you the truth?' Perilla said. 'When she denied knowing in advance that Ruso intended to kill Bolanus?'

I'd been wondering myself about that. I might only have the lady's word for it, but it made sense, especially taking into account her behaviour immediately afterwards when she'd 'found' the body. Plus the fact that nothing in my dealings with her had suggested she'd been a willing accomplice. Besides, she was dead; we could afford to give her the benefit of the doubt.

'Yeah,' I said. 'I think she was telling the truth. Sulpicia was just caught. She had to make the best of things.'

'The poor woman,' Perilla said quietly.

'Oh, I wouldn't go as far as that, dear.' Marcia was frowning. 'I'm sure that had she really tried she could, like poor Lucius, have found some way of extricating herself from the business without implicating her lover. And Abudius Ruso did remain her lover, did he not, Marcus?'

'Yeah,' I said. 'So I'd imagine, anyway.'

'There, then.' Marcia sniffed. 'I'm sorry it ended as it did for her father's sake, but I've very little sympathy for the girl herself. You younger folk may disagree, and you're free to do so, but in my opinion there's too much moral laxity in the modern world.' She fixed Persicus with an icy glare. 'Isn't that so, Paullus?'

'What? Ah . . . yes, Aunt Marcia. I quite agree. Absolutely.'

Persicus coughed into his napkin. 'Marcus, to change the subject a little: you'll be going to the festival tomorrow yourself, I assume?'

I shook my head. 'Uh-uh. I've got a prior engagement. A wine tasting in town.'

Marcia's glare disappeared. 'Not at Pontius's, surely?' she said.

'Yeah. Yeah, that's right.'

'He invited you himself? Pontius, I mean?'

'Yeah, about ten days ago.'

'Well, well!' The old woman smiled. 'That's an annual event in itself, quite a long-standing tradition locally. Also, Marcus dear, it's a great honour to be asked. They don't usually invite strangers, especially not Romans.'

'Cheeky buggers,' Persicus murmured and reached for the wine jug. 'Honour's the other way round, if you ask me. They're a clannish lot these bloody Latins.'

'You didn't mention this, Marcus,' Perilla said. 'What is it, exactly?'

'Oh, it's quite straightforward, Perilla,' Marcia said. 'Everyone involved pays a few silver pieces as an entrance fee, some of which goes for the wine and the rest to the winner. Each contestant has a card with the names of ten wines on it, and there are six wines which have to be matched with the correct names on the card. I've never attended myself, of course, but it sounds like fun.'

Perilla smiled. 'Marcus will certainly enjoy it,' she said. 'Who are the contestants?'

'Just the locals. But they're all wine-drinkers, naturally, and they know their stuff. Also, all the wines are Latian. That's part of the event. I understand it's a . . . well, a sort of regional counterpart to the Latin Festival proper.'

'Which is why they keep us out of it, I suppose,' Persicus said sourly. 'Mind you, Marcus, boy, I can't say I blame you. Given the choice I'd rather sink a few cups of wine in comfort than trek all the way up Mount Alba to slit a few sheeps' throats any day.'

'Well, I wish you luck, Marcus dear, in any case,' Marcia said. 'As I said it's a great honour to be asked, and in a way you're representing Rome.' She turned back to Persicus. 'Incidentally, now Abudius Ruso is gone who *is* taking over the organisation of the festival?'

'One of the other aediles.' Persicus cracked a walnut. 'Most of the work's done already, mind, so—' He stopped and his gaze shifted to the door behind me. 'Good gods!'

I turned. It was the Princess, looking like something the cat had dragged in, in a tunic that was three-quarters-over mud and torn down one sleeve. Her pal Clarus was standing in the doorway. If anything, the lad was in an even worse condition, and he was staring at Persicus in his consul's mantle with an expression of pure horror on his face. I glanced from one to the other and grinned.

'You remember Marilla, of course, Paullus?' Marcia said calmly. 'Marcus's and Perilla's adopted daughter?'

'Uh . . . yes. Yes.' Persicus was still goggling. 'Ah . . . how are you, m'dear?'

'Very well, Consul.' The Princess gave him her best social smile through a good half-inch of grime. 'I'm sorry. I'd forgotten you were coming tonight.'

'What the hell happened to *you*?' I said, trying not to laugh.

'We were coming home when we saw a cow stuck in a bog. You know the one at the edge of Gratus's meadow, Aunt Marcia, where the hurdles are broken?' Marcia nodded, her lips tight. 'It took us *hours* to get her out. Is there any dinner left?'

'Not in here, dear,' Perilla said firmly. 'And certainly not while you're in that state. Go and ask Meton.'

'All right.' She turned. 'Come on, Clarus.'

She left, dragging the Medusa-struck Clarus with her by the arm.

There was a painful silence.

'How old *is* that girl now, Aunt Marcia?' Persicus said finally.

'Sixteen.' Marcia was coring the last quarter of her apple. Her eyes were lowered, but I could see she was trying her best not to laugh as well.

'Sweet Jupiter! Does she make a habit of pulling strange cows out of bogs?'

'Not so as you'd notice. Only when they wander in of their own accord.'

'That so, now?' Persicus cleared his throat. 'And the . . . ah . . . the boy would be one of your slaves, yes?'

'Oh, no. Clarus is a friend.'

The goggle came back in earnest. 'A *friend*? And you *allow* it?'

'I don't see why not, Paullus, and nor should you,' Marcia snapped. 'He's a very nice boy, they have interests in common and I've known the family for years. The father's a doctor, of sorts.'

'The boy's father is a bloody *doctor*?' Persicus's voice had risen to a squeak. 'A *freedman*?'

I took a sip of wine. 'Nothing wrong with that, pal,' I said easily.

That got me a look like I'd offered him a salted slug. 'Nothing *wrong*? Good gods, it's immoral! And, Aunt Marcia, you'll forgive me for saying this but a girl of that age and of her background should be in Rome, not pulling bloody cows out of bogs out here in the sticks! Especially if she's taken to fraternising with young men of that class!'

'You mean we should give her the same social opportunities as Sulpicius Severus gave his daughter?' Perilla said quietly.

'Yes, of co—' Persicus stopped, and coloured. 'That's unfair; you know exactly what I mean. It's unnatural.'

'Seems perfectly natural to me,' I said. 'And the girl's happy enough.'

'That has nothing to do with it! Perilla, when you were her age what were you doing?'

'Becoming engaged to Suillius Rufus.' Perilla's voice was still quiet, but now there was a dangerous edge to it. 'You remember him, Paullus?'

Oh, bugger. This wasn't getting us anywhere, and tempers were definitely frayed. The guy had a point, of course – sixteen-year-old girls from good families didn't normally run around wild smeared with mud and worse to the eyeballs, especially with freedmen doctors' kids in tow – but I couldn't see it was doing the Princess any harm. Quite the reverse. Still . . .

'Perhaps you have a point, dear,' Marcia said diplomatically. 'Certainly it's something to think about. And now I really do feel we should change the subject; tell us what's happening in Rome these days with that dreadful Sertorius Macro in charge.'

They talked politics, while I switched off and drank my wine.

Well, it could've been worse; at least the Princess hadn't introduced our senior consul to Dassa. Even so, I had my moment of sympathy for Ruso: maybe it would've been better if he and Exuperius had beaned the elitist bugger the next day after all. They might've been doing the civilised world a favour.

30

Perilla would've come to Pontius's to cheer me on, but it was an all-male bash and I didn't like to seem pushy, especially when Marcia had said it was an honour to be asked. Castrimoenium wasn't Rome, and women in country wineshops either get the disapproving eye or, if they're alone and on the lee side of presentable, half a dozen propositions before they make the counter. I'd checked on timings a couple of days previously and the sun was just into its second quadrant when I crossed the market square.

Big local event was right; the place was packed to the door and beyond already. I got a few surly looks when I pushed through the crowd, but most of the punters were friendly enough and I even had a few nods from guys I recognised as regulars. Not that everyone there was: Pontius must've pulled them in from all over the region.

'Hey, Corvinus!' The man himself was behind the bar setting out cups. 'How's it going?'

'Okay.' I glanced at the rack behind him. It'd been cleared of everything but six numbered jars. Above each of them was pinned a label, the wrong way round so you couldn't read what it said. Yeah, that was clear enough. What did puzzle me, though, was a roped-off area to one side with ten wine jar bungs laid out in a line on the floor. 'Everything's set, I see.'

'Sure.' He handed me a card and a small wax tablet and stylus.

'We're just about ready to go. Only one more contestant to turn up and that's it.'

I took out my purse and paid over the entrance fee. Then I looked at the card. Fregellan, Formian, Veliternian, Fundanan, Arician ... Bacchus! We'd got a good selection here right enough; not all top-bracket wines by any means, but a good regional cross-section. There were a couple I wasn't too familiar with, mind, but—

'Morning, Corvinus.'

I turned. 'Oh, hi, Gabba. No problems?'

The ugly-looking three-times champion winked. 'Quietly confident,' he said. 'Still, it's the taking part that's important, right?'

'Seems pretty popular, certainly. All these guys contestants?'

'Nah. Some of them are just here to watch. There're only a dozen of us, last count. Mind you, some of the buggers don't take it seriously. They're only here to throw as much wine past their tonsils as Pontius'll let them get away with.' He looked round the room with the eyes of a connoisseur. 'I'd reckon there's just three in it excluding us. Old "Lucky" Maecilius over there in the corner' – he nodded towards a toothless octogenarian sitting on a bench and clutching a stick – 'he's getting a bit past it, but he knows his wines. Farms up by Six Cedars, used to win regular until eight or nine years back when he swallowed a mouthful of goat liniment by accident and ruined his palate. The bald-head next to him's Clovanus. He's a wine-blender in Lanuvinum. The third one's the red-nosed guy talking to himself. That's Titus Caesius.'

'What does he do?'

'He's a drunk.'

'Uh ... right. Right.' I glanced at the roped-off area. Each of the bungs was resting on a numbered card. 'By the way; what exactly are these for, pal?'

His ugly scare-the-crows face broke into a grin. 'You mean you don't know?'

'No. Why should I?'

'But I thought—'

'Here she comes now!' someone at the door shouted. There was an immediate stir of interest.

She?

I turned round. The press of punters had moved aside, leaving an alleyway between the door and the bar. Down it shambled a familiar apelike figure trailing a sheep on a rope. I watched in disbelief as Meton reached into his belt-pouch, took out five silver pieces and slapped them down on to the counter. Pontius gave him his card and wax tablet without a murmur.

'Uh . . . Meton?' I said.

He glared at me; which was our misanthropic chef's standard expression. 'Yeah?'

'You . . . ah . . . competing in this?'

'Nah. Just the sheep.'

My ears; there had to be something wrong with my ears. Unless the world had gone completely mad. 'Ah . . . I'm sorry, friend. I thought you said "just the sheep" there. Stupid, eh?'

'Yeah, I did.' He turned back to Pontius. 'You want to get started?'

Sweet immortal gods! I tried again. 'Meton?'

'What?' The glare went up another notch.

'Let's be very clear about this. You're entering Dassa in a *wine-tasting competition*? As a *contestant*?'

'Sure. Why not?'

'Because she's a fucking sheep, pal, that's why not!'

Pontius was over beside me so fast he blurred. 'That's enough, Corvinus,' he said quietly. 'There's nothing in the rules against a sheep taking part. Besides' – he dropped his voice even further – 'if you tried to stop it the punters would lynch you. Okay?'

'Too bloody right we would,' the guy next to me growled. 'She's paid her money like everybody else. Give the sheep a chance, Roman.'

I didn't believe this. Jupiter's holy scrotum, was I the only sane person in the room? Still, it explained what Meton had been up to with his ovine pal in the kitchen all this time. The woolly bastard had been in training.

Well, I was a guest here, after all. If the locals wanted to play silly buggers then it was fine by me. This time, though, when it was all over I really would scrub out Meton's omelette pan with wire. I'd have a private word with the Princess, too: five silver pieces wasn't chickenfeed to a slave, and I'd be interested to find out who'd subbed him.

Pontius had brought a handbell out from under the counter. He rang it and the wineshop went suddenly quiet.

'Okay, gentlemen and . . . uh . . . lady,' he said. 'You know the rules. You have six numbered wines here and you match them to the names on your card. The man or . . . ah . . . sheep who gets the most right wins the pot. Clear?' There was a chorus of yeses and one bleat. 'Fine. No cribbing of answers, no asking guidance from the referee – that's me – and no crapping on the floor by any of the contestants. And may the best man or . . . uh . . . sheep win.'

Oh, great; there ain't nothing like impartiality.

Pontius had half filled the cups on the counter with the first wine. I picked one up, but I didn't try it straight away. Like everybody else in the room I was watching Dassa.

Instead of the cup she had a soup-bowl. Meton led her into the roped-off area and set the bowl down in front of her. She lowered her head, puckered her lips and *sucked* . . .

The wine disappeared. Right to the bottom of the bowl.

Meton had stepped back, but he was holding the tablet and stylus ready. Dassa wandered over to the bungs and sniffed her way along the line. Finally she went back to the third and gently but with great deliberation pushed it out of line with her nose.

Meton made a note on the tablet and the room let out its communally held breath while Dassa trotted back to the bowl and licked it clean.

Impressive, I had to admit; weird, yeah, but impressive none the less. Oh, sure, the situation wasn't quite clear-cut: we were matching a taste to a name on a card while all Dassa had to do was match it to the smell on the bung from the appropriate jar. On the other hand, I reckoned in terms of task difficulty human and sheep were more or less starting even. It all depended on who had the better nose for wine . . .

I caught myself. Bacchus on a tightrope! I was getting as bad as the rest of them!

I took a sip from the cup. Yeah, this one was easy-peasy: thin and dry with a distinct grassy aftertaste. Latian, sure, but a long way removed from one of the top wines on offer, which was probably why Pontius had given us it first. Definitely Arician, which was interesting. On our card Arician was number five. Either Dassa's bungs were in a different order or the sheep was whistling through its ears. I noted down 'I – Arician' on my wax tablet and noticed that most of the other punters were scribbling away happily as well. We were on the nursery slopes here.

I dumped the rest into the receptacle provided – no point in tanking up on that stuff – while the majority followed suit.

Pontius poured the second wine: pale, straw-coloured with a hint of green. I sipped at my half cup while I watched Meton go through the bowl routine. Easy-peasy again. Although this one was an improvement, it wasn't one of my favourites: dry as a bone, slightly acidic with a gravelly roughness which made it better for swigging with cheese and pickles than spending time over. Definitely Signinan. I marked the tablet and glanced over at Dassa. She hadn't had any trouble with this one either, or so it seemed: she was already pushing the last bung but one out of line.

On my card Signinan was number eight. I took a proper swallow – at least it wasn't cat's-piss like the Arician – tipped the rest into the bucket and wandered over to Pontius.

'The sheep's are in a different order from ours, right?' I said.

His eyes narrowed. 'Sure they are. What did you expect? I told you: cribbing answers is against the rules. You buggers can hide your tablets, she can't. Fair's fair, Corvinus.'

Oh, Father Liber! 'You saying anyone would be stupid enough to crib from a fu— from a *sheep*?'

'Why not? Some of these bastards'd take any help going.' He pulled down the next jar. 'No point making it easy for them, is there?'

We were venturing very close to the spinning edge of sanity here. I took a covert look round. Sure enough, two or three of the punters were eyeing events in the roped-off area closely, and one of them was smoothing over what he'd written with the blunt end of his stylus and writing something else down instead.

'How're you doing so far, Corvinus?' That was Gabba, pouring the dregs of his own half cup into the slops bucket.

'Okay,' I said. 'No problems.'

'So I'd hope. Pontius always starts us off on the easy ones just to work the lads in. The next four should be more tricky.'

Meton was coming up to the counter with Dassa's bowl.

'Ah . . . just as a matter of interest,' I said as he set it down. 'How did you manage the training?'

That got me a slow glower. ''S a professional secret, that.'

'Oh, come on, Meton! I'm impressed!'

The glower became a satisfied smirk. 'Got a friend works for a wine shipper in Ostia. He let me have a few samples. I been using them.'

'Yeah? How did you swing that?'

'Told him I wanted them for you. Expanding household stocks. Mind you' – he picked his nose with a horned, hairy forefinger – 'the sheep din't need much training. She's a natural, is Dassa.'

I remembered the story about the brute getting into her former owner's neighbour's cellar and accounting for four jars of the guy's best wine without touching the rest. Meton would've heard it too, and given the weird bastard's devious thought processes I should've seen this coming. Shit.

'That was . . . uh . . . pretty smart of you, pal,' I said.

He inspected the finger and wiped it on his tunic. 'Yeah,' he said. 'Yeah, I thought so.'

Pontius had hefted down the third jar and was pouring for the punters. I held out my cup. Meton got the bowl half filled and took it back to Dassa's corner.

I sipped. Bugger; Gabba was right. This one wasn't easy, not at all: again, not a top wine, middle of the range, sweeter than the Signinan but not by much, with less acid and more fruit. Overtones of peaches. I consulted my card. It had to be one of the wobblers, Labicanan or Gabianan; either of them might fit, but because they weren't wines you met up with all that often in Rome I wouldn't plump for one over the other. I tried another swallow, but that didn't help . . .

Hell, toss for it. I wrote '3 – Labicanan' and looked round. Well, I wasn't alone: there were two or three puzzled faces and scratched heads, although Gabba didn't seem too worried, nor did the wine-blender or the drunk. 'Lucky' Maecilius had tripped over his stick on the way back to his seat, dropped his cup and was demanding a refill.

Dassa sucked up her half bowlful, trotted over to the first bung and shoved it forward. Meton consulted his card and jotted a name down on the tablet. No hesitation on the sheep's part yet, either. I was beginning to get a bad feeling about this.

On the other hand, four and five were easy. We were into the top bracket here, no question: real stars, full-bodied, aromatic, with lots of mileage, both near the top of every Roman wineseller's list. Four was Fundanan, five Alban.

Only one to go.

It was a real killer. Pontius, the bastard, had thrown us a googly to finish. So far, we'd been moving up the quality scale with the wines becoming fuller and more rounded the further we went. With the last, we were back in the middle bracket with a vengeance, and the first sip was like drinking vinegar. Even Gabba was frowning. I took a mouthful, swirled it around to let the taste settle, then spat into the bucket and tried again.

It had to be the second wobbler: certainly it wasn't any of the other four still on the card because them I could've placed. No point changing horses now. I wrote down '6 – Gabianan' and crossed my fingers.

Pontius had been filling six numbered jugs from the flasks. 'Okay,' he said. 'You've got ten minutes to try any you're not sure of. Then we collect the tablets.'

This, evidently, was the moment most of the punters had been waiting for. There was a concerted rush for jugs four and five, apart from the guy I'd seen cribbing from Dassa on wine number two who was tanking up on the Arician. 'Lucky' Maecilius was right in there at jug five, using his stick as a very offensive weapon. Ruined palate or not, the old bugger knew quality when he tasted it.

'You get them all, Corvinus?' Gabba said. I'd noticed that when Pontius had made his announcement he'd been standing right next to the fourth jug. Maybe coincidence, but I doubted it.

'Three and six were problems.'

'Is that so, now?' Gabba's eyebrows lifted. 'Well, you might have to be a local for them two right enough. I wonder how the sheep did?'

I looked across at the roped area. Half a dozen of the bungs had been pushed out of line. 'She lasted the course, anyway,' I said.

'Got to hand it to your chef.' Gabba sipped his Fundanan. 'No one ever thought of entering her before.'

'Yeah, Meton's something else.' If I had my way, when I got him home the bugger would be hamburger, for a start. I topped up my cup with what I hoped was Gabianan – the Alban and Fundanan jugs were both empty – and carried it over.

Meton was scratching the nape of Dassa's neck while she licked the bowl. He looked up and glowered.

'Dassa, uh, get them all, pal?' I asked.

'Sure. I told you, she's a natural.'

'Even that last one? The . . . ah . . . Gabianan?'

Meton looked past me and yelled, '*Referee!*'

Pontius came over. 'Yeah?'

'I want to lodge a complaint. Our confidentiality's being infringed here.'

Pontius opened his mouth. I held up my hands, palm out. 'Okay. Okay, I'm sorry. It was just a question, right?'

I took my cup back over to the counter, but there wasn't anything left barring the Arician and some very happy punters.

Five minutes later, Pontius rang the bell and collected in our tablets. Then he turned round the labels above the jars . . .

Hell.

'Stop being silly, Marcus,' Perilla said. 'After all, it wasn't an outright win. Gabba had all six right as well.'

'Lady, I have been bested in a wine-tasting competition by a fucking *sheep!*' I settled against the couch cushions and took a morose swallow of Setinian. At least Persicus wasn't there to gloat; he was dining out this evening with the other nobs. 'Gabba doesn't matter. He's human, I can take that.'

'It was a fair contest. And don't swear. Especially with Marilla present.'

'Oh, I don't mind.' The Princess was sitting in her favourite Gallic wickerwork chair, grinning. 'Dassa's very clever, I told you that. Besides, you'd've got all six too if you'd had the third and the sixth round the other way.'

'Thanks, Princess. That's a great consolation.'

'Don't be childish,' Perilla snapped.

I ignored her. 'So what's Meton buying with his winnings? A solid silver egg-whisk?'

'He only took a percentage,' Marilla said. 'Meton is very fair.

In any case, he made a lot more than a quarter of the prize money on the side bets.'

I stiffened. 'Side bets? What side bets?'

'Didn't he tell you? That was the whole idea. He's been laying bets with the locals for ages.'

'That Dassa would win?'

The Princess hesitated. 'Ah . . . not exactly. That she'd get at least as many right answers as you did. It's why he had Pontius invite you in the first place. He got quite good odds before people started to be more wary.'

I goggled at her. Jupiter on a fucking handcart! I'd been set up, right from the word go! I put my cup down and yelled, '*Bathyllus!*'

The little guy softshoed in. There hadn't been an appreciable pause; not that that surprised me, mind, because Bathyllus has the super-major-domo ability to materialise where he's wanted wherever he's been in the house previously. On this occasion he could've been listening in the corridor, sure, but I'd've thought the bald-head would consider that beneath him.

'Yes, sir?' he said.

'Bring Meton in here! Now!'

'Ah . . . yes, sir.' He turned to go.

'Wait a moment, Bathyllus,' Perilla said. 'Marcus, I don't think that is a terribly good idea.'

'You may not, lady, but personally I think it's a peach. And chewing the bastard's balls off is just the start.'

'How long would you say we could survive on turnip rissoles, then?'

That stopped me. She'd got a point; like I said before somewhere, you don't mess with Meton, not without thinking six times first. The rule is, count to twenty then forget it. Which is just what I did. Much though it hurt, Meton was sacrosanct.

I sighed. 'Okay, little guy, order countermanded. As you were. Go and polish the spoons.'

'Yes, sir.' He exited.

I took a swallow of Setinian. 'The locals're going to laugh about this for years. Even the ones who've lost their shirts.'

'Don't exaggerate, dear.'

'Who's exaggerating? Like Marcia said, I was representing fu—. . . I was representing Rome. We could be seeing the start of a folk-tale here: Roman beaten by sheep. Like the Gauls and the geese. I will *kill* Meton.'

'Nonsense. It was only a bit of fun.' She turned to the Princess. 'What are you buying with Dassa's share of the prize money, Marilla?'

'I thought a pair of earrings.'

'You don't wear earrings.'

'Not for me. For Dassa.'

'Ah.'

'Or do you think a collar would be more appropriate?'

'Yes. Yes, I think perhaps it would.'

Bathyllus shimmied back in. 'Dinner will be served shortly, sir. I've already told the Lady Marcia. Suckling pig stuffed with green beans, tripe with a cinnamon-nutmeg sauce, roast quails with a hazelnut stuffing, asparagus stewed in wine and a selection of spiced cakes, fresh fruit and Alexandrian dates in poppy-seeds and honey for dessert.'

My eyes widened. 'All that, pal? I thought the senior consul wasn't dining this evening.'

'He isn't. Meton has also provided a carafe of twenty-five-year-old Alban to go with the pig, sir. With his compliments.'

Holy gods! That wasn't dinner, that was a banquet! Yeah, well; a peace offering, obviously. Not a bad lad, Meton, and Rome was big enough to stand a few knocks; Persicus would be missing out, too, which was an added plus. I'd bet whatever he was getting, nob dinner party or not, it wouldn't be a patch on one of Meton's peace-offering specials.

Twenty-five-year-old Alban, eh? Maybe I'd let the bastard live after all. So long as he hadn't set a place for Dassa.

Author's Note

Coincidences happen.

The story is just a story, with no historical basis whatsoever. Nevertheless, any author, if asked, will have tales of odd coincidences and similar, unconscious overlaps of fact and fiction which find their way into the plot and only emerge later: I've experienced several of these myself in the course of writing the Corvinus books, notably in connection with the original choice of the principal characters' names for *Ovid* and my floorplan of Tiberius's villa on Capri in *Sejanus* where they were downright eerie and still bring a tingle to the back of my neck. In this case the coincidence involved the Alban Brotherhood.

I made the name up, selecting it because it reflected both the long-vanished Latin town of Alba Longa and the Gaelic name for Scotland (there were – surprise! – very distinct parallels between the Latins' historical relations with Rome and Scotland's with England, which, given the original plot idea of a nationalist group hijacked by the villain for reasons of his own, were far too convenient not to use). However, while doing my bit of research on the Latin Festival I came across a set of inscriptions discovered at Bovillae referring to the 'Fratres Albani'; which, of course, translated means the Alban Brotherhood.

Not that the Bovillan Fratres and my version had anything else in common but the name, so we're not quite in the

Ovid and *Sejanus* bracket; still, it's another one for the collection, isn't it?

My thanks again to Roy Pinkerton, my wife Rona and the staff of Carnoustie Library. I've no doubt there are factual mistakes somewhere in the book but if you did happen to spot one (or, embarrassingly, more than one) then I hope they didn't spoil the story for you, especially if your name is Lyn Williams. They are, naturally, completely my own fault.

DAVID WISHART

WHITE MURDER

'Uh ... Dad?' Young Lucius's face was chalk white. 'Dad, I think he's dead.' It took a moment to register. Then Renatius dropped the towel and was through the door in five seconds flat; and the rest of the wineshop, including me, were about two seconds behind him.

When Pegasus, racing mega-star and lead driver of the Whites faction, is found stabbed to death in the alleyway beside Renatius's wineshop, Marcus Corvinus is already on site. The local District Watch – crooked to a man – claim that the killer's motive was simple theft, but Corvinus knows it wasn't.

Tracking the murderer down with the often-unwilling help of his wife Perilla takes him deep into the murky world of Roman chariot-racing with all its secrets, skulduggeries and scams; and his task is not made any easier by the fact that in the process he has a lovesick major-domo, an invisible dagger and Mount Etna to contend with.

Praise for WHITE MURDER:

'Wishart creates a pungent, throbbingly vibrant Rome'. *Highland News Group*

'The amiable Marcus Corvinus ... wisecracks his way through each mystery with great style. A delightful read.' *Huddersfield Examiner*

'well-written, easy-to-read tale, ful of innate humour and pace ... with intriguing twists and turns. David Wishart ... has a deep knowledge ... of Imperial Rome.' *Historical Novels Review*

'A real gripping mystery yarn with a strong vein of laconic humour.' *Coventry Evening Telegraph*

HODDER AND STOUGHTON PAPERBACKS

DAVID WISHART

LAST RITES

'Right,' I said. 'So what can I do for the chief Vestal, pal?'

The Axeman was flexing his hands like he was squeezing a couple of those wooden balls wrestlers use to strengthen their grip. 'I'm to take you to the Galba place,' he said.

'Is that so, now? And why would you do that?'

'Because there's been a death.'

I stared at him. Jupiter, not again! Five minutes back in residence at the Hub of the World and we were already hitting corpses.

The body of a young woman, with her throat cut, is found the morning after the nocturnal rite of the Good Goddess – an all-female ceremony strictly out of bounds for the male of the species. Hoping to avoid to scandal, Senator Lucius Arruntius calls in Marcus Corvinus to do some discreet sleuthing.

Praise for David Wishart:

'With the toga-wearing sleuths of Lindsey Davis and Steven Saylor prowling the alleys of Ancient Rome, is there room for Wishart's Marcus Corvinus? On this evidence the answer is resoundingly in the affirmative.' *The Times*

'His learning shines through. He has a feel for ancient times yet uses modern dialogue. This neat trick manages to combine the atmosphere of the ancient world while moving the story quickly and assuredly on. Highly recommended.' *Yorkshire Evening Press*

HODDER AND STOUGHTON PAPERBACKS

DAVID WISHART

OLD BONES

I sat down on one of the couches.
'So, Stepfather,' I said. 'Who did you kill?'
'He didn't kill anyone!' Mother snapped. 'Don't be silly!'
I sighed. 'Okay. So who didn't you kill?'

Marcus Corvinus doesn't seriously think that his stepfather is a murderer. Priscus wouldn't hurt a fly. But he did discover the corpse, and was caught clutching the murder weapon, so proving the old man's innocence presents quite a challenge. Not at all Marcus's idea of a holiday . . .

The victim had enemies enough, a cuckolded husband among them. As usual, Marcus needs the brains of his lovely wife Perilla to untangle the more complex threads of the investigation; but even so, he catches many a red herring before hooking the murderer.

Praise for David Wishart:

'With the toga-wearing sleuths of Lindsey Davis and Steven Saylor prowling the alleys of Ancient Rome, is there room for Wishart's Marcus Corvinus? On this evidence the answer is resoundingly in the affirmative.' *The Times*

'Witty, engrossing and ribald . . . it misses nothing in its evocation of a bygone time and place.' *Independent on Sunday*

'His learning shines through. He has a feel for ancient times yet uses modern dialogue. This neat trick manages to combine the atmosphere of the ancient world while moving the story quickly and assuredly on. Highly recommended.' *Yorkshire Evening Press*

HODDER AND STOUGHTON PAPERBACKS